Welcome to
TIM DORSEY'S

Hammerhead Ranch Motel

Books by
Tim Dorsey

FLORIDA ROADKILL
HAMMERHEAD RANCH MOTEL
ORANGE CRUSH
TRIGGERFISH TWIST

And in Hardcover

THE STINGRAY SHUFFLE

Hammerhead RANCH MOTEL

TIM DORSEY

HarperTorch
An Imprint of HarperCollins Publishers

This is a work of fiction. Names, characters, places, and incidents are products of the author's imagination or are used fictitiously and are not to be construed as real. Any resemblance to actual events, locales, organizations, or persons, living or dead, is entirely coincidental.

HARPERTORCH
An Imprint of HarperCollins*Publishers*
10 East 53rd Street
New York, New York 10022-5299

Copyright © 2000 by Tim Dorsey
Excerpt from *Orange Crush* copyright © 2001 by Tim Dorsey
Back cover author photo by Janine Dorsey
ISBN: 0-380-73234-3

First HarperTorch paperback printing: June 2001
First William Morrow hardcover printing: August 2000

HarperCollins®, HarperTorch™, and ♦™ are trademarks of HarperCollins Publishers Inc.

Printed in the United States of America

Visit HarperTorch on the World Wide Web at
www.harpercollins.com

10 9 8 7

For Eugene Morse

Let us consider that we are all partially insane.
It will explain us to each other.

—*Mark Twain*

Acknowledgments

Again, a debt is owed to my agent, Nat Sobel,
and my editor, Paul Bresnick,
for helping me order in finer restaurants.

Prologue

*f*lorida's beauty creates the illusion of civilization.

It is a thin but functional veneer, like fake-wood contact paper stuck to flimsy particle board. Glistening condos, palm trees down the median, corkscrew water slides and waiting lines of retirees spilling onto restaurant sidewalks at four P.M., hoping for a shot at an early-bird $3.95 Sterno tray of Swedish meatballs. Spring training, mermaids, trained whales. *Brave New Disney World,* where commercial microbiologists try to isolate the DNA responsible for bad thoughts and free will. Space shots and orange juice with more pulp and roadside hot dog vendors in T-backs causing traffic mishaps at the latest apparition of the Blessed Virgin Mary, who chose to appear this time in squeegee residue on the plate glass of a financial tower on U.S. 19.

Late one Thursday toward the end of the twentieth century, a white Chrysler New Yorker drove up the Florida Keys on the way to Tampa. Behind a secret panel in the trunk was a spare tire, a jack and a metal briefcase containing five million dollars. Under the bumper was a homing device. The Chrysler's innocent occupants didn't have a clue.

A small concrete booth painted a graffiti-resistant government tan sat near the base of the Sunshine Skyway bridge. Its green-tinted windows beveled outward like an air traffic control tower. The Skyway spanned the mouth of Tampa Bay with a massive arch that climbed so steeply into the thin, clear air that motorists said it was like taking off in a DC-10. Pleasure boats made small white trails through the wave caps far below.

Inside the booth, state safety officer Chester "Porkchop" Dole stood at the stainless steel sink and rinsed his favorite coffee mug, which remained in his right hand at all times. It read: "Ask someone who gives a shit!" The window AC unit began to clatter, and Dole whapped it with precision.

On paper, Dole's job was to monitor the bridge for hazard. In reality, Dole's job was to *preserve* his job. A nineteen-year public servant, he was the equivalent of a fat, hundred-year-old alligator. No natural predators left. Just as long as the gator didn't change his proven routine in a spasm of senility and chase executives around the thirteenth green at Innisbrook. Not to worry with Dole. He was master of the unvaried, safe pattern that didn't deviate into unknown adventures of genuine work. His attitude toward his job station was that of a felon at the crime scene: Don't touch anything and don't stay a minute longer than absolutely necessary. Paperwork wasn't filled out,

reports weren't read, ringing phones kept ringing.
His bosses, a pyramid of progressively paranoid career preservationists, gave him high marks.

Dole stared out the windows, making sure the
hand not holding the coffee mug stayed in his pocket.
He became an expert on every detail of his solitary
outpost that had nothing to do with his job. To the
south, the Skyway bridge dominated everything. It
was Tampa Bay's defining landmark, like the St.
Louis Arch or the Seattle/Dallas/Calgary Space Needle. Dole studied the Skyway's twin isosceles triangles of yellow suspension cable all day long—a big
sundial, backlit in the morning, bleached bright with
vertical shadows at high noon, glowing a burnished
orange in late afternoon and then a soft scarlet at
sunset. Finally the bridge was the negative image
against the indigo sky, and the headlights came on
and trickled across the span like illuminated water
droplets sliding down monofilament fishing line.

Dole sipped from the mug. Tanker ships sailed in
from the Gulf of Mexico, fly fishermen cast on the
flats, sailboats tacked around Pinellas Point, and dolphins splashed in the channels. There was the monu-
ment to the crew of the USCG *Blackthorn*, lost in a
foul-weather collision in '80. And the stub of the old
Skyway bridge, now a fishing pier. A sign: "Please
do not clean fish in restroom."

Inside Dole's booth was a bank of nine-inch
black-and-white video screens feeding live from remote cameras at various pressure points along the
Skyway. They monitored for breakdowns, wrecks,
fog conditions, suicide jumpers and terrorism. But

Dole wasn't monitoring the surveillance screens because he was monitoring his portable color TV set, laughing at Toto the Weather Dog doing a funny dance on the anchor desk of a local newscast. Toto was an eight-year-old half-blind Chihuahua who appeared in a variety of anthropomorphic costumes and predicted the weather. Tonight Toto was shaking in a hula skirt in a manner consistent with a sixty percent chance of rain and a UV index of seven, according to weatherman Guy Rockney.

Following a recent spate of fatal tornadoes and windstorms on Florida's west coast, both the U.S. Weather Service and local television stations faced pressure to upgrade their Doppler radar and other early-warning technology. Four of the region's major stations spent heavily on new equipment. The fifth, Florida Cable News, picked up Toto at the pound for the cost of the shots.

Florida Cable News saw its audience share increase sixteen percent on segments with Toto. The loss was spread evenly among stations with the expensive new equipment. Those stations saturated the air with ads desperately trying to explain the importance of adequate wind-shear detection.

Toto kept dancing them right over to Florida Cable News.

Early one October evening, the technology investment paid off. The Weather Service and four stations picked up a quick-forming front moving east of Tampa with funnel clouds. The warnings went out. Hundreds took cover and were saved. Florida Cable News, instrumentally blind to the twisters bearing down on its viewers, sent the audience to bed with a happy little jig from Toto in a spandex aerobic outfit and a promise of a pleasant evening and a sunny tomorrow.

Florida Cable News wasn't responsible for the entire death toll, just part. Just enough to spell Toto's demise. The end was hastened when weatherman Guy Rockney joked on the air that some of his viewers had gone on a "Florida Double-Wide Sleigh Ride."

That did it. Toto and Rockney were history before Rockney could remove his clip-on microphone. It lasted a week. Until the specific gravity of letters and phone calls and, most important, the ratings plunge was too much to withstand. Both were reinstated and the ratings at Florida Cable News rebounded stoutly. The other stations responded by hiring a cast of trained cats, ferrets, chimpanzees and marmosets.

Chester "Porkchop" Dole was a loyal television viewer. He couldn't be lured away by cheap imitations; he was sticking with Toto, the cheap original. On this December evening, Dole was working the short-straw second shift. But he made the best of it, howling with laughter and pointing at Toto on the little TV. He slapped his knee with the hand that wasn't holding the coffee mug. He wheezed and coughed and laughed some more as Toto pirouetted in a tutu atop the News-Flash Anchor Desk, and the entire News-Flash Anchor Team chuckled with manufactured sincerity.

As the anchor team waved good night and the camera pulled back, weatherman Guy Rockney secretly jabbed Toto with his weather pointer, and Toto resumed dancing for the fade-out. Dole broke up laughing again and waved back at the anchor team. He never once thought of glancing over at the bank of surveillance monitors, especially not monitor number five, trained on the peak of the Sunshine Skyway bridge.

Johnny Vegas was chasing a blue moon across Tampa Bay.

The Porsche's top was down, it was almost midnight and he was doing ninety on the Gandy Bridge, but it was still too hot. It was another typical heat wave that sweeps Florida every December, baffling the tourists and mocking the natives. What's wrong with this state, Johnny wondered, wiping beads of sweat from a line under his pompadour.

Johnny passed a bait shop on the west side of the Gandy. The stuffed snook on the sign wore a Santa hat; in the parking lot were eight plastic flamingos with reindeer antlers pulling a bass boat. Johnny adjusted the bow tie on his tux. He passed a billboard urging him to have eye surgery in a strip mall. More decorations. Inflatable snowmen in bikinis and wise men with sunglasses and elves on water skis. Johnny turned down Fourth Street toward the St. Petersburg bayfront, hoping *she* would be there.

They had met three hours earlier, on the other side of the bay in Tampa's Channel District. It was an after-hours black-tie fund-raiser at the new Florida Aquarium. The lights were low, the stars flickered through the aquarium's landmark glass dome, and the free liquor flowed as only free liquor can. A promenade of snob cars pulled up for valets at the aquarium entrance. Saabs.

The facility herniated debt, and the fund-raising party was another backhanded effort to get in the black. The aquarium was conceived by politicians and backed with tax revenue, which meant the operation was dumber than dirt when it came to surviving in the real economic world. A marketing corporation hired by the City of Tampa—the same one that advised the city to tear down a perfectly good football stadium and build a new one right next door with tax dollars—concluded that the same strategy was the only way to rescue the aquarium.

"Gentlemen!" the report's author addressed the city council. "We must destroy the aquarium in order to save the aquarium!"

The proposal was tabled in a close vote.

On this sticky December evening, casino tables crowded the horseshoe crab tank, and a makeshift dance floor squeezed through the mangroves next to the otter pool. The turtle ponds began to fill with crumpled napkins and cigarette butts. The in-house joke: We draw the line at having sex with our animals. *Except during bonus pledge hour!*

Johnny Vegas's Porsche screeched up in front of the aquarium. Ahead of him in the valet line was a mega-stretch limousine; on its doors were five multi-colored interlocking rings. A dozen members of the International Olympic Committee—scouting Tampa Bay for the 2012 games—got out of the backseat. A smiling reception team of exotic dancers immediately stuffed unidentified envelopes in the suit pockets of the Olympic Committee and led them off to special guarded VIP rooms.

A valet jumped in the limo and sped off. It was Johnny's turn. He pulled the Porsche up to the curb, jumped out and flung the keys hard, sidearm like Phil Rizzuto turning the double play. The keys deflected off the fingertips of the celebrity volunteer valet and hit him in the teeth.

"And don't fuck with the stereo! It's set how I like it!" Johnny barked as the mayor of Tampa dabbed blood off his gums with a handkerchief.

Johnny adjusted his tux, stretched his neck side to side, and strode into the aquarium with the air of a horny adolescent.

Johnny was the man other men hate. A young, bon vivant party hound, impeccably dressed and visibly rich with no visible means of support. His tan was a little too good and his haircut a little too long and sexy to get respect in any business setting. It drove chicks wild. Not those who mattered, of course. None of the educated, accomplished women would take such a man seriously. These were the real prize ladies—mature, focused, substantial in conversation and content. In short, the prizes the other men already had—their wives. Johnny only held attraction for the others, the giddy young bubbleheads with the short skirts and boob jobs who drooled over him. The married men thought: Damn him all to hell!

But Johnny had a dark secret. Even in the realm of gigolos and trust-fund playboys, where everyone scored so frequently it blew the bell curve, someone had to bring up the rear. It was Johnny. He had no problem getting runners on base; he just couldn't bring 'em home. Nothing, nada, zip, doughnuts, goose eggs. It was part Johnny's immaturity, but it was more. Events seemed to naturally conspire against him. Whenever he was close, had a willing babe in his crosshairs, there was always a massive disruption. It was uncanny. Johnny was charting new horizons, entire lost continents, in involuntary *coitus interruptus*. Forest fires near Daytona, prison escape manhunt in Orlando, circus elephant rampage in Clearwater, and the red-tide marine kill off Sarasota: "Hey, where are you going? It just smells a little fishy!"

Playboy Johnny Vegas, the Accidental Virgin, currently was trying to woo women with his Porsche. Until recently, he tracked his quarry with an orange-and-aqua cigarette boat customized with Miami Dolphins insignia. Then he ran aground and had to get it floated off a shoal in the Marquesas and later crashed it into a floating reggae bar near Dinner Key. The Dolphins sued him when women complained he was impersonating the quarterback. There were insurance problems and storage fees and barnacles, and the reggae bar filed a lien, and it went on and on until Johnny finally threw up his hands and thought, I'd almost rather *not* get laid.

But tonight at the aquarium everything was clicking with an unblemished ingenue in a strapless evening dress who had the supermodel prerequisites of being tall and sticklike. She said her name was If.

They flirted on the edge of the dance floor, near the marsh. A disco ball and revolving colored footlights disoriented the egrets, who flew out of their ponds and into the bar and restrooms. At the front of the dance floor was a mobile broadcast booth of local radio station Blitz-99, which was DJing the fund-raiser in a publicity swap. Blitz-99 had the hottest disc jockey in Tampa Bay, Boris the Hateful Piece of Shit.

That really was his name, at least according to files in Hillsborough Circuit Court, where Boris legally changed it in a ploy to get around persistent fines from the Federal Communications Commission. When regulators brushed aside the legal maneuver, the radio station compromised, and each time Boris said his name on the air, the last part of the word "shit" was bleeped out by a horn from a Model T automobile.

Boris objected that the compromise was a sellout of values.

Market research, however, showed the distinct Model T sound increased his name recognition, and the horn became the logo for a line of freebie T-shirts, bumper stickers and beer-can insulators.

In the late 1990s, the biggest things going in radio were shows that featured either mean-spirited, intolerant rants or sophomoric sexual innuendo. In a revolutionary breakthrough, Boris combined the two. He became all things to all sexually frustrated malcontents.

Half of Boris's audience was easily titillated teenagers. His trademark was the call-in confession in which kids graphically described sexual experiences that Boris would grade for arousal and imagination; then he would send them on their way with a plug for God-fearing Americans of European stock. The other half of Boris's audience was voyeuristic fifty-year-old bigots.

Church groups were enraged, editorial writers had infarctions, city councilmen passed resolutions and then smiled for photographs.

Boris responded with a packed press conference on the steps of City Hall. "It's First Amendment, baby! I'm an artist!" he yelled, gripping the rubber-ball end of a large brass horn. Dozens of middle school and junior high fans cheered from the sidewalk. Plainclothes Klansmen set up an interactive booth.

Boris pointed at the kids and looked into the TV cameras. "The youth of America will not have their rights trampled. Don't mess with Boris the Hateful Piece of Sh—AHH-OOOO-GAH!"

Boris's notoriety exploded, and his appeal began overlapping all demographic lines. If you wanted to draw a crowd to your event, you hired Boris for a guest appearance. And you got your money's worth, because although Boris was just under five and a half feet tall, he was just over four hundred pounds, most of which was not adequately bathed. Standing still in air-conditioning, Boris perspired like a yak. While songs played, Boris sat like a statue in his DJ chair with arms crossed, wearing dark sunglasses, a beatnik Jabba the Hut.

In the mutual-approval symbiosis of celebrity and fan, people constantly approached Boris as he sat motionless: "You're the greatest, man!" "You're a genius!" "You tell it like it is!"

Boris never acknowledged them—just continued sitting rigid, arms crossed, staring straight ahead in his sunglasses.

"Man, that is so *cool!*" said his fans.

It was a different story if it was a young girl. Then Boris broke his pose and whispered in her ear. The girl would yell over to her friends something like "Hey, guess what Boris just asked me! He's a riot!"

They didn't get it. They thought it was part of the act. No, Boris would say, I'm serious. I really want you to do that to me.

"You can't be serious," replied the last girl. "But you smell."

"Of course I smell. I'm a piece of shit!"

"Get away from me, you fat freak!"

Boris shrugged and leaned back and crossed his arms.

Johnny Vegas stood next to the wetlands exhibit and said to no one in particular, "Isn't that Boris the Hateful Piece of Shit?"

"Yes it is," came a reply. "And you wouldn't believe what he just asked me to do."

Johnny turned and gazed into the emerald-green eyes of If, who tossed an empty plastic champagne flute into the otter tank. Responding to ancient genetic memory, Johnny sheep-dogged her over to the bar. The TV was tuned to Florida Cable News.

FCN was in Daytona Beach reporting the phenomenon of college student balcony falls. And it wasn't just hotels anymore—anything of altitude would do: overpasses, parking decks, scoreboards at sporting arenas. While the FCN reporter spoke, a computer illustration showed the side of a beachfront hotel and a dotted line arcing from the top floor down to a large X on the pavement painfully shy of the swimming pool.

Johnny turned to If. "Did you know that because of Florida, architects have had to recalculate the set-back distance of swimming pools from hotels?"

She shook her head.

"It's true," he said. "They used to go by standard Mexican cliff-diving clearances and then add a percentage as a deterrent. But spring break queered the whole equation. All the drinking. Everyone's depth perception is fucked."

"What kind of yutz would dive from the fourteenth floor?" asked If.

"I'd rather hit something with my speedboat," said Johnny.

"You have a speedboat?" If asked, her face lighting up.

"Used to," Johnny said with dejection. "It's now being raced around Biscayne Bay by Rastafarians smoking marijuana cigars."

"Oh," she said, and her smile dropped along with her eyes.

Johnny stared at the floor, too, and idly scraped at a piece of gum with the point of his Italian shoe. Then a thought. He looked back at her and offered tentatively, "I have a Porsche."

"Not a nine-twenty-four, I hope," she said with reserve.

"No way! Nine-eleven. Convertible."

"Airfoil on the trunk?"

"And Luther Vandross on the CD."

If began to purr, and Johnny tried to picture her in the cheerleading outfit he had in the back of his closet. If said she had to hit a party across the bay— meet a few guys from her office and string them along, purely as an investment in her career. But she'd love to meet him, say, in two hours? She gave him directions, a late-night piano bar in St. Pete, a little walk-down joint below street level on the bay-front.

Johnny glanced back at the TV. The newscast had moved into the weather segment, and he laughed and pointed at the screen. "I love that dog. He cracks me up."

If looked up and saw Toto the Weather Dog spinning in a ballerina outfit and began laughing, too. "That's too much! How do they think of this stuff?"

Johnny smiled and bade If farewell, but in his heart he knew she wouldn't be at the piano bar. It was the classic brush-off.

He'd forgotten about her as he trolled the party without result. Two hours later, with no further success in hand, Johnny hopped in his Porsche and drove for the piano bar, a slave of groundless hope, calling on God in the night air: "Please, please, please, please, please . . ."

Seconds after Johnny left, Boris cued up "Train" by Quad City DJs. Patrons filled the dance floor, which shook with the nondancelike, orthopedically inadvisable twitching and stomping of rich white people. The aquarium staff lined the sides of the crowd, clapping in rhythm and blowing traffic-cop whistles.

Amid the swirling lights and dry-ice fog, there was a tremendous crash—then a huge cannonball splash in one of the tanks. People looked around, but the loud music and light show aggravated the confusion. Someone glanced up and saw a jagged opening in the middle of the aquarium's glass dome. It was simple deduction from there. The imaginary path of gravity led down from the dome to the alligator tank, where a large object floated. The staff turned up the house lights, and the crowd pressed against the glass walls of the tank for an underwater view. What was it? Where did it come from? There were no tall buildings nearby and no air traffic patterns overhead.

The waves from the splash lapped against the tempered glass and churned up bottom gunk, hazing the view. Two docents climbed down to the tank from a maintenance ladder. Guests began to make out bits of brightly colored cloth with a floral pattern, a tan Birkenstock, purple fanny pack and Roger McGuinn/Byrds sunglasses.

"It's . . ." someone said, then filled with dread, ". . . a college student!"

*J*ohnny drove slowly through the empty downtown streets of St. Petersburg, the Porsche jostling on the brick road as he scanned boarded-up buildings for a street address. Johnny wondered how he had been reduced to this: junior nooky cadet, sniffing around a ghost town on poontang patrol. I deserve better, he told himself. I have a trust fund! And he thought about the family business of scamming the elderly into life insurance for which "you can't be turned down! Your rates will never go up! And there's no physical! Don't make the mistake of waiting until it's too late!"—and then an old woman in the TV ad cries over a checkbook and a photo of her dead husband. Johnny swelled with pride.

As the numbers on the abandoned buildings approached the appointed street address, Johnny heard piano tinklings and eggnog laughter echoing from around the corner. He turned right at the light and pulled to the curb beside an iron staircase railing leading below the street. Standing at the top of the stairs, next to a small red "Piano Bar" sign, was If. She leaned against the wall quite sultry, sipping a jumbo martini. Her eyelids were at half-mast. She slugged back the last of the martini with a whipping action of her neck, took two steps toward the Porsche and threw the martini glass back over her shoulder. It was supposed to smash against the brick wall, but it missed and broke a window too. Things happened simultaneously. If stumbled toward the car. People came running up the stairs. Johnny tried to start the already running Porsche, and it made an expensively bad sound.

Johnny was at his indecisive, fumbling best as If climbed in. "Let's get out of here," she told Johnny. "I need to be fucked hard."

A bouncer ran up and grabbed If's door handle. Johnny pressed the gas pedal, and the bouncer was left spinning on his back in the street like a break dancer.

If peeled her dress over her head as they cleared the southbound tollbooth for the Sunshine Skyway. The bridge began to ascend, and If unzipped Johnny's pants with her teeth. He knew he had to hurry. He reached over the top of her head and pressed buttons to call up the exact song he wanted on the stereo. It had to happen perfectly, the right spot of the ideal tune playing at the precise moment they crested the bridge for the maximum view. He punched the controls quickly for Lynyrd Skynyrd's "Free Bird." But the part of the song he wanted was the fantastic guitar solos toward the end, and they were almost to the bridge's apex. Shoot, he thought, it's all happening out of synch! It's falling apart! Maybe if I slow below a hundred. He digitally fast-forwarded through the song until finally, almost at the last second, everything was aligned. He wanted to tweak the volume up a little, but If's increasingly bobbing head made it hard to reach. To make it louder, Johnny would have to mash her face down really hard leaning over her. Screw it, he thought, I'll live. The song's guitar triplets screamed from the Alpine speakers, and Johnny scanned the panorama of distant lights from ships and beach towns, and his pre-orgasmic ego said, "My sphere of influence." Then it was back to shaking and moaning and trying to keep track of the steering wheel.

Johnny didn't see the parked car until it was almost too late. A white Chrysler New Yorker without emergency flashers sat half in the breakdown lane,

half in Johnny's lane. Johnny screamed and swerved
left into the retaining wall. The Porsche scraped the
cement barrier for three hundred yards, spraying a
dramatic shower of sparks, but it helped slow the car
without wrecking. There was no harm except exten-
sive body damage and a socially awkward moment
after they stopped when Johnny found If's head
turned a little too far in an undesigned direction and
inextricably wedged between the seat and the bottom
of the steering wheel.

"Hold on, let me get some tools from the trunk,"
Johnny said and hopped from the car.

If tried to wiggle loose. "Hurry! It hurts!"

Johnny lathered the sides of her head with grease
used to pack bearings, and her head snapped free
with the sound of a finger popping a cheek. They
stood for a silent moment of relief, catching their
breaths, then realized they had forgotten about the
parked Chrysler that had started it all. They turned
and looked back up the bridge.

Chester "Porkchop" Dole was flipping channels on
his TV and complaining about the lack of quality
programming when he accidentally glanced up at the
safety monitors.

He screamed.

Chester dove for the radio and knocked over the
microphone. He'd never used the radio in six years at
the bridge. He pressed buttons and switches until he
got deafening feedback, and pressed more until it
stopped. He keyed the mike and begged for help

without protocol. He forgot to release the microphone button to hear a reply. When he heard no reply, he panicked and gripped the button harder. Everyone in the greater Tampa Bay area who owned an emergency scanner turned up the volume.

"Help! Help! I'm at the bridge! Oh, please! Why won't anyone answer me! Why are all of you doing this! For the love of Jesus! Fuck me!" Followed by long, loud crying.

On the wall was monitor number five, and on the screen a man in a tux and a young woman in a strapless evening dress with a large, dark stain on the side of her head walked apprehensively up the bridge. Ahead was a white Chrysler New Yorker with scorch marks down the side, parked southbound. The Chrysler's passenger stood between the vehicle and the bridge railing. He flicked a Bic lighter and held it to a strip of rag hanging out of a wine bottle and tossed it in the open passenger window.

A fireball. The car crackled and was engulfed, sending swirls of sparks up into the bridge's suspension.

As Johnny Vegas watched a lunatic Molotov his own car, he thought the man might as well take a flamethrower to Johnny's romantic life. He hadn't lost his virginity yet. Some decent oral foreplay, but that wasn't official under Queensberry rules. When the Chrysler's driver climbed onto the bridge railing, Johnny's heart skipped. Pleeeeeeeease don't jump. It's almost impossible to get a woman amorous after something like that. Men, sure. They're in the mood after mass executions. Literally, there *is* no wrong time. But Johnny knew women were different. He

had been on the business end of enough aborted
trysts to know that far less than this can throw a
woman's emotions tottering out of that carefully nur-
tured trajectory needed to get her through the window of opportunity and into the sack.

A highway patrol car skidded to a stop behind the
Chrysler and the trooper jumped out. "Why don't we
talk about this?" he said calmly. Back on the patrol
car's radio, Johnny heard a frantic, sobbing voice:
"Oh, sweet God in heaven! Please, somebody answer
me! Mother! Mother, where are you! Why did you
leave me, Mother?"

Back in the safety booth, horror swept up the spine
of Chester "Porkchop" Dole, and a cold, sallow flush
hit his face. Dole could handle the drama on the
bridge. What unraveled him was the knowledge that
the smooth boulder of fate was about to roll over his
nineteen years of public service. The safe routine of
his job had been varied, the universe altered.

A journeyman state employee, Dole had the bureaucratic survival instincts that told him how to lat-
eral most responsibility, dodge most blame, cover
most ass. But there was one error so costly it was to
be avoided above all else. It was known as Death-by-
Headline. No matter what you do in public life, no
matter how gravely you blow it, make sure it's in a
nebulous way that takes a lot of obscure argot to explain. Even if you get a bunch of people killed, as
long as they die in eight-syllable words with no con-
venient puns, alliterations, rhymes or homonyms.
There's nothing worse than screwing up in a way that
makes a snappy, pants-around-the-ankles newspaper

headline that wins some poor copy editor the hundred-dollar prize for the month.

Dole saw just such a headline coming together on the screen. The Chrysler's driver, dressed in a complete Santa Claus outfit, leaned forward, spread his arms wide and dove off the Sunshine Skyway bridge.

"Shit!" Johnny Vegas said under his breath as Santa disappeared over the side. Then a light went on in his head. He would turn this to his advantage. Yes, he thought, I'll console her. I still have a chance to hump her till she craps the bed by being incredibly sensitive and caring.

Johnny took off his coat and draped it around If's shoulders. He patted her head and leaned it against his chest. "Now, now," he said, "everything will be all right."

They turned around and started walking back to the Porsche. They heard a deep air horn from behind. A semi tractor-trailer had come upon the scene too fast and couldn't stop. Johnny and If pressed themselves against the guardrail as the truck blew by. The truck ran over the Porsche, flattening it out like a beer can, and dragged it a quarter mile.

First there was silence, then the sniffling started, and Johnny closed his eyes for what he knew was coming. If's crying erupted, building in hysteria until she emitted a shrill, warbling sound previously only heard in rutting minks.

*T*he ends of *The Little Mermaid* slippers poked across the front-door threshold and into the moder-

ately humid eighty-two-degree December morning.
Mrs. Edna Ploomfield, a little older than the temperature, bent down on the step of her Beverly Shores
condominium to get the paper. She read the top headline, "Sad-Sack Santa Swan-Dives in Seasonal Sunshine Skyway Suicide." She turned back into the
house, closed the door and shuffled across the living
room to the kitchen. The television set was on the
local morning show *Get the Hell Out of Bed, Tampa
Bay!* As she passed the set, state safety officer
Chester "Porkchop" Dole was on the screen being interviewed live about his vain but heroic efforts radio-
ing for help after keenly observing the Skyway
jumper. It was such an impressive TV performance
that Dole probably would have salvaged his career.
Except he was absentmindedly holding his "Ask
someone who gives a shit!" coffee mug prominently
for the cameras.

Mrs. Ploomfield's condo sat on a thin ribbon of
barrier island on the Gulf of Mexico. It towered
thirty stories and, with the other condos, formed a
wall along the shore. The only road running up the
island was Gulf Boulevard, and across the street was
an old Florida neighborhood of single-story concrete
houses with white tile roofs. The landscape was flat,
bright and hot. The yards were mostly white stones,
with palm, hibiscus, bougainvillea, croton and schef-
flera. Some homes had sets of windows wrapped
deco-style around the corners. Front doors were
jalousie, and everything was whitewashed. Address
numbers over the doors were flanked by pink sea
horses or blue sailfish or yellow scallops. Herons

wandered through yards, pecking on windows for handouts.

The condominium residents thought they lived in paradise. The only problem was everyone else. All those cheesy houses across the street and that awful Hammerhead Ranch Motel next door that they couldn't manage to close down.

Mrs. Ploomfield lived at 1193 Gulf Harbor Drive in a first-floor unit of Calusa Pointe Tower Arms. There was little traffic this morning, only a brown delivery truck at the curb. A man stood outside the passenger door and checked the address against his clipboard. He leaned in the van and grabbed a floral arrangement in a ceramic manatee and a two-foot-long box of chocolates, red and green, with thick gold ribbon. He headed for unit 1193; a second man stayed behind the wheel and idled the engine.

Mrs. Ploomfield had just gotten back to the kitchen table with the newspaper. She was scooping out canned nibiets for an aged Chihuahua when the doorbell rang.

"Coming," said Mrs. Ploomfield, and she began cross-country skiing in her slippers across the terrazzo. A few minutes later, she arrived. She cranked the jalousie. "Who is it?"

"Florida Flowers 'n' Fudge." The man crouched down to see Ploomfield eye to eye through the slowly opening slats of translucent glass. "I have a delivery."

"Who's it from?"

"Is this eleven ninety-three?"

"Yes."

There was a growling.

The man bent down even lower to look through the jalousie, and he saw a small dog.

"That looks exactly like Toto, the mutt on TV."

"It *is* Toto, and he's not a mutt. I take care of him for my friend, weatherman Guy Rockney. Now, I want my candy and flowers. And I don't like your attitude one bit."

"I hate that fucking dog."

Mrs. Ploomfield's hemoglobin seized up like a piston, and it took several moments before she reconstituted. "What? What did you just say? I want your name right this second, young man. I'm going to ruin your life!"

"I go first," said the man. He ripped open the candy box and pulled out a sawed-off Remington shotgun with a twelve-shell drum clip.

"Oh, my," said Mrs. Ploomfield. She slowly cranked on the jalousie window. It was a quarter closed when the man racked the shotgun and the clip fell out. Shells rolled across the concrete porch.

"Hee, hee, hee! You dropped your bullets," said Mrs. Ploomfield, still cranking arthritically. Half closed. The man leaned down and began reloading, a little faster than Ploomfield had expected.

"My goodness," she said, cranking faster. Three-quarters closed.

The man racked the shotgun again, but in his hurry the top shell of the magazine was not aligned to the feed lever, and it jammed. Mrs. Ploomfield finished closing the window and began shuffling back across the room.

The man unjammed the gun and fired with beer-ad gusto. Splinters of glass sprayed the room. "Oh, my heavens," said Mrs. Ploomfield. He fired again and again. A large swan-shaped vase exploded in front of Mrs. Ploomfield and a statue of a Persian cat behind her.

He kept firing and kept missing, all kinds of ugly ceramic shit blowing up. The smoke clouded his view, and the man used the barrel of his shotgun to knock out the triangles of broken glass around the inside edge of the jalousie door. He ducked his head and stepped through the opening. When he looked up, he saw Mrs. Ploomfield reaching into a bric-a-brac shadow box on the wall. Old-fart antique country junk, the man thought. He swept specks of glass off his shirt with the back of his hand and checked his magazine, making sure there would be no jam this time. When he looked up, he saw what Mrs. Ploomfield had been reaching for: In the largest compartment in the middle of the shadow box was her late husband's antique .45-caliber Peacemaker revolver. She wheeled and shot the man square in the chest, and he fell back through the hole in the door.

The gunfire drew neighbors from the condo units and the houses across the street. When they saw the van's driver dragging his dead partner and the shotgun back to the truck, they hit the ground and ducked behind square bushes.

The driver heaved the body through the passenger door and threw in the shotgun. He walked casually around the front of the van and climbed in the driver's seat. He leaned forward and turned up the radio. "New Sensation" by INXS pounded out of the truck and off the houses. The driver bobbed his head to the beat as he put the truck in gear and chugged down the street, running over a garbage can as he turned the corner. The neighbors watched the van until it disappeared, then slowly emerged and tiptoed toward unit 1193.

"I got one! I got one!" Mrs. Ploomfield shouted from her doorway. "I got one of the cocaine men!"

1

Lone headlights appeared in the blackness five miles away.

They were high-beams, illuminating the sea mist through the slashed mangroves and crushed coral down the long, straight causeway toward Miami. The rumble of rubber on tar grew louder and the headlights became brighter until they blinded. The Buick blew by at ninety and kept going, red taillights fading down U.S. 1 toward Key West.

It was quiet and dark again. An island in the middle of the Florida Keys. No streetlights, no light at all. The low pink building on the south side of the street was unremarkable concrete except for the hastily stuccoed bullet holes and the eight-foot cement conch shell on the shoulder of the road, chipped and peeling, holding up a sign: "Rooms $29.95 and up."

No cars in front of the motel; the night manager nodding in the office. The beach was sandy, some broken plastic kiddie toys, an unsafe pier and a scuttled dinghy. The air was still by the road, but around back a steady breeze came off the ocean. Coconut palms rustled and waves rolled in quietly from the Gulf Stream. Parked behind the motel, by the only room with a light on, was a black Mercedes limousine.

Voices and an electrical hum came from the room, number seven. Inside, personal effects covered one of the beds—toiletries, carefully rolled socks, newspaper clippings, sunscreen, postcards, snacks, ammunition—meticulously arranged in rows and columns. The hum was from the Magic Fingers bed jiggler that had been hot-wired to run continuously. The voices came from the TV that had been unbolted from its wall mount and now sat on a chair facing into the bathroom, tuned to *Sportscenter*.

In the flickering blue-gray TV light, a figure sat in the bathtub behind an open *Miami Herald*. Two sets of fingers held the sides of the paper—a front-page splash about a drug shoot-out in Key West and a missing five million in cash—and smoke rose from behind the paper. An old electric fan sat on the closed toilet lid, blowing into the tub. Something about the Miami Dolphins came on ESPN. The man in the tub folded the paper and put it on the toilet tank. He grabbed the remote control sitting in the soap dish on the shower wall. The slot in the top of the soap dish held a .38 revolver by the snub nose. "Nobody messes with Johnny Rocco," said the man in the tub, and he pressed the volume button.

The bather was tan, tall and lean with violating ice-blue eyes, and his hair was military-short with flecks of gray. He was in his late thirties and wore a new Tampa Bay Buccaneers baseball cap. In his mouth was a huge cigar, and he took it out with one hand and picked up an Egg McMuffin with the other. He checked his watch. Top of the hour. He clicked the remote control with the McMuffin hand and surfed over to CNN for two minutes, to make sure nothing had broken out in the world that would demand his response, and then over to A&E and the biography of Burt Reynolds for background noise while he read the *Herald* editorials. He put the McMuffin down on the rim of the tub and picked up the cup of orange juice. On TV, Burt made a long football run for Florida State in a vintage film of a forgotten Auburn game. The tub's edge also held jelly doughnuts, breakfast fajitas and a scrambled egg/sausage breakfast in a preformed plastic tray. On the toilet lid, next to the fan, was a hardcover book from 1939, the WPA guide to Florida. Inside the cover, the man had written his name. Serge A. Storms.

Like now, Serge was usually naked when he was in a motel, but it wasn't sexual. Serge thought clothes were inefficient and uncomfortable; they restricted his movements, and his skin wanted to breathe. Nudity also cut down on changing time, since he was constantly in and out of the shower, subjecting himself to rapid temperature changes, alternating hot and cold water rushes that reminded him he was alive and cleaned out the pores to keep that skin breathing, feeling new.

Serge hesitated a second in the tub, mid-bite in the McMuffin. He couldn't think of what to do next, not

even something as simple as chewing. Too many
ideas raged at once in his head, and his brain grid-
locked. He was paralyzed. Then the congestion
slowly unclogged and he resumed chewing. When he
realized he could move his arms again, he reached on
top of the toilet tank for a prescription bottle. He
shook it, but it made no sound, and he tossed the
empty in the waste can beside the sink, a bank shot
off the ceramic seashell tiles. Hell with it, he thought,
I'll go natural. If it gets too strange, I'll run to a drug
hole and score some Elavil that crackheads use to
come down after four days on the ledge. Serge had
started feeling the effects of not keeping up with his
psychiatric medication.

And he liked it.

He got out of the tub and opened the back door of
the motel room and walked out under a coconut
palm. The breeze dried the sweat cold on his skin. He
looked up into the nexus of palm fronds and coconuts set against the Big Dipper and a sky of brilliant stars over the water, away from the light
pollution of the mainland. Serge said: "There's a big
blow a-comin'."

Serge went back inside and slept all day in the
motel tub, and his skin shriveled. Two hours before
sunset, there was a loud beeping sound in room
seven. Serge awoke in alarm and splashed around as
if he'd discovered a cottonmouth in the water. He
jumped from the tub and into his pants without tow-
eling off. The beeping sound came from a metal box
on the dresser, an antitheft car-tracking device. Serge
threw on a shirt and packed a travel bag in seconds.

He didn't close the door as he ran out with shirt open and shoes in his hands. He threw the bag and shoes in the front of the limo and sped away from the motel.

Serge caught up to the white Chrysler on the Long Key Viaduct and closed quickly as they passed Duck Key. They hit the next island. At mile post 66, they passed the historic marker for the Long Key Fishing Club, whose president was Zane Grey.

Serge became jittery and started to sweat. He looked over his shoulder and wiped his brow.

"Damn!" He smacked the steering wheel with both palms. He did a fishtailing U-turn on U.S. 1 and raced back to the roadside marker. He jumped out of the limo with his camera and took three quick snapshots, then hopped back in the driver's seat.

He caught sight of the Chrysler again coming off the Channel Five Bridge into the Matecumbes. At mile 73, he saw the resort hotel coming up on the right. Serge stepped on the gas and summoned the will to resist, locking his eyes on the Chrysler. He began to vibrate. His face reddened from backbuild of blood pressure. He finally shrieked and took a hard turn, skidding into the parking lot at the gas pumps. He wound his way through the resort grounds to the waterfront and the Safari Lounge. He burst inside the bar with the camera. The bartender and patrons stopped and looked. Serge took quick pictures of the walls displaying old photos and mounted heads of exotic game the bar's owner had gotten on hunting trips to Africa with Ernest Hemingway. Then he ran out.

Back on the road, he was about to leave Islamorada and still hadn't reacquired the Chrysler. At mile 83, Serge saw the stone Whale Harbor Tower. He banged his forehead on the steering wheel three times, then grabbed the camera.

*f*lorida was on fire and Johnny Vegas didn't care.

He was in room four of the Rod and Gun Lodge in Everglades City, trying to score with a lithe spokesmodel for fattening beer products he'd picked up at an MTV promotional show-your-ass-athon in Miami Beach. The Florida Marlins had just won the World Series, whose rich celebratory tradition often peaks with fans mistaking police cruisers for piñatas. When the spokesmodel began nibbling Johnny's ear on Ocean Drive, he didn't want to take any chances. The specter of mob misbehavior inspired Johnny to shove her in his Porsche and immediately put a hundred miles between them and Miami. They headed west into the glades on the Tamiami Trail. Johnny stopped at a megaplectic convenience store frequented by airboat operators and survivalists with inscrutable politics. He purchased cheese, bread, crackers, a four-dollar bottle of champagne, plastic cups, Vaseline, duct tape and ribbed Day-Glo rubbers, and he winked with conspiracy at the cashier. Back on the road, Johnny cranked up Sheryl Crow.

"*. . . I think a change . . . would do you good . . .*"

He sped past Miccosukee Indian chickee huts on the two-lane shoulderless highway, flawlessly filling the plastic cups with champagne to demonstrate the sports car's fine European suspension; the model squeezed Johnny's crotch, stress-testing his sleek Italian slacks. They pulled in at the rustic mosquito lodge on the western edge of the Everglades, surrounded by miles of nothing but peace. The buzz of crickets relaxed Johnny as he stuck the key in the knob of their room.

It had been a dry, brittle autumn, and a rash of lightning strikes sparked forest fires in sixty-six of sixty-seven counties. The winds drove the blazes across highway breaks. Civic events were canceled and motels evacuated from Tallahassee to Homestead. A fire line advanced on the mosquito lodge.

Gigi the spokesmodel returned from the hotel bathroom naked, but her eyes watered hard.

"What's that smoke?" she asked between coughs.

"Nothing," said Johnny. "Just a pig roast or a citronella tiki torch, to keep bugs away." He leaned her back on the bed and tried to stroke her breast with a gentle, feathery touch, but she kept bouncing around from full-body hacking. More smoke came through the window seals and under the door. Johnny started coughing, too, and he grabbed a handkerchief and put it over his mouth and nose as he prepared to penetrate.

Gigi stopped him. "I can't breathe!"

Johnny pulled her off the bed and pinned her on the varnished wood floor that had historic character.

"I saw a public safety message once where Dick Van Dyke said to get down below the smoke line," said Johnny.

"To survive," said Gigi, "not to make love!"

The was a sharp knock on the door. "Emergency management! Anyone in there?"

"Yes! Help!" said Gigi.

"No! Nobody's here!" said Johnny. "We're okay. Go away!"

"Mandatory evacuation! You have to come out!"

"We're fine!" said Johnny. "I'll sign a waiver. Slip it under the door."

The officials opened the room with a pass key. They wrapped Gigi in a towel and administered oxygen as they led her to an evacuation van. Johnny straggled behind, clenching his fists. "I was this close. *This close!*"

Johnny followed the van in his convertible Porsche to the command post outside the burn zone, where Gigi was checked out by field medics, who gave her bottled water and fire safety pamphlets, and she turned and gave Johnny a stare that could freeze hydrogen.

$\mathcal{T}$he black Mercedes 420S limousine was doing a hundred when it clipped the gopher tortoise, which spun on the heel of its shell and tumbled violently as it skipped down the road. It came to rest. The tortoise poked its head out of the shell and looked around the edge of the Tamiami Trail in the Everglades.

Serge had seen the tortoise and tried to avoid it. He lost control of the limo and bounced through the sawgrass a bit before coaxing it back on the pavement. The limo's steering column was missing its plastic collar, and Serge's ignition key was a slot screwdriver. A crumpled tag lay on the floor from the Key West Police impound lot. Serge thought he should probably ditch the limo, since it would draw attention, but he didn't because, one, he was nuts, and two, it had gizmos.

The sun went down, a deep red beach ball over Naples, and Serge raced through the glades waiting for the back of a white Chrysler to show up in his headlights. In the Chrysler's trunk was five million dollars in drug money. It was in a metal briefcase hidden behind a panel over the wheel well, unknown to the car's innocent occupants. In fact, nobody knew it was there except Serge.

Serge speculated there was more missing drug money around Florida than buried pirate treasure. The illegal drug industry flows hundreds of millions of dollars in and out of Florida every year. It's all in cash. It's moving around constantly. It must be concealed every step of the way or ditched in an emergency. And most of the people hiding and retrieving it *are on drugs*. They do a few lines or bong hits and go back and say, "I could've sworn it was under this rock . . . or was it that one?"

This time around, someone had tried to make off with five million in cartel money being laundered through a Tampa insurance company. That someone was dead now. Serge had seen to it. But before Serge could move in, the man had tossed the money in the trunk of an acquaintance's car. . . .

The *Miami Herald* sent three reporters to Key West and two more up to Canaveral to cover the story. Eleven bodies so far. One sap shotgunned in a

Cocoa Beach motel room, three tied to cement
blocks in the ocean, another floating with a doll's
head in his windpipe, and four more machine-
gunned in a Key West bed-and-breakfast, three of
whom were members of the Russian mafia from Fort
Lauderdale. A man was run over outside the stadium
in Miramar by a car with a dead stripper in the trunk.
Rumors said the killings were over five million in a
missing briefcase. Nobody knew whether the briefcase or the money really existed, but that didn't stop
everyone in Key West from clearing out of the bars
and tearing the island apart. As more and more bodies turned up, another rumor began to circulate about
the money.

   It was cursed.

Sean Breen and David Klein headed home fishless
again, their record intact. The breadth and complex-
ity of each fishing failure was increasingly impressive. This time they had gone all the way to the Keys
and spent a couple thousand to not catch fish.

   They had overlearned the sport. They studied drag
and line and leaders. There were tides and feeding
patterns and how to read the water. They boned up on
"the presentation of the lure" like it was a plaque at a
Rotary luncheon. Too much thinking and not enough
fishing.

   They didn't care. Fishing wasn't about *catching*
fish. It was about trolling the flats with a silent electric motor, watching the barracudas and sharks and
tarpon. And the colors: down in the Saddlebunch

Keys, ten miles from Key West, the bright pastel green puddled up in the cracked cakes of clay . . . fluorescent aqua near the mouth of Newfound Harbor . . . raw umber shining off the coral through the shallows at Ramrod Key.

They had a heck of a fish story to tell when they got back, except that everybody had heard the whole thing already on the news. The big fiasco down in the Keys. They got special commendations from the mayor and a gold trophy from the city council for basically being in the wrong place at the wrong time—and staying alive in the cross fire while the bad guys bumped each other off. It was a chance for local officials to put smiling faces on the tourism nightmare. All that was behind them now.

Sean and David were one hundred ninety miles from Tampa, crossing the Everglades at dusk. They had just passed Ochopee, home of the smallest post office in the United States, when they saw a commotion up ahead. There were men in the road and a bunch of cars parked askance on the shoulders. They noticed a glow on the horizon, and their headlights caught wisps of what they first thought was fog. There was a line of blinking amber lights ahead on wooden barricades. A sweaty man with a reflective yellow vest and a blackened face stepped into the middle of their lane and put his arms out toward the car, ordering them to stop. David and Sean pulled over and saw a firefighting team on the side of the road taking water; some were tended by paramedics.

A wildfire was raging across the Everglades, and a stout northeastern wind had whipped it toward the

Tamiami Trail. Soon flames came into view and scrub burned to the edge of the pavement. A National Guard helicopter swooped overhead. A team of fire-fighters staggered out of the smoke in a sawgrass ditch and collapsed. The firefighters who had been resting got to their feet and disappeared into the smoke. Tourists who had been stopped by the road-block took snapshots and video. A young man in Italian slacks cursed and pounded his fist on the hood of a Porsche.

David and Sean stood on the side of the road next to a panther-crossing sign. They watched the fire jump to the other side of the road, and the highway became a tunnel of flame filled with smoke. The wind gusted and shifted again to the east, and the fire leaned toward them. The resting firefighters got to their feet and motioned the motorists back to their cars. They yelled for everyone to evacuate east. The fire would be burning where they now stood within twenty minutes.

Sean and David turned and started back to the Chrysler. It was the first time they noticed the black Mercedes limousine parked behind it. They were a few yards away when the Chrysler's headlights suddenly came on and the engine roared to life. They jumped back as the car lurched off the shoulder of the road and sped past them. Firefighters ran into the highway, waving for the driver to stop. They dove out of the way as the Chrysler splintered the wooden barricades and disappeared into the wall of flame.

2

*N*ear the end of 1997, at longitude twenty degrees west and latitude ten degrees north, the waters of the North Atlantic Ocean reached a comfortable eighty degrees Fahrenheit, and vapor filled the air. The trade winds blew robustly and the barometric pressure dipped. Convection began to convect. The earth rotated, as it has for billions of years, and the force of the spinning imparted the Coriolis effect on the atmosphere. Nobody was there to see it happen, but lots of air and water molecules started turning slowly like a child's top the size of Iowa.

Three thousand miles east of Florida and four hundred miles west of Dakar on the coastal tip of Africa sit the Cape Verde Islands. There are fifteen islands in the chain, ten large and developed, five not. In Cape Verde they grow coffee beans, bananas and sugar cane, and they catch tuna and lobster. They won independence from Portugal in 1975, and many residents practice animism, the belief that everything in nature has a soul. The monetary unit is the escudo. Four of the five smaller islets of Cape Verde are uninhabited. But on the fifth is an aboriginal, nonviolent people who live in thatched huts atop stilts on the beach. The people are simple hunter-gatherers, subsisting on fish and mollusks and, until this century, a hairless feral dog that ran wild on the island.

Because of Cape Verde's remoteness, its tiny indigenous dogs have experienced quirky evolution, much like that of the Galapagos turtles, and they've developed extremely sensitive inner ears to detect predators. In the year 1897, a terrific tropical cyclone threatened the island late one night after everyone had gone to bed. When the barometer plunged from the impending storm, the painful pressure in the dogs' delicate ears caused them to screech and jump up and down across the island. The villagers were awakened by the yelping little animals twirling on their hind legs in the middle of the village. Then they noticed the leading edge of the hurricane coming ashore.

The storm demolished every hut, but the entire population had enough warning to move upland to the center of the island and was spared. The good-luck dogs were given an indefinite reprieve from the island people's cuisine.

Exactly one hundred years later, at the end of November, the last month of the official hurricane season, the village chief brought out the ceremonial dog after dinner. It had been a light hurricane season for the islands, and there had been no need to press the dog into service. He lived the good life in his own hut and had grown quite fat on the grateful and excessive amount of food the island people provided. Tonight, however, the chief had a feeling in his bones. The sky was strange, the fishing futile, and the birds were flying into things.

Following a dinner of stewed mollusk, the chief arrived with the sacred dog in a bamboo cage. The dog was dressed in his ceremonial costume. The inhabitants of the island were a carefree people, and the only thing they wore was a thong woven from palm fronds and bound tightly between the legs. The dog's costume was a smaller version.

The chief placed the cage atop a tree stump and said the magic incantations. He lifted the door of the cage and the dog scampered under a bush and started chewing off the painful thong. There was no dance of the dog in the village circle. The chief raised his arms and decreed that the sacred dog had spoken: All was safe on the island.

Shortly after midnight, the village was awakened by a newly formed hurricane ripping huts off their stilts. Everyone was able to climb to safety, due to well-timed panic and mad scrambling. But dog was back on the menu.

A childless Colombian couple named Juanita and José Cerbeza moved into a four-bedroom million-dollar waterfront home in Tampa's prestigious Culbreath Isles community.

The residence had been the original model home for the Tampa Bay Tile Company. It had a Spanish tile roof and a circular driveway of brick-red paver tiles that curved around the giant fan of a traveler's palm. The front porch was a colorful mishmash of broken porcelain and pottery set randomly in the mortar. The spleen-shaped swimming pool had a rim of violet ceramic bullnose tile and a large patio of glazed Mexican tile. From the pool was a clear view of Tampa Bay over a seawall capped with coquina tile.

The moving van arrived Saturday night. The Cerbezas began hand-to-hand combat Sunday morning.

José was a small, powerfully packed man with a falsetto voice and explosive temper. In contrast, Juanita was a woman of impressive avoirdupois, and if she could ever hold José still, she'd squeeze the breath out of him. Necessarily, José's strategy was jab-and-run, and he danced around Juanita and darted in and out of the reach of her bologna arms, registering sharp jabs in the kidneys that caused her to make the birthing sounds of a Cape buffalo.

The clash was the age-old balance of the natural order, size against speed, and it was a fascinating thing to watch. However, early on a Sunday morning in one of Tampa's toniest neighborhoods, the residents had yet to acquire an appreciation for a South American midget screaming Spanish profanities like Frankie Valli and sucker-punching a fat woman into submission between the jacarandas.

The police drove Juanita and José away in separate patrol cars.

Hours later—calm restored and bail posted—the

couple was released at sunset for a tearful reunion outside the Orient Road Jail. They took a cab back to Culbreath Isles and embraced again on the red-tile driveway before going inside.

An hour later they were back at it on the front lawn, and a careless José got a little too close. Juanita began crushing him in a Kodiak hug.

Neighbors with cell phones filled the sidewalks as Juanita caved in José until his cries became mere peeps. Before police could respond to the eleven simultaneous 911 complaints from Culbreath Isles, a black Beemer pulled up to the house and cut the headlights. The engine and parking lights stayed on. Two men in gray jogging suits got out. They raised their right arms, fully extended, and aimed SIG 9mm automatic pistols, the P-210 model with the attractive scored wooden grip. They fired ten to twelve shots each, and the silencers gave the gunfire a docile, metallic *ka-ching ka-ching* sound that made it seem not quite real to the neighbors.

The BMW sped away, and the neighbors slowly approached to inspect the lifeless pile of José and Juanita.

*T*he Diaz Boys were crazy.

Three brothers and a cousin, they had smuggled, trafficked, extorted and strong-armed their way around Tampa Bay for fifteen years. They were the last of their breed. The average shelf life of their peers was three years, and the Diaz Boys had out-

lived them all. The Garcia Brothers, the Rodriguez
Brothers, the Uptown Gang, the O'Malley Triplets,
the Caballero Siamese Twins and Octopus Boy.

The Diaz Boys were lucky, because it certainly
wasn't brains. They were the statistical exception
that proves the rule, and they were completely psy-
cho. Whenever a light touch of sophistication was required, they kicked the door in. Their brazenness
survived the odds the way the occasional drunk can
weave across a freeway and not get splattered.

Florida still had its scars from the cocaine eighties.
Prison expansion, after-care centers, foreclosed waterfront mansions, luxury yachts in dry dock. Like
Germany after the war—lots of people fleeing to
South America, abandoning cars, houses and artwork. Stashes of currency and gold were plastered
into walls or buried at the base of a crooked tree.
With a single haul of coke worth up to a hundred million dollars, smuggling methods became the stuff of
Florida lore. Expensive airplanes and speedboats
were ditched after a single shipment. When customs
agents began giving "swallowers" laxatives at the
airport, surgeons sewed the coke into their legs. Law
enforcement had thought they'd seen it all.

Then came disposable real estate.

Smugglers set up "moles" in posh waterfront
Florida homes with docks. The moles were married
couples, and they'd live at the home about a year.
They were given a sailboat and told to use it often.
Every expense paid. All they had to do was blend in
and keep a low profile until the day their "uncle" vis-

ited and went sailing with them at sunset and came
back after dark with the boat riding much lower in
the water.

It was simple in theory and profoundly problem-
atic in practice. The people the Diaz Boys recruited
could not for the life of them keep it together a full
year. They went loopy from the wealth and drugs,
partying and attacking each other in front of the
neighbors. They tried using local talent—gringos—
but the results were the same except the screaming
on the front lawn was in English. Hundreds of thousands invested in one mole house. Poof! Wasted in a
single violent incident that traumatized the whole
block and ensured the couple's every move would be
watched closely from then on. The Diaz Boys had
had it. In the last year alone, there'd been five aggravated batteries and a DeLorean driven into a swimming pool. When José and Juanita Cerbeza didn't
last two days in Culbreath Isles, the Diaz Boys had
already made their decision.

A green Jaguar crested the hump of the Gandy
Boulevard Bridge heading across the bay from St.
Petersburg to Tampa. A few fishermen worked nets
and rods on the old Gandy Bridge, now closed down,
running alongside the new span. The illuminated red
letters of "Misener Marine" glowed on the shore and
reflected in the choppy midnight water.

Two men sat in the front seat of the Jag and one in
the back.

"What do you think? Should they tear down the old Gandy or leave it up for a jogging trail?" asked the front passenger.

"I don't jog," said the driver.

"Sake of discussion."

"Leave it up, I guess."

"Why don't you take your arm in from the window and roll it up?"

"You cold?" asked the driver.

"No, I don't want you trying to signal the police or other drivers." He pushed the six-inch barrel of the .44 Magnum into the driver's ribs.

"Look, you got the wrong guy. I sell insurance. Check my wallet. Check the glove compartment."

The driver certainly looked like the insurance type. Conservative, neat black hair in a business cut. On the handsome side, a rough-hewn Burt Lancaster type. Light acne scarring, but only enough to add character. Five-eleven, one-eighty. White oxford shirt rolled to the elbows, now soaked in sweat, and an awful maroon tie with flying squares all over it.

"Fuck you, Fiddlebottom. You owe us fifty grand. That coke had been cut. You think we're stupid? You think we didn't have someone inside in Opa-Locka test purity? Fifty grand. That's the cost of a ten-point step."

"I got kids! A wife! Will you look at that wallet? You're making a mistake. You got me mixed up with someone. . . . Look, I won't tell anyone. You've got me scared to death. I'll just be happy to get out with my life."

"Which ain't gonna happen!"

"I'll give you fifty grand myself."

"Hell no. Fifty K is nothin' to the boss. But you shit on him. He wants you to stop using his oxygen. We're gonna take you out by the port. You don't give us any trouble, we'll do you a favor and put two in the back of your head. You won't feel a thing. You fuck around, we shoot your knees, then we'll do the rest slow with knives. All above the neck."

They were coming off the bridge.

"Slow to thirty-five and stay in the left lane," said the passenger.

"We turning left?" asked the driver.

"No. I don't want you to sideswipe a parked car or a pole. You're starting to get desperate, and I know what's going through your head. Maybe thinking you'll hit something and I'll fly into the dashboard and lose my gun. Well, if I don't get you, Lou back there will."

The driver looked over his right shoulder. Lou, the silent one, smiled. He had the perfect angle on the driver, aiming a .45 automatic that lay sideways atop the back of the passenger seat.

"We had a guy try to crash us once," said the front passenger. "Veered for a mailbox. We saw it coming and Lou popped him behind the ear. We hit the box and got banged up pretty good, but we laid the guy over in the front seat to cover the bullet hole. When everyone rushed up to the car, we yelled for an ambulance. All they saw was this guy and a lot of blood. What's new? Blood in a friggin' accident? By the time the paramedics turned him over and saw the entry wound, we'd disappeared. So whatever's going through your mind, you won't be fast enough."

The driver shook visibly.

"I'm telling you, you got the wrong guy. This is a horrible mistake. I want to see my family again!"

"Don't lose it on us," said the passenger. He jammed the barrel harder into his ribs. "Don't fuck up now, Fiddlebottom."

"You know what model Jaguar this is?" asked the driver.

"What?"

"You know what model this is?"

"How the hell should I know? It's *your* car."

"That's right, it is."

They approached the light at West Shore Boulevard.

"Just shut up," said the passenger, growing annoyed.

"You should have taken me in your own car instead of carjacking me. You don't know anything about this Jag."

"I said, shut up!"

The driver turned and stared the passenger straight in the eyes. The passenger started to get angry but something gave him the creeps. "What's wrong with you! Watch the road!"

The driver didn't speak right away. While staring at the passenger, the driver saw everything he needed with peripheral vision. He imperceptibly turned the wheel to the left. He smiled and said in a calm voice, "We only have one air bag."

When the passenger heard the horn, the oncoming cement mixer was only feet away.

The last thing the passenger heard: "You shouldn't have called me Fiddlebottom."

The passenger went through the windshield and into the grille of the truck. Lou, recently of the backseat, only made it halfway out the windshield behind his buddy. His moaning was a faint gurgle, the lacerations superficial, the internal injuries mortal.

The Jag's driver awoke from unconsciousness and shook his head to clear the fog. He pushed away the deflating airbag. His white oxford was splattered with blood. He checked quickly—not his. He sighed. "I have *got* to get out of the cocaine business."

He saw two police officers rushing toward his door, and he started crying. They told him to stay still—they'd have the door pried open in no time. He looked up at them through tears. "I was carjacked!"

3

The Diaz Boys didn't exactly outlive everybody. There was this one other guy.

Harvey Fiddlebottom kept telling himself he had to get out of the cocaine business.

Since the salad days of the 1980s, Fiddlebottom had branched out into the comparatively harmless fields of wire fraud, election tampering and stolen car parts. But his voracious greed-streak kept bringing him back. Fiddlebottom had mixed luck in the trafficking business. His deals regularly went awry. On the other hand, he always came out alive.

He sat by the pool at the Hammerhead Ranch Motel and read a newspaper article about another shipment of cocaine intercepted on I-75. To Fiddlebottom, it was a hundred-thousand-dollar loss. Goddamn the Diaz Boys! He had let them talk him into it again. He threw the paper down in disgust.

"I've got to get out of the cocaine business!"

Harvey Fiddlebottom's name belied his brutality. He hadn't always been a tough guy, but his name made it inevitable. It had that certain musical texture that invited daily butt-kickings from his classmates. By senior year they had created a monster. Violent threats, school hall beatings, weapons charges. After his expulsion, Fiddlebottom decided he needed a fresh start, a bigger gun and a new name. It had to be a special name. Something to command respect, strike fear. One word, like Cher. He grabbed an old city map of Pensacola and read down the street index until he found something he could live with. He filed the necessary papers with the county clerk. The former Harvey Fiddlebottom walked out of the courthouse, puffed up his chest and strolled back into life a new man. The new man swore he'd kill anyone who called him by his old name. From now on, he would only answer to *Zargoza*.

Zargoza got into the drug business in the mid-1980s. The Diaz Boys needed a mole for a piece of disposable real estate. Tommy Diaz had gone to Tampa High School with Zargoza and remembered his brutal tendencies from senior year. Banging taunting kids' heads into walls. Now that was style.

They knocked on the door of his second-floor apartment on grimy Hillsborough Avenue. Zargoza opened up shirtless, wearing blue boxer shorts with smiling sharks, hair uncombed, eyes not ready for the light of day, gun in hand.

"Hey, Fiddlebottom, we got a proposition for you," said Tommy Diaz.

Zargoza raised his pistol and the Diaz Boys pulled theirs. Point-blank, standing against the rusted turquoise balcony railing, afternoon traffic going by.

"Nobody calls me by that name anymore! From now on, it's Zargoza!"

"Zargoza what?" asked Tommy.

"It's like Cher," said Zargoza.

"Zargoza Bono?"

"No, you fucking idiot! Just Zargoza."

But the gun and the cursing were a language the Diaz Boys understood and respected, and they told him he was the right man for the job.

"We'll call you Carmen Miranda if it makes you happy," said Tommy. He handed Zargoza a thick brown envelope and Zargoza peeked inside.

For eighteen months, Zargoza managed the run-down Hammerhead Ranch Motel on the Gulf of Mexico near St. Petersburg. After three successful shipments of cocaine, the Diaz Boys moved on to new property and gave Zargoza the motel deed as a tip.

Hammerhead Ranch was falling apart, but that was its charm. The entrance was the gate of an Old West corral—two upright posts connected at the top by a wooden plank with the name of the motel and the cattle brand "HR" burned in a circle. In the middle of the plank was the stuffed head of a hammerhead shark with a rope lasso around its neck. The motel was a single-story L-shaped ranch house. The building stayed white, but the color of the trim changed every other year. Pink, blue, yellow, orange, seafoam green. It was originally the Golden Palm Inn, built in 1961, then the Coconut Grove, the Whispering Palms Lodge, the Econo-Palm Motor Court and Herb's Triple-X Honeymoon Hideaway ("in the palms"). Then the owners got back from a trip through Texas on Route 66. They'd driven by Amarillo and seen the ten half-buried cars at the landmark Cadillac Ranch, and the rest is roadside Florida kitsch history. The owners contacted charter fishermen and taxidermy shops and in three months had purchased ten stuffed hammerhead sharks, which they planted in a row behind the swimming pool.

The owners thought it would increase business, but it only increased the number of people who stopped, posed for snapshots and drove off.

As the nineties dawned, Zargoza saw the beginning of the end of cocaine. The Diaz Boys did not. Zargoza diversified, and in five years he had parlayed his drug proceeds into enough savvy criminal enterprises that he pulled even in wealth and stature to the Diaz Boys. As the nineties waned, the only reason Zargoza would buy into a coke run anymore was uncontrollable avarice and the sporadic favor he owed the Diaz Boys in return for having used their muscle to limber up stubborn clients. And, though nobody would admit it, they liked to hang out together, mainly to bust each other's balls for old times' sake. Surviving fraternity brothers, the Last of the Mohicans. Sometimes they drank at the motel bar and sometimes they drag-raced after midnight around the bay.

Zargoza had a small chop shop in Ybor City and a hand in a nursing home Medicare scam, but most recently he concentrated on the boiler room telephone bunco operation he had set up at Hammerhead Ranch. He gutted and connected the last four rooms of the motel into a giant office and furnished it with military surplus desks, telephones, copiers and postal meters. Zargoza's callers worked sucker lists that cost up to fifteen bucks a name. The room hummed with the overlapping patter of con men.

"This is your lucky day, Mrs. Castiglioni! You're our grand prize winner. Now just give us your credit card number so we can verify eligibility and pay our modest processing fee. . . ."

"No, you won't wait to ask your husband when he comes home, and we won't wait either, Mrs. Shoemaker, because this offer is only good for the next five minutes! You're not a loser, you're a winner! And your husband will be so proud of you. Now, I want you to start reading that credit card number when I count to three. One . . . two . . ."

"You're king of the world, Mr. Boudreau! This is your big day! Do you believe in God, Mr. Boudreau? . . . Good, because God wants you to get out that credit card. . . ."

The con men made regular runs to the coffee machine but didn't pour any coffee. Zargoza may have been against the drug business, but not *drugs*, and he provided his phone operators with an unlimited supply of complimentary cocaine. It was an expensive experiment, but Zargoza immediately saw profits spike due to increasingly predatory salesmanship.

"Feeding them coke was the smartest thing I ever did," Zargoza told Tommy Diaz as he gave a tour of the operation. "Look at 'em intimidating those old bastards. Check out that satanic sparkle in their eyes. You don't get that from Folgers."

Zargoza stopped at the coffee stand and dipped a flat wooden stirring stick in a pile of white powder. He stuck it under his nose and snorted.

His arms flew out, and he fell against the wall, shattering a full-length motel mirror. He pawed at his stinging nose like a dog that just stuck his snout in a fire-ant hole.

"Jesus! Who put the fucking nondairy creamer in the cocaine jar?"

"Sorry, Z," said one of the phone men. "The coke's in that other jar today."

"Let's get some labels on this stuff. God knows what's in Coffee-mate!"

"Sure thing, Z."

Zargoza turned to Tommy. "You got to get out of cocaine, man. It's passé. It's just not chic anymore. Brings too much heat. Now, wire fraud—that's where it's at.

"We send out fake insurance invoices and credit card bills. We scare old people into buying home security systems that we get at Radio Shack for a fifth the price—say stuff like 'Did you know Mrs. Crabtree on the next street was anally raped by winos?' We mark up water-filtration systems eight hundred bucks, tell the old bags they need it or they'll grow kidney stones like avocados.

"For a while we took out second mortgages on houses we didn't own. Amazingly easy. Get a fake driver's license, find a nice home and start calling mortgage brokers. The business is so competitive they almost make you take the money at gunpoint. They Xerox your license and hand you the cashier's check. They don't even take you to the house to make sure you have the keys. So you cash out the check and you got a month's head start until the home-owner gets a new payment book in the mail and calls the mortgage company and says, 'What the hell's this?' "

Tommy Diaz nodded approvingly.

"The key is not to get too greedy in any one scheme," continued Zargoza. "I've survived through diversification—getting out of every scam just a little bit early, before the authorities catch on. Since it's not violent crime, the complaints have to reach a crit-ical mass in some government office before it comes off the back burner. By spreading out the scams, you spread out the complaints. . . . I tell ya, this new gen-eration coming up"—he made a dismissive wave of his arm—"they reject many lucrative areas of crime simply because they're not glamorous enough."

They walked by a table where a man sat hunched over cartons of eggs working with a counterfeit USDA ink stamp.

"I still got the chop shop in Ybor City, to anchor the portfolio, but otherwise I'm only expanding in the white-collar sector," Zargoza told Tommy. He reached into a file and handed Tommy Diaz a docu-ment from the secretary of state's office.

"Amalgamated Eclectic Inc., a Florida corpora-tion," said Tommy, reading the fine official certifi-cate. "Impressive."

"Wait till you hear about my latest venture. Sweepstakes. Look at this great mailer! Big letters: 'YOU'VE WON MILLIONS!!!' Gets 'em every time. I was receiving the offers so often myself that I figured they had to be making money."

"Who's this in the little picture on the mailer?" asked Tommy Diaz.

"Some has-been personality. I figured I needed a celebrity endorsement. All the stars these old people remember—they're nobodies today. You can get 'em to endorse anything real cheap."

"Sounds like you've thought this all out," said Tommy.

"You know the best part? You meet a much better class of people in this line of work. In the drug business everyone's a backstabbing scumbag looking to rip you off or turn you in. But in telephone fraud, your victims are all sweet, polite, law-abiding citizens who would never think of taking advantage of you. Why can't everyone be like that?"

The two stared out the back window in quiet contentment and watched a white Chrysler New Yorker with scorch marks down the sides pull up to the motel office.

4

*H*ammerhead Ranch had a wonderful, sweaty Florida seediness to it. The bargain pricing drew an interesting cast, who slinked around the pool and the bar. The sidewalk outside the rooms had orange-brown rust stains from the sprinklers. Rooms one to eleven ran parallel to the beach along the long part of the motel's L layout. Zargoza's four-room boiler operation occupied rooms twelve to fifteen—the short part of the L that ran toward the water. Every room had a story to tell.

Room one: It was 1971. A forty-year-old man stood on a bright afternoon in the Fra Mauro highlands. His name was Edgar Mitchell. He held what looked like a long-handled gardening tool and he slowly scooped up a few little gray rocks and some dirt. Then Mr. Mitchell got in a rocket ship and flew to the third planet in our solar system, called Earth. The United States government looked at the moon rocks for a while and gave a few of them to a man named President Nixon. Mr. Nixon gave some of the rocks to people who ran other countries, to try to get them to like him. He gave one rock the size of a Cocoa Puff to a man at the top of the government of Honduras. The Honduran head of state was ousted in a violent coup and the rock fell into the hands of a rebel leader named Ché Gazpacho, who put it in a special case on his credenza. Gazpacho was killed a week later when the military regained control during the chaos following a hotly contested soccer match in the capital of Tegucigalpa. The moon rock was grabbed by one of the lieutenants storming the rebels in the presidential palace, who was forced to give it to the general who entered the room behind him, who in turn was forced to give it to his long-legged mistress, who was using sex as a weapon and had unrealistic expectations of a singing career. The mistress gave the rock to an incompetent theatrical agent in the Dominican Republic named Shecky, who was later discovered in a filing cabinet in sixty feet of water. The rock turned up six months later in the lint and Wrigley gum wrappers at the bottom of a hooker's purse at the Hemingway Marina in Cuba, and she used it to get smuggled aboard a sailboat piloted by an American with a press visa who curses the day he put the rock up for collateral during a scag relapse in a leather bar on South Beach. The rock found its way to a pawnshop in Dania, where it sold for fifty dollars in food stamps. It changed hands three more times in a tight circle of people in the porn industry before ending up in the possession of a man who was trying to arrange a black market telephone auction from room one of Hammerhead Ranch.

Room two: Twenty-seven blue cardboard crates of legal-size files covered both beds. Lunch hour. Three unindicted co-conspirators in business suits anxiously fed documents into a ninety-nine-dollar shredder just out of the box from Office Depot.

Room three: A Balkan war criminal tried to unload three hundred loggerhead turtle eggs to an aphrodisiac salesman from Terra Ceia.

Room four: Twenty-one undocumented Haitians huddled silently as their cruise director, Captain Bradley Xeno, brushed his teeth in the mirror and hummed "Tequila."

Room five: Six federal agents sat around the edges of the beds eating Chinese-to-go and guarding an underboss in the witness protection program.

Room six: A delicensed surgeon stacked twenty thousand in cash in his briefcase and prepared to saw off the right leg of a man afflicted with the rare condition apotemnophilia, the sexual desire to have limbs removed.

Room seven: A Japanese businessman filled a hollow surfboard with a five-year supply of shark cartilage extract in gel caps.

Room eight: An unemployed auto mechanic named Leo barricaded himself and refused to come out, although he had done nothing wrong and nobody was looking for him.

Room nine: Three Cubans swallowed condoms filled with large American currency folded into tiny squares and triangles.

Room ten: Two men tried unsuccessfully for the

third day to sell a highjacked truckload of thirty thousand Motorola beepers.

Room eleven: Three Anglos in taste-proof floral shirts randomly tested seven kilos of cocaine packed in Sharps medical waste dispensers. Three Latinos in matching yellow guayaberas stood across from them, cramming bundles of hundred-dollar bills into the side of a Naugahyde golf bag.

Rooms twelve to fifteen: Zargoza went over the day's wire fraud receipts as a dozen con artists worked the phones. There was a loud thud against the wall coming from room eleven, then a series of smaller thumps and some yelling. A door slammed.

"What the hell?" said Zargoza.

On the other side of the wall in room eleven, bricks of coke and hundred-dollar bills were strewn across the floor and both beds. A Mexican standoff. Two of the men in floral shirts stood in one corner of the room, MAC-10s drawn. The third crouched on the floor with a pistol-grip Mossberg shotgun. The three Latinos aimed back with Rugers.

The door of eleven crashed open and four men in black ninja outfits ran into the room pointing sub-compact machine guns at both the Anglos and the Latinos. They wore night-vision goggles. It was the afternoon.

"I can't see anything! Are the lights on?" said one ninja, slapping the top of his goggles. He reached in a Velcro compartment on his right thigh, pulled out an underwater flare, cracked it and threw it on the floor, setting the carpet on fire.

"I still can't see anything. What's happening?"

The head ninja glanced sideways at his colleague and back at the men he was covering with his machine gun. He whispered out the corner of his mouth: "Lens caps."

"What?"

"Oh, for cryin' out loud!" the leader said. He turned and ripped the night goggles off the ninja's head and stomped out the carpet fire.

Then he aimed his weapon again at the floral shirts and guayaberas. "Okay, back to live action! Everybody drop your guns! You're all under arrest! We're U.S. special agents from the U.S. Special Agency."

"No, you drop 'em—*you're* under arrest!" said one of the floral shirts, showing a badge. "Florida Bureau of Investigation! This is a double-reverse, flea-flicker sting operation!"

A guayabera said, "No, both of *you* drop 'em! You're all subpoenaed! We're from the special prosecutor's office!"

"Are you freakin' kidding me?" said the ninja leader. "We're all cops?!"

A fist pounded from the other side of the wall. It was Zargoza. "Hey, what's all the racket in there! Knock it off!" he yelled, and he went back to weighing out cocaine on a triple-beam scale.

"You shut up!" a floral shirt yelled back through the wall and hit it with the butt of his shotgun. "I'll kick your ass!"

"I'm the owner!" yelled Zargoza. "Settle down or I'll call the police!"

The head ninja told them to cool it. This farce didn't need a fourth jurisdiction of cops.

"Sorry. We apologize," the leader yelled through the wall.

"That's better," shouted Zargoza, spooning cocaine. "We try to run a civilized place here."

The three teams of cops filed out of the room and took up a row of stools at the bar by the motel pool. They ordered strawberry daiquiris and watched a TV weather report on a new hurricane moving steadily across the Atlantic after slamming the Cape Verde Islands.

"Doesn't anyone sell cocaine these days?" asked an agent in a floral shirt. "I mean, besides undercover cops?"

"It's out of style," said a ninja with night-vision goggles propped on top of his head like sunglasses. He licked whipped cream off the end of a flamingo swizzle stick. "I don't think you can buy it in Florida anymore."

The Hammerhead Ranch Motel was a sandspur between the toes of everyone who lived next door in the spanking-new high-rises of Beverly Shores.

Condominiums, someday, will be the stuff of Florida nostalgia, but not yet.

Before it incorporated, Beverly Shores was the classic beach town. A row of one-story mom-and-pop motels built in the early sixties. All nondescript and modest except for the few dollars that went into corny neon signs. Alligators in top hats and dancing swordfish. Several of the motels carved out niches with foreign visitors. There were signs with maple leafs and Union Jacks, and one had an insane Bavarian with crossed eyes, playing a glockenspiel.

Hammerhead Ranch was the only one left. The others were all gone, demolished one by one to clear the path for the advancing column of condos that would become the City of Beverly Shores.

One of the condominiums had a twin, curved design like a W; one was stair-stepped. There was traditional Mediterranean, a towering spaceship and another that looked like the Watergate. One was a rhombus.

Half had the word "Arms" in the name. Total, nine hundred fifty units, average cost, six hundred thousand. Population: spite.

The residents were exceedingly fortunate and comfortable, which brought them to the inescapable conclusion that they needed to be pissed at someone. They were mad at people who drove down the public street in front of their condos, and swimmers who swam in their public ocean and beachcombers who combed their public beach. The phenomenon was so pronounced across Florida that such residents had a nickname: "Condo Commandos." The particular residents of Beverly Shores took it to a new level.

A nine-year-old overthrew a Frisbee behind one of the buildings, and it sailed a few yards across the city limits of Beverly Shores. A woman manicuring a shrub picked up the plastic disk, cut it in half with pruning shears and threw the two unaerodynamic pieces wobbling back at the boy.

The residents put aside a few hours each day to complain about being screwed by welfare mothers.

Every fall the storm season washed the beach at Beverly Shores out to sea, and every spring the Army Corps of Engineers sent in barges to dredge sand off the bottom of the Gulf and pump it back to shore. It cost millions of dollars and, coupled with their federally subsidized flood insurance, made the residents of Beverly Shores the biggest welfare recipients in the state. All the government required in return, to legitimize spending tax dollars on beach restoration, was public access to the already public beach.

It was an outrage.

The residents planted small trees to obscure the beach parking signs at the tiny access areas. When people continued showing up, they stole the signs at night and blamed outside agitators. They presented a united front of frosty stares at anyone who parked in the small public lot between their buildings; the mayor yelled at them if the parking job was out of alignment, and he yelled if it was not. The residents drove golf carts everywhere, with loud horns.

They were the luckiest people on the island, and they filled days of endless leisure in paradise by being petty, quarrelsome, obsessive and vindictive. They woke up difficult, had a whiny lunch and went to bed not backing down for shit.

When nobody from the outside world was doing them wrong, they turned on each other, and the courthouse brimmed with lawsuits and unfounded criminal complaints. Florida Cable News regularly rifled the legal briefs for a dependable stream of feature stories. There was the condo association that wouldn't let the disabled vet hang an American flag on his balcony for Memorial Day. And the child in the wheelchair sued for running over a sprinkler head. And the arrest of two women on the beach for breaking the beverage prohibition by drinking coffee during a morning stroll. Florida Cable News cameras were live in the courtroom for the weighing of Muffins, the not-so-miniature poodle who had eaten herself right up to the condo's fifteen-pound pet weight limit. But Muffins became nervous under the camera lights, and her shaking produced a range of readings from fourteen pounds fourteen ounces to fifteen pounds two ounces. Muffins then relieved herself in the scale, triggering motions from both lawyers on whether the bonus should be included in the weighing. The judge ordered a continuance and stomped off the bench in a huff. The stories were so frequent that Florida Cable News had an on-screen logo—"Beverly Shores 33786."

Almost all the incidents at Beverly Shores were minor. There were exceptions. One resident was watering the flower bed outside his ground-floor unit, and the resident upstairs, his archenemy and nemesis Malcolm Kefauver, the mayor of Beverly Shores, came up and needled him about the shade of blue of his wife's hair until Malcolm got a face full of hose water. The soaked Mayor Kefauver ran back in his condo looking for a weapon and grabbed the first thing he found. The man with the garden hose saw the mayor return, and he took off running.

It was an impressive shot. At a range of thirty feet, the fleeing condo owner was nailed in the derrière with a lawn dart. He went down to his knees like a rhino hit with a tranquilizer gun, then fell face first in the Bermuda grass. They both filed civil and criminal complaints, which brought out the TV people again.

And so went the golden twilight years at Beverly Shores.

5

C. C. Flag stared out of his third-floor office in Los Angeles. He daydreamed and squeezed a small exercise ball with one hand; with the other he held binoculars to ogle a woman on the eighth floor of the landmark Capitol Records building across the street. He relit a cigar and stuck the antique gold lighter in the breast pocket of his elephant hunter jacket. Got to cut down, he told himself, and blew smoke rings at the ceiling.

The office appeared more spacious than it was from the paucity of furniture. Like someone was moving out, only it was supposed to be taste. Flag sat in an ultramodern chair that looked ready to buckle. It had a thin frame of shiny alloys invented on the space shuttle and was covered with a film of polymers. His desk was a triangle of safety glass atop a giant golf tee. The only other furniture was the retro bar and antique Coke machine. The floor was oak parquet. Ceiling tracks of boron spotlights emphasized the framed photographs of Flag covering the walls. Flag with Buddy Holly, Flag with The Who,

Flag with Hendrix, all carefully cropped, just before security grabbed Flag and his personal photographer.

For his sixty-four years of unhealthy living, time had not been unkind to Flag. He was a large, husky man, but his paunch was modest. His hair was thick, his complexion bent toward ruddy, and he always dressed as if he were on his way to Mayan ruins. Thick pants tucked in the tops of high, rugged boots. Double-stitched shirt, wide-brimmed hat, riding crop.

C. C. was making a comeback from obscurity after his heyday as "America's Daddy-O of Rock 'n' Roll." Flag gave himself the nickname because no one else would. Dick Clark was much more popular. Flag had tried everything: jokes, cash giveaways, sexy women, on-location dances. Nothing worked. Then he stumbled on a gimmick that would forever vault Flag into the rock 'n' roll pantheon of distant also-rans. One Saturday afternoon in 1958, Flag became the first person in rock music history to destroy musical instruments at the end of a performance. He just forgot to tell the band ahead of time. It was a melee.

News of the brawl boosted viewership the following week, when Flag and three stagehands beat the crap out of the crooning group the Wind-Breakers. After that, the show was forced to adopt an all-record format. But the brief excitement was enough to keep Flag's career from dwindling out for another three years.

Flag's elbowing personality hadn't been heard from in decades until the mid-1990s, when he turned up at four A.M. on the ex-celebrity infomercial circuit. He was still recognized by the same demographic burp that had watched his dance show as kids and now was the target audience for advertisers of denture adhesives, confidence-inspiring undergarments and term life for the near-dead.

His phone rang. Flag pressed the button that activated the speakerphone, which he prized for its irritation value. His secretary said someone was here to see him. Then he heard his secretary yelling out in the hall. "Stop! You can't just barge in there!"

Flag's office door flew open and slammed into the wall. A courier from Insult to Injury Process Servers stormed into the room and tomahawked a subpoena into Flag's chest. "Consider yourself served, defendant-boy! Have a nice fucking day!"

The federal indictment was from the Middle District of Florida, *United States v. C. C. Flag and Hammerhead Ranch et al.* It looked like C. C. Flag was going to take that Tampa vacation ahead of schedule.

Flag's biggest celebrity endorsement was a magazine sweepstakes out of Florida. Apparently the contest people had exaggerated a little too much in their mass mailing, and a handful of elderly people from across the country were showing up in person to claim their million-dollar prizes.

In the seventh game at the Tampa Jai Alai Fronton, Testaronda II dropped an easy killshot.

"Shit-on-a-keychain!" shouted Zargoza as he tore his quinella tickets and threw them in the air over his ten-ounce sirloin and vodka tonic. C. C. Flag, wearing a Daktari expedition ensemble, had just arrived from Tampa International Airport. He sat down at Zargoza's table in the Courtview Club on South Dale Mabry Highway.

"I can't believe they're gonna close this place down," said Zargoza. "Nobody goes to jai alai anymore. There's no respect for *the old ways*."

"No luck?" asked Flag.

Zargoza grumbled. New jai alai players trotted out into a presentation line on the court before the next game and saluted the crowd with their cestas.

Flag looked at the row of players. "I hear you're supposed to bet on the one that takes a dump."

"Wry."

Flag turned to face Zargoza. "Why am I getting subpoenaed?"

"Because you're a toad!" said Zargoza, suddenly raising his voice. "And not just your regular happy garden toad, but one of those lumpy, putrescent amphibious tumors you find under a bunch of rotted lumber in a ditch next to a closed-down industrial plant. . . . How's Marge and the kids?"

"They're fine, Z . . . but I'm worried. . . ."

"Take a chill pill," said Zargoza. "It'll blow over."

"You said it would never come to this. You said you'd diversified so the complaints would be spread out. . . ."

"It's that damn Dick Clark and Ed McMahon scandal," said Zargoza. "It's gotten too much press. Everyone who does any kind of sweepstakes fraud is getting unfairly tainted."

"Dick Clark again," said Flag. "I should have known!"

They were engrossed in the next jai alai match when Flag unexpectedly began crying. "I can't go to jail!"

"Stop it! You're embarrassing me!" snapped Zargoza. "Don't make me bitch-slap you!"

Flag settled into a light whimper, shoulders popping up and down.

"I have another job for you, unless you're going to start crying again," said Zargoza.

Flag said he was okay.

"Good. Get over to Vista Isles. Their nursing home division wants to get rid of the Medicare residents and replace them with private payers. They're losing fifteen grand a bed per year. Guess who got the removal contract?"

"How are you getting rid of them? You're not killing them, are you?" asked Flag.

"Of course I'm not killing them!" said Zargoza. "I'm, uh, *liberating* them. Don't worry. I've got some hired muscle handling it. I trust these guys—we go way back. What they do is—"

"I don't want to hear the details," interrupted Flag, covering his ears with his hands. "I'm a respectable businessman!"

"Then it's settled. Get over to the nursing home and meet the staff, shake hands with the Q-Tips, hang out, show you care," said Zargoza. "There's not much to do now, but management is bracing for when someone notices the radical shift in Medicare beds. It's the newest trend in the industry, and advocates for the elderly are watching closely. People are difficult like that."

*Z*argoza had emptied twenty beds in two months. The management at Vista Isles was surprised and thrilled.

"It's nothing," said Zargoza. "What we do is—"

"No, no, no! Don't tell us how you're doing it!" said Vista Isles president Fred McJagger, waving both hands at Zargoza. "As long as you're not killing them. You *aren't* killing them, are you?"

"Nope. What I do is—"

"Don't tell me!" shouted McJagger. "I can't know these things. I'm a respectable businessman!"

What Zargoza *was* doing was driving them out of state. Most were senile or had Alzheimer's. He'd strip them of ID and pack them in vans. Then he'd drive north and scatter them around bus stations from Macon to Shreveport.

It was the perfect cover. Old people wandered away from group homes every day in Florida. Barely made the news anymore. They were impossible to identify unless fingerprints turned up something, and even then, none of the victims could remember anything—nothing could lead back to Hammerhead Ranch. As long as Zargoza was handling it, the plan came off without a hitch. But then other business endeavors distracted him. The nursing home scam was going so smoothly, he decided to franchise it out to the Diaz Boys, who got greedy and lazy and elimi-

nated the long drives out of state. They started cutting
the patients loose at bus stations around Tampa Bay.

Zargoza's desk was the largest in the boiler room. It
was made of teak and stood at the west end of the operation. Zargoza sat behind the desk with reading
glasses halfway down his nose, writing out a series
of checks for Amalgamated Eclectic Inc. On the
other side of the desk were three Spartan chairs,
which held three of his goons. The first wore a T-shirt
that read, "It's not the heat—it's the stupidity"; the
second wore an "I'm with stupid" shirt with an arrow
pointing at the third goon, who simply wore a plain
white T-shirt with a large cherry Slurpee stain in the
middle that, at a distance, made him look like a
Japanese flag. The three goons were silent and uncomfortable. Zargoza made them wait.

Finally Zargoza looked up and took off his
glasses. He began reaming them out. They were in
charge of Zargoza's chop shop in Ybor City and they
had not stolen a car all week and only four the entire
month.

"You call yourselves car thieves!" yelled Zargoza.
"You have twenty-four hours to turn this around or
it's the egg-stamping detail for you."

The three unproductive car thieves looked over
at the depressed goon stamping inferior eggs in a
listless manner, and they winced. Egg-stamping
was considered the lowest social stratum in the
boiler room, and an air of disgrace enveloped the
position.

* * *

Serge stepped out of the shower in his room at the Hammerhead Ranch Motel. He had just arrived minutes earlier and compulsively went right for the tub. Now, he toweled off and happily strutted across the carpet in his new skin. He slipped on swim trunks and drew the curtains open to admire the Gulf of Mexico. Instead, he saw three men in T-shirts patching out of the parking lot in a scorched Chrysler New Yorker. Serge let out a terrified, sucking scream. He ran out the door and into traffic on Gulf Boulevard. He stopped on the center orange line, looked around desperately, and dashed the rest of the way across the street. At the curb was a small building in the shape of an ice cream cone, and a man was at the pass-through window ordering a Neapolitan "Brain Freeze." The customer's beige Montego was parked next to him with the keys still in it, and Serge jumped in and sped off.

The Chrysler was four blocks ahead in stop-and-go traffic, but Serge kept it in sight and caught up on the Howard Frankland Bridge. He shadowed the trio over to a brick warehouse in Ybor City, where he watched them pull the Chrysler into a freight bay at the warehouse. One of the goons looked around outside suspiciously before pulling down the roll-top garage door.

Serge drove to a Home Depot and then back to the motel to make preparations.

Midnight. Serge looked more handyman than cat burglar. He peeled back the bottom of the chain-link surrounding the warehouse and rolled underneath with a full toolbelt and a spelunker's flashlight on his forehead. Slow, patient work with a mini-hacksaw and bolt cutters got him through the garage door and into the freight bay, and a simple lock punch popped the Chrysler's trunk. He checked behind the panel over the wheel well; it was still there, next to the jack and crowbar—a Halliburton briefcase with the exquisite pewter satin finish. He opened the case to check on the money. All there. Serge salvaged the small homing device off the Chrysler's bumper—he could never waste a cool gadget—and crammed it in the side of the briefcase. Then he let himself out quietly from the back of the warehouse, but the three goons were waiting and jumped him. They clocked him in the head with a piece of rubber tubing and used a monkey wrench to play his rib cage like a xylophone. Two held him down while the other opened the briefcase. The pair restraining Serge were so mesmerized by the sight of the money that they unconsciously released their grips and walked in a trance toward the cash.

Serge took off and dove under the fence, rolling in a single motion and coming up running on the other side. He didn't stop sprinting until he hitched a ride on Adamo Drive with an anhydrous ammonia tanker heading for the port.

As Serge went one way, the car thieves went the other. They jumped in a Bronco and raced out of the warehouse lot, taking Nuccio Parkway downtown.

The one riding shotgun flicked on the map light and opened the briefcase on his lap—to make sure they hadn't been seeing things—and they all drank in another long look. The cash was crammed so tight it practically blew the lid on its own. Wall-to-wall packs of hundreds still in bank bands. Their hearts beat like snare drums. They stared hard at the money, and the driver had to swerve at the last moment to miss an Alzheimer's patient stumbling off a curb at the bus station. They pulled over in the dark by the railroad trestle over the Hillsborough River for an emergency meeting. First they needed to stash the money. Then they agreed to keep word of the briefcase an airtight secret. Absolutely not a word to another soul. And they wouldn't spend any of the cash for a while, either. Maybe wait six or seven months in case there was any heat. They'd play it smart. Because they were smart guys.

6

Five miles away from the car thieves' warehouse, an unrestored white Rambler sat in a small south Tampa parking lot.

It was just another day in paradise for Sidney Spittle.

Sid sat behind the wheel with his arm resting in the open window. The upholstery was red and split. It was a Wednesday.

The parking lot was half empty and there was light traffic on the minor artery through Tampa's Palma Ceia neighborhood. Two teenage girls cutting school walked by on the sidewalk. Sid smiled at them; they called him a schmuck. Sid laughed. Nothing could ruin his day. He had a cold beer in a Styrofoam koozie between his legs and a newspaper propped on the steering wheel. The late-morning Florida sunshine warmed his arm in the window. The AM radio was tuned to Jamaican music, "Electric Avenue." Tropical flowers bloomed on the landscaped islands in the parking lot, and egrets perched on trash cans. What an existence. He turned the paper over to the weather page to check the temperatures in Sheboygan, Bangor and Duluth (14, 1, −8). There was a tracking chart and a small article about a new hurricane with a fifteen percent chance of striking Florida. Sid stuck his face out the window into the sunlight and smiled. "Ain't gonna be no hurricane." He folded the paper over to the races at Tampa Downs and creased it sharply. He took another swig of cold beer, clicked open a ballpoint pen and went to work picking losers.

Sidney Spittle was the Twenty-First-Century American. He completed the nation's transition from a culture molded by sacrifice and hard work to a bunch of cranky, unobliged brats. The Roosevelt Americans of the Depression and World War II were gone. So was rugged individualism, self-determination, Ellis Island, manifest destiny and the American Dream.

Now there was Sid the Fuckhead.

Sid was living off the national inheritance, of which he was unaware and ungrateful.

Sid was a twenty-eight-year-old doughboy. Not fat, just soft in the gut, face and work ethic. He grew a dark mustache so he wouldn't look like a complete dick, and it made him look like an insecure complete dick. Exercise never crossed the man's mind. Sid had gotten up that morning at a leisurely nine o'clock, a little earlier than usual because he was working today, which he did three days a month tops, and then only for a couple of hours. At other times, Sid dressed like a slob, but this morning he wore a natty charcoal suit, and his hair was organized.

Sid looked over the top of the newspaper. The glass front door of the local branch of Florida National Bank opened, and Mrs. Deloris Hastings, a venerable and bent-over ninety year old, walked out in slow motion without the aid of a cane. Sid put down the paper and started the Rambler. He waited patiently for Deloris to get to her car, but her pace was so excruciatingly slow that Sid began to give her body English.

Once in traffic, Mrs. Hastings drove a precise and unvarying sixteen miles per hour for twenty blocks, having signaled for her eventual left turn immediately after leaving the bank parking lot. A steady stream of traffic flowed around Mrs. Hastings to pass. Except Sidney Spittle.

When Mrs. Hastings pulled into the driveway of her 1923 bungalow, a Rambler pulled in behind her.

"Who are you?" Deloris asked as she got out of her car.

Sid flashed a gold badge as he walked up the driveway. His tie was thin and pinned to the bright-white button-down shirt with a bald eagle tack.

"Norman Kauffman, Federal Investigation Department Agency."

"What do you want?"

"I'm here to protect you," said Sid. "Let me give you a hand." He took her by the arm and helped her into the house.

"You're such a nice young man," she said. "Could I get you some tea?"

"Maybe some other time, ma'am, but right now I'm on business. My department is investigating a suspect who preys on the elderly. We could use your help."

"My help? What can I do? I'm ninety years old."

"There's a teller at the bank who is stealing from seniors. We want you to go to the bank and make a withdrawal. He's the last one on the right. We'll have people watching."

"You want me to be a decoy?" she asked. "Like on *Hunter*?"

"Exactly."

"I don't think I can. What if there's shooting?"

"There won't be any shooting. This guy is strictly nonviolent. Besides, we'll have people all around for your safety. The person in front and behind you in the bank line will be our undercover agents. But of course they're such pros that they'll look ordinary. They'll never acknowledge you, and you can't talk to them. How much can you withdraw?"

"I only have three thousand left in savings until my next Social Security check. . . ."

"You better get all of it because this guy won't make a move unless the stakes are right. He rarely goes for less than five grand. You have any CDs?"

"Two, but I was saving them for an emergency."

"This is the emergency," said Spittle. "Mrs. Hastings, your people need you."

*D*eloris Hastings was two feet shorter than everyone else in the bank line. She turned and smiled at the construction worker behind her. She leaned and whispered, "You people do such fine work."

The carpenter leaned down to her and whispered back: "Thank you."

When Deloris got to the last teller, she handed over her paperwork, and the teller smiled warmly. Then he stopped and looked puzzled at Mrs. Hastings's face. It appeared an angry sneer was curling up at the corner of her mouth. Either that or she'd gotten some bad cottage cheese.

"Are you okay, Mrs. Hastings?" he asked.

"I'm fine!" she groused. "I'll bet you sleep just fine at night!"

Sidney Spittle waited around the corner in his Rambler and followed Deloris back home once he had determined everything was jake.

"I got it! I got it!" Mrs. Hastings said in her living room. She dumped the money from her purse onto an old desk. "I hope you put him in jail and throw away the key!"

"With the help of citizens like you, we just might," said Sid. He took a midsize office envelope from his jacket pocket and stuffed the money inside.

"What I'm doing is putting this money in a special envelope and I'm going to mark it, and then I want you to take it back to the bank."

Sid bent over the desk and wrote "Mrs. Hastings" on the envelope with a thick black Magic Marker. As he straightened up, he had his back to Hastings. During the brief moment, Sid switched the envelope of money with an identical envelope stuffed with blank pieces of paper that was premarked "Mrs. Hastings" with the same felt pen. God, this was too easy, he thought. It was one of the oldest scams, but it never stopped working. There was an endless supply of old people who were trusting, eager to follow rules and ready to assist authority. When would they wise up?

He held the packet out to her. "Okay, now go back to the bank."

As Deloris took the packet, someone honked a horn outside. Spittle walked to the front window and peeked out the curtain, and he saw a green Geo parked in the driveway behind his Rambler, half hanging out in the street.

"Shit!"

The honking resumed—beep, beep, beeeeeeeeeep.

"Something's come up," said Spittle. "I gotta run."

"What about catching the bad guys?" asked Deloris.

"That'll have to wait."

The horn outside went silent.

"What am I supposed to do now?" Deloris asked.

Sid kept glancing at the front door, starting to show the first tremors of panic. "Look, I really gotta go."

Deloris asked, "But what—"

The front door opened without a knock, and Sid cringed.

There she stood. Patty Bodine. The seventeen-year-old runaway that Spittle started diddling last week on Indian Rocks Beach. She was a thin waif of a thing with long, straight dirty-blond hair and lots of freckles that made her look even younger. She was sorta cute, but her lower face had a nagging ursine quality that Sid couldn't quite get around. Her loose jeans rode low on her hips and the tight tangerine junior miss top exposed her midriff and pierced belly button. She tapped one of her dirty bare feet impatiently and smoked a Marlboro red. "What's taking so long? *Come on!*"

Sid's facial muscles tightened as he clung to composure. Underage girls were such great lays, he thought, but the immature crap he had to put up with—it just didn't seem right.

"You're messin' up my gig!" said Sid. "Go wait outside!"

"You've got the money, right?" said Patty. "What's the big deal? Just take it and let's go!"

"What's going on?" said Deloris. She looked inside her envelope and saw the stack of plain pieces of paper. She looked up. "You're not a cop! Gimme my money back!"

"Let's go!" yelled Patty, tugging on his right arm.

"I want my money!" yelled Deloris, grabbing his left arm.

Sid was dumbstruck by the turn of events.

Before he knew it, Sid had turned and decked Deloris with a right cross to the nose delivered as hard as he could. She dropped at his feet like a fifty-pound sack of russet potatoes. Her delicate vascular network had ruptured and begun to fill out the area under her eyes and across both cheeks with a deep purple just under the skin.

"Ooooo, gross!" said Sid. He leaned over and studied Deloris as she moaned.

"What are you waiting for?!" asked Patty.

"Think we should call an ambulance?"

"Don't tell me you care what happens to her!"

"No, I care what happens to *me*!" said Sid. "If she dies, this is a murder rap."

"Fuck her!" said Patty. She reached on top of the TV and grabbed a brass statue of the gentle Saint Francis holding a songbird on his finger, and she bashed Deloris in the head. That stopped all but the slightest movement in the old woman, so Patty did it again. This time Deloris fell completely still.

"There! She's dead," said Patty. "Now there's no decision to make. Can we *finally* go!"

"Jesus Christ!" Sid yelled, stumbling backward in shock. "You're one cold cunt!"

"You hit her first."

"But that was self-defense!"

*M*rs. Hastings never felt a thing. She didn't die right away like Patty thought. First she went into a coma. Six hours later, about the time that brain swelling put a coda on Mrs. Hastings's ninety years, Sid was on his fourth Corona at a table in the back of a beach dive called The Wharf Rat. Patty had made a whining pain in the ass of herself wanting to go to the beach, but Sid said he needed some beer first to settle his nerves from what he had just witnessed. He placated her with two of Deloris's hundred-dollar bills, and Patty smiled for the first time all day.

"This calls for a suck!"

Sid looked around the dim bar. "Okay," he said and pulled out the chair next to him, and she crawled under the table.

The Wharf Rat was the kind of place where the waitresses worked in wet T-shirts and sold five-dollar joints on the side, which was overlooked by the bartender, who sold forty-five-dollar half-grams in the men's room. The music was too loud, the room too dark, and the only pool table was warped.

An hour later, Sid's nerves were sanded down smooth and he was feeling pretty good about himself. He had even gotten over his anger at Mrs. Hastings. The five thousand meant he wouldn't have to work again for weeks.

A drink arrived, and the waitress in the wet T-shirt told him it was compliments of the men at the next table. Sid looked over. He saw three sloppy-drunk losers in T-shirts. He reluctantly raised the drink in a gesture of thanks, but they were too far gone. They had an entire bottle of scotch on their table, half pouring, half spilling their own drinks. He recognized them. They were regulars, just like him. But he had never liked their looks, and they didn't socialize.

Sid soon noticed he was having trouble getting served. At first, the waitresses merely hovered around the three drunks. Then they dropped all pretenses; service to the rest of the bar ground to a halt as every waitress stopped and joined the circle around the three men, waiting to jump at their command. Sid saw they were tipping with hundreds. The bartender came over and led the trio to the bathroom, and they all came back out smiling.

"Arriba! Arriba!" they yelled.

Sid slid his chair over to their table. "What's the celebration, fellas?"

"We're richer than King Tut," said the closest one, his pupils dilated different sizes and his mouth and tongue out of synch. "We just found five million big ones!"

"Shhhh! Shhhh! Shhhh! Shhhh!" said the second, his head rolling around in its neck socket. "That's a seeeeecret! We can't let anybody know it's out in the car! . . . Ooops!" And he covered his mouth with his hands as if they were faster than the speed of sound.

"But I'm your friend," said Sid.

"Yesh, he'sh our friend!" slurred the third one.

*L*ate the next morning, the first of the car thieves awoke in bright sunlight on the wooden floor of their Ybor City warehouse apartment, where they'd passed out just before daybreak.

He looked around, groggy. What happened? Snatches of memory filtered back. He remembered some guy back at The Wharf Rat helping them into a cab and paying the driver, then the ride back to the warehouse and the inebriated struggle up the steps, the three of them leaning against each other, an unstable tripod holding itself up. They must have made it into the apartment and lost consciousness on the floor because that's all he could remember. He couldn't remember anything at all about . . . the money! Where was the money? That bastard in the bar must have stolen it!

The car thief tried to spring up from the floor but couldn't move. He looked down and saw his entire body spooled tightly head to toe with hundred-pound-test fishing line, his arms pinned by his sides and his legs bound together. He looked over at his two comrades on the floor next to him wrapped in the nylon line.

"Hey, you guys! Wake up! There's trouble!"

The other two came around slowly at first, but then awoke all at once when they realized their situation. They thrashed around in panic.

"I wouldn't do that if I were you," said an unfamiliar voice. "That line will slice you to ribbons."

A stranger walked into the room from the kitchen and sat on the couch. He was wiry and casual, sitting there with a leg crossed, reading a *Tampa Tribune*. On the front of the newspaper the thieves saw a big headline, "Keys Killer Sought," and a large photo that matched the man holding the paper.

"Who are you?" said the first thief. Then he stopped and studied the stranger. Something familiar. "Hey—you're that guy we jumped last night coming out of the warehouse."

Serge set the paper down. He leaned forward on the edge of the sofa cushion and spoke softly. "Where's my money?"

"What money?"

Serge reached around the side of the couch and slid a toolbox into view. He opened it and removed a pneumatic staple gun.

"Oh, *that* money. We don't have it anymore. Some guy took it."

Serge's voice was understated: "Where's my money?"

"I told you, we don't know where it is."

Serge didn't say a word. He got down on the floor and sat cross-legged next to the men.

"What are you going to do to us?"

Serge raised a single finger to his lips for them to be quiet. Slowly and with deliberate theatrics, he removed items from the toolbox and set them on the floor. The men lifted their heads the best they could to get a better look. A roll of metal wire, tubes of commercial solvents and epoxies, arsenical soap, gauze, highly elastic putty, steel wool and quick-dissolve surgical suture. The three faces went white. One of the thieves fainted, and his head hit the wooden floor with the clack of a billiard break.

Serge went into the kitchen and came back with two buckets and a large plastic mat, which he unrolled on the floor. He turned on a small electric air compressor.

Serge went to work with diligence, industry and master craftsmanship. Before the hour had passed, Serge had been told every single detail the thieves could remember about the money, and a few more they made up. Serge knew they weren't holding back. But it was too late; nothing could stop him once he was into one of his hobbies.

"Ever been to Ocklawaha?" Serge asked as he turned off the compressor.

Wide stares in response.

"You haven't? You don't know what you're missing—gotta go sometime. It's just up the road a ways between Orlando and Ocala. Famous four-hour shootout. That's where Hoover's G-men finally tracked down the notorious Ma Barker Gang. They raided their empty hideout in Chicago and found a map of Florida with Lake Weir circled. On January sixteenth, 1935, they surrounded the house. A two-story antique wooden place with a traditional cracker porch. It was a crime in itself that they put three thousand bullets in it. Afterward, they found Fred Barker and Machine Gun Kate dead, and the locals later sold postcards showing their bodies at the morgue."

The car thieves continued staring in blank terror as Serge put down a tube of epoxy and picked up the staple gun. "What?" said Serge. "None of this registers? And you call yourselves criminals?"

Serge sighed in disappointment as he made a deft cross-stitch with the suture. "What about Giuseppe Zangara? Ring any bells?"

Still nothing.

Serge threw up his arms. "If we can't remember our own history, what kind of state will we have to live in?"

He began rubbing with the arsenical soap. "Okay, but I'm only going to go through this once, so listen up. It was 1933, the place: Miami. Zangara was an unemployed bricklayer who had a chronic stomachache that he blamed on capitalism. To me, it sounds like he had some other problems, if you get my drift. Anyway, on Monday, February thirteenth, Giuseppe buys a pistol in a pawnshop. He's just about to leave for Washington to shoot Hoover when he hears FDR is planning to visit Florida, so he decides to save gas money. President-elect Roosevelt is giving a speech in Miami's Bayfront Park. Giuseppe is only five feet tall, and he gets a chair to stand on. Suddenly he yells, 'Too many people are starving to death,' and opens fire. But he picked a crappy chair to stand on, and it wobbled. He missed Roosevelt and hit five other people, mortally wounding Chicago mayor Anton Cermak. . . ."

Serge made a final suture stitch and sat back to admire. "There!" he said, and smiled proudly at the three men, seeking approval.

Four hours later, the trio lay on the floor, quiet, still alive for a little while longer. Three disbelieving mouths frozen open.

One of the thieves had a late resurgence of survival instinct, and he began to twitch on the floor.

"See, now you're wiggling around! Ruining all my work!" Serge let out a frustrated sigh and picked up the staple gun again.

7

On July 27, 1943, in a small tavern in Bryan, Texas, a group of English and American pilots sat around the tables knocking back drafts in tall, cold mugs and talking about the approaching hurricane. Someone suggested evacuating the AT-6 Texan trainers because the planes were so delicate. A few of the pilots had flown heavier planes in combat—Spitfires, Corsairs, Helldivers—and the discussion turned into a trashing of the little Texan.

Many of them had a good laugh, but not Major Joe Duckworth. The Texan was his plane, and he said the AT-6 was good enough to fly right through the middle of the hurricane.

He had just walked into the ambush of the barroom dare.

As the storm approached, the only navigator on the airbase was Ralph O'Hair, and he soon found himself sitting behind Duckworth in the tiny single-propeller plane as they took off from southeast Texas and into the Gulf of Mexico. They rose to five thousand feet. Just off the coast the sky darkened, and the lashing rain drummed the metal fuselage like they were in a kettle. The plane rocked and vibrated, and there was less and less light outside the cockpit until it was completely black. The men became quiet. The worst was the unknown—they were in uncharted territory. Nobody knew what happened to an aircraft as it neared the churning core of a hurricane. The plane's body oscillated like both wings were about to snap. Then, an explosion of bright light all around. They were in a large, clear circle of sky, and the wall of the storm ran all the way around. They were in the eye. Duckworth and O'Hair had just made aviation history. The Hurricane Hunters were born.

Fifty-four years later, Major Larry "Montana" Fletcher of the 403rd Air Wing piloted his plane across the twenty-fifth parallel, heading over the Atlantic toward the Cape Verde Islands. The aircraft was the pride of the Hurricane Hunters' fleet, a magnificent silver Lockheed-Martin WC-130 Hercules, and Montana was their best pilot.

They were three hours out of Keesler Air Force Base in Biloxi, Mississippi, and the sky was bright and cloudless.

The crew of seven from the 53rd Weather Reconnaissance Squadron was a tight-knit but sundry lot. Major Fletcher was from the beaches of Southern California—the steady, all-American leader type with blond hair, a close shave and a square, dependable jaw. The copilot was ex–Lieutenant Colonel Lee "Southpaw" Barnes, a crusty and foul-mouthed veteran with hangover stubble and a footlocker of vintage *Playboy*s who had been demoted for moral turpitude so unsettling that the Air Force conveniently lost all records. His job was to repeatedly tell Montana he "couldn't fly for shit." The flight engineer was Milton "Bananas" Foster, the highly excitable yet gifted mechanical wizard. Marilyn Sebastian was the plucky aerial reconnaissance officer, as tough as any man, *but every bit a woman*. The navigator was Pepe Miguelito, the forlorn youth with a pencil mustache and unending girl troubles. The weather officer was "Tiny" Baxter, the massive country boy from Oklahoma with simple but strong values. The instrument operator was William "The Truth" Honeycutt, a former all-services bantamweight champion.

The WC-130 Hercules made a loud, continuous hum as it flew southeast above the Atlantic. According to coordinates from the National Hurricane Center in Miami, the storm that had just ripped through Cape Verde would break the horizon in less than a half hour.

Baxter silently double- and triple-checked his weather charts with drafting tools. Pepe Miguelito's lip quivered as he read another Dear John letter.

"I got a *baaaaaaad* feeling about this mission," said Milton "Bananas" Foster. Then he began crying. "We're all gonna die!"

Marilyn Sebastian shook Foster by the collar. "Be a man!" She slapped him, then kissed him hard.

Back in the cargo hold, Honeycutt skipped rope in his boxing trunks.

At zero seven hundred hours, the edge of Hurricane Rolando-berto began to rise out of the sea, larger and larger.

"Oh my God!" yelled Foster.

"Easy now," said Montana. He adjusted the rudder to bring the course around east.

Ex–Lieutenant Colonel Barnes glanced up from his latest copy of *Skank.* "You can't fly for shit!"

As the plane reached the outer bands of the storm system, the wings began to shake. Montana's heart rate remained level as he deftly banked the plane left to minimize crosswinds. They entered clouds and the cockpit went blind. All instruments from here on. The drone from the engines and vibrations from the storm became deafening.

"Baxter?" Montana said into the microphone of his intercom headset.

"Go!" Baxter said into his own headset.

"Sebastian?"

"Go!"

"Barnes?"

"Fuck yourself."

"Honeycutt?"

"Go!"

"Miguelito?"

"Go!"

"Foster?"

Whimpering.

Barnes turned around and smacked Foster with his rolled-up stroke magazine.

"Go!" said Foster.

Montana wrapped a scarf around his neck and adjusted his goggles. "Okay. This is it. Hold on."

The plane banked back right and shook savagely. A forgotten coffee cup slid off a shelf and broke. The blind view out the cockpit darkened. The glass cover on the altimeter cracked. There was a spark, then flames from the weather console, but Baxter hit it quickly with a Class C fire extinguisher.

Montana raised his chin and spoke solemnly into the headset. "It has been a privilege flying with all of you."

Then nobody spoke. The violent shaking of the fuselage seemed to go on forever.

When they had almost given up hope, there was a bright flash and the Hercules punched through the interior wall of the hurricane and into the calm, clear eye of Rolando-berto. A cheer went up in the cockpit. Baxter hugged a tearful Miguelito; Barnes hugged Foster. Sebastian unexpectedly found herself in Honeycutt's arms. They looked deep into each other's eyes, remembering that weekend in Baton Rouge. Marilyn's eyebrows raised up in poignancy and she opened her mouth, but Honeycutt shook his head. "No, don't say anything." They let go and went back to their stations.

Montana radioed Miami with news of their success.

8

Way up north in the Gulf of Mexico, the very tip of Florida's panhandle meets the Alabama border on a remote barrier island named Perdido Key. In the middle of the island, right at the state line, is a ramshackle roadhouse built in 1962 called The Flora-Bama Lounge. It is an outpost of sorts—a peculiar, isolated place standing in relief against the bright, flat landscape of shore and ocean. It takes persistent driving and a good map to get to, and the people who make it there are not in a hurry to get anywhere else. An old peach windsock flaps over the roof to aid customers who arrive by parachute and seaplane.

On an uneventful day late in the year, at exactly noon, a burly old man with white hair and beard sat on the last barstool at the Gulf end of The Flora-Bama. He looked out the back door at the waves and laughing gulls. His name was Jethro Maddox, and he was on his eighth Bud.

Jethro's tired eyes scanned the Redneck Riviera.

"This is like Paris in the twenties," he told the bartender, who was distracted by a TV tracking map showing a newly formed hurricane.

"A man can be destroyed but not defeated!" Jethro lifted his beer and drained it all at once and then looked at the can. "I have drunk you, beer, and I thank you. We are now one. . . ."

Jethro smacked the empty can on the bar and burped with abandon. "There is no shame in a belch if it is the truth. . . ." And he promptly toppled backward off his stool and disappeared from sight.

The bartender heard muttering from the direction of the floor—"Ouch! *Galanos!* I will kill you!"—and he leaned over the bar looking for Jethro. "Are you okay?"

Jethro stood and whisked off his sweater and fit his fishing cap back on his head. "I am fine," he said and remounted the stool. "A man will hurt, but he must forget his hurt. The great DiMaggio played with hurt, and there was a grace when he struck out that others do not possess when they connect hard. . . . We will drink to DiMaggio. Another cold one. . . ."

As the bartender popped the top on another can, he heard a deep drone high above and stepped over to the window and looked up. "Must be a hurricane plane returning to Keesler."

"Ah, brave aviators. They are a noble crew filled with the vigor of their youth," said Jethro, "and they will never feel more alive and proud than when they face the knowledge of death."

* * *

$\mathcal{W}$e're all gonna die!" screamed Bananas Foster in the cockpit of the WC-130 Hercules ten thousand feet over The Flora-Bama Lounge.

Nobody paid any attention. They were all reading books, writing letters or doing tedious chores on the boring return flight over the Gulf of Mexico. Ex–Lieutenant Colonel Barnes scraped diligently with a quarter on an ancient scratch-and-sniff foldout in one of his magazines, but instead of an arousing bouquet from the southern female glands, all he got was a musty attic.

Sebastian and Honeycutt stared together out the lower windows in the cargo hold, tracing the shoreline with their eyes. They tried to identify the features of the Florida panhandle. Santa Rosa Island, Pensacola Bay, the Naval Air Station, Perdido Key. There was a scattering of cotton-puff clouds far below, throwing shadows on the ground, and they could make out the white wake of a shrimp boat in the Gulf. They could even see teeny-tiny cars driving along the coast, and they wondered where those people's lives were headed.

$\mathcal{A}$ red Alfa Romeo convertible sped east along the shore of the Gulf of Mexico on Route 292, Free's "All Right Now" blasting from the stereo. Two tall, athletic, college-age women looked up at the plane in the sky and wondered what was going on in those lives.

They were the kind of women who were sexy at a range of a quarter mile, and their loose hair blew and snapped in the wind with a wild coquettishness. They wore big T-shirts over bikinis, and their sunglasses were cheap and cool. They gave off wanton vibrations. The scene could have been from a devil-may-care, coming-of-age independent flick that takes the jury award at Cannes, or maybe a tragedy-strikes-good-kids-in-a-small-town made-for-TV movie that opens with Meredith Baxter Birney staring through drizzling rain on a windowpane, popping pills and wondering when it all started to go so horribly wrong.

The driver was Ingrid Praline, a twenty-one-year-old blonde from Alabama with Scandinavian blood, and in the passenger seat was LaToya Olsen, a military brat from the Bronx.

Ingrid's hair and cheekbones recalled Ursula Andress in *Dr. No*. She often braided her hair into pigtails and wore denim bib overalls, and the giant Lolita package gave men hemorrhagic fever. LaToya favored a young Lena Horne; she had the face of an angel, especially the eyes, and she often kept her hair pulled back in a bun, but now it was down.

The two had most recently worked at a Piggly Wiggly in Tuscaloosa, where their boss was a spitting-mean little bumper car of a woman. She hated Ingrid and LaToya on sight because they had potential, and she gave them all of the most undesirable chores. The pair first met on rubber-glove duty corralling an errant bowel movement in the men's room.

They immediately became inseparable. LaToya

was the talkative one and Ingrid was the mental sponge. Ingrid was far from dumb, but she had grown up in a crippling parochial environment. Her mother was Olga Svjörlvladablatt, a hardworking third-generation Swedish immigrant, but her father was Jebediah "Jeb" ("Bo") Praline, fifth-generation Jim Beam, and global knowledge was viewed in their home as a new strain of syphilis that the line of Praline men had yet to build up a natural resistance against.

In contrast, LaToya had seen it all. She had been everywhere as a Navy kid. Subic Bay in the Philippines; Rota, Spain; and Naples, Italy, before spending her teen years at an intelligence station near London, where she picked up her British accent. She talked a streak about the outside world, and Ingrid could never get enough.

That's how the nicknames started. After a month, they stopped using their given names altogether. Instead, Ingrid always called LaToya "City," and LaToya always called Ingrid "Country."

"Pensacola is actually older than St. Augustine, but it wasn't a continuous settlement, so St. Augustine gets all the attention," said City. "There's a bar over on the mainland called Trader Jon's. It's a freakin' aviation museum, but Trader is getting on in years and they may have to close it down. The customers are trying to save it. . . ."

They passed a pile of shells outside an oyster shack and a man at the shoulder of the road using a tire iron to take out his frustration on a broken-down Pontiac Firebird. City called attention to the sea oats and boardwalks and dunes of sugar-white sand. "The sand is so white because it's finely ground quartz." They passed a "Welcome to Florida" sign.

City pointed at the beach side of the road. "That's The Flora-Bama Lounge, home of the Interstate Mullet Toss. . . ."

A young man beat on his Firebird with a tire iron as a red Alfa Romeo blew by. He dropped the iron and began marching east along the beach highway on Perdido Key in a mixture of anger, confusion and fear.

It was the worst day of Art Tweed's life.

Art had begun the day in Montgomery, Alabama, where he worked as an accountant for the state. His full name was Aristotle "Art" Tweed. He was from a rural family, and his parents had named him Aristotle in the hopes that it would imbue intelligence in the manner that "Biff" would not. His parents raised him good-natured, gullible and tragic, and he felt obligations to the community that were almost quaint in their rarity. He had grown tall and skinny with lots of freckles and a short mop of red hair that was a shocking orange shade more often found on puppets than people.

Art Tweed's problems started that morning when the phone rang.

"Oncology Department, Montgomery Memorial Hospital. Is this Art Tweed?"

"Yep."

"Just need to go over some lab results," said a

woman's voice. "As a follow-up to your physician's consultation, we received a second confirmation from the lab today that the neoplasm is indeed malignant and inoperable. Do you have any questions?"

Art stopped eating his Cap'n Crunch. "Neoplasm?"

"Tumor, pancreatic."

"What?"

"This is Art Tweed, twenty-eight years old, correct?"

"Yeah, but—?"

"The Art Tweed who recently had tests at Montgomery Memorial?"

"That was just a routine physical for the state insurance pool."

"You don't know you have a tumor?"

"Tumor?"

"Oh my. The chart shows an initial consultation. You never discussed this in person with a doctor?"

"Nope."

"Whoops," said the woman. "I think I've just made a terrible mistake. It's my first week on the job. I wasn't supposed to say anything before you met for counseling with a physician."

Art fell apart. He began yelling.

"Please calm down," said the woman. "You're making this very hard on me."

"How long do I have?"

"Sir, if you're not going to—"

"I'm the one with the tumor!"

"Well! Aren't *you* the self-centered one! Everything is me, me, me."

"How much time?"

The woman harrumphed. "Four weeks! I hope you choke on 'em!" And she hung up.

Art had been driving in the Pontiac ever since. No particular route or direction, just a three-hour anxiety meltdown behind the wheel watching his life before his eyes, wiggling at the end of a stick. He ended up at the Gulf of Mexico and made a left. He was finding it increasingly difficult to stay within his lane and freak out at the same time, and he was just about to pull over when the Firebird threw a rod on the Alabama side of Perdido Key.

He crossed the Florida state line on foot and saw a pay phone outside a tavern. He felt in his pocket but only came across paper money.

The tavern was a wooden building that appeared to be falling down and going up at the same time. Old and rickety, but with newer additions built on hodgepodge over the years, and the result looked like it was hammered together by enemies of the owner. Rip Van Winkle walked out the front door and climbed on a Harley. Art caught the door before it closed and went inside The Flora-Bama Lounge.

He spotted the bartender at the far end of the place and headed for him as he pulled ones from his wallet. Early Aerosmith—the good stuff—was on the juke—*"Take me back to south Tallahassee . . . down cross the bridge to my sweet sassa-frassy . . ."* Art told the bartender his car was history and he needed quarters for the phone.

The bartender was making change when Art noticed the only other person in the bar, a burly old man with white hair and beard, wearing a sweater and fishing cap. Art turned away to avoid conversation, but it was too late.

"You appear to be on a journey. I am on a journey, too. Sit and appreciate some alcohol with me and we will journey together."

"What the hell's he talking about?" Art asked the bartender.

The bartender shrugged and handed Art his change and a Bud. "It's on him."

The man slid his stool over to Art and held out a hand. "Name's Jethro Maddox. A name is what a man makes of it, not what others may make of him. I sometimes write my name in my shorts—"

"Right, right," Art said impatiently, and quickly shook the hand. He snatched his change off the bar and took a fast sip of beer. He put the can down and turned toward the door. Something made him hesitate. He decided he'd better have another sip for the road, and he reached back for the can. He took a second sip, paused, and started gulping.

"You remind me of my greener days, when I, too, had unquenchable appetites, or was that Gertrude Stein? It doesn't matter. It was Paris in the spring and the wine made me burn with desire, and then I beat a mime with the bottle—"

"Please stop talking," said Art.

Art then experienced an unusual rumble of emotion moving up his chest, and the next thing he knew, he was facedown on the bar sobbing like a baby.

"Cowards and men do not cry the same, and a man can cry with dignity and not confuse the two. But when women get going, they can sometimes throw ashtrays with the velocity of Sandy Koufax, and it is best to leave the house."

"Will you shut up!"

"It is a woman that is causing you this pain, is it not? I was married to four, which is also the number of wisdom teeth I was separated from, and they caused me much less distress in the end."

"Shut up! Just shut up!"

But Jethro Maddox did not shut up and Art did not stop crying until the fourth round of beer. Art didn't want to say anything, but it just blurted out—about how he was dying and the engine blowing on his car, and then more sobbing.

"We are all dying," replied Jethro. "I do not say that without compassion, for death is in a hurry with you. Find something worth living for and grip it by the neck with both hands. . . . I have found something, and it has changed me forever."

"Don't tell me—Hemingway."

"Of course, Hemingway. Touched my soul. Once I started reading, I could not stop until I finished it all."

"I had to read it in school," said Art. *"The Sun Also Rises, The Old Man and the Sea."*

"What?"

"His masterpieces."

"No, no!" said Jethro, waving Art off as if he were talking foolishness. "I haven't read a word of that stuff. I'm talking about the Hemingway biographies. I've read all twenty-three."

"But if you never read him, how come you talk like—"

Jethro cut him off, reaching in his pants and producing a Berlitz pocket reference book: *English–Hemingway/Hemingway–English.*

"The Papa mystique made me question my existence," said Jethro. "That is why I joined the Look-Alikes. They are my whole life now."

"Look-Alikes?"

"We gather in Key West every year for the look-alike contest at the Hemingway Festival. There are something around three hundred of us, with a permanent colony living in trailers down on the island. A British entertainment consortium discovered us and signed us up. We tour five months a year."

Jethro pulled a business card out of his pocket and handed it to Art. "Jethro Maddox, assistant regional manager, Hemingways Unlimited Ltd. . . . Live appearances, historic anniversaries, ground-breakings, movie extras, children's birthdays."

"That's an old card. We don't do the birthdays anymore since last time when a couple of the guys threw up in the kiddie pool and on the bunnies."

Something on the television caught the bartender's attention and he turned up the volume. A newsman appeared on the screen, talking dramatically into a weatherproof microphone as he walked along a beach.

"*. . . This is Florida Cable News correspondent Blaine Crease reporting to you from the Cape Verde Islands, where the latest hurricane spawned during this treacherous season has dealt a devastating blow to the simple people who inhabit this remote atoll. . . .*"

The camera panned with Blaine as he moved through the village. He came upon some stilts without a hut on top. A campfire burned in front of it, and a small animal the size of a Cornish game hen turned on a makeshift rotisserie.

"*. . . The destruction and the hardship is so severe that the residents have been reduced to cooking their own pet dogs! . . .*"

The people sitting around the campfire behind Blaine couldn't have looked happier.

When the report ended, Jethro Maddox stood and picked up a ratty canvas bag. "It's time we got going. This is a moveable feast."

But Art was still immobilized by intermittent sobbing.

"We'll never get to Kilimanjaro with that attitude." Jethro grabbed him under an armpit and coaxed him off the stool. He led Art to the parking lot and got him into the passenger seat of his blue Malibu, then went to the driver's side and climbed in, and they began heading east across the panhandle on Highway 98.

They entered Okaloosa County, "Florida's Finest Beaches," and drove through Fort Walton and Destin. Recent storms had taken bites all up the coast. Some homes were still set back high and safe with wide beaches; elsewhere, waves lapped the stilts. They entered Walton County, "The Best Beaches in Florida," and drove through the movie-set town of Seaside, featured in *The Truman Show*. They entered Bay County, "Florida's Most Beautiful Beaches," and came to Panama City, spring break territory. Jethro eyed the motel balconies. "Life has a cruel way of taking the youngest and the brightest." The balconies were enclosed in bars and cages to prevent the brightest from falling on their heads.

They continued east. Fighter jets buzzed high above Tyndall Air Force Base. They hit Gulf County, no motto. The waterfront housing was spare and humble as they approached Port St. Joe. They stopped at the Indian Pass Trading Post near Cape San Blas and ate shellfish in Apalachicola, down on the elbow knot under Florida's panhandle.

In the restaurant, Art spoke for the first time since The Flora-Bama. "Where are we going?"

"It is not the destination but the journey."

Art stared sadly at him.

"Okay, we're going to Tampa. I have a gig with the Look-Alikes."

It had all the makings of a Girl Power roadtrip, "Daytona or Bust."

Steppenwolf was on the stereo as City and Country headed out of Apalachicola after a seafood lunch.

"If this were the early 1800s, we'd be in the third-largest cotton port on the Gulf," City told Country. "The bridge and half the things in town are named after Dr. John Gorrie, the first person to figure out how to make ice cubes."

After Apalachicola, erosion had its way with the highway. There was no beach, and the waves hit the side of the road and sprayed cars. Some sections of road had collapsed in the sea and been repacked with new tar. There was no shoulder. If the wheels went out of the lane, they rolled into the water.

City drove with one hand, then the other, pulling her T-shirt off over her head and revealing a purple bikini top. She put on a tennis visor. In the passenger seat, Country slouched way down and stuck her feet up on the dash. She pushed a floppy hippie hat down over her long hair. She had a white tank top from a Jacksonville radio station and white shorts, and she watched the road over the top of raspberry-tinted Janis Joplin glasses perched at the end of her nose.

They stopped for gas and cheddar popcorn.

"I taught my Rottweiler Chinese," the Miami man ahead of them at the cash register told his friend.

"Get outta here."

"No lie. You know how everyone in Dade is buying vicious dogs because of crime? I read where burglars are giving the dogs commands, because everybody uses the same ones—sit, stay, heel—and houses are cleaned out while expensive pit bulls and German shepherds stand there stupid."

"Why Chinese?"

"Can't use Spanish. Half the burglars in Miami are bilingual."

"How do you say *sit* in Chinese?"

"I'm not gonna tell *you*!"

Back on the road, City and Country talked bad romance.

"Remember that one guy you thought was Mr. Right because he drove up for your date in an expensive Lincoln?" asked Country. "Then he took you cruising back and forth across campus for three hours and activated those low-rider shock absorbers that bounced the front wheels two feet off the pavement until it nearly detached your retinas."

"Very funny," said City. "Okay, remember that guy who came to pick you up with an entirely new haircut?"

Country stopped laughing and cringed. Shaved into the side of her date's head: "Ingrid," with a heart and a dagger through it. He'd seemed normal enough when he asked her out—then he arrived with that crazy shit carved in his skull. "How do ya like it?" he asked. Country plotzed in the doorway.

And their date still lay ahead. A dinner so painfully uncomfortable for Country that everything tasted like packing peanuts. Then an evening at the 4-H fair. Country returned home at midnight, quickly locked the door and threw a giant stuffed animal across the apartment.

"Nice panda," said City.

"Shut up," said Country.

The red Alfa Romeo sailed through a yellow light in Perry and kept going east.

*T*he traffic light in Perry turned red, stopping a blue Malibu.

Jethro Maddox checked his roadmap, then stuck it back in the visor. "When you took vacations as a small child, did you ever play the license-plate game?"

Art didn't respond. The light turned green and Jethro made a right onto U.S. 19.

"I now enjoy a similar game when I am on the road—Pick the Fugitive," Jethro continued. "It works very well in Florida. Anyplace you are on the highway, there must be a hundred fugitives come through a day. . . . You study the people in the other vehicles and try to determine who is on the lam."

Art couldn't help but look around at the traffic, and Jethro joined him.

Cars full of suitcases and colorful rafts, with "Heart of Dixie" license plates, Florida Gators wheel covers and Fob James for Governor bumper stickers. There was a truckload of fruit pickers riding in back with a load of cantaloupe and marijuana; a retired couple from Newark muling stolen gems; a cold-call bauxite salesman with Michigan fraud warrants, driving a station wagon eaten up by harsh winters in Saginaw. Three runaway teens from Texarkana in a hot Taurus; the deposed president of Paraguay in a Chevy with bad transmission; and an ex–KGB agent stranded in Florida during the Soviet collapse who was now a freelance troubleshooter for the Broward County Democratic Committee.

"I pick that one," said Jethro. He pointed at a van with a faded Molly Hatchet mural.

Inside the van were two sour-smelling men—a couple of open beers and loaded pistols on the greasy upholstery between them.

"I'll bet the discussion in that van has just drifted into speculation about how much cash liquor stores keep on hand," said Jethro.

". . . About five hundred dollars just before the night drop," the van's passenger told the driver.

"I have seen it with alarming frequency," Jethro told Art. "It is a well-worn path: The Downward Spiral into Paradise. They all follow the same internal riffraff gyroscope and drag their traveling cavalcade of dumbness across the Florida state line for a final stand that only ends in crime tape and headlines. . . ."

". . . Maybe six hundred bucks on the weekend," said the van's driver.

Jethro grabbed a day-old newspaper off the floor-board and handed it to Art. Strong-arm robbery. Exploitation of the elderly. Church funds missing. Handicapped woman raped. Four-year-old bludgeoned to death by boyfriend while mother went to buy crack.

Art became troubled. He looked up from the paper and resumed examining the nature of the traffic around him. He realized he had spent far too much time in the small pond; he never knew the outside world was so upsetting. His small-town values and obligations to the community kicked in. The knowledge that he would soon die gave Art a chance to be selfless and do something positive for the world before he left.

"Have you considered my advice?" asked Jethro. "Have you thought about something that moves you? Something to focus your energies?"

Art had. He became obsessed with the number of bullies he saw.

He decided to kill one of them.

9

Zargoza waited ten minutes at the glass front door with the "Sorry, we're closed" sign. He daydreamed and gazed at the drawbridge over the viridian sailboat channel. A gold Dodge Viper rolled into the gravel parking lot of B. F. Skinner Taxidermy.

"What are you doing here so early?" the driver asked Zargoza as he got out of the car.

"I need a repair job, B. F." He pointed to the stuffed hammerhead shark sticking out the back of his pickup truck. The end of one of the shark's eye pods was snapped and dangling.

"Damn college kids," said Zargoza. "One shimmied up the thing last night and lost his balance and grabbed for something on the way down. Fucked up my shark. Kid landed on his neck, went to the emergency room. Guess who he's gonna sue."

"It just ain't right," said Skinner, unlocking the door. He hit switches near the entrance and fluorescent tubes flickered on in sequence and filled the large room with unnatural light. The taxidermy shop was an open studio with a high ceiling. The walls were white, and there was a row of generous transom windows just under the ceiling. Only a blond pine desk near the door and long, neat work shelves in the back. The minimalism set off the trophy fish. Finished jobs covered the walls. The fish still curing hung by their tails from a ceiling rack running down the center of the studio.

"Damn fine work," said Zargoza, looking at a sailfish, king tarpon and hammerhead shark hanging in the middle of the room, almost completely dry. He admired the sail—the iridescent rainbowing in the ultramarine ridges—and the silver scaling of the tarpon. Zargoza walked up and touched the shark tentatively, but it was still tacky.

"That's a great hammerhead," said Zargoza. "I'll double whatever you're getting for it."

Skinner rummaged through a mess of yellow papers and mail on his desk. He looked up. "I don't know who that's for. I'll have to check with Jeff. He must have come in over the weekend and done them."

"Jeff sure has improved since you took him on," said Zargoza. "This is some of the best work I've ever seen. . . . And these eyes—they're so lifelike. It's almost like the fish knew he was doomed."

Zargoza walked around the tarpon. "I like what he did with bodies, too, full musculature. Lumpy, but in a menacing way, like a boa constrictor after it's swallowed something."

Zargoza squatted down and stuck his face under the hammerhead to admire further.

Skinner was opening a bank statement and almost

impaled his hand with the letter opener when Zargoza screamed. He looked up and saw Zargoza on the ground, trembling and unable to speak, pointing up at the recessed mouth of the hammerhead. Inside the shark's mouth was another mouth, a human mouth.

*T*he coconut telegraph running through the Gulf Coast's criminal subculture came alive.

Sidney Spittle was enjoying a morning beer at The Wharf Rat when word swept through the bar about the three regulars found taxidermied alive over at B. F. Skinner's. His hands shook, and a sweat broke out at his temples. He got up and made it to the pay phone by the pool table, where he dropped his quarter and it rolled under a jukebox. He retrieved another from his pocket and used two shaking hands to get it into the slot, and he dialed.

"Baby, I'm at The Wharf Rat. Something bad's happened. No, not now, not here. In an hour. . . ." Sid stopped and looked around. He turned his back to the pool room and whispered.

". . . I love you. Be careful," and he hung up. He scanned the room again and left briskly through the screen door in the back of the bar.

A customer sitting at a table next to the screen door had his nose in a 1952 *Life* magazine. When Spittle went by, the customer stuck the magazine under his arm and followed Sid out the door.

As the screen slammed shut, Zargoza and his trav-

eling goon squad skidded to a stop in the parking lot
out front.

The bartender got his cocaine six steps below
Zargoza and the Diaz Boys, and he wanted to score
points. He also wanted to avoid the unspoken penalty
of later being found to have withheld information.
Upon hearing about the dead car thieves ten minutes
earlier, he immediately phoned in a tip to Zargoza
that the three had been bragging about five million
dollars the night before and tipping everyone in sight
like John Gotti. They had been hanging out with another regular, and the guy was back this morning,
acting peculiar—he only knew his first name, Sid.

"Where is he?" Zargoza shouted as he crashed
through the front door of The Wharf Rat.

The bartender pointed at the back door. "Just left."

They ran out the back and saw Sidney Spittle and
another driver pulling onto Gulf Boulevard. They
sprinted around front to Zargoza's German sedan.

It was a slow-motion O. J. chase down the barrier
islands of the Gulf Coast. Serge had retrieved the
scorched Chrysler in Ybor City after dealing with the
car thieves, and he drove under the speed limit in
the right lane. Two cars back in the left lane was
Team Zargoza. Neither was aware of the other and
neither wanted to make a move on Spittle until they
saw him with the briefcase.

They took a bridge to the mainland and drove
across the Pinellas Peninsula. They caught the Gandy
Bridge over the bay to Tampa and followed the Lee
Roy Selmon Expressway downtown. Took nearly an

hour, everyone stressed going so slow hanging back from Spittle.

Sid parked in front of the bus station, looked around and went inside. Zargoza parked a block away, Serge at the corner.

Spittle took a chair with his back to the wall and pretended to read a travel brochure. He peeked over the top and scoped the place. So far so good. He got up and walked around for a more thorough recon, checking out the facilities. An old scale, your weight and lucky lottery number, twenty-five cents. A vending machine dispensing artificial stimulants, artificial depressants and temporary tattoos. A schedule board, arrivals, departures. Western Union, for the broke and the shameless, to renew old friendships with the endearing three-A.M. phone prostration for five hundred dollars. Out on the loading platform, thick with diesel fumes, a bus from Richmond idled and someone in uniform was flinging sawdust on a Night Train regurgitation. Sid took a seat again in the station and decided to wait and watch. The terminal reminded him of visiting day at the state prison. The chronic inability to master life hung in the air like a toxic mist. Something about the manner of travel. Good news comes to Tampa rarely and by divine intervention, but bad news arrives every day on the bus. The luggage definition was casually regarded: gunnysacks, laundry bins, pillowcases, Glad bags and liquor cartons. Woody Guthrie made them sound like romantic troubadours over the radio, but in person the image was a bit too jarring for Sid to burst into hobo songs.

Two Tampa cops came in the front door and walked slowly down the rows of molded plastic chairs, comparing waiting passengers with mug shots of Serge A. Storms. Various fugitives began to fidget and perspire in their seats. The stress got the best of a young work-farm escapee with bushy hair and an acoustic guitar. He jumped up and was grabbed immediately. He tried to put up a fight with the instrument, but the cops easily took it away and smashed it like balsa wood to a smattering of applause. They led him off in cuffs. The clock on the wall continued ticking.

A half hour later, Sid was confident the coast was clear. He got up and walked to the lockers. He scanned the station a last time before opening number seventeen and removing a metal briefcase.

When Sid turned back around, he saw a man in a chair on the other side of the station staring at him over the top of a newspaper. The man quickly looked back down. A hot flash of dread surged through Sid and he had to focus hard to walk as if each leg weighed two hundred pounds. He made it to a chair and sat down next to a girl reading a *Sixteen* magazine with Leonardo on the cover. He set the briefcase on the floor next to his feet. He was still on the other side of the terminal, but he had a clear view of the man with the newspaper. The man looked at Sid again over the top of his paper and back down quickly. Sid then noticed there was a whole damn row of men peeking over newspapers.

Sid's heartbeat shook his whole body. He and the

men furtively watched each other for five minutes. Sid suddenly grabbed the briefcase and raced for the bus station's exit onto Polk Street. Zargoza and his goons threw their newspapers in the air, pulled guns and ran after him.

There was a yellow Checker cab at the curb, and Sid clutched the briefcase to his chest and literally dove through the open back window.

The cabbie turned around. "Never seen *that* before."

"Get me out of here!" yelled Sid.

"Sure thing."

The cab patched out from the curb, and Sid looked out the back window at Zargoza and the goons standing in the street, shaking their fists at the cab and shouting.

Sid turned back around, slumped in the seat and let out a deep breath of relief. "Take me to the airport."

"You got it," said Serge, and he turned on the meter.

*B*ack inside the bus station, everyone was in Florida mode—here we go again!—hitting the deck when the goons pulled their guns and started hurtling through the terminal.

As the cab peeled away and the men stood yelling in the street, the waif named Patty Bodine stopped reading her magazine article about Leonardo Di Caprio. She picked up a second, identical metal briefcase at her feet and calmly strolled out the exit doors on the other side of the bus station.

* * *

Serge had Sidney Spittle's undivided attention.

Sid was chained up around the armpits and elbows. Another chain wrapped tightly around his hips and knees. Each chain was extended loosely and fastened in opposite directions so that Sid hung like a hammock. He almost looked comfortable.

There wasn't any challenge to the interrogation. In the first minute, Spittle was ready to confess to the Lindbergh kidnapping. He told Serge everything about the money, about making the switch at the bus station with his girlfriend, Patty, and about their planned rendezvous later that night.

Serge had one last question. Who were those guys chasing you?

"You don't know?" Sid said incredulously. "That's Zargoza's crew!"

Serge said thank you and taped Sid's mouth shut. Then he sat back on the catwalk and ate a Snickers bar and waited. He fiddled with his electronic tracking device and shook it, but the sensor stayed in the middle. Why wasn't it picking up the briefcase? Something must be jamming it. Must be the weather—all the electricity in the air.

Serge's blinking increased and he sat paralyzed for a moment.

When movement came back into Serge's body, he asked Sid, "Did you know the first barbecue was held in Tampa?"

Sid just stared bigger.

"It's true," said Serge. "In 1528 a stranded Spanish

explorer named Juan Ortiz was marked for death by
Harriga, the Timucuan Indian chief in Tampa Bay—
mainly because another Spaniard had earlier cut off
the chief's nose. And we called *them* savages. . . .
Anyway, they decided to roast Ortiz alive over a fire
pit that the Indians called *barbacoa*—and that's how
we got barbecue!"

Serge smiled broadly with satisfaction and his
eyebrows raised in an expression that said, "Impressed, eh?"

Then Serge's face got serious again. "Oh, I almost
forgot. Cool footnote alert: Ortiz didn't die. He was
saved by one of the chief's daughters, who had the
hots for him and begged her father to let him go.
The episode was later stolen for part of the story of
Captain John Smith. And it became the legend of
Pocahontas."

Sid was a mask of silent terror.

"What? Don't believe me?"

Sid began screaming mute under the tape, but the
noise was soon drowned out by the air horn of an approaching sailboat. Serge got all excited like a kid at
the circus. Water splashed below and cars droned
above on the metal grating. A gap of moonlit sky
opened over Sid's stomach and he was lifted up into
the air, the two spans of the drawbridge rising and
separating, each chained to a different end of Sidney
Spittle.

It was the last flight out.

Patty Bodine, the underage girlfriend of the very

late Sidney Spittle, was like ice water. Not a flutter, totally calm, sitting in a blue styrene seat in Airside D at Tampa International Airport with five million dollars on her lap.

It was shortly after midnight, and the airside was empty. Vacuum cleaners going. One last guy schnockered in the lounge.

The flight was the second leg of a Fort Lauderdale red-eye to Chicago, and the Whisperjet had just taxied to the accordion boarding arm. A ticket agent walked to the gate and unhooked the velvet cord. Patty and five other weary people stood up.

Patty pulled her boarding pass from a hip pocket. She was at the end of the short line, and she felt something poke her in the back.

"Where are you going?" asked Zargoza.

He turned her around and marched her back up the airside, and they caught the monorail to the main terminal. When the doors opened, Patty fell to the floor of the car and screamed and flopped around. "They're gonna kill me!" The other passengers stared. Zargoza and his goons stuck their hands in their pockets, looked around innocently at the others and smiled, like they didn't know her.

As the doors were closing again, Patty sprang out of the car. Zargoza lunged and grabbed the back end of the briefcase, and it wedged in the closing doors of the monorail.

"Let go!" they both shouted on opposite sides of the doors. They struggled fiercely and Patty lost her grip. Zargoza fell over backward with the briefcase, and the monorail doors snapped shut.

"Get her!" Zargoza yelled at his goons.

"Dammit!" Patty said under her breath as she saw the briefcase disappear into the monorail car. Then she saw the goons banging on the doors, trying to pry them open. She began backpedaling slowly, then faster and faster. One of the goons found the emergency button and the hydraulic doors hissed open. Patty turned and dashed full speed through the main terminal with the goons twenty yards behind. She bolted out the front of the airport to curbside and jumped in a cab.

"Get me out of here!"

"Ten-four," said Serge.

Zargoza stood and stretched in the morning air, sipping hot coffee just outside the office of Hammerhead Ranch. He thought: A good night's sleep, that's all I needed to calm my nerves. That's when he heard the first siren.

An out-of-breath goon ran across the parking lot. "Boss, I think you better come see this."

Zargoza walked around the motel to the drawbridge over the inlet, where authorities had just discovered what was left of Sidney Spittle.

"Jesus!" Zargoza yelled.

Sharks pooled under the bridge and rubberneckers pulled over to be sick en masse.

Zargoza walked back to the motel and another goon came running from the other direction.

"Boss, come quick. You better see this."

Zargoza walked around behind Hammerhead Ranch toward the swimming pool.

He suddenly screamed and fell to his knees. Then he held a hand over his mouth reverently and whispered: "The Curse."

He faced the row of ten hammerheads. In the hole where Zargoza had removed the broken shark, there was now a replacement, a gleaming new hammerhead with the primordial eye pods seamlessly epoxied to the sides of Patty Bodine's head.

10

Serge A. Storms was the native.

Born and raised.

Serge thought Florida in the sixties was a great place and time to grow up. He mythologized his childhood. All the objects in his memory had bright, shimmering outlines and they bloomed against backdrops of perfect cerulean sky or aquamarine sea. In his memories, there was no sound except a hot, melancholy wind. As a young boy, he wandered foot-loose around beaches and causeways, stomping through mangrove bogs, pretending they were the La Brea Tar Pits. He climbed the Jupiter Lighthouse on a field trip. He broke into JFK's boarded-up bomb shelter on Peanut Island in the middle of Lake Worth Inlet. He dangled mullet heads off the Singer Island drawbridge with a cane pole, making sharks jump for dinner. Sometimes he fished from atop pier pilings on the Loxahatchee River. He always looked upriver, to the bend where it disappeared. All the kids knew better than to go up the Loxahatchee. That was Trapper Nelson territory. Nelson came to the area in the

1930s and built a primitive cabin on a remote bank of the river, where no road could reach. He made a living skinning furs and made a reputation as the Wildman of the Loxahatchee. To the adults, he was a crazy old hermit, but to Florida schoolchildren who repeated his story over and over, he was the Maximum Boogeyman.

One day when Serge was eight, he stole a rental canoe and paddled up the river. He entered a tree canopy, and the eyes of alligators bulged from the water like knots on cypress knees. He lifted his paddle and glided silently, listening. He came around another bend and the cabin appeared. Serge was still and quiet. No Trapper. He paddled with stealth, hugging the far bank, craning his neck for any sign of the wildman.

Serge heard movement behind him, and he turned to the near bank. There was Trapper, silent, with a slaughtered boar.

"Aaaaaaaaaaaaaaaaaaaaaa!" Serge yelled, and paddled like a mad bastard back to the boat launch.

The undetected canoe theft was Serge's first taste of the criminal life. Twelve years later he began a series of short jail terms for petty larceny and simple assault, and a year at Starke on a coke charge. He avoided anything longer by reason of insanity. It was an easy call. Even expert state witnesses hired to rebut defense psychiatrists would spend five minutes interviewing Serge, then go back to the prosecutor and say, "Are you kidding? I can't testify this guy's normal."

Serge's face was inviting and intense. It betrayed

his surplus of energy and told you he was completely alive every waking moment, fully engaged in life, gripping it with white-knuckled fists. He would invariably end up back at Chattahoochee, the high-security state mental hospital for the criminally insane.

There was nothing mean about Serge. In fact, there was an abundance of compassion. He had empathy for any living thing, felt its pain and joy as his own. It was just a problem of wiring. His overload of energy caused him to get a little too excited at times and he would fritz out. It short-circuited his conscience and he would perform horrific acts in a detached manner, as if he were watching it all on a TV set at the other end of the room. In the same five minutes, he could be exceedingly tender and frighteningly brutal.

The better psychiatrists in the Florida correctional system loved Serge. They recognized the pathology, just hadn't seen it to this degree. A mixture of schizophrenia and attention-deficit, with a dash of dissociative. It was simply a matter of fine-tuning the chemicals in his brain, like the tracking on a VCR. It generally took a cocktail of four antidepressants and psychotropic drugs to even him out. When he was leveled, he was like an enthusiastic, sweet little kid.

The problem was that the medication dimmed his wattage. Serge would either hide the pills in his mouth or throw them up later. He didn't want anything messing with his gray matter; he liked the hum inside his head too much—the free commerce of thoughts and images streaming back and forth, occasional bursts of genius flashing inside his skull like heat lightning over Tampa Bay on a warm August evening.

Serge's first admission to Chattahoochee came in the early eighties after he was picked up at Cypress Gardens. A night watchman discovered him practicing synchronized water ballet in the Florida Pool, the famous swimming pool built in the shape of the state just north of the water ski ramps.

The police called in a state psychiatric team when Serge refused to come out of the pool, claiming he was Esther Williams rehearsing for the hit 1953 MGM musical *Easy to Love*.

Soon a crowd of cops and park officials had gathered. Serge lay on his back in the pool and made "water angels." The theme park wanted to avoid publicity at all costs. They conferred quietly and asked if anyone knew what the heck the intruder was talking about.

"He's got his facts right," the park publicist chimed in. "Part of that movie was shot in this pool. But that's ancient trivia. Most of our own employees don't even know that."

A voice from the pool turned the group. "Cypress Gardens, two hundred botanical acres on the shore of beautiful Lake Eloise. Florida's first theme park, established 1936 . . ."

The publicist eventually coaxed Serge out of the pool on the pretext of an audition for *Skirts Ahoy!*

*T*rapper Nelson was found dead by his cabin in the late sixties, and all the children whispered it was something sinister. He was shot, they said, maybe suicide, maybe murder.

In 1995, Martin County sheriff's department and game officials began hearing strange rumors. Trapper Nelson wasn't really dead. The body they found more than two decades ago was some unfortunate soul who had wandered into Nelson's camp, and Trapper had since dug in deeper. Canoeists reported a shadowy figure darting about the banks or sometimes in the windows of Trapper's old cabin. The hermit's local status eclipsed legend.

A week later, deputies dragged Serge into the sheriff's station, wearing furs and smeared with dried animal blood. He kicked and he screamed. "But I *am* Trapper Nelson! Lemme go!"

So began Serge's most recent stay at Chattahoochee. After two months, prison psychiatrists got together to discuss Serge's case. He was their favorite, most charming patient, and they couldn't stand to watch what was happening.

They got a visiting specialist from Austria to put Serge under hypnosis.

Serge babbled and grunted as he lay on the couch. He began pitching violently and they had to hold him down. His mumbling increased to a high-speed torrent of incomprehensible sonic hash.

"Someone get a tape recorder!" yelled the shrink gripping Serge's ankles.

Hours later, after Serge was back in his cell under sedation, the psychiatrists met with a police evidence tech. He tinkered with the tape recording on a special machine, adjusting the treble and reverb and turning the speed way down. When the tape played at a fraction of its original rate, they began to detect human speech.

"Florida: literally, abounding in flowers, named by Ponce de León. Statehood granted in 1845, first governor William D. Moseley"—the voice became more excited and angry—"flowing from the waters of the Kissimmee River to Lake Okeechobee and through the Everglades into Florida Bay. Along the way, nurturing a low, flat petri dish of extreme people. The rugged, the hopeful and the damned. Ridiculed as the place with no roots, no native residents and no culture, the land of shuffleboard and the nonregional, TV weatherman accent. But they're not laughing anymore. Cocaine, Castro and carpetbaggers castrated with grooved grapefruit spoons that say 'Life's a Beach' on the handle. New residents are interned in hot, dusty trailer parks populated entirely by assholes from Illinois. We get hit with storm after storm and walk through the rubble, whistling 'Dixie' and applying sunscreen. How does that stack up against *your* commonwealth? We don't have *great potatoes,* we're not the *garden state,* we aren't proud to wear furry hats with earflaps and '*Live free or die!*' We're a twenty-four-hour, dead-bolted, hair-on-the-back-of-your-neck, free-continental breakfast, death-wish vacation of a lifetime, not from concentrate. State motto? *'Behind you!'*

"It's an experiment in natural selectivity. We're breeding a hardier genetic strain of American to build on the Forty-niners and Plains settlers in Conestoga wagons. The new Florida Sooners, Jimmy Buffett's Grapes of Wrath Tour. Thousands come every year but few make the cut. Most are on vacation, but others are on business. And some are simply running toward the light. Men with beaten-dog looks driving carloads of dirty-faced kids. None of this is new to the old-timers. The outsiders just started coming here in big enough numbers to get the word out. But it's been going on for hundreds of years, ever since the Europeans hacked and diseased the Indians in the name of God and gold, searching for the Fountain of Youth, which was recently discovered in the middle of a roadside attraction in St. Augustine. From the conquistadors and the Seminole Wars to the Civil War Battle of Olustee. The two Henrys—Flagler and Plant—running train tracks down both coasts. The railway that went to sea figuratively in 1912 and literally in the hurricane of 1935. Hemingway stumbling, scribbling and brawling his way through the Keys. German U-boats off Fort Myers. Jackie Gleason with a pitching wedge, launching divots the size of toupees. Cape Canaveral became Cape Kennedy until we said, 'What were we thinking?' and changed it back. . . . The '68 Republican Convention. The '72 Miami Dolphins. Claude Kirk, Reubin Askew, Walkin' Lawton. Sinkholes, phosphate, citrus canker, Anita Bryant . . . the horror . . . the horror . . .''

And Serge passed out.

The technician turned off the tape, and the Austrian psychiatrist was stunned. "We must help him!"

The next day the Austrian met Serge for a one-on-one. Serge sat on the edge of the couch, rocking back and forth, listening to his Walkman. The psychiatrist leaned down and took the earphones off Serge's head and pressed the stop button.

"Can we begin?" the doctor asked with a smile.

The session was unproductive for the first hour. Serge wanted to talk about the fall TV lineup. He said he'd submitted a script to *Friends* where everyone gets killed, but he hadn't heard back yet.

"I'm sure it's a fine script. Now about your childhood . . ."

Shortly into the second hour, the doctor stopped talking and began looking around the room. He inspected his own hands, front and back, in minute detail. Serge knew it was time. He had scored some acid off a minimum-wage bedpan polisher and slipped the microdot of orange barrel LSD into the doctor's coffee at the beginning of the session.

"I hope this has been helpful to you," said Serge.

The psychiatrist looked up from his palms with a question on his face.

"This role reversal," said Serge, getting up from the couch. He began taking off his patient's uniform. "I think you'll make a fine doctor someday. Now, if I can have my clothes back . . ."

The psychiatrist got up slowly. He took off his shirt and slacks and handed them to Serge and put on the patient's clothes.

Serge got dressed and adjusted his bow tie and glasses in the mirror, looking spiffy. He slicked his hair with mousse. He looked back at the doctor and saw a quivering mass of Jell-O.

Serge had anticipated the possibility.

"Okay, I have to escape now. But I want to make sure you're all right," said Serge. The doctor was suffocating with dread. Serge clipped the Walkman to the doctor's elastic waistband and pressed play.

"This is the *Sergeant Pepper's* album," said Serge. "You've got the right guys in the control tower to talk you down—they're pros. A lot of positive messages. Just keep playing the tape over and over."

Serge placed the earphones on the doctor's head and checked the clock. Shift change fifteen minutes ago. New staff. They hadn't seen Serge and the doctor come in the room. Serge pressed the intercom, and two large guards arrived.

The guards were suspicious anyway. "Hey, you look familiar!"

Just then the Austrian started running around the room making British ambulance sounds before perching on top of a desk like a gibbon and chattering his teeth.

Serge shook his head sadly and made notations in a patient file.

The guards wrote off their doubts and grabbed the psychiatrist and dragged him back to Serge's cell, where he listened to *Sergeant Pepper's* twenty-two times.

Serge flushed his medicine down the toilet and walked out the front door of Chattahoochee, disappearing into the general population of the state of Florida.

*A*t daybreak, Serge opened the door of room one at Hammerhead Ranch and took a deep, satisfied breath of salt air.

"Another day of life. Thank you, God."

He went jogging up Gulf Boulevard, not for exercise but from impatience. He ran across the drawbridge, waving at the cars and the fishermen. The tide was just coming in and the shorebirds scurried on the shoals in the pass. A deep-sea fishing boat motored back from an overnight cruise, loaded down with mackerel, tuna and sharks. Serge waved from the bridge, and the captain sounded his air horn. The more Serge saw, the more he wanted to see, and he ran faster.

He was in a full sprint when he came off the bridge, and he ran up to the row of news boxes in front of a breakfast diner shaped like an Airstream. A fat man wearing a baseball cap that said "Old Fart" came out of the restaurant, working a toothpick in his mouth like he was picking a lock. Serge smiled and pulled a quarter from his pocket as he bent down to a green newspaper box.

Serge suddenly jumped back and made a startled yip. There it was again, his face on the front page, third day in a row. "Manhunt Widens for Keys Killer." Can't they give it a rest? You go and do a little spree killing and they never let you forget about it.

Serge ran back to Hammerhead Ranch doubletime, looking over his shoulder. He locked the door, watched Florida fishing programs all day on TV and took a nap.

He awoke after dark and poured himself a tall glass of orange juice. He sat up at the head of his bed and leaned back against the wall. He grabbed the remote control and turned on the TV.

Serge's picture immediately filled the screen, and Serge spilled juice in his lap. Florida Cable News correspondent Blaine Crease said the suspect, Serge A. Storms, had been sighted in the Tampa Bay area and a team of FBI agents was en route from Quantico, Virginia.

"That's the problem with the media today," Serge complained out loud. "Too much bad news—always focusing on the negative." He clicked the TV off and made a mental note to write a letter to the station, requesting more upbeat stories.

"I gotta get out of this room."

Serge jumped in the scorched Chrysler and headed for the Howard Frankland Bridge. As he started over the bridge, he took in the sparkling lights of Tampa across the bay, the rivulet of cars cresting the bridge's hump, and the jets landing at Tampa International. He was in his zone. He turned on the radio, to add a soundtrack.

"... We interrupt this program to bring you an update on the manhunt for the spree killer from the Florida Keys. Authorities are now certain he's trapped in the Tampa Bay area. They're setting up roadblocks on all major highways out of town and posting agents at bus stations, train depots and the airports. ..."

This is getting ridiculous, Serge thought. Time to hit the eject button. He hated to do it, but he would have to leave Florida, at least for a little while, until things cooled down.

After the bridge, Serge got in the exit lane for the

airport. As he approached the terminal, three police cars raced by. I'll have to hurry, he thought, but I still have a chance if I can get through before they establish a perimeter.

Serge skidded into long-term parking and took the Tony Janus Shuttle to the terminal. Serge held on to the subway-style pole in the shuttle and involuntarily recited from memory. "Tony Janus: Aviator who began the world's first regularly scheduled airline route, St. Petersburg to Tampa, 1914."

Serge walked calmly through the concourse. Every couple of minutes, officers ran by. Serge checked gate after gate, concourse after concourse, but each time police were set up before he got there. He turned and headed back toward the exits, but now the cops were there too. More trotted through the terminal. "Shit," Serge muttered and put his head down and walked into the cafeteria.

He grabbed a tray and stood in the chow line, looking up at the menu board of food priced like jewelry. *"I'd rather do time!"* he said, and walked out without a purchase. More cops. He ducked in the newsstand and nonchalantly rifled a glossy magazine that delved into the courage of John Travolta and tastier pound cake.

He held the magazine up to his nose and peeked over the top of Travolta's head, looking for an angle.

He studied arriving travelers. Businesspeople with jet lag, middle-class vacationers back from middle-America, glassy-eyed relatives arriving for a funeral, skiers back from Aspen, golfers back from Pebble

Beach, nuns, and four illegal Asian immigrants slip-
ping past customs posing as Chinese nuclear spies.
Everyone rolling suitcases with wheels, moving with
purpose.

A distinguished businessman rolled his suitcase
into the bar across from the newsstand, and Serge
kept an eye on him. The man had touches of gray at
the temples that made him look senatorial, but he
was in fact the front for a Pacific conglomerate selling counterfeit gold-crown car air fresheners. The
man took a seat in the airport bar, ordered a Harvey
Wallbanger and wolfed Spanish peanuts from a ster-
ling service bowl. Two seats down was an elegant,
tall brunette of obvious sophistication, who initiated
conversation.

After five minutes of small talk the salesman was
discreetly propositioned by the call girl. The pair left
together for the airport hotel. Serge's eyes swung
across the concourse. No cops at the elevator to the
airport hotel—they were expecting a fugitive to flee,
not put up for the night.

Serge put down the magazine and began following
the businessman forty feet back. He looked around.
Off to his right, a cop was moving toward the hotel
elevator. Serge picked up his pace.

The businessman and call girl were in the elevator,
smiling at each other, waiting for the doors to close.
The cop was talking in his walkie-talkie, just arriving
at the elevator. Serge was fifteen feet back. The doors
started closing.

Serge called out toward the elevator and began
running: "Mr. Johnson, wait up! The office has been

trying to reach you all day!" He jumped through the closing elevator doors as the cop turned to say something.

"I'm not Mr. Johnson," said the businessman.

"I know," Serge said, and smiled and then looked up at the ascending floor numbers over the door.

The businessman made an unheard joke to the call girl, and they both laughed at Serge's expense. Serge turned to them and nodded and grinned.

The doors opened at seven. The businessman got out a magnetic plastic card and opened a room across from the elevators. Serge headed down the hallway, looking for the stairwell.

Serge had walked down to the fourth floor when he heard two cops coming up the stairs. He ran back up to seven and down the hall.

When Serge burst into the hotel room with gun drawn, the businessman was sitting on the edge of the bed in a Santa Claus outfit, and the hooker was on his lap wearing altar boy vestments.

"I can explain . . ." the man began.

Serge cut him off with a pistol whip. "I don't *want* to know. Just gimme all your money and ID."

He had another thought. "And gimme that red suit, too, while you're at it."

11

*W*elcome *Miami Vice* fans!" read the pink-and-aqua banner over the hotel entrance on Miami Beach.

In the lobby, dealers sat behind dozens of card tables, doing brisk business. Jan Hammer CDs. Philip Michael Thomas 8×10s. Ferrari Matchbox cars. Board games, coffee mugs, police badges. There was a line of people with luggage waiting to check in at the front desk, wearing Ray-Bans, pastel T-shirts and white Versace linen jackets.

Later that evening in the auditorium, a man who did not look remotely like Don Johnson was onstage playing Sonny Crockett. A woman dressed like a prostitute played Gina.

Suddenly, "Gina" ripped off her wig and threw it to the ground.

"I didn't get my GED just to play a prostitute!" she yelled.

Don Johnson grabbed her wrists and said he loved her.

The audience whistled and applauded.

It wasn't part of the script. The woman ran out the

side door of the hotel, and the man followed.

He found her sitting and crying in his convertible parked on a side street off Ocean Drive. It was a pink Cadillac Eldorado. Running the length of the car down to the tail fins was an airbrushed *Miami Vice* logo and the words *Lenny Lippowicz—The Don Johnson Experience*.

Lenny Lippowicz was the pride of Pahokee, Florida. He dropped out of high school and bounced around as a spot welder in the shipyards and Ploeşti petroleum storage compounds of Jacksonville, Tampa and Fort Lauderdale. He did a little bartending, worked a carnival in Margate, and stinted as an unqualified dive operator off Boca Raton.

He got fired from the dive boat after a bad head count left a never-found tourist behind at sea, and he drove west across the swamp. He stopped at an authentic Indian Swamp Village, where he bought authentic tribal garb woven by authentic Chinese political prisoners. When he got to Fort Myers, he put on the colorful Indian outfit and walked into the administrative office at Sunken Parrot Gardens and applied for alligator wrestler.

"What are your qualifications?"

"Look at this fantastic outfit!"

He was hired on the spot.

Lenny figured the trick to gator wrestling was keeping them fat and happy, and he fed them so much they lay around the pond drowsy all the time like a living room full of uncles after Thanksgiving dinner.

Lenny arrived in the morning and moved the red

plastic hands on the fake clock that said, "Next show at . . ." He got into his Indian costume and dragged annoyed alligators around by the tail. He picked the frailest and tucked the end of its jaws under his chin. He stuck out his arms—"Look, Ma, no hands."

It was a pleasant life and Lenny started to like the costume. Then he was fired again. One of the alligators got away while Lenny was smoking a joint behind the serpentarium, and it ate one of the parrots, which wouldn't normally have gotten Lenny fired except it ate the only one that could roller-skate.

The next day, Lenny went to the newsstand down the block from his apartment and saw a small article in the local paper about the alligator eating the bird.

A few days later Lenny stopped by the same newsstand and noticed a London tabloid with a vibrant cockatoo photo on the cover. A big story with a giant headline: "Gator Chomps Miracle Bird in Florida Feather Fest!"

The Weekly Mail of the News World had lots of dramatic details and described the parrot roller-skating for its life down a handicapped ramp at the gift shop with the gator in hot pursuit. Lenny knew the sensational details were all made up. But it was great copy.

"I can do this!"

Lenny launched his new career as freelance Florida correspondent for the sleazier side of Fleet Street. He wrote a fake résumé and exaggerated stories. He struck oil. The Brits went ape for anything Florida. The stories the tabloids wanted most:

tourists attacked by narco-criminals with machine guns, alligators, the Everglades stinkfoot, old-time gospel preachers caught with transvestites, tourists attacked by alligators, tourists attacked by stinkfoot, flesh-eating bacteria in Jacuzzis, and coconuts found growing in the likenesses of the royal family.

Lenny had a beat-up yellow Cadillac, and he headed down to Miami. He called it the *newsmobile*. He got a roll of two-inch masking tape and taped the word PRENSA across his windshield as if he were driving around war-torn Latin America, which he was.

He grabbed a plastic milk crate behind a Publix in Pompano and used it to organize his files and maps on the passenger seat. He let the *Herald, Sun-Sentinel* and *Post* bird-dog his stories and then he'd swoop in with the newsmobile to add the profitable details. He soon found he didn't need embellishment. The truth already stretched credibility. He covered the sheriff's deputy who hid in the closet videotaping his prostitute wife with public officials; the federal agent who broke up an exotic animal smuggling ring by dressing in a gorilla suit; the man found floating off Miami Beach surrounded by twenty bobbing bales of coke—said his boat sank and then these bales just came floating by. The fisherman in Islamorada dragged from the shore and drowned because he refused to let go of the rod after hooking a large fish. The Miami supermarkets that fought shoplifting with cardboard cutouts of police officers, instructing employees to move them to different aisles every hour to create the impression they were patrolling. Lenny dutifully tucked the newspaper clippings in the plastic crate at stoplights on A1A.

Then he got too bold. He started staging events. He illegally fed wild gators in retention ponds and canals until they were sluggish. He flipped them on their backs, tied them up and threw them in the backseat of the newsmobile. Then he released them at shopping plazas and busy intersections, taking photos of the resulting mayhem and filing prewritten stories.

He got caught. The newsmobile was impounded, and he lost his fake press credentials.

Lenny was allowed to wear his Indian costume in jail on religious grounds. He bribed a guard to take his photo through the bars. *The Weekly Mail of the News World* published a story about a Native American from the swamp who was arrested for protesting European encroachment by releasing alligators in populated areas. Lenny used the money from the story to pay court costs and get the newsmobile out of impound.

Lenny was living the Florida Dream. He knew the state well and he'd find safe, isolated roads and sleep in his car. Another sunrise and another day of journalism. He bought a laptop for a hundred dollars from a junkie on Biscayne Boulevard. He collected facts during the day and typed stories into the laptop at night in the bars. Over the course of the evenings, between the rum and the joints in the parking lot, the amount of writing became increasingly lean.

One night Lenny picked up a flyer left on the bar.

He had been chatting with the woman on the stool next to him—said her name was Angie—and she looked over his shoulder at the pamphlet. The first annual *Miami Vice* convention in the art deco district on South Beach.

"I love *Miami Vice*," she said.

"You do?" he said with a smile.

Lenny had his newest rap.

He bought a loose white Italian suit and Gucci loafers. He took the newsmobile in for an off-the-books pink paint job. He turned it into a convertible with a demolition saw and glued strips of packing foam over the jagged metal along the top of the windshield and where the side window posts had been. He stuck pink and blue neon tubes under the chassis.

The *Miami Vice* convention started well enough until Angie broke down onstage. Out in the car, Lenny managed to get her to stop crying and he got in and started driving to their next gig in Tampa. She gave him the silent treatment all the way across the Everglades and up I-75. When he got to Tampa Bay he pulled off at the fishing pier, hoping maybe if he could get her alone in a romantic setting and turn on the Johnson charm. . . .

$\mathcal{T}$he fresh salt air stung Lenny Lippowicz's nostrils as he gazed off the end of the fishing pier and into Tampa Bay just after midnight. He looked up at the Sunshine Skyway and the flashing red and blue lights of the emergency vehicles bunched together at the top of the bridge.

He turned around and watched Angie's angry hips in red-leather hot pants as she walked barefoot away from him under the row of crime lights running down the pier, toward shore. She had a pair of bright green spiked heels in her right hand, and he colored her gone.

Lenny sighed with a hard exhale through his nose and watched her, now tiny at the foot of the pier. He listened to the waves. He rolled the end of a filterless Lucky Strike in his mouth, gripped it with his lips and didn't light it. The cold ocean wind blew through his hair.

Lenny leaned against the concrete retaining wall at the end of the pier and looked into the blackness. The pier used to be the old Skyway bridge until a ship hit its supports in a storm in '80 and collapsed the middle span. When they built the new Skyway next to it, they ripped out most of the old bridge except the ends and converted them into fishing piers. Lenny looked up again at the emergency lights flashing on the bridge and wondered what had happened. A Coast Guard helicopter arrived and hovered with a search beam aimed down into the water.

Lenny was alone on the pier. Waves plopped against the cement supports in the darkness thirty feet below. He pulled a joint from his pocket but he couldn't get it lit in the breeze from the bay, so he crouched down behind the concrete wall and fired it up.

When he stood again, another head popped up simultaneously from the outside of the retaining wall. Lenny screamed in surprise and the other man screamed too, and the man lost his grip and fell thirty feet, splashing back into the bay. Lenny leaned over the railing and saw the man climb back out of the water again and up one of the pylons like a telephone repair man. A Santa Claus cap floated in the water behind him.

The man pulled himself over the railing, turned around and reeled in a soaked black parachute trailing behind him. He wrung out the chute and bundled it in his arms.

"Don't hurt me!" Lenny said, and covered up his face.

"I'm not gonna touch you," said Serge, and he threw the wet chute in the backseat of Lenny's Cadillac. Serge walked to an oil-drum garbage can in a corner of the pier and retrieved a small brown paper sack hidden down in the garbage. Serge unpacked the contents: khaki shorts, sandals and a short-sleeve yellow shirt with an M. C. Escher pattern of angelfish turning into juvenile delinquents. He changed into the dry clothes.

Lenny slowly lowered his arms. "Who are you?"

"I'm *the messenger,*" said Serge. "The one you've been waiting for."

Lenny took another slow drag on his joint. "Far out."

Serge climbed into the passenger side of the Cadillac and Lenny got in behind the wheel.

Serge pointed down the pier, back toward land. "Step on it, toke-meister."

And Lenny hit the gas.

*O*n the edge of the Hillsborough River, in a large open room on the second floor of the Tampa Tribune Building, the skeleton night crew tapped away at computer keyboards.

A young copy editor just out of college named Kirk Curtly worked the rim. He opened a computer file from the directory containing stories that needed headlines written. Kirk had been gently prodded by his supervisors to be more specific in his headlines. On the other hand, he was roundly praised for never having incurred a dreaded correction, which he achieved through inspired vagueness. Kirk tapped his chin with the Montblanc pen he'd gotten for a graduation gift and never used, since everything was done on computers. He typed the headline "Panel Studies Plan." He looked at its structure and rhythm on the screen. He smiled with satisfaction and sent the story along to the typesetters. He called up another story and tapped his chin again. He typed "Official Mulls Options." Curtly had a mental Rolodex of short, bureaucratic terms that were perfect for narrow headlines over one-column-wide stories, and he searched for such thin articles in the headline directory to show off his arsenal. It went this way for much of his shift. "Board Picks Member," "Senate Takes Flak," "Gov Eyes New Trend," and his proudest effort: "Pols Nix Proxy Prexy Tap."

Shortly after midnight, a late news story wormed its way through the *Tribune* computer system until it came to the headline directory. Kirk looked around. All his colleagues were writing heads on other stories. Only one story left that wasn't being worked. It wasn't one column. It ran in big type all the way across the top of page one. Kirk's hands were unsteady as he opened the file. He read the story. A man in a Santa Claus suit had jumped off the Sunshine Skyway bridge. He began typing. He finished, sent the story along, got up and walked into the men's room, where he suffered a forty-minute failure of nerve.

The story and headline moved with the speed of light to the copysetter, who was overworked and had exactly eight seconds to proof everything before pressing a button in the upper right of his keyboard, which fired electrons through the building and made the story spit out on a roll of silver-nitrate paper from a machine in the blue-collar section of the building. The page composers, who had exactly six months before their jobs would be sucked out of them by microprocessors, ran it through the waxer and slapped it on the master page, which was photographed by a giant camera, burned into a metal plate and clamped on the huge rollers of the printing press, and hundreds of thousands of copies rolled down conveyor belts to trucks waiting at the loading dock to bring the news to you.

12

═══════════════════════════

*I*t was a hot, clammy afternoon in Biloxi. Keesler Air Force Base was dead. There were no missions for the Hurricane Hunters and no wind, and the air sat heavy on the town. The Prop Wash Bar only had ceiling fans.

Ex–Lieutenant Colonel Lee "Southpaw" Barnes filled his mug from a pitcher of draft and looked across the bar at the group of airmen sitting around two tables near the dart boards. It was the crew of the *Rebel Yell*, the fierce rivals of Montana's plane. The crew stared back at Barnes and his colleagues, and a few began to chuckle derisively.

"I hate those fuckers," said Barnes. "They think they're hot shit."

Marilyn Sebastian leaned up against the jukebox, wearing flight pants and a tight combat-green tank top with a large oval of perspiration between her shoulder blades. Her fiery red hair was out of its usual ponytail and fell over her shoulders. She punched up a Patsy Cline tune and swayed with far-away thoughts. She wrapped her lips around a long-neck beer and took a hard pull.

One of the members of the *Rebel Yell* made a wise-crack and his table broke up. He smiled and stood and strolled over to Marilyn with the cockiness of the oxygen-deficient.

Both crews watched as the airman whispered something to Marilyn, who continued staring into the jukebox. He leaned a second time and whispered something else. Without warning, Marilyn had him by the forearm, with leverage behind his elbow, and smashed his face into the front of the jukebox.

"Bitch!" the airman shouted from the dusty floor.

Both crews sprang out of their chairs. Ex–Lieutenant Colonel Barnes grabbed a whiskey bottle by the neck and smashed it against the bar, cutting tendons in his favorite hand.

Suddenly, the air base's claxons sounded, and Montana's crew was all business. They grabbed their gear and sprinted in formation across the tarmac. The wheels of the Hercules were off the runway in eight minutes.

Four time zones ahead, Hurricane Rolando-berto began to sputter. The cooler waters of the mid-Atlantic sapped its strength, but the National Hurricane Center wanted visual reconnaissance before they downgraded it. It did a loop-de-loop more than a thousand miles due east of Montserrat and languished in random, constantly changing directions, its tracking chart looking like someone with DTs got hold of an Etch A Sketch.

Weather officer "Tiny" Baxter bandaged the ex–lieutenant colonel's damaged hand. Montana took a wide swing at twenty thousand feet around the storm system. Miami was right, he thought, no longer a defined eye. It was becoming completely unorganized. Milton "Bananas" Foster radioed the report back to Florida; then he began screaming "Mayday!" until Barnes wrestled the microphone from him.

Armed with the report, the books at the National Hurricane Center were officially closed on Rolando-berto.

*B*ack in Aristotle "Art" Tweed's hometown of Montgomery, Alabama, lived a man named Paul.

Paul was passive.

He was built for it. At five foot four, he never weighed more than a buck-ten—a small, rumpled man in a similar suit. He had thin gray hair that he kept covered with a black fedora, and his voice was hesitant, barely above whisper. Paul's was the soft face of the full-time victim. All his features were on the small side, and the fifty-eight years of aging did not etch harsh lines and cracks, but gentle folds. Pink webs of capillaries and other blood vessels were visible on his cheeks and chin. His complexion was extra pale, not quite sickly, but you wouldn't be surprised if he fainted at any moment.

Paul was a nice guy, to a fault. He was a shy, considerate, deferential, rule-following worrier. He was worried about lawsuits and IRS audits and madmen. He drove slow in the right lane, never took a pen from work, ate extra fiber and overfed parking meters. He was obsequious to telephone solicitors.

When Paul walked by, people thought: The meek shall inherit the earth, but only if their parents were ruthless bastards.

Paul had worked the past twenty-three years as a claims adjuster at Fidelity Insurance, which was trying to cheat on Paul. Even with paltry two percent annual raises, Paul's salary had grown to a decent level, and Fidelity wanted to replace him with a younger, cheaper worker.

They gave Paul a six-month buyout, which killed his pension in the fine print. Fidelity didn't mention that the buyout put the company on dicey legal ground and he had every legal right to refuse, which most of his co-workers did. The gracious offer was designed to take advantage of people like Paul, who rolled over on command.

Paul soon found the six-month buyout was based not on his current salary, but on a mathematically suspect twenty-three-year index, and in today's dollars Paul received the equivalent of two paychecks. He went to work selling shoes at the Mega Mall.

Paul's wife was not passive. She was a thirty-six-year-old loud bottle blonde with qualified good looks, possibly sensual, but not elegant. Put it this way: She'd be the best-looking woman you could expect to find at ten A.M. in a bar, which was where she went every day after Paul left for work.

They were newlyweds, and they hadn't had sex since the wedding night, which she only did for tax reasons.

She married Paul because he owned his house outright, and her lawyer/lover estimated the shortest

possible time she had to stay married to Paul to have
a realistic legal shot at getting half. It was a modestly
priced place when Paul purchased it in the sixties,
but the area had become exclusive Cloverdale, and
the house had appreciated wildly.

On the first day Paul's wife was in the eligibility
zone for a fifty-fifty split, she asked for a divorce,
and for the first time in memory, Paul said no.

On the second day, Paul came home and found her
naked on the dining-room table, her lawyer riding
herd. "Well, if it isn't Mr. I-won't-give-my-wife-a-
divorce. How was work today, honey?"

She got her divorce.

Paul was forced to sell the house and move into a
cramped apartment on the Atlanta Highway, closer to
the shoe store.

Since he was a teen, Paul found refuge during difficult times in the pages of hard-boiled mystery nov-
els. He read Dashiell Hammett, Raymond Chandler
and Mickey Spillane. He watched Robert Mitchum
on the big screen. A private detective—it was all he
ever wanted to be. He fancied his life a dog-eared
twenty-five-cent paperback, a dame, a shot of bourbon and no regrets. But he never followed his passion
because he found out it might involve confrontation.

After the divorce, he began plowing through Philip
Marlowe and Mike Hammer. He drove to the shoe
store imagining he was cruising through the City of
Angels in the fifties. At work, he pretended every
woman customer was a floozy with a hard-luck story
who only needed a good slapping.

During his third Monday on the job, Paul was lacing up oxfords with a gritty, hard-boiled savoir faire. Three truants ran through the shoe store, grabbed the left oxford and played keep-away from Paul. Paul repeatedly jumped in the air, trying to grab the shoe the youths held over their heads. "C'mon, guys!"

The youths grew bored and shoved Paul into a promotional pyramid, and he went sprawling on the floor in an avalanche of Hush Puppies. Even his customers laughed. He'd had it. If life was going to kick him in the teeth anyway, he might as well be doing what he loved.

Paul dipped into his proceeds from the sale of his house. He hung out a shingle and had his name painted in gold block letters on the window of his office door. His enthusiasm for the job started paying off in any case that had no possibility of human contact. Tracking lost assets, researching ancestry for probate, taking surveillance photographs of empty buildings. Because Paul was so terrible with people, his other senses began to compensate, and Paul learned he had an almost mystical clairvoyance when it came to inanimate objects. Word got around, and Paul was sought out by law enforcement and the private sector for a specific kind of case. He began making headlines. "Lost Gems Located After Eighty Years," "Murder Weapon Recovered from Lake," "Human Skull Found in Victory Garden."

Paul was patted on the back for his results and then browbeaten over the size of his bill, and his net rates became the cheapest in town. But with each success, Paul became more confident and assertive. A metamorphosis was taking place. Of course in Paul's case, it was all relative; there could only be so much change.

He became Paul, the Passive-Aggressive Private Eye.

One afternoon in November, Paul was sitting in his office with his feet up on the desk, asking questions of one of those large novelty eight balls that tell fortunes. An answer floated up in the ball's liquid window. "Fat chance." The phone rang.

It flustered Paul and he threw the eight ball over his shoulder and out the third-floor window. He grabbed the receiver.

*A*t four-oh-five on a cool fall afternoon, the public information officer of the Montgomery, Alabama, Police Department called the assignment editors of the collected capital press corps. He announced a "walkout." A walkout was a staged event where a police department assembles reporters and walks a suspect out in front of the cameras, at the optimum photographic angle and light, just in time to lead the six or eleven o'clock broadcasts. Reporters are supposed to yell, "Why'd ya do it?!"

At four-fifty, in front of a compressed line of still and video cameras, two husky officers escorted a handcuffed teenage girl out of the police station to a waiting jail van. The girl had ratty hair down in her face.

"Why'd ya do it?" a dozen reporters yelled in harmony.

The girl answered with the middle digit.

The snarling teenager seen on the six o'clock news across the great state of Alabama that night was the incorrigible daughter of the senior records keeper at Montgomery Memorial, a good, hardworking woman trying to straighten out her child. So she took her to work on a recent Friday afternoon and left her in an auxiliary records office to do her homework . . . where she logged on to the hospital's confidential computer files and telephoned twenty patients, falsely informing them of positive HIV tests, malignant growths, late-stage leukemia and something she made up called "brain worms."

Officials at Montgomery Memorial Hospital had been trying for three days to track down the twenty patients. They had reached eighteen. The nineteenth had shot himself in the head that morning. That left only one.

They tried the home phone but got no answer, so they sent someone out to his house. There was no car in the driveway and nobody answered the door. They couldn't find Aristotle "Art" Tweed.

Neighbors hadn't seen Tweed around in at least a week, so the hospital asked the police to trace his long-distance phone calls, credit-card charges and ATM withdrawals. The credit-card company already had an eye on Tweed, who, although not over the limit, had begun to amass charges with a frequency and eclecticism that tripped the company's security software designed to detect cards that had fallen into the hands of binge criminals.

At the behest of the hospital's civil attorneys, a private detective was dispatched to bring in the nomadic Mr. Tweed before he could incur any liability.

When Montgomery Memorial Hospital was advised to retain a private eye to track down Art Tweed, they followed the same corporate philosophy that guided patient care: cut cost regardless of result. Any law firm worth its salt would have known that the particular private detective selected by Montgomery Memorial was not right for this type of job: It involved people, not inanimate objects. However, the hospital had also retained the cheapest law firm in town, and there were no objections. They dialed the phone.

"I'm on the case," said Paul, the Passive-Aggressive Private Eye. He put on a fedora, got in his black Ford Fairlane, put "The Peter Gunn Theme" on the radio and headed for Florida.

/ have attained a humility that involves no loss of pride," said Jethro Maddox, just after passing gas in the blue Malibu heading down U.S. 19.

Art Tweed quietly stared out the passenger window, saddened by all the bullies in the world.

They were in the Big Bend, where Florida's panhandle makes the wide turn south into the peninsula. There were no more beaches, no postcard scenes. A small rusty bridge spanned a gorge. Art saw a brown highway sign at the river that had a bunch of music notes and the name Stephen Foster. As they crossed the Suwannee River, Art looked down and saw a handmade wooden canoe knifing the glass surface of the water.

The gas needle was on *E,* and Jethro aimed the Malibu for the turn lane and the old gas station with a tin awning.

On the gas station's porch was a whiskered man with a large carving knife, whittling a table leg into a tree branch. "Ain't no way that Hurricane Rolando-berto is gonna hit Florida! I can feel these things. I got the shine."

"All the weather reports indicate otherwise," said Jethro.

"They also said we landed on the moon, but that was TV tricks." The old man leaned and spit. "You've been brainwashed by whitey!"

"But *you're* white," said Art.

"Bah!" the man said in a crotchety voice, dismissing Art with a careless flick of the knife. He got up and went inside.

Jethro and Art stepped over a lactating Labrador in front of a rusty Yoo-Hoo machine and followed the man into the station.

Jethro pulled out a Visa card and asked for fifteen bucks of regular unleaded.

"We don't accept charge cards," said the old man, displaying undependable teeth.

Jethro pointed out the window at the Visa sign on the gas pumps.

"The distributor put that up," said the old man. "It's only good at participating dealers. I'm not a participating dealer."

"What determines whether you are a participating dealer?"

"Whether I feel like it." He lit a filterless cigarette and pulled a piece of tobacco off his tongue. With an insulting slowness, he picked up an open gold can of Miller High Life next to the register.

"Okay," Jethro said in resignation. "Can I get the key to the restroom?"

"Are you buying any gas?"

"No, I am going to a participating dealer."

"Then you're not a customer. Can't you read the sign? Restrooms for customers only."

Jethro took a deep breath and looked at the ceiling. "A man must sometimes summon patience when there is no reward for doing so."

"And no Hemingway in here either!" said the old man.

As the clerk talked, Art noticed he had clumps of hair sprouting like pods of lichen from unexpected anatomy, and he knew it would be an image he would have trouble shaking.

"You wanna take a crap? Buy something! Whatever you want—doesn't matter to me—Ding Dongs, pickled eggs . . ." The old man patted the big green glass jar next to the lottery machine.

The sound of the old man's voice became softer and softer inside Art's head until there was no sound at all—just his lips moving. Art's stare tightened to tunnel vision around the man's head. Then he heard a deep, unfamiliar voice inside his skull: *He should die! You should kill him!*

"Hey! What's wrong with your friend?" the clerk

asked Jethro. "He's actin' kinda weird. I don't think I like how he's lookin' at me. . . . Both of you, outta here!"

They backed out of the store like gunslingers retreating from a hostile saloon.

Jethro turned to Art in the car. "There are many roads to dignity, and one is called *character*—"

"Just drive," said Art.

Jethro pulled back onto U.S. 19 and Art turned on the radio.

"Hey, boys and girls, this is Boris the Hateful Piece of Sh—AHH-OOOO-GAH! reminding those of you who are old enough to hit the ballot box to make sure you vote yes on Proposition 213. . . ."

"What's *this* about?" asked Art.

"Foreign immigrants are taking away your jobs and sponging off your tax dollars! It's time we stood up for America and put a stop to it!"

"Intolerant bastard!" said Jethro. "When I was in Spain for the civil war—"

"Shhhh!"

As Art listened to Boris, his eyes locked on the radio, and his gaze went to tunnel vision. Boris's voice slowly faded out and was replaced by a new, deeper voice inside Art's head. Art was listening.

*C*ity and Country could feel they were getting close.

They were eastbound, driving through the backroads of Florida without streetlights. The night wind was too cold and they had the convertible top up. They hadn't seen another car in miles; Bruce Spring-

steen's *Nebraska* tape was in the stereo on low. State
Road 16 was narrow and empty, and they rode high
beams as they crossed girders over the St. Johns
River at five A.M. Twelve miles later, they saw something bright and green in the distance that said they
were out of the woods. The on-ramp sign for Interstate 95. They caught the highway below Jacksonville and headed south.

They soon passed the last St. Augustine exit. The
stars were gone and the black sky was replaced with
dark blue. By Palm Coast, daybreak was definitely
on the way, and they crossed over to the seaside A1A
highway. At a stoplight, the pair threw the latches;
Country turned around and stood in her seat as she
pushed the convertible top back. They were in twilight, and they couldn't distinguish where ocean left
off and sky began. They kept glancing left, and a thin
red line soon defined the horizon.

When they hit Daytona, they drove right out on the
sand. The early-bird beer-funnelers whistled and cat-
called, and City and Country waved back. After the
novelty of driving on sand wore off, City drove up
Main Street. They parked across from the cemetery
at Boot Hill Saloon. A hard-core biker hangout. They
walked in and all heads turned. But the girls knew
the score—places like this were harmless as long as
nobody smelled fear, and the two strolled with reckless attitude to a pair of barstools. They ordered
whiskey. It was seven A.M.

"Shit," muttered an impressed biker three stools
down, and turned back to a conversation with a hit
man. City studied a photograph over the bar. Three

smiling bikers with their arms over each other's shoulders. Underneath was a plaque: "In memoriam. Stinky, Cheese-Dick and Ringworm. Killed by yuppies."

The door opened and a flabby insurance type with an untucked polo shirt stood frozen in the doorway with a Tipper Gore wife. Both looked like deer in headlights—one of the moments where someone knows they're in the wrong place, but they don't know which is worse, running or sticking it out. They took hesitant steps forward, their feet crunching the peanut shells covering the floor, the only sound in the room. They stopped under the unlaundered bras and panties hanging from the ceiling. Fear stunk up the joint. Several bikers got off their stools. The couple changed their minds and ran.

But there was a difference between fearless and dumb . . . take the Georgia Tech theology student in a Hog's Breath T-shirt and the English major from the University of Tennessee, who finished off an all-night drink fest by falling from their hotel balcony. However, their room was on the first floor, and they simply rolled on the lawn, got up, and walked to Boot Hill Saloon. The Georgia sophomore was Sammy Pedantic. The English major in the Volunteers letterman jacket was Joe Varsity, and he was telling Sammy about his thesis comparing the Styron-Mailer literary schism to the East-West rap feud.

"Mailer might do a drive-by?"

"He's got the temperament."

"But he can't do this," said Sammy, and he stuck a full longneck beer in his mouth and raised it in the air without hands and drained it. Then he opened his mouth, and the empty bottle fell and bounced off the bar.

Three Latin men in sharp suits came in the door, and the bikers picked up their beers and cleared out of the way. The three sat down next to Joe and Sammy, who were trying to balance small stacks of quarters on their noses.

City and Country were getting a little blitzed. They ordered more whiskey and smoked cigarettes like amateurs.

Soon the Latin men left the bar, and Joe and Sammy looked around the place and spotted the two women.

"Oh, no!" said City. "They're coming over here!"

"Hi, girls! Mind if we join you?"

"Yes."

Joe and Sammy sat down.

The guys talked nonstop for twenty minutes while the girls faked yawns and tapped their watches. "So that's the deal," said Joe. "These three Latin guys are paying us to drive their Lexus across the state, and they're even throwing in a couple of motel rooms on the beach. We just need someone to drive our car. What d'ya say?"

City talked real slow and annoyed, like she was dealing with the simple. "Why don't one of *you* drive the Lexus and the *other* drive your car?"

"Cuz then we can't drink beer and party on the way over," Sammy said like it was obvious. "It wouldn't be a roadtrip."

"Who were these guys with the Lexus?"

"Great guys! . . ." said Sammy. "What were their names?"

City looked out the side window at their Alfa Romeo. A police cruiser drove by slowly, then stopped and backed up.

"Please, you gotta come with us," said Sammy.

The officer got out and started walking around the Alfa.

"On second thought, it's not such a bad idea," said City. "Where's your car?"

"Right across the street." Sammy pointed. "When can you leave?"

"How 'bout right now?"

13

The Diaz Boys had a big shipment of cocaine headed for Tampa Bay, and they decided to try one last time to make a drop at a rented home.

They sat down their newest mole couple, Mr. and Mrs. Ramirez, and told them about all the other couples they had placed in rented homes, only to screw up. The Diaz Boys let them know in no uncertain terms exactly what the score was.

"What's the score?" said Mr. Ramirez.

"We just told you!"

Ramirez wasn't really their name and they weren't really married. They were Miguel Cruz and Maria Vasquez from Colombia, both in their late fifties, who had recently immigrated to the United States with green cards arranged by the Diaz Boys with hefty bribes. They posed as a married couple. To make the arrangement more credible and unassuming, they were accompanied by a sweet great-grandmother, who was actually Margarita de Cortez, the vicious Mata Hari of Venezuelan politics from the 1940s, who was rumored to have been making love to the fi-

nance minister when she stabbed him in the heart
with the spike of a German kaiser helmet that he had
begged her to wear to bed. But now she was just another harmless old lady in her eighties on Florida's
Gulf Coast—Mrs. Edna Ploomfield, the live-in
mother-in-law.

The Diaz Boys repeated what the penalty would
be if there were any more mistakes—just in case
there was any confusion. The Ramirezes nodded ea-
gerly that they understood and that everything would
be fine. Thank you for the opportunity—you won't
regret it. They shook hands and made pleasantries
until they noticed Margarita de Cortez sitting silently
off to the side. Everyone stopped talking and looked
over at her.

"I need a smoke," she said. "And a drink. And a
man."

*M*r. and Mrs. Ramirez moved into Calusa Pointe
Tower Arms, unit 1193. They couldn't have been
more thrilled about living in the United States. They
wanted to be part of the American Dream. They
signed up for citizenship classes.

But above all else, Mr. and Mrs. Ramirez remembered what the Diaz Boys had said, and they kept to
themselves and were gracious in all social situations.
It came naturally. Their enthusiasm for being in the
land of the free bubbled over, and they were exceedingly pleasant to all their neighbors, who reacted
with surliness and sweeping expostulations. The
Ramirezes couldn't understand how people who had

so much could be so bitter. But they figured it was just another facet of American culture they did not yet understand but would soon come to appreciate.

After a few months, the Ramirezes got the odd feeling that things had changed. Their neighbors' normally crappy outlook had become one of suspicion and standoffishness. One day the Ramirezes were walking back to the unit with grocery sacks when they saw Mrs. Ploomfield standing in her nightgown just outside the door of unit 1193, pointing down the hall at one of their neighbors. "Yeah, you! I'm talking to *you*, motherfucker! . . ."

Mrs. Ramirez screamed and dropped her brown bag of vegetables. She leaped over the zucchini squash and ran up the walkway.

Edna Ploomfield was still yelling down the hall at the neighbor as Mrs. Ramirez hustled her inside: "You're dead! You hear me? Dead!"

Mr. Ramirez brought up the rear and bolted the door. The couple quivered and stared at Edna in disbelief.

"What are you doing?" yelled Mr. Ramirez. "Do you want to die?"

Mrs. Ploomfield spit on the floor with disdain and shuffled toward the kitchenette.

Everyone in Calusa Pointe knew Mrs. Ploomfield and they avoided her. Just the opposite in the bar next door at Hammerhead Ranch, where she made lots of friends. One of her drinking buddies was Guy Rockney, the weatherman for FCN, who owned a penthouse at Calusa Pointe.

Rockney told Ploomfield he had a problem. He

had come up with this great idea at the station for Toto the Weather Dog. The station gave him a raise but also made him take care of the pooch, which was running and peeing all over the penthouse and chewing up his shoes. He tried everything. Books, videos, obedience school. No matter what he did, he just couldn't get the dog to behave. Could Toto live with her? He'd pay.

"Of course," she said. "I love animals."

Mr. and Mrs. Ramirez returned to Calusa Pointe from the drugstore and found a small Chihuahua wearing a Florida Gators cheerleading outfit, pompoms tied to its paws, sitting quietly in the corner.

"Stay!" Mrs. Ploomfield commanded, and the dog stayed.

*T*he mayor of Beverly Shores was shrinking.

This much was confirmed when he was fingerprinted and photographed for attempted murder with a lawn dart, which was dropped to simple assault. The news vans converged on Calusa Pointe again. Malcolm Kefauver had lost at least an inch since the last news story. He was now only five foot two, and his clothes had become so baggy they were in style.

The judge told Malcolm he expected more from a mayor, even if it was just the smallest incorporation in three counties. In addition to the lecture, Malcolm got probation and a hundred hours of picking up litter on the beach, which he accomplished by attaching a lawn dart to the end of his cane.

Malcolm Kefauver was up for reelection. The

city's vote total each year averaged one eighty-eight. Elections at Beverly Shores were wonderful occasions. Rows of folding plastic chairs filled the community rooms of the condominiums, and red-white-and-blue banners covered the walls and the podiums like the cabooses of whistle-stop trains. There was always a strapping turnout at candidate forums because of the likelihood they would degrade into talk-show donnybrooks.

Kefauver approached the podium. He was running for mayor as a Republican. The mayor and the city council did little more than argue over trash pickup, pool hours and the weight limit of pets. This didn't stop Kefauver from issuing a tirade against the intangibles tax, foreign aid and the cultural elite in Hollywood that was conducting a systematic campaign to undermine the God-fearing values that built the condominiums of Beverly Shores. The crowd applauded politely.

As the clapping died down, someone in back yelled, "What about your arrest, Manson!"

Someone else: "Yeah, Dillinger, will your criminal enterprise be part of your administration?"

Laughter and hooting.

"Lies!" retorted Kefauver. "The distortions of commies and fags!"

"What are you talking about? You hit Mr. Goldfarb in the butt with a lawn dart. He's a retired Army major with ten grandkids!"

"That's right!" another woman yelled. "And why did you try to evict my dog, Muffins?"

"Oh shut up!" replied another heckler. "Your dog's a mangy bitch!"

"She is not!" the woman responded. "But your wife has four martinis with lunch, not including the flask in her purse."

"What are you saying!"

"She's a lush . . . and she swims out to troop ships!"

"Why you . . . !" The man started climbing over rows of folding chairs until others restrained him, and someone gaveled an emergency adjournment. Everyone decided definitely not to miss the next meeting.

Normally, Kefauver's arrest would have ensured the election would be his personal Waterloo. However, the Democratic candidate was a woman named Gladys Hochenburger. At the next meeting, Kefauver attacked the Black Caucus in Congress and the U.S. military policy of not using its bombs more. Then Gladys took the podium. She shuffled papers and adjusted her reading glasses. She pointed at Kefauver and said, "This man's an impostor! The real Malcolm Kefauver died in the middle of last term and has been replaced by a man from New York named Danny DeVito. That's why his clothes don't fit and he looks like he's shrinking!"

The crowd started buzzing.

"Danny DeVito the actor?" someone yelled out.

"Who?" asked Gladys.

"The actor."

"No," said Gladys. "Danny DeVito the replicant. I

heard about him during *The X-Files*. Agents broke in on a special frequency that only I could hear."

Kefauver was back in the race.

But it would still be close. Despite Gladys's interesting bearings, she immediately inherited the built-in Jesse Ventura constituency in every precinct as the yahoo/sabotage candidate.

Until now, reporters never considered covering the Beverly Shores campaign. With Malcolm and Gladys in the race, every network had a mobile transmitting van outside the polling station at the Calusa Pointe condominiums.

On election night, Gladys took the lead on early returns, and Florida Cable News broke in from coverage of the governor's race. But as the absentee snowbird votes were tabulated, Malcolm pulled off a narrow, four-vote victory. When the TV camera lights went on, Malcolm pledged conciliation. "I will reach across the aisle in my administration for bipartisan cooperation to work for the common good of the people of this great city."

After the speech, Malcolm Kefauver set about identifying exactly who among his neighbors had voted against him and how he would prepare his cold dish of revenge.

*T*he next morning at Calusa Pointe Tower Arms began with a hard knock on the front door of unit 1193.

A second firm knock. "I know you're in there!"

Mrs. Ramirez opened the door and smiled. "It's Mayor Kefauver, from 2193, right above us. How nice to see you, Mr. Kefauver! Congratulations on the election!"

"Knock off the bullshit. I know you voted against me. How dare you!"

"But . . . but . . . how do you know how we voted?" asked Mrs. Ramirez. "It's supposed to be secret. The sanctity of the ballot box."

"Sanctity, shmanctity," said the mayor, stepping into the living room, uninvited. "Guess what? We peeked! We have to do things like that because you immigrants are sneaky. You think you can just fall off the banana boat and start voting in *secret*?"

"But that's what they taught us in citizenship class. We would be regular Americans. We could vote and have constitutional rights and everything. We just couldn't be president."

"But we could be in the cabinet," added Mr. Ramirez, "like the great Mr. Kissinger."

"Save it for the next load of greaseballs!" interrupted the mayor. "You're all a bunch of friggin' wetbacks as far as I'm concerned, and we don't want your kind here! I'm going to make your life a living hell until you . . ."

Mrs. Ramirez felt someone grab her from behind and shove her out of the way, and Edna Ploomfield stepped up to the mayor.

"Wetbacks? Greaseballs? You don't even know your racist geography. Your slurs missed by a whole goddamn continent both times, you ignorant fuck!"

She gave him a fast, two-handed shove in the middle of his chest and he stumbled backward. Ploomfield advanced and stood up to his chest again.

"You wanna dance with someone, cocksucker?" She gave him another hard shove and he stumbled back again, too surprised to know what to do.

She shoved him again, and he stumbled again. On a bookshelf she saw the rocks glass of scotch she'd been drinking, and she grabbed it.

"You sonuvabitch!" She threw the scotch in his eyes. Since the mayor had been shrinking, he was now right at Mrs. Ploomfield's eye level, and she smashed the glass into his forehead, opening a large cut over his brow. He fell in the doorway and pressed his hands against his head to stop the bleeding, and Edna jumped on his back. She grabbed him by the hair and bounced his head on the sidewalk until the Ramirezes pulled her off.

When the police arrived, Kefauver was sitting up holding his forehead and screaming about the psychotic old lady who attacked him. He reeked from the booze splashed on his face and shirt.

Edna Ploomfield hobbled to the door and a young policeman helped her by the arm. "Oh, my, my. Thank heavens you're here, you nice officers," she said in a delicate, creaking voice. "That terrible man threatened us. Ohhhh, I'm just a sweet little ol' lady, and he was mean to me. He fell and hit his own head because he was so crazy and drunk . . ."

"You're putting on an act, you old bag!"

". . . just like that," Ploomfield said, and pointed.

"We've heard enough," said the sergeant in charge,

and they handcuffed the mayor and took him away in a patrol car, but not before the TV crews arrived and pointed cameras in the back window and yelled in unison, "Why'd ya do it?"

*T*he Diaz Boys held an emergency meeting right after watching the mayor of Beverly Shores being driven off in a squad car on the nightly news. Tommy Diaz told Rafael and Pedro to take the shotguns, and he gave them a map to Calusa Pointe, unit 1193.

"How do you want it handled?" asked Rafael.

"Just knock on the door."

"Then what?"

"Shoot whoever answers."

14

*T*hree weeks into December, the meteorologic tragi-comedy known as El Niño produced two markedly abnormal conditions in the Lesser Antilles. The trade winds exceeded the annual average by five miles per hour, and the water temperature rose two degrees. The changes were imperceptible to the islanders living in the region. But they made the critical difference when the remnants of a barely organized and forgotten storm system limped into the area. Overnight, Rolando-berto roared back to life and came ashore on one of the Leeward Islands, where the residents did not possess a prescient dog, but instead relied upon a goat wearing an Ohio State sweater bestowed as a peace offering in 1977 by a shipwrecked alumnus who mistook the natives for cannibals.

Before the goat could ring the bell on its neck, Rolando-berto promptly dispatched the animal through the side of a quaint and gaily painted barn, and entire villages were leveled without warning.

News of the death toll in the Leewards whipped Florida into action and cranked up the state's Hurri-

cane Industrial Complex. Commemorative "I survived Rolando-berto" T-shirts were printed in advance, and shelves were stocked with packing tape,
weather radios and splatterproof party ponchos.
Water was bottled, plywood nailed, and candles and
batteries shipped in by tram. TV advertising time
was purchased to demonstrate two-hundred-dollar
panes of miracle glass that could withstand coconuts
fired from special cannons. Florida Cable News
bought a new wardrobe for Toto.

*N*ews of the hurricane was playing in hi-fi in the
Lexus, and Sammy Pedantic changed the station to
techno-dance.

"Those were great guys," Joe said as they drove
through Orlando on I-4. "What a deal—just drive
their car across the state to Tampa Bay and give it to
their cousin and we get five hundred bucks."

"I've heard about this before—rich people actually
pay someone to drive their cars city to city. It's like
house-sitting. Except there's no house."

"Plus a free weekend on the beach!"

"And chicks, too!" Sammy turned around and saw
City and Country driving eight lengths back in their
maroon Mercury Cougar. He popped two beers and
handed one to Joe. "Now, this is living."

They concentrated on drinking for a moment, then
threw the empties onto the leather backseat. Joe
burped first, then Sammy, then it became a contest.

"You know anything about the Gulf Coast?"
asked Joe.

"Are you kidding? It's ten times better than the East Coast. And Miami has nothing on Tampa. We're lucky we fell into this deal."

"How do you know all that?"

"Those guys told us, remember?"

"That's right."

"There is a God," said Sammy.

"And he has plans for us," said Joe.

On the way through Orlando, Joe and Sammy began hearing a peculiar sound inside the dashboard, but it didn't seem to be affecting the car's performance. They continued southwest on Interstate 4, past a collision of money and architecture. Castles and resort hotels and imperial pagodas. Wild West sets and Polynesian discos. Artificial beaches and heliports. Down both sides of the highway, like the master growth plan of a small, oil-producing state. Pirate ships and towers of terror. Giant Las Vegas signs: "Buffet $4.99." Reptile petting farms, go-cart tracks. Fun World, Fun Mania, Fun 'n' Sun. And it wasn't even Disney yet. The Great White Shark was still ahead; these were just the remoras and trash fish that clean its teeth and suck the scales for sidestream commerce.

They hit heavy traffic, then construction, and the boys lost City and Country just past the American Gladiators Dinner Theater.

"Where'd the girls go?" asked Sammy.

"Shhhh!" said Joe, trying to listen to the engine.

They noticed the engine sound growing louder as they drove through Lakeland. It was a rhythmic noise, a whap-whap-whap like a baseball card in the spokes of a bike. Joe leaned toward the dash.

"I've heard engines about to go, and this doesn't sound the same," said Joe. "We're pretty close to Tampa. We'll make it."

He was right. It wasn't the engine. The problem was the air-conditioning. One of the fan blades was rubbing. Only a little at first. The blade had shifted slightly and began clipping some plastic in the cowling. As the clipping wore on, the plastic became frayed and gave the fan blade more to dig into, which tore up more of the plastic.

By the time they took the exit ramp into downtown Tampa, the puttering sound filled the car. Sammy read the map and said where to turn. Joe made a right on Polk, and Sammy pointed at the bus station a block ahead. "That's where we're supposed to meet the guy's cousin."

Something they didn't know: The plastic that the fan blade was clipping wasn't supposed to be there. It was the tight outer binding of a kilo of cocaine. As Joe and Sammy rounded the corner, the slightest aperture opened through the last bit of plastic wrap and a thin, invisible current of coke blew out the vents.

Sammy sniffed the air. "Smells musty in here."

The fan now had something to work with. Once that first hole had broken the seal, the blade ripped open the rest in short order like a Christmas present.

Suddenly, the air conditioner blew a swift, solid cloud of white dust that filled the passenger compart-

ment, blinding and choking them. Joe began hitting
parking meters and garbage cans all down the right
side of the street until he crashed into the back of a
van outside the bus terminal.

A police officer ran from a sandwich shop. The
electric windows rolled down and a thick cloud of
cocaine billowed out. Joe and Sammy opened their
doors and fell to the ground, gagging. The officer
pulled his gun.

In all, the cocaine in the air conditioner and other
parts of the Lexus tipped police scales at just over
four hundred and ten pounds, a weight which, under
new federal law, required a roomful of politicians to
appear at the press conference announcing the ar-
rests. Seven hours into the interrogation of Joe and
Sammy, a team of detectives, prosecutors and city officials met secretly in a conference room at police
headquarters. Something had happened for the first
time in their collective crime-fighting experience.
Suspects found in a car full of drugs—actually covered *in* drugs—appeared to be innocent. But since
they had already held the press conference, the two
young men would have to be convicted and imprisoned.

While they discussed the case, a corporal walked
around the conference table with plastic fast-food
sacks, placing a child's Happy Meal, complete with
toy prize, in front of each top official. The embattled
and paranoid chief of police looked around the room
at a Who's Who of Tampa's power structure. He

looked down at the Happy Meals in front of them and thought: This is political—someone in the department is trying to make me look like an idiot. The officials discussed legal and strategic options and made a decision. They would let the suspects go and keep them under surveillance.

The surveillance team, however, lost Joe and Sammy in the heavy traffic of TV and radio vans following the suspects, so they had to break off and track them on live TV back at police headquarters. Outside the command room, a disgruntled police major slipped a corporal a hundred-dollar bill for making the chief look like an idiot with the Happy Meals.

After nightfall, when the news helicopters returned to the airport, Joe and Sammy were kidnapped outside a convenience store in Dunedin by a van with TV news markings. Inside were their new friends from Daytona Beach, the Diaz Boys, three brothers and a cousin.

"Hey, you're really drug smugglers!" Sammy said as the men gave them injections of sodium pentothal.

They drove to a motel room, where Joe and Sammy were tied to tropical chairs. The men made drinks and got the hockey game on TV. Under the truth serum, Joe and Sammy told them about the police interrogations. A man arrived with a deli tray and chips.

"Did you go by the wedding rental shop?" asked Tommy Diaz.

"I forgot," said Juan Diaz, still holding the platter of cold cuts and cheeses.

"Better get going before it closes," said Tommy.

"How come I always have to go?" asked Juan. "It's because I'm the cousin, isn't it? The rest of you are brothers, so it's always 'Send Juan to do it.' "

"Absolutely not," said Tommy.

"You know who I feel like?" said Juan. "Norman Durkee."

"Who the hell's Norman Durkee?" asked Rafael.

"You don't know, do you?" said Juan. "He was the guy in Bachman-Turner Overdrive whose name wasn't Bachman or Turner."

"He just played piano," said Tommy Diaz. "The piano guy never counts. In concert, they're always way over on the side in the dark, with the guy who plays those tall bongos and the three chicks singing backup."

"What about Rick Wakeman from Yes?" countered Juan. "Or Keith Emerson from Emerson, Lake and Palmer?"

"Those were keyboard-dominated bands," said Tommy. "BTO was wall-of-sound guitar."

"Excuse me?" Sammy interrupted. "Is this a Latin thing?"

Everyone glowered at him, including Joe Varsity.

"Sorry," said Sammy. He grinned nervously, then made a straight face.

Tommy turned back to Juan. "What are you talking about? You're one of us! Your name's Diaz, too! We're the *Diaz* Boys!"

"Yeah, but it could be the Diaz *Brothers*. Like in *Scarface*! I know that's what you've really always wanted. Like the Garcia Brothers and the Rodriguez

Brothers. You only let me in the group because you felt sorry for me and you promised my mom."

"Where do you get these ideas?" said Tommy. "You're family!"

Tommy gave Juan a big hug and kissed him on both cheeks. "I don't want to hear any more of this foolishness. Now get going before the wedding shop closes."

Juan wiped a tear and smiled and rushed out the door.

As soon as he was gone, Rafael Diaz said, "Let's get rid of that guy. Then we can finally be the Diaz *Brothers*."

"I can't," said Tommy. "I feel sorry for the guy and I promised his mom. Besides, he runs all the errands."

"Can we at least change the *s* to a *z*?" asked Rafael. "We could be the Diaz Boy*z*."

Tommy Diaz looked at Rafael like he had an extra nose. "Okay, follow me carefully. We smuggle cocaine. We don't sing fuckin' doo-wop."

Juan Diaz returned from the wedding shop in thirty minutes with a giant box of deflated balloons and a floor-standing tank of helium. Everyone drank heavily watching the hockey game. They untied Joe's and Sammy's hands so they could eat roast beef sandwiches and drink beer. There weren't enough chairs so Juan had to sit on the cooler because he was the cousin, and he complained about having to get up every time someone wanted a beer.

"It's because I'm the cousin, isn't it?"

"Nonsense!"

They all cheered when the Lightning scored the

go-ahead goal in the third period. After the game, Florida Cable News' Blaine Crease appeared on TV at the top of the Sunshine Skyway bridge.

"*. . . And this is where the bloody trail of the Keys Killer came to an end, where he jumped to certain death and was swept out to sea in the powerful currents at the mouth of Tampa Bay. . . ."*

Crease stopped to pull a folded piece of paper from his pocket.

"*. . . Just before he decided to take his own life, the notorious murderer wrote an exclusive letter to me, Blaine Crease. . . ."*

Crease put on reading glasses, held up the letter and began reading:

" *'Dear Mr. Crease, You report too many depressing stories. More happy news, please. Warmly, Serge A. Storms.'* "

Crease dramatically whipped off his reading glasses. *"Obviously the rantings of a seriously deranged mind! . . ."*

Tommy Diaz and the others started filling balloons with helium, tying them off and letting them float up to the low ceiling.

The men took turns inhaling helium and talking funny.

"I didn't know drug smugglers were so much fun," said Sammy, hair disheveled and head bobbing from the injection. "I thought you'd be mad at us."

"No, we're not mad," Tommy said and took a hit of helium.

"So, you're not going to kill us?"

"Oh no," Tommy said like Donald Duck, "we're still going to kill you."

One of the men went outside and got two beach loungers from the patio next to the pool. They tied and taped Joe and Sammy into the loungers and attached a hundred balloons to each.

"Hey, what are you guys doing?" asked Joe Varsity.

Nobody answered. They kept tying on more balloons and taping Joe and Sammy more securely to the beach loungers.

"Okay, this is starting to not be funny anymore," said Joe.

More balloons.

"Are you trying to make us blimps?" asked Joe. "It'll never work. You can't lift a person up with regular party balloons."

Just then, Sammy floated away from his handlers. His hands were tied to the sides of the lounger, and his nose mashed up against a hanging lamp.

"Stop clowning around," snapped Tommy. "Get him down from there."

Sammy wasn't coming out of the drug as quickly as Joe, and he giggled as they retrieved him.

"I heard about this before," Sammy told Joe. "Some guy up in Georgia was laid off at a factory. So he got loaded at his daughter's wedding and tied a bunch of balloons to a cot and grabbed a leftover bottle of champagne and took off. He brought a frog gigger with him to pop balloons one at a time when he wanted to come down." Sammy turned to the Diaz Boys. "You're gonna give us giggers, right?"

"No giggers," said Tommy, not looking up, tying off another balloon.

"What'll happen to us?" Joe asked from the outskirts of panic.

Sammy answered. "We'll go up real high and black out from lack of oxygen and then die. Or the balloons will explode from the low atmospheric pressure and we'll crash and die. Even odds which will happen first."

Joe started crying.

"I hear Tampa Bay is beautiful from the air at night," said Sammy.

Tommy Diaz cracked the front door to the room, stuck his head out and looked both ways. "Coast is clear."

Joe sobbed and Sammy giggled as the men jockeyed with the loungers like Macy's parade ground crews. They bumped into each other in the close quarters of the motel room and Sammy got wedged in the doorway. Rafael Diaz shoved from the rear and a few balloons popped as Sammy came free and shot up into the night air faster than they had expected. "Wheeeeeeeeee."

Then it was Joe's turn, but he went up screaming and crying.

Some people in the bar heard the commotion and looked out the window, but didn't see anything. Two doors down, City and Country thought they heard something and stepped out of their rooms onto the sidewalk. City checked her watch and shook it. "Where can those guys be?"

Sammy drifted out over the Gulf, but Joe caught a thermal crosswind and blew back across the bay toward Tampa, over the big green glass dome of the Florida Aquarium.

15

Lenny had been staying with Serge the last two days in room one of Hammerhead Ranch. From the moment they jumped in Lenny's Cadillac on the Sunshine Skyway fishing pier, there was instant hypergolic chemistry.

Serge upon arriving in the room: "First we establish a bivouac. I'll deploy my gear over here by the TV and check the escape routes; you fill the tub with ice. . . . If we do it right, the room should look exactly like we're on a stakeout."

"This is so great!" said Lenny.

Serge cleared the wicker writing table with the round glass top and laid out precision tools, electrical meter, soldering iron and snacks. He began taking apart the homing signal receiver, trying to figure out why it wasn't picking up the briefcase. Soon he had the guts all over the table, frayed wiring sticking out everywhere, looking like it would never work again. Serge talked to himself. "It's gotta be something simple, like a bad rheostat. . . . Hmmm." He stuck his tongue out the corner of his mouth in concentration.

He plucked a semiconductor off the chassis with nee-
dle-nose pliers like a kid playing the old Milton
Bradley game Operation. In the background, Lenny
was a one-man bucket brigade, making repeated trips
from the ice machine to the tub with the motel's tiny
plastic ice pail.

"These things don't hold shit," said Lenny, dump-
ing his twentieth bucket of cubes.

"That's so inconsiderate guests don't hog all the
ice."

"Some people spoil it for everyone."

Lenny dumped another bucket, and the ice finally
crested the top of the tub.

Serge finished reassembling the homing receiver,
extended the telescopic antenna and turned it on.
Nothing. "Piss." Serge turned it off and tossed it on
the near bed. "Supply run!"

"Check!" said Lenny, and they sprinted out the
door.

They had been tooling around the barrier islands
ever since in bursts of aimless but urgent activity.

On the third day, Serge slouched in the passenger
seat at an open drawbridge on the Pinellas Bayway.
His arm was over the side of the car, slapping the
"Don" in "The Don Johnson Experience" in time
with the music. He looked up to the sky and made a
scrunched face.

"My spider senses are tingling. . . . First time I felt
like this I was three, just before Betsy hit."

"Betsy?"

"One of the craziest hurricanes on record. Labor
Day weekend 1965. It was first spotted by a Tiros

weather satellite, and it curled up near the Bahamas. Then it continued tracking northeast, out to sea, and Florida breathed a sigh of relief. Everyone got out their barbecues and went swimming. But Betsy stalled out there. Everyone gulped hard and kept watching the TV reports in disbelief as it did a complete U-turn. Nobody had seen anything like it. Betsy headed right back at south Florida with hundred-and-forty-mile-per-hour winds. . . ." Serge swirled his arms.

"What happened?"

"Raked the bottom of the state. My family huddled in the hallway of our house. Everything got real dark and quiet. I was a little kid so I thought it was fun, but I remember it was the first time I had seen the grown-ups afraid. A small palm tree came through our living-room window, and my mother screamed. We rode it out, but seventy-four others weren't so lucky."

"Wow," Lenny said softly.

The drawbridge closed and they began moving again. Serge fished in the glove compartment and found a Phil Collins tape, and he stuck it in the stereo. They passed the Pelican Diner.

" . . . *I can feel it comin' in the air tonight—hold on . . .* "

"This is too cool," said Lenny. "It's like we're on the exact same page. I need another joint."

Lenny grabbed a doobie paper-clipped behind the visor and tried to light it but couldn't. "Same thing on the pier. I need a new lighter." He pulled into a convenience store.

Back on the road, he lit the joint on the first try with a small, windproof acetylene torch on a keychain, $9.99.

"You shouldn't waste your money on crap like that," said Serge, playing with the laser pointer on his own keychain.

"In the long run, paraphernalia pays for itself," said Lenny.

"I used to know someone like you," said Serge.

"What's he like?"

"He's dead."

"Oh," said Lenny. They stopped behind a Rolls-Royce at a red light, waiting to turn onto Gulf Boulevard.

"Why were you trying to fake a suicide the other night?" asked Lenny. "Need to ditch some business partners? Meet your wife in the Bahamas to split the life insurance? Jump bail?"

"I don't know what you're talking about," said Serge.

"It's obvious. I mean, don't get me wrong. It's brilliant, too. Not like the guys who dive from short bridges and leave stupid notes or torch their boat in the Gulf at night and row ashore in rafts and they're suspected right away and turn up two weeks later in Cancún. But nobody can survive a fall from the Skyway, so you *have* to be dead. Your prints are all over the car you left up there. And best of all, they got your fatal jump on videotape on the bridge surveillance cameras. Except the part about what was inside Santa's belly. Where'd you get a black parachute, anyway?"

"Pez Easter egg coloring."

Lenny nodded.

"Wonder why this light's taking so long," said Serge. He stretched his neck to look forward in traffic.

Their lane had the green arrow, but the Rolls-Royce ahead of them didn't move. Then the arrow was red again.

"Goddammit!" said Serge. "Now the light has to cycle again. What's going on in that car?"

Serge grabbed the top of the convertible's windshield and stood up. He grumbled and sat back down and fidgeted. The driver of the Rolls was talking on a cell phone while simultaneously trimming nose hair with tiny scissors. Serge could see the driver stop to inspect his nostrils in the lighted mirror on the back of the sun visor, then resume trimming.

"Try to hang on," Serge whispered to himself, twisting nervously in his seat. Then he noticed the Rolls' two bumper stickers: "God is my copilot" and "Get a job!"

"You know, that's pretty unsafe, putting a sharp object in your nose at a red light," said Serge. "You never know when someone might rear-end you."

Serge reached over with his left leg and tapped Lenny's gas pedal, and the Cadillac lurched forward and popped the bumper of the Rolls. The windows of the Rolls were up, but everyone near the intersection could hear the terrible screaming anyway.

"You might want to pull around him," Serge told Lenny. "I think there's some kind of problem in that car."

They crossed the bridge at Johns Pass as a casino boat headed out to the edge of territorial waters.

"I love how we're holed up in the room," said Lenny. "I do it as often as I can. What about you?"

"Only when I have to."

"I mean for fun," said Lenny. "You know, you want to break the routine, so you drive across town and check into a seedy motel and pretend you're on the run. Act mysterious, arouse people's suspicions, maybe *rock star* the room. There's a lot of style you can put into being a fugitive. It's a damn American art form!"

"Turn here, David Janssen."

"Where?"

"Here!"

Lenny checked his watch as Serge sprinted in and out of the video store and vaulted back into the passenger seat without opening the door. "Two minutes, eight seconds," said Lenny.

"Gotta get it down under a deuce," said Serge.

They skidded into the parking lot of a thrift store, and Serge raced in. Two minutes later, he hurdled back into the car and threw a T-shirt in Lenny's face. Lenny held the shirt out and read the front. "Treasure Island Police Athletic League." Serge had an identical one, and he had already stripped off his other shirt and was wiggling his arms through the holes of the new one.

"Put that on," said Serge. "Whenever I'm fleeing and eluding, I hit the thrifts for local law enforcement T-shirts. Makes traffic stops go much smoother."

Back in the motel room, Lenny shoved more bottles and cans down into the ice-filled tub. Coke, Sprite, orange and grapefruit juice, Bloody Mary mix, Budweiser, Heineken, Absolut, Finlandia. Serge arranged a row of Florida keepsakes along the back of the writing desk. Above them he taped an autographed black-and-white photo of a scuba diver to the wall.

"Who's that?" said Lenny, shotgunning a beer on the way out of the bathroom.

"Lloyd Bridges," said Serge. "The immortal Mike Nelson from *Sea Hunt*. Originally, Nelson operated out of Marineland in California. But later he went freelance, and they shot several episodes in the Florida Keys, which made him technically eligible for inclusion in my shrine."

Lenny reached into the shrine and started to pick up a *Flipper* thermos, but Serge slapped his hand.

"It's burned into my mind," Serge continued. "The end credits of every episode, Bridges sailing off in his boat, the *Argonaut,* and then the trademark emblem of Ziv Productions."

"You have a good memory."

"That's because I don't smoke that shit you do. I wouldn't want to be abnormal."

Lenny looked again at Bridges's smiling face in the yellowed photo and the inscription, "To my pal, Serge."

"This is all very interesting, but why put his picture up?"

"Inspiration. It's important to build on the shoulders of the giants."

Lenny poured vodka, lit a joint and took some speed.

Serge duct-taped the edges of the curtains to the wall, taped over the message light on the phone and the battery indicator on the smoke detector.

"What are you doing?" asked Lenny.

"Establishing theater conditions. I hate it when people watch a great movie at home with a bunch of lights on. Wrecks the whole medium. If there's any other light source in the room except the film, it completely ruins it for me."

Serge unplugged the pine-scented nightlight in the bathroom and taped over the blinking "12:00" on the VCR. Lenny took a small brush out of a nail polish jar and painted his joint with a brownish liquid.

"What are *you* doing?" asked Serge.

"Putting hash oil on this doobie," said Lenny. "I've been refining the technique. The speed counteracts the dovetail-drowsiness of the weed and the depressant effect of the alcohol. The booze files down the rough edges of paranoia from the pot and hyperagitation from the amphetamine. And the marijuana heightens self-awareness to prevent you from pulling something stupid that the liquor and pills are trying to talk you into."

"What if you, like, didn't do any of that stuff, then you wouldn't have to worry about neutralizing all the bad effects?"

Lenny looked at him blankly. "What are you talking about?"

Serge popped *Goldfinger* in the VCR, and Lenny got ready for another pill.

"Look! Look!" said Serge, pointing out the scene

where Bond meets Goldfinger in the Fontainebleau in Miami Beach. Serge's yelling startled Lenny, and he inhaled the pill and began choking. He staggered, clutching his throat with one hand and bracing himself against the TV with the other.

Serge hit pause on the remote, stood up without urgency and gave Lenny a roundhouse kung fu kick in the solar plexus. The pill flew out and plinked off the TV screen.

"Now the movie's ruined," said Serge. He went over to the writing table and immersed himself in the tedium of taking apart and reassembling the homing signal receiver for the fifth time since they got to the motel.

"What are ya doin'?" Lenny asked.

No answer. Serge wore safety goggles, and the soldering iron gave off a tentacle of smoke when he touched it to a capacitor.

Lenny reached under the bed and pulled out a sturdy nylon travel bag with zippers, pockets, compression bands, D-rings and Velcro.

He suddenly had Serge's attention by the short hairs. "What's that?" Serge asked, unplugging the soldering iron and coming over to the bed.

"My special bag," said Lenny. "It's got more little pockets and compartments than I have stuff." He dumped the contents onto the bed. "Take out all my crap and—boom!—molded rubber bottom and insulated sides. It becomes a cooler—perfect for the barfly on the go!"

"Cool!" said Serge.

"I got something even better," said Lenny. "Put out your hands and close your eyes."

"They're closed."

"No peeking," said Lenny.

"I'm not peeking! Hurry up, already."

Lenny reached out and placed a small plastic cube in Serge's cupped hands. Serge opened his eyes.

"It's just a rock in a clear plastic box," said Serge. "What's the deal? Does it have a gem inside? A core of Uranium 238?"

"No, it's just a rock. But it's where it's from that's special."

"Give."

"The moon."

"Baloney!" said Serge. "It's against the law to own moon rocks—they're all in government vaults. All eight hundred and fifty pounds from the six landing sites."

"And where else?" Lenny asked with a smile.

"All except the ones the president gave as personal gifts to foreign dignitaries."

Lenny's smile broadened.

"Get outta town!" said Serge, and he punched Lenny in the shoulder.

"I hear it's from Honduras. Look, it's got this nifty certificate, too."

Lenny pulled a wallet from his back pocket. He opened the bill section and removed a piece of paper that had been folded six times and had a circular coffee stain. Serge recognized the authentic Richard Nixon signature.

"You sonuvabitch," Serge said, and he punched Lenny again. It hurt a little, but Lenny kept smiling.

"How'd you get it?"

"I fronted a guy a lid of weed in Deerfield Beach, and he couldn't pay me back. You know how it gets, after you have to bug a guy over a pot debt long enough, they start getting mad at you like *you're* the one who's in the wrong. So we're there in his apartment, stoned again—*my* weed of course—and I say, 'Look, it's been three weeks. Put up, man. Show some good faith. Whatever you got. A lottery ticket, a burrito—I just need some collateral.' So I follow him into his room and he pulls out his sock drawer, and taped to the back is this rock."

"What are you doin' with it here?" asked Serge.

"I'm gonna sell it. I've been making some calls to get an auction together. I bet it can fetch at least ten large on the black market."

"Like hell you're gonna sell it!"

"Why not?"

"Cuz I'll kick your ass if you do! You know what you got there? That is the coolest! If I had one, I'd never sell it. I'd keep it in a special container with the rest of my special stuff."

"Why?"

"To look at. You know, when you get the mood some nights to get your special stuff out and put it on the table, and you sit there and look at it and play with it, move it around . . ."

Lenny had a puzzled look.

"What?" said Serge. "Didn't you have any hobbies when you were a kid?"

"So what am I supposed to do with it?" Lenny asked.

"If it'll bring ten grand, so will a fully authenticated counterfeit moon rock. I can get this certificate touched up at Kinko's and we'll run off a bunch. Then we'll get a few Lucite display boxes with little pedestals inside, like they use to show off autographed baseballs. We'll sell the rock over and over again."

"Where we gonna find more rocks?"

A red Audi driven by Tommy Diaz slowed on Gulf Boulevard and turned into the driveway of Hammerhead Ranch.

"Aaaaaauuuuuuuu!" Tommy yelled, and cut the wheel, barely missing two men crouched low to the ground in the parking lot.

Lenny looked up from the pavement as the Audi swerved by, barely missing him. "I think we're too far out," Lenny told Serge. "We're gonna get run over."

The pair duck-walked to the side of the motel parking lot, picking up rocks as they went.

"How about this one?" Lenny asked, holding up a smooth white river rock used in decorative landscaping.

"Are you still high? At least make some attempt to select one that looks real. That certificate is only gonna fool 'em so much."

Serge sorted through some rocks next to a garbage can, and he picked one up and held it in front of his face. "Okay, here we go. We're cookin' now!"

"How's that rock better than mine?"

"Look at it! Think basaltic, igneous—use your imagination. This could be from an ejecta blanket on the Sea of Storms. See the perforated texture? Intense heat, geological trauma! A few more of these and we're in business!"

Serge leaned back down and sorted meticulously through the rubble among the butts and bottle caps.

"You gotta be careful selling space stuff on the black market," said Serge. "Local cops and even the FBI shouldn't be a problem, but you don't want to mess with the National Aeronautics and Space Administration. Just ask the shrimper who's talking to rats in his jail cell."

"What happened?"

"They were on a trawler dragging the North Atlantic for shrimp when they snagged a tiny metal box. The shrimper cracked it open and found some personal effects and a few crew patches that said 'Challenger.' Their nets had hit a small skid of debris that hadn't been found after the space shuttle blew an O-ring in '86. The guy goes back to Cocoa Beach of all places and tries peddling the box around the pawnshops. He's asking twenty grand, and he ends up settling for something like thirty bucks."

"Not too shrewd," said Lenny.

"That's why they're the underclass," said Serge. "So the pawnshop owner calls NASA, and the next thing the guy knows, he's walking down the sidewalk on A1A when ten agents come out of thin air and gang-swarm him. . . . All that scientific nerd stuff you hear? Total garbage—these boys don't play."

They stopped talking and went back to collecting rocks.

A half hour later, Serge was still at it, subjecting every pebble to the same intricate degree of scrutiny. Lenny was totally bored and cranky.

"I think this is a lot more work than we have to go through," he whined. "At a certain point it's just not worth it anymore."

Serge turned around with a handful of rocks. "It's not a question of whether crime pays. It's whether you enjoy your job. That's the key to life."

An hour later, Serge and Lenny lay on their backs on their motel beds. Serge held the moon rock above his face, moving it around in the air, making rocket-thruster sounds with his mouth.

Lenny was on the bed next to the window, head toward the door. Serge had given him his keychain laser pointer to play with, and Lenny held it up above him, shooting the beam around the room and out the window.

"This is the coolest," said Lenny, waving the red light around. "Since we're gonna sell counterfeit moon rocks, I really don't need the original. Wanna trade for the laser?"

"Deal!" said Serge.

They each reached out an arm into the little aisle between the beds and did a pinky shake to make it official.

16

It was ninety-two degrees by noon.

Zargoza reclined on a chaise lounge next to the pool at Hammerhead Ranch. He wiped sweat off his forehead and thought, I know this is Florida, but we're heading into the holiday season for heaven's sake. His swimsuit was a golden tan and a short length last in vogue in 1973. He had a sheen of sunscreen butter on his rugged, hairy chest and read the *St. Petersburg Times* through postmodern sunglasses that looked like welder's goggles. It was early afternoon, no clouds or haze, and the sun was full strength. A group of children splashed and shrieked in the pool.

Four swimsuit models lay on their stomachs on Budweiser beach towels. Their bikini tops were untied as they read paperbacks with vibrant covers, *Done Deal*, *Bones of Coral*, *Skin Tight* and *The Mango Opera*. Just behind Zargoza's chair, a constant flow of Japanese, French and German tourists stopped and posed for pictures in front of the row of stuffed hammerhead sharks and then drove away.

Zargoza had a tall, sweating glass of grapefruit juice on the boomerang cocktail table next to his lounger. A cheap transistor radio played "Lawyers, Guns and Money." Zargoza took two Valium, the blue ones, and chased with the grapefruit. He was becoming a nerve case, thinking too much about the five million in the briefcase. Obviously drug money. Someone doesn't lose that and not come looking for it. And, apparently, someone already had. Taxidermied alive? Ripped apart under a drawbridge? Zargoza shivered at the images. Those weren't murders; they were messages. Definitely cartel work. It was only a matter of time.

Zargoza hadn't been sleeping well. He kept waking up in the night obsessing about the briefcase, worrying it wasn't hidden well enough. He couldn't go back to sleep until he moved it again, and late each night he ran around the grounds of Hammerhead Ranch in his Devil Rays pajamas, the briefcase in one hand and a pistol in the other, making everything worse. "What was that?" Zargoza would spin around, aiming the pistol at imaginary shadows, dramatic music playing in his head. The curse was getting to be too much. Not to mention the Diaz Boys, the sweepstakes subpoenas and the simmering scandal at the nursing home. Zargoza decided right then to set C. C. Flag up as the fall guy; prosecutors can't resist the headlines of bagging a celebrity.

Zargoza took another sip of grapefruit juice. He finished the *Times* and picked up a *Weekly Mail of the News World* left on the next lounger by a British tourist. Zargoza lifted the grapefruit juice again, gulped and put it back without taking his eyes off the tabloid. He couldn't believe the stories.

First, a coke brick explodes in a car driven by a college student. Then the same student crashes through the glass dome of the Florida Aquarium. Finally, an unidentified Latin male with a shotgun is killed in the doorway of a condominium by an eighty-year-old woman with a hundred-year-old gun. The stories had the Diaz Boys' fat fingerprints all over them. Shit, Zargoza thought, the British are covering this better than we are. He looked over the articles again. They all had the same byline, correspondent Lenny Lippowicz.

He turned the page and saw another story by Lippowicz about a frantic treasure hunt in Key West for a briefcase full of drug money. A giant headline: "The Five-Million-Dollar Curse!"

"AAAAHHHHHH!" Zargoza screamed and dropped the paper like it was on fire.

Panic turned to anger. Zargoza picked up the paper and shredded it, crunching the pieces into a ball and slamming it to the ground. "Fuck! Fuck! Fuck!"— spitting the words as fast as he could, losing breath, standing there shaking next to his lounger.

Tommy Diaz had terrible timing.

He drove up in a red Audi, and got out looking shaken.

"What's wrong with *you*?" asked Zargoza.

"I almost ran over two guys duck-walking in your driveway!" said Tommy, sitting down on the side of the lounger next to Zargoza.

"You always were a shitty driver," said Zargoza.

He reclined again and closed his eyes. Minutes passed. Tommy looked at the patio around the loungers, wondering what the deal was with all the torn-up newspapers. Zargoza finally sat up again and faced Tommy.

"Do you have any concept of *subtlety*? Any aptitude at all for the soft touch? Is there a feather in that quiver of yours, or is it all sledgehammers and battering rams with you guys?"

"What do you mean?"

Zargoza threw up his arms.

They were distracted by a loud racket. Some hammering and a buzz saw. Both turned and looked out on the beach behind the Calusa Pointe condominiums next door. They saw a furious level of construction as if the Seabees were building a Coral Sea airstrip. Half the noise was coming from where a massive temporary stage was being erected. The rest of the noise was from people getting plywood ready for the hurricane.

"What's that about?" asked Tommy, pointing at the lighting masts going up over the stage.

"It's their stupid anti-immigration rally tomorrow," said Zargoza.

Two workers hung a large cloth banner across the back of the stage. "Proposition 213: Because they just don't look right!"

"Chowderheads," muttered Zargoza. He grabbed the grapefruit juice and chugged the whole thing and wiped his mouth with the back of his arm.

Tommy Diaz didn't say anything. He set a small object down on the cocktail table.

"What's that?" asked Zargoza.

"It's a beeper," said Tommy.

"I *know* it's a beeper, you dumb shit," Zargoza said. "When I say 'What's that?' I mean, what is it in the technical context of 'Why should I give a flying fuck?' "

"It's going to make us rich," said Tommy.

"What? You're putting up microwave towers?"

"No. We stole these. A whole semi full. When we unload them, we'll make a fortune."

"It has zebra stripes," said Zargoza.

"They all have zebra stripes."

"All?"

"All thirty thousand," Tommy said proudly.

"Jesus, you got thirty thousand beepers with zebra stripes. How do you ever expect to unload them?"

"Because they're Motorola," said Tommy. "People want quality."

"They don't want zebra stripes."

"Yes they do."

"No they *don't*! Maybe they want their favorite color, but not this nightmare. It's hideous. Might as well be covered with 666s."

"Maybe some people won't like it, but there'll still be plenty of other customers."

"Look, you got only two markets for this thing," said Zargoza, counting off on his fingers. "One, zoologists, and two, that hooker chick in *Get Christie Love*. That's it. End of story. Fade to black."

Tommy Diaz was crestfallen. "What am I gonna do with 'em?"

"That's your problem," Zargoza said as he lay back down and closed his eyes.

"Well, it's kinda *our* problem. They're all in room ten."

Zargoza sprang up. "What!"

"Easy, easy. We had to get rid of the truck. It was bringin' a lot of heat."

"Bringin' a lot of heat? As opposed to what? Dropping some kid through the roof of the aquarium?"

"We weren't thinking right on that one. We were drinking and I got a little dizzy from the helium."

"Jesus! You're all over the papers. And if you go down, I go with you. You guys need to lay low for a while. Watch some cable TV. Catch up on *Law & Order.* You staying in room ten?"

"Can't," said Tommy. "It's full of beepers."

Zargoza's head fell to his chest in frustrated exhaustion.

Tommy got a funny look on his face, like he was debating whether to say something. "You didn't happen to come across five million dollars by any chance?"

"Five million? Are you kidding?" said Zargoza, and he laughed artificially.

"You wouldn't hold out on us, would you?"

"Never!"

"Word on the street is it's from the Mierda Cartel," said Tommy.

"Mierda?" said Zargoza. "That means *shit* in Spanish."

"Apparently they didn't research the name well enough."

They both lay back down on their loungers and closed their eyes. They were quiet a few minutes.

Tommy finally lifted his head. "I notice you don't carry a beeper."

17

Serge hunched over and turned a jeweler's screw-driver, the last step in reassembling the homing signal receiver, which he was doing for the eleventh time in three days. He turned it on again. Nothing again.

"Dammit! What's the deal?" He grabbed it in his right hand and smacked it on the writing table a few times. He stopped and waited. Still nothing. He had it over his shoulder, ready to fling at the wall, when the indicator lights began flashing and the beeper began beeping.

Serge looked out the window of room one. Zargoza was walking by on the sidewalk with a briefcase, every few steps spinning around in paranoia like a street crazy.

Serge ambled down to the jetty next to Hammerhead Ranch. A few dozen people fished at the end of the rocks, a wide mix of heritage and walks of life, getting along famously. A rapper with a Snoop Dogg

T-shirt showed a skinhead how to tie off a new lure. Serge's theory was that you could end the world's troubles by going to the hot spots and handing out fishing poles.

He watched the people with saltwater casting rigs and buckets and stringers. Three men without shirts cast from the last rock of the jetty. Waves rolled in every minute, threatening to sweep them off. But there was a large tidal pool at the base of the rock, which sucked the waves down and blasted a spray high in the air in front of them.

To the left, on the beach side of the jetty, children and families played in the swim area, roped off with buoys. A small boy with a new dive mask was face-down in the knee-deep water, studying shells and schools of tiny translucent fish that changed direction abruptly and in unison.

Midway on the jetty, Zargoza had climbed down the boulders to the water line, where there were no other people, looking around nervously and jamming a metal briefcase in a cranny between the big rocks.

Serge arrived on top of the jetty without a sound and called down to Zargoza. "Nice weather."

"Auuuuuhhhhh!" Zargoza yelled, jumping up in surprise. He put his hand over his pounding heart. "Don't *do* that!"

"You're the owner of the motel, aren't you?" asked Serge.

"Who wants to know?" said Zargoza, climbing back up the boulders.

"I'm a guest. Room one."

Serge smiled broadly and Zargoza didn't like the looks of it.

The car thieves and Sid and Patty had been child's play. But he hadn't fully appraised this Zargoza cat yet. Might be a more worthy adversary. Serge decided to bide his time and draw the thing out in a war of nerves, maybe even use a little "rope-a-dope," and his mind suddenly unanchored and floated back thirty-three years to Miami Beach, a young underdog named Cassius Clay going crazy at the weigh-in, pounding on Sonny Liston's limo at the airport, then beating Liston like a rug at the Convention Center. . . .

"Hello? Hello? Anybody home?" asked Zargoza.

Serge snapped back to the present. "Sorry. I was in Miami."

Zargoza took a step back and gave him a wary look, but they were interrupted by a loud mechanical noise. They both turned and looked up the inlet. It was a growing buzzing sound, high-rpm engines like dirt bikes. Or Jet Skis.

There were four of them. Lots of colors, expensive swimwear and shirts with designer markings. Luxury dive watches on their wrists even though they weren't divers. Huge scuba knives strapped in spring-loaded scabbards on their calves even though they never had any use for them. They did doughnuts in their personal watercraft, accompanied by "Wooooooo!" and "Yahoooooo!" Then another flat-out run in formation across the mangrove flats and toward the jetty. A rapidly approaching jackass armada.

"No nautical training, no understanding or respect for maritime courtesy," said Serge. "Everyone with a boat knows the unspoken code you live by. The waterways were the last refuge of *honor*."

Zargoza nodded gloomily. "Now I know how the outlaw bikers felt when these dingleberries started showing up on Harleys."

On the first pass, the Jet Skiers snapped two fishing lines. Then they had the courtesy to come back and snap three more. By the third pass, they had driven every fish out of the inlet. People on the jetty slammed down their poles. The Jet Skiers whipped around the end of the jetty, and only providence saved them from the submerged boulders they didn't know existed. They ran over the swim ropes and through the family bathing area, forcing a mother to snatch her two-year-old out of a blow-up turtle and dive toward the beach. They passed between shore and the small boy in the swim mask with his head down in the water.

The Jet Skiers stopped up the beach and one pulled a small fabric cooler off his shoulder. He opened it and tossed beers to his buddies. They killed them fast and chucked the empties in the water.

"Did you see that?" said Zargoza. "They almost ran over that kid. And they littered."

Serge walked over to a garbage bin and pulled out a few soda cans and filled them from the faucet at the fish-cleaning table. He walked back and rejoined Zargoza out on the rocks. They could hear the high whine of the engines on their return trip. The Jet Skis rounded the end of the jetty one by one.

"I love Florida sunsets," said Serge. "Every time the sun goes down it gives me renewed hope for tomorrow."

Serge made practice swings with his arm, gauging the weight of the can. He lobbed the aluminum cylinder in a practice shot and it splashed ten yards out from the rocks. "Now you try."

Zargoza made practice swings of his own to get the feel.

Serge studied his stance and motion. He pointed at the Jet Skiers yelling and doing more doughnuts at the end of the inlet. "What's happening to this country?"

"No sense of sacrifice," said Zargoza. "They live right up to the edge of their means, buying Jet Skis they ride two days a year. Fancy cars, Rolexes, all show. They eat their seed corn."

"In Texas, they have a saying for people like that," said Serge. "Big hat, no cattle."

Zargoza got ready with the soda can. He reached his arm back.

"Say, you hear anything about the cursed five million dollars that's in the papers?" asked Serge.

Zargoza became unnerved and bricked the shot ten feet off target.

Serge walked over and grabbed Zargoza's arm like a golf instructor, and he swung it in a slow pendulum to demonstrate technique.

"The mistake people often make is to try to add too much velocity. That way you lose accuracy," said Serge. "What you want to do is put all your effort into aim. At the speeds they're going, they'll supply all the velocity you'll need. Finesse it. Air it out in a nice arch like Rip Sewell's old ephus pitch for the Pittsburgh Pirates."

Zargoza reloaded with another can. The first Jet Skier approached, and Zargoza let it fly. The skier didn't notice as it missed wide and long.

The next Jet Skier was about to go by. Serge tossed the can in a two-handed lob from between the legs—a basketball free throw out of the fifties. The sound was a sickening thud as the can broke across the bridge of the man's nose and knocked him backward off the Jet Ski like a horseback rider hitting the bottom branch of a tree.

The jetty broke into laughter.

The other three Jet Skiers circled and grabbed their friend out of the water. One skier pulled him aboard, and then the other two moved toward the rocks where Zargoza and Serge stood. They went for their scuba knives. Zargoza produced a pistol, and the men beat a panicked retreat, leaving the fourth Jet Ski bobbing nose down in the water.

"You know," said Zargoza, tucking the pistol back in his waistband and turning to Serge, "you're a lot of fun to be around."

"That's because I'm a people person."

18

Wild green parrots squawked and flew in circles against the bank of clouds that glowed orange and violet at dusk. They swooped in front of the condominium and settled atop one of the tall Washingtonia palms that lined the road, evenly spaced like streetlights.

Edna Ploomfield watched the parrots at sunset each evening from her back porch at Calusa Pointe. Or she watched the herons. Or the oystercatchers, kingfishers, skimmers, stilts and plovers that strutted at low tide.

But tonight she ignored them because she was being interviewed on Florida Cable News with Toto about her shooting of one of the infamous Diaz Boys.

"Tell us again how Toto handled all this," said correspondent Blaine Crease.

"He was fine," Ploomfield said in her little ol' lady voice. "So then I went for the gun on the wall—"

"And where was Toto?"

"On the floor somewhere. So I grabbed the gun and spun—"

"What was Toto wearing?"

After the camera lights were turned off, Mrs. Ploomfield said good night and went into her kitchen and freshened up her scotch. She shuffled to her bedroom and set the glass on the nightstand. She climbed into bed, propped herself up with three pillows and watched a *M*A*S*H* rerun. She turned off the TV with the remote. Then she looked over at the lamp on the nightstand and clapped twice, and the light went out.

But unknown to Mrs. Ploomfield or anyone else at Calusa Pointe, there was a second clapper in the room. It was under her bed, wired to blasting caps and fourteen pounds of dynamite, and a millisecond after the lamp went out, Mrs. Ploomfield was blown straight up through the ceiling and into the condominium of the incredible shrinking mayor of Beverly Shores.

Zargoza was sitting in the bar behind Hammerhead Ranch when a tremendous explosion at the condominium next door rocked the place. Liquor bottles rattled and two wineglasses at the edge of the sink fell and broke. Zargoza remembered that two hours earlier he'd seen someone who looked vaguely like Rafael Diaz run out the back of Calusa Pointe and up the beach.

"Fuckin' Diaz Boys," Zargoza grumbled to himself. "I want those beepers out of here!"

Zargoza got up from the bar and went back to room twelve, where his boiler room operation was

winding down from its dinner-hour fever pitch. He
gathered his goons away from the telephones, and he
half-sat against the side of his oversize desk. He read
from a leather organizer, giving the day's rundown of
business and who wasn't up to quota.

As Zargoza spoke, a bright red laser dot slowly
traced along the wall behind him and settled on his
forehead. The goon standing closest to Zargoza tack-
led him to the ground. Another ran to the window
and peeked out. "It's coming from one of the motel
rooms."

*W*hen the door crashed open in room one of Hammerhead Ranch and four men with automatic pistols
burst in, Serge was on the far bed, packing the moon
rock into his toiletry bag. Lenny was lying on the
other bed, having just stuck the keychain laser in his
hip pocket. His head was toward the foot of the bed,
and he bent his neck backward and looked upside
down at the four men sticking gun barrels in his face.

"What I do?"

*S*erge and Lenny sat handcuffed to chairs in room
twelve as Zargoza paced and talked to himself and
his men played cards. He slugged down sour mash
and marched around the room and cursed.

"You back-stabbin' chickenshit!" Zargoza yelled
at Serge. "We had all that fun with those Jet Skiers—
pretending to be my friend and everything—and the
whole time you were planning to kill me! Someone

sent you after the five million, didn't they? Well, I don't have it!"

Zargoza paced some more, and he grabbed a bag of potato chips away from one of his goons and began chomping.

"Look how jumpy I am—I'm gaining weight!" He threw the bag of chips back at the goon. "What am I gonna do with these guys? If I can't handle this, how will I ever keep the Diaz Boys in line?"

He was interrupted by a loud voice from the back of the room.

"Fuck the fucking Diaz Brothers!" Serge shouted, veins bulging. "Fuck 'em all! I bury those cockroaches! What did they ever do for us?!"

Two goons turned their guns on Serge. "We should waste him! Teach him to shut his mouth!" one said. Then, talking to Serge, "For your information, it's the Diaz *Boys,* not Brothers."

"No," said Zargoza, "that's not it. He's doing Pacino from *Scarface*. I love that movie!"

"Say hello to my little friend!" said Serge.

"Did you see *Miami Blues*?" asked Zargoza.

"Ever been in a lineup?" asked Serge, making a tense Fred Ward face. "You own a suede sports coat?"

One of the goons was patting down Lenny, and he found the personal laser in his hip pocket. "Z, look at this."

Zargoza shook his head and started laughing. "Uncuff 'em. They ain't hit men. I haven't figured out what they actually *are,* but it ain't assassins."

"I'm supposed to be Don Johnson," said Lenny.

19

It was two A.M. when Zargoza, Serge and Lenny walked out of Zargoza's office at Hammerhead Ranch. Serge retrieved his camera bag from room one, and they all got in Zargoza's roomy BMW M3, Serge riding shotgun and Lenny in the middle of the backseat.

Serge immediately began fiddling with the fur-lined handcuffs dangling from Zargoza's rearview mirror.

"I can't believe I met you guys," said Zargoza. "It's like we're all tuned in to the same Florida wavelength."

They drove east, back onto the mainland and across the St. Petersburg peninsula until they came to the Gandy Bridge leading to Tampa. As the Beemer headed over the water, Zargoza called up a CD on the stereo, "Abacab" by Genesis.

"This is one of my favorite things, one of those little pleasures you have to make for yourself," he said.

Zargoza looked over and noticed Serge and Lenny leaning forward in anticipation, waiting for him to continue.

"Oh—I love driving across the Tampa Bay bridges after midnight, playing my music. Sometimes I'll make loops and go over the different bridges and sometimes I'll go all the way down to the Skyway if I'm really jazzed. Say, you hear someone dressed like Santa jumped the other night?"

Lenny said yes and Serge said no.

"I remember crossing this bridge years back in my Jag. Piled it into a cement truck. Seems like a lifetime ago."

Zargoza looked at Serge, and then back at Lenny sitting in the backseat with an unlit Lucky Strike in his mouth.

"You need a light," Zargoza said, reaching for the dash.

"Don't smoke," said Lenny.

Zargoza gave Lenny a double take, then went on. "These bridges are wonderful at night. They're practically empty, and the views over the bay are mesmerizing."

Zargoza opened a console between the seats and thumbed through a dozen CDs. "The hardest part is picking the right tune. For the bridges, I prefer haunting music."

"Haunting?" asked Lenny.

"Yeah," said Zargoza, "music that touches something preternatural inside. You can't quite put your finger on it, but it awakens a nonverbal sense of horror in your unborn soul."

"Like the Spice Girls?" asked Serge.

"I'm trying to be serious!" snapped Zargoza. "I'm talkin' about Peter Gabriel, Pink Floyd, Jeff Beck . . ."

Lightning forked in the distance toward Plant City, and it inspired Zargoza to pick Bad Company's "Burnin' Sky" for the next tune. He increased the volume and everyone stopped talking and grooved, letting the moment happen.

Zargoza saw the flashing red and blue lights in the rearview mirror. "Damn!" he said. "That'll kill a buzz!"

Zargoza stood next to his car in the breakdown lane as the officer studied his driver's license. He looked up at Zargoza. "We clocked you at ninety."

Inside the car, Serge got the homing signal receiver out of his camera bag. It began flashing as soon as he turned it on. He panned it around and the flashing light went solid when he pointed it at the Beemer's trunk.

Zargoza stood silent outside the car as his ticket was written, but he finally lost it. He made two fists and pounded them on the roof of his car and yelled. His radar detector was stuck onto the left side of the windshield with suction cups, and he reached into the car and tore it loose. The officer went for his gun, but when he saw Zargoza come up with only the detector, he left the Glock holstered.

"Damn piece of no-good cheap crap," he said, rapidly winding the coiled wire around the detector. "Frickin' four hundred dollars of unreliable shit!" He wound way back like Carl Yastrzemski and let the detector fly out into the bay, and it made an unseen splash somewhere in the dark water.

The police officer pointed toward the sky. "We got you with the airplane."

After the officer pulled away, Zargoza tossed the ticket out the window and sped toward south Tampa. He hit the mainland and cued "Biko" and fired up a brown onyx pipe of Aztec design. "Opium, anyone?"

"Trying to cut down," said Serge.

"Don't mind if I do," said Lenny.

They drove through the back streets under the Lee Roy Selmon Expressway, named after the Tampa Bay Hall of Fame football star.

"What's going on over there?" asked Serge.

"They're tearing down the aquarium," said Zargoza. "Making way for the new one."

"But it's brand new," said Serge.

"They must know what they're doing."

The BMW cruised by the hockey arena, closed and dark, but the marquee was still lit. "Dec. 17: Southeast Figure Skating Finals/Dec. 18: Lightning vs. Rangers/Dec. 19: Nuremberg Trials on Ice." Zargoza turned west on Kennedy Boulevard, in front of the old Tampa Bay Hotel.

"Stop!" yelled Serge.

Zargoza hit the brakes. "What? What?"

But Serge had jumped out of the car with his camera and taken off running into the trees in Plant Park. Zargoza and Lenny peered into the darkness but couldn't see anything. Suddenly there was a quick series of bright flashes.

"Someone's shooting!" said Lenny.

"I didn't hear anything," said Zargoza. "Must be the camera flash."

Serge reappeared out of the trees and jogged back to the car.

"What was that about?" asked Zargoza.

"I've been meaning to get that one for a while," said Serge. "There's a big oak tree down there where Hernando de Soto held talks with the Indians in 1539."

Zargoza stared at him. "Where do you get this stuff?"

Serge stared back. "Doesn't everybody know that?"

A half hour later they were in Ybor City. Serge was quickly out of the car again without warning.

"I wish he'd stop doing that," said Zargoza.

"Best not fight it," said Lenny, watching xenon strobe flashes light up the street around the corner at Café Creole. "When he's in his zone, you get out of his way or you get trampled."

Serge jumped back in the car, all smiles.

"What this time?" asked Zargoza. "Indian shell mound?"

"Don't be silly," said Serge. "The geology's all wrong. That used to be the old El Pasaje restaurant, where José Martí stayed last century while planning to kick some butt in Cuba. He's my role model. . . . This is also where the Buffalo Soldiers went on their rampage. Remember them? The highly decorated military units? They were staying in Tampa, getting ready to ship out to Cuba for the Spanish-American War. Elsewhere they were received like heroes, but here the innkeepers and bar owners discriminated against them 'cause they were black. Here they are, ready to go fight for America, and these locals are acting like bozos, so the Buffalos tore the place apart. Good for them."

"Are you set? Can we go now?" Zargoza said rhetorically.

"Ooops," said Serge. He was out of the car again, running across Ninth Avenue and up Fifteenth Street, and Zargoza was forced to follow slowly in the car.

"I give up," said Zargoza.

"Be glad you weren't his parents," said Lenny.

"Good point."

Serge leaped back in the car and Zargoza looked at him without speaking.

"Cigar factory established by city namesake V. Martínez Ybor circa 1885," said Serge. "Recognized it from an old Burgert Brothers print."

"I'm putting a shit-stop to this," said Zargoza. He reached down by his left side, throwing a switch that activated the BMW's child-safety locks.

They drove off and Serge played with the radio. A jazz station, an all-night Lightning hockey postgame show, and Blitz-99.

"Hey, boys and girls, this is Boris the Hateful Piece of Sh—AHH-OOOO-GAH! reminding you that the big vote on Proposition 213 is only days away . . ."

"That's that stupid anti-immigration amendment again," said Zargoza. "Everyone's pissed 'cause we're going bilingual."

"Doesn't anybody study history anymore?" said Serge. "Florida was colonized by Spain. *English* is the foreign language here."

"I'm counting on you! Vote yes on Proposition 213! . . . Because they smell funny!"

"What kind of trip is this guy on?" asked Lenny.

"Not sure," replied Serge. "We may have just slipped through some kind of white-trash worm-hole in the time-space continuum."

Zargoza glanced again at the backseat. "I been meanin' to ask: What's with the *Miami Vice* getup?"

"I'm the Don Johnson experience."

Zargoza laughed again. "You look more like James Woods."

"It's not look. It's heart."

"Okay," said Zargoza, humoring him. "Show us some heart."

Lenny cleared his throat in the backseat. *"Listen, pal! I don't do this for kicks! It's a job, and when it's over, I walk as far away from it as I can!"*

Serge and Zargoza snapped their heads toward the backseat. "My God," said Serge. "It's *him*."

They drove randomly around Tampa Bay, admiring the views.

"Face it, Rico, we're just small-time players in a high-stakes game, where the rules are made by people we can't touch!"

Serge directed Zargoza up Fifty-sixth Street until they came to an uneventful honky-tonk.

"What's so great about this place?" asked Zargoza.

"Keep it in your pants," said Serge.

They went inside and the place was dead. Idle dart boards and pool tables. One drunk chick swayed slowly by herself on the dance floor to a country song about lost love and lice.

Serge ordered drafts for Lenny and Zargoza and a mineral water with a twist for himself. Serge drained the water in one pull and slammed the glass down.

"Kill those," he said. "We're on the move," and he ran out the door.

Back in the car, Serge told Zargoza to go north and hang a Louie on Busch Boulevard.

They pulled into a lounge that was an afterthought to the package store. A dive on a resigned stretch of the boulevard. Only two other people and an unidentified smell. The side door was open to the humid night. Yellowish crime light in parking lot and a fresh wreck up the street that was closing two lanes, the ejected body still in the street. A cop squatted next to it and felt for a pulse.

Serge ordered drinks again, but this time Zargoza declared he would not be rushed.

"No problem," said Serge. "We've arrived."

"Arrived *where*?" said Zargoza.

"You've just completed the *Goodfellas* tour of Tampa," said Serge. "Remember the Martin Scorcese movie? The part where Robert DeNiro and Ray Liotta got arrested in Tampa? In the movie they threatened a guy with a gambling debt by dangling him over the lion fence at the Tampa Zoo, which was actually the Lowry Park Zoo. That was Hollywood. In reality, they kidnapped him from that last bar we were at, pistol-whipped him in the car on the route we just took, dragged him into this place and stuffed him in that storage room"—Serge pointed across the bar. "It was October eighth, 1970."

Lenny leaned over and whispered to Zargoza: "He has incredible recall."

"How do you know all this?" asked Zargoza.

"The zoo scene didn't feel right, so I pored through the microfilm morgue at the library. I found the clips from the original case. There they were, defendants Henry Hill and James Burk." Serge snapped his fingers for effect. "DeNiro's and Liotta's characters in *Goodfellas*. All the facts were identical except instead of the zoo there were these two bars. The names of the lounges had changed but I was able to track them down through old city cross-indexes."

Serge jumped off his stool in excitement and made a sweeping gesture with his right arm. "Scorcese put Tampa on the map!" Then his expression shifted. "Come to think of it, really wasn't a very positive light."

He rubbed his chin. "You know what would make a better movie? All the people getting killed over the five million dollars that's floating around in a briefcase."

Zargoza spit up his drink, and Serge handed him a napkin.

"I gotta hit the can," said Serge.

He was gone awhile. Zargoza went looking for him.

"What are you doing?" shouted Zargoza, walking out in the parking lot, finding Serge messing around by the Beemer's trunk.

"You had a little wax buildup." Serge buffed a spot with his elbow. He smiled; Zargoza squinted back. Lenny came out and the three got in the car.

"Where to?" Zargoza asked.

Serge knew Tampa after midnight. Not the night-clubs. The rest. When he was having one of his spells, he would go until he dropped, so places with quirky hours were essential. The print shops, the study halls at UT and USF, all-night fishing spots, the Dale Mabry coffee shops, the cafeterias in the Tampa General and St. Joseph's maternity wards, the twenty-four-hour post office at the airport. He listed the options out loud.

"Anything else?" asked Zargoza.

"There's the three-day nonstop revival," said Serge.

"We do need grace," said Zargoza.

"I have sinned," said Serge.

They pulled off the causeway into a sea of cars parked outside an auditorium bathed in floodlights. Inside, the show was in full swing, the man on the stage talking fast, stiff-arming people in the fore-head, knocking them over. His burly assistants/bouncers worked the crowd with collection baskets. Zargoza hung back at the rear of the hall, but Serge grabbed Lenny by the arm and made for the stage, to be healed.

The preacher had already selected a group of twelve, but Serge and Lenny jumped right up and took their place at the end of the line. The preacher saw them, but didn't want to mess up a good thing. He worked his way down the row, interviewing each person with a microphone over the PA system.

"And what is your name, my brother?"

"Serge."

"And what is your affliction?"

"I'm crazy."

The preacher started to ask another question but thought better of it and skipped to Lenny.

"And what is your name, my brother?"

"Lenny."

"And what is your affliction."

"I have a problem with weed."

The preacher raised an arm to the crowd and bellowed into the microphone, "He has a problem with the evil weed, tobacco!"

"No, preach, I mean pot," said Lenny.

"He has a problem with the demon weed mareeee-juana!"

"Well, I wouldn't really say *demon*."

"He is caught in the fangs of dope! He wants to rid himself forever of its scourge!"

"Actually, I just want to cut down," Lenny said, patting his stomach. "I'm starting to get a bit of a gut from the munchies."

The preacher furrowed his brow at Lenny and then backed up on the stage to address the group as a whole.

"Do you believe in the power of the one true living God?"

"Yes!" the group said together.

"Do you reject Satan and all his works?"

"Yes!" the group said again.

"Yes!" said Serge. "Except for Led Zeppelin's fourth album."

The preacher glared at Serge.

Serge shrugged his shoulders. "It's a classic."

Large hands grabbed Serge and Lenny from behind and they were given the bum's rush by security.

Zargoza made a break from the back of the auditorium for the parking lot, and he already had the car in the circular drive when the doors burst open and Serge and Lenny hit the pavement.

On the other side of town, at the studios of the Florida Cable News network, Blaine Crease was summoned by the news director for an emergency three-A.M. meeting.

Correspondent Blaine Crease was the undisputed journalistic star of the upstart news network. He was brilliant with delivery, big on flash, short of facts, reckless with accuracy and destined to go places. As the newest network on the block, FCN needed to grab attention, and Crease was their guy. A former stunt man, he reported every story as if danger were all around. He was the master of the "newsman as fearless participant" feature story. He went on SWAT team raids, got in the tank with killer whales, threatened to fistfight murderers during jailhouse interviews, rappelled from small buildings, and ate with a large fork from the latest lot of recalled food.

Crease often appeared on camera scuffed up, bruised and bleeding, usually because he had rolled himself on the ground just before going on the air. If the story lacked drama, he'd set up a wind machine just off camera. It could be a piece about geranium season, but Crease would be leaning into the wind, fighting for balance to hold the pose that made his hair look dashing in a gale. He wore combat fatigues, flak jackets and helmets whenever it was unnecessary. But most of all, Crease liked to ride loud, fast things. Ambulances, fire engines, boats, planes.

Consequently, Crease was beside himself when the news director of FCN called him into the office in the middle of the night and gave Crease the assignment he'd been waiting for all his life.

"Good, glad to hear it," said the news director. He left the room and returned shortly with a small metal cage.

"What's that?" said Crease.

"You're taking Toto along."

"Like hell I am! It's demeaning! I'm the star of this network!"

"Now you listen to me!" said the director. "You may be the highest-rated *human* on the network, but this dog butters our bread. . . . Catch!" The director threw a box of liver snaps hard into Blaine's chest.

20

===

*Z*argoza roared up in his BMW just as the bouncers tossed Serge and Lenny out of the all-night revival. They hopped in, and Zargoza sped out of the driveway.

"You're right about Zeppelin's fourth album," Zargoza told Serge. "It rules."

Serge launched into air guitar of the album's first cut, "Black Dog." Zargoza joined in playing drums on the steering wheel. Lenny growled with a Kmart Robert Plant, but it was serviceable.

"Hey, hey, mama said the way you move—gonna make you sweat, gonna make you groove!"

Serge made guitar sounds with his mouth and Zargoza pounded on the wheel.

". . . been so long since I found out, what people mean by dinin' out!"

Serge resumed the scorching guitar part again, but Zargoza had a funny look on his face.

"Whoa! Whoa! Stop it! Hold the fuckin' train!"

The others fell quiet.

"What was that?" Zargoza asked Lenny.

"What?"

"That lyric. Did you say '*what people mean by dinin' out*'?"

"Yeah."

"That's not how it goes."

"Yes it is."

"No it isn't, you boob. It's *down and out*."

"No it isn't," said Lenny.

"What kind of shithead are you?" said Zargoza. "Jimmy Page is choppin' the most savage guitar licks ever laid down, and you think Plant is singing about not getting out to White Castle enough?"

"I didn't give it much thought," said Lenny. "I figured they were very busy in the recording studio and they ate a lot of takeout."

"It's *down and out*!" said Zargoza. "He's talkin' about the struggle of the common man!"

"Now I'm hungry," said Lenny.

"Me too," said Zargoza. "Let's find a place."

Lenny fired up a tubular joint—"so I can taste my dinner." They turned onto U.S. 19, fast-food row, and pulled in the drive-through lane at the new fried-chicken-skin joint.

Lenny was quite high now. "This is the best place!" he said. "They get rid of all the damn meat so you just get the skin. That's all we've ever wanted. That's all we've ever asked for."

He took another hit.

"Why do they say the drinks are *king*-size, like that's the biggest possible comparison. Look at Prince Charles—no superlatives spring to mind there," said Lenny. "You wanna get my money? Start talking about a dictator or a conqueror. Like Attila-sized, or Stalin-sized! . . ."

"What the fuck's he talking about?" Zargoza asked Serge.

"Free-associating," said Serge. "I've seen this sort of thing before. Verbal incontinence. Just vomiting words."

"When does it stop?" asked Zargoza.

"It doesn't," said Serge. "Not without intervention."

Zargoza glanced back at Lenny and then at Serge. "We're up next at the ordering microphone. You need to suppress that shit with prejudice."

Serge turned around and gave Lenny the mondo eye, which made Lenny extremely paranoid, and he became quiet.

"That should do it," said Serge. "He'll go on an introspective journey now. But be prepared. We may hear weeping."

Zargoza rolled up to the menu board. The small metal speaker came on. "May I take your order?"

"Yes," said Zargoza. "I'd like your mega-combo meal . . . number twelve. Do I get the Galactic Massacre playing pieces with that?"

"Yes, you do."

"Okay, and I'll take the extra-crunchy fried chicken skin on a stick . . ."

Lenny leaned over the side of the car toward the speaker.

"Hitler-size my french fries!"

"What?" said the speaker.

"Saddam-size my apple pies!"

"Can you repeat that?" said the speaker.

"Shut that motherfucker up!" Zargoza yelled at Serge.

"Excuse me?" said the speaker.

"I wasn't talking to you!"

Serge climbed in the backseat and grabbed Lenny in a full nelson.

"Where were we?" Zargoza asked the clerk.

"Number twelve, chicken skin on a stick."

"Can I substitute cole slaw for the mashed potatoes?"

Lenny broke free from Serge and leaned out the car again. "Ho Chi Minh my chicken skin!"

"I'm getting the manager," said the speaker.

Zargoza floored it through the drive-through, snapping off a sideview mirror.

"Goddammit!" he yelled as the car bottomed out onto U.S. 19. "I was hungry, too!"

They headed back across the Howard Frankland Bridge and took West Shore down to Gandy.

A red Audi with tinted windows pulled alongside at a stoplight.

Zargoza looked over. "Twats!"

"What is it?" said Serge.

"Those damn Diaz Boys!"

The light turned green and both cars patched out and drag-raced all the way to Bayshore. At the red light, the Audi's tinted windows went down and shotguns appeared.

"What's this about?" Zargoza shouted at Tommy Diaz.

"Safety inspection," said Tommy. "You wouldn't

mind if we checked your trunk, would you? We've been hearing rumors. Beemers sometimes have expensive loose objects back there that could create a hazard."

"Sure," said Serge. "But you'll have to race us for the opportunity."

"We don't need to race. We have the guns."

"You also have the tiniest balls this side of the squirrel family," said Serge. "I was thinking of cutting 'em off and feeding 'em to my poodle as a new between-meals treat, since they're not too filling."

"Don't ya just love this guy!" Zargoza called out the window.

Tommy Diaz was in a barely contained rage. "Okay, we'll race! First one down to those psychedelic fish at the bridge to Davis Islands!"

"Hold on," said Serge. He turned to Zargoza. "You got that opium pipe?"

"Sure," said Zargoza. He handed the pipe to Serge and cranked up "Free Ride" on the stereo as he gunned the engine. Tommy Diaz gunned his engine, too.

Serge leaned out the window. "Peace pipe," said Serge. "Anyone for some good opium?"

"Back here," said Rafael Diaz, reaching out the passenger window behind the driver. He hung way out the door to take the pipe from Serge. Just as their hands met, Rafael noticed one end of a set of fur-lined handcuffs around Serge's hand. Serge quickly clasped the other end around Rafael's left wrist. He turned back to Zargoza. "Hit it!"

"Roger!" Zargoza floored the gas. Screaming came from the other car and Tommy gave it the gas, too.

The cars stayed tight as they wound along the waterfront route, Serge smiling, Rafael ashen and whimpering. Zargoza intentionally drifted the BMW to the left, and Tommy Diaz mirrored his moves. Zargoza popped the left wheels up on the grassy median. Then he had the whole car in the median, doing fifty, and kept drifting. Tommy Diaz was forced to drift with Zargoza unless he wanted to lose Rafael. Serge laughed like a lunatic, but the other car had gone silent.

Zargoza drifted left until he had forced the Diaz car onto the median as well. This was the same median where city leaders had decided to move a series of abstract modern sculptures, and the next one coming up was a jumble of sharp pieces of round metal, a giant serrated Slinky. Now the other car came alive again, pointing ahead and screaming, begging with Serge. Rafael was more than halfway out the window, and the others held him in the car by his legs.

Just a few seconds to go. Serge casually got out the key.

"Whoops," he said, and jerked forward like he'd dropped it. He smiled and showed he still had the key. "Just kidding." A second left. Serge turned the key and he and Rafael shot apart. The two cars parted high-speed around the sculpture, Zargoza ending up on the wrong side of the median in the oncoming lanes. He swerved around a taxi and jumped the next median, crossing back in front of the Diaz Boys as both cars raced around a hard left curve, then a right, neck and neck. Tommy Diaz gunned it and took the inside as they went into the last turn. Zargoza opened it up and passed him as they went by the psychedelic fish.

They both hit the brakes, skidding into the parking lot at the boat launch, and everyone jumped out and drew guns. Zargoza aimed a shotgun across the hood of the BMW and tossed a pistol to Serge.

"You fucking sons of bitches!" yelled Tommy. "Cocksuckers of whores!"

"Easy now," said Serge. "You're mixing your metaphors."

"We should kill all of you!" said Tommy.

"Hey, guys," said Lenny. "It looks like I'm not needed here. I'm free to go, right?"

Everyone: "No!"

"Shit-eating dogs!" said Tommy.

"Yeah, yeah, yeah," said Serge, he and Tommy pointing guns in each other's faces a foot apart.

"Open the trunk!" said Tommy.

"You lost the race," said Serge. "Bite me."

"The race is under protest," said Tommy.

"You think this is NASCAR?" said Serge.

"Interference with another driver."

"No way," said Serge. "These are Ben-Hur rules."

Nobody spoke for a solid minute, guns still leveled.

"Next time!" snapped Tommy, and he started walking backward to the Audi. The other Diaz Boys followed his lead, and they slowly climbed inside, still aiming guns.

Tommy started the engine. He began pulling away and stuck his head out the window. "You're dead! You're all fucking dead!"

"No, you're the ones who are fucking dead!" shouted Zargoza.

"No, you're fucking dead!" yelled Tommy, pulling into traffic.

"No, you're fucking dead!"

"You're dead!"

"You're dead!"

"You are!"

"You are!"

"Fiddlebottom!"

"Don't call me that! It's Zargoza!"

"Fiddlebottom!" yelled Tommy, his voice trailing off in the distance.

"Come back here—I'll kill you!"

Some guns were fired in the air as the Audi disappeared around a bend.

Serge turned to Zargoza. "I take it there's some history here."

"Fuckin' tradition," said Zargoza. "We've been racing for years. Before that we were in a bowling league, but they won't let us play anymore."

"Go figure."

21

Shortly after Serge and Lenny had set up their bunker in room one, City and Country showed up at Hammerhead Ranch, unable to find the two guys they were supposed to meet from Daytona. They considered it a plus.

City and Country loved Hammerhead Ranch the second they drove up. Between the beach and the open-air bar and the pool and freezing air-conditioning in the room, they had everything they needed for a much-needed vacation.

They didn't leave the motel grounds for the first two days except to walk across the street to the Rapid Response convenience store. Actually it was more of a run. They were barefoot, and the sun had turned the pavement to hot coals. It started out: Wow, this hurts a little, and then, How fast can I move and still be lady-like? By the time they hit the shaded sidewalk in front of the store, they were both in gangly, loping gallops, and when they got inside they made fun of each other.

It was a regulation Florida convenience store. A

man talked to invisible people at the newspaper boxes as a drug deal occurred by the car vacuum. There was a quiet aridness to the place, like a dusty tumbledown gas station with a squeaky metal sign swinging in the sagebrush outside Flagstaff, except with a row of bright beach rafts out front. No shortage of crap inside, either. Inflatable rings with horsey heads, umbrellas, sunscreen, novelty cans of Florida sunshine, suggestive postcards, beach towels with unicorns and Panama Jack and Jamaican flags, and a tall spinning rack of paperbacks next to the Great Wall of Beer. City opened the cooler and stuck her face in with eyes closed, and a cloud of frosty air fogged the glass. City grabbed a four-pack of passion fruit wine coolers. The clerk looked seventeen with fresh row crops of acne. A healthy self-image prompted him to shave his skull, grow a goatee and tattoo his neck with barbed wire. He installed what looked like tiny trailer hitches in his pierced eyebrows and smoked sub-generic cigarettes.

A police officer walked in and tipped his hat. City and Country tensed up and looked away. The cop bought a Wild West gunfighter magazine and caffeine tablets and tipped his hat again and left.

"How are you ladies today? Finding everything all right?" the clerk asked with a smile that revealed another trailer hitch in his tongue. The accent was Scottish.

City and Country put the wine coolers on the counter and grabbed two ice cream bars from the minicooler by the register. City smiled back at the clerk. His name tag said "Doom."

"Hope you're having a wonderful time on our island," he continued. "We pride ourselves on the
peacefulness out here."

He took a horrific double drag on his cigarette and
scratched his cheek rapidly like a mouse.

The pair left the store, and Doom watched through
the glass as they bounded across the street. He
looked down and kicked the ribs of the tied-up and
gagged clerk stuffed under the counter.

"Where's the goddamn safe?"

City and Country put the wine coolers on ice and
took paperbacks out to the bar. They grabbed a table
in the corner by the ocean. It was midafternoon,
siesta time, and the bar was empty. Fine by them.
Everywhere they ever went, men flocked. They ordered a fad Mexican beer because they wanted to
play with the lime slices. They set the beers on the
windowsill and leaned their chairs back and began
reading. It was shift change on the beach—the last of
the morning people packing it in, the afternoon people setting up.

When the wind was still, they heard the yells of
high school kids throwing Frisbees in the surf, and
when it wasn't, they heard the bar's license-plate
wind chime. Then they heard this odd, sucking sound
that they couldn't quite place. It was near. They put
the books down and looked around but couldn't lo-
cate it. They stuck their heads out the open window
and it grew louder. They looked straight down.
Lenny Lippowicz sat on the ground with his back
against the side of the bar, glancing around nervously

and rapid-fire toking on a roach he had curled up in his hand.

"What are you doing?" asked City.

"Aaaaauuuuuuuu!!!" Lenny yelled.

The roach joint went flying and Lenny spun and ended up on his back in the sand.

"Don't *ever* sneak up like that!" he said. "Oh man, now my head's in a bad place, and I have to get my heart rate down.... Can I have a sip of your beer?"

Country handed him her bottle and he killed it.

"Hey!" she yelled.

"Sorry, I'll pay you back," he said, sifting through the sand for his roach and coming up with cigarette butts and a diamond ring.

"Damn! It's lost!" he said. "Now I have to go back to my room for another. You wanna join me?"

"To smoke marijuana?" asked Country.

"That's the plan, and I'm the man."

She looked at City and shook her head. "We can't!"

"Definitely not!" said City.

"I've never done it, and I'm never going to," said Country.

"Me neither!" said City.

Five minutes later they were cross-legged on the floor in Lenny's room, smoking a fattie.

"We shouldn't be doing this," said City.

"We're so bad," said Country.

"Don't talk—hold the smoke," said Lenny.

"What's that music? It's so great!" said City. "It's the best music I've heard in my whole life."

"I think it's ABBA," said Lenny.

Country tried to talk but each time she opened her mouth, she broke up laughing. "What I'm trying to say . . ."—helpless laughter—". . . I don't know why it's so funny . . ."—more laughter—"but I'm starving!"

"Me too!" City giggled.

"I don't have anything, just a moldy old box of Cheese Nips in my suitcase."

"Give it to us!" Country shouted. They didn't wait for an answer before tearing apart the luggage and attacking the orange box.

"Got anything else to eat?" City said with a dry mouthful of masticated crackers.

"You guys are *so* stoned!" said Lenny.

"No we're not!" said City.

"You are too!"

"I don't feel a thing," said Country.

"First music, now food," he said. "That's two out of the Big Three."

"What's the third?" asked City.

Lenny was about to respond when Country slammed into him on the blind side like a crack-back block. She knocked him to the floor and ripped open his belt and zipper.

"City, quick! Help me hold him down!"

"I'm not resisting!" said Lenny.

City came up behind Lenny and knelt over his head, pinning his arms with her knees. Country pulled off his pants and then hers and mounted him. Fifteen minutes later, she and City switched places.

An hour later City and Country were back at their

regular table in the bar. Four fresh empties lined the sill, and they drank Bloody Marys, chewing the celery stalks as if they were smoking cigars. Their eyes were red and glazed. The bartender arrived with a platter of Hurricane Andrew Nachos—tortilla chips fanned out in the circular swirling pattern of a cyclone and smothered with picante and melted cheese. They devoured it without the aid of utensils. Halfway through the nachos, with mouths full, they waved the waiter over and ordered smoked mullet. When that arrived, they asked for the dinner menu.

Lenny walked like a zombie into the bar.

The bartender recognized him and pointed over at the women. "Hey, check those two in the corner—they're eating me out of the place. . . . Lenny? . . . Lenny?"

Lenny didn't answer. He staggered through the bar and walked out the back door, where he sat down in the sand with a dazed smile until the sun went down.

The next morning, Lenny opened the door to go out for a paper and City and Country were already standing there. They each held out a five-dollar bill. Country said loudly, "Can we buy ten dollars of pot?"

"Shhhhhh! Jesus!" Lenny replied. He looked around quickly and yanked them into the room, then closed and bolted the door.

An hour later, City and Country were down the street at the International House of Belgian Waffles. They sat at the semicircular corner booth with a fire-rated capacity of eight. Covering the table were blueberry flapjacks, silver-dollar pancakes, sunny-side-up eggs with steak, French toast, scrambled eggs and hash browns, a side order of link sausages, a small bowl of whipped butter and pouring jars of maple and boysenberry syrup.

Back at the hotel, Lenny lay in his jockey shorts spread-eagle on the bed, unable to move. He was in love.

22

Major Larry "Montana" Fletcher of the 403rd Air Wing pulled up to the guard shack at Keesler Air Force Base in Biloxi, Mississippi. There was a long line of cars ahead and some type of commotion at the front. Montana stuck his head out the window to see what was going on.

One of the guards jumped back from the car at the head of the line and pulled his gun on the driver. The driver exited his vehicle with his hands up. He was decked out in nonregulation combat fatigues, flak jacket and helmet, a press pass clipped to his breast pocket. Another guard went to the passenger side of the car and removed a small cage holding a dog.

Montana laughed. He got out of the car and walked to the guard shack. He checked the name on the press pass and turned to the guard. "It's okay, fellas. He's with me." The guards saluted.

"Mr. Crease, it's a pleasure," said Montana, extending his hand. "I've been expecting you. I'm a big fan. Why don't you pull your car up to that building and I'll be right with you."

A half hour later, Montana and Crease shouted back and forth over the propeller noise as they walked across the tarmac to the mobile staircase waiting at their plane.

It was a magnificent silver Lockheed-Martin WC-130 Hercules. Montana's particular plane was nicknamed *The Rapacious Reno*.

"I named it after Janet Reno," Montana shouted as loud as he could. "She's a native of Miami, the home of the National Hurricane Center."

Crease stopped and was shaken at the sight of the World War II–style nose art on *The Rapacious Reno*. Instead of a cheesecake pose, Reno had flying tiger jaws with pointy teeth dripping blood, and Crease recognized the reading glasses and smart haircut of the seventy-eighth attorney general of the United States. Behind the flying tiger head was a mural depicting Reno's life—courtroom scenes, childhood memories of south Florida.

"I painted it myself," shouted Montana. "I'm a big admirer of hers—a classic Florida pioneer. She gets a lot of criticism and bum raps from people who don't know anything about her."

"What's she doing in this part of the mural?" asked Crease.

"Building a log cabin."

"Did she ever build a log cabin?"

"I dunno," Montana said, and ran up the staircase.

The planes of the 53rd Weather Reconnaissance Squadron had an additional staff position. It was the instrument operator—technically known as the drop-sonde operator—and on *The Rapacious Reno* that job fell to William "The Truth" Honeycutt. The dropsonde is a small metal cylinder sixteen inches long and three inches wide containing a microprocessor, a radio transmitter and a small drogue parachute. The dropsonde operator's primary responsibility is to release the electronic tube into the eye of the hurricane to measure temperature, humidity and pressure. Through triangulated telemetry with ground stations, the device also registers wind speed and direction. Under intense pressure from the Air Force public relations office, the 53rd Squadron reluctantly conferred the position of "honorary dropsonde operator" to FCN correspondent Blaine Crease.

Honeycutt was supposed to coach and supervise Crease. Instead, Crease made Honeycutt carry his TV camera and follow him around the plane to film him performing important-looking tasks. Crease was beside himself with joy; his only regret was that he had to carry Toto everywhere in a kangaroo-style nylon pouch on his stomach. Crease sat in the copilot's seat and at the navigator's table, the reconnaissance post and the weather console. Honeycutt had to keep filming and refilming Crease because crew members constantly leaped into the picture to grab Crease's arms before he threw levers and switches he knew nothing about.

"He's gonna make us crash! We're all gonna die!" screamed Milton "Bananas" Foster.

"Get that limp-dick the fuck out of here!" yelled Lee "Southpaw" Barnes.

Pepe Miguelito sat in the corner weeping as he listened to "Breaking Up Is Hard to Do" on his personal radio.

"Now, now. Everyone settle down. Everything will be all right," Montana said in a steady, calming voice. "Honeycutt . . . Honeycutt? . . ."

Honeycutt stopped shadowboxing in the back of the cockpit. "What is it, sir?"

"Honeycutt, why don't you take Mr. Crease back in the hold and teach him about the dropsonde?"

"Yes, sir," said Honeycutt.

At zero nine hundred hours Zulu, the Hercules entered the Tropic of Cancer. At nine hundred thirty, the crew crossed the twenty-second parallel three hundred miles west of Havana. The plane was buffeted as the WC-130 entered the edge of the cyclonic system. More than three weeks after forming near the Cape Verde Islands, the hurricane was tracking across the Caribbean Sea, threatening the Gulf of Mexico.

"We're all gonna die!" yelled Foster.

Marilyn Sebastian grabbed him by the collar and shook him violently. "Get a grip on yourself! Be a man!" She slapped him. She was about to kiss him when Honeycutt grabbed her. "This is for Baton Rouge," he said and took her in his strong arms and their mouths met. Montana coolly banked left, into the clockwise rotation of the hurricane, to minimize the crosswinds. He edged his way back right, flying closer and closer to the eye of the storm.

"Look!" said Baxter, pointing out of the cockpit. There was a sudden break in the clouds. "Check that eye wall. What incredible stadium effect. This one has to be at least a three on the Saffir-Simpson Scale."

"It's a four," said Montana. "Hold on. I'm going to take it through and come back for another pass. The plane punched into the eye wall on the other side.

Back in the cavernous cargo hold, Crease listened to the entire lecture Honeycutt gave about the drop-sonde and paid absolutely no attention.

"Yeah, yeah, okay, okay," Crease said impatiently. "So where is the little tube? Where's the door I throw it out?"

"I just told you," said Honeycutt. "It's dropped by hydraulics from an automatic external hatch. You never see the thing. All you do is press a button."

"That's not good television," said Crease. "You mean there's no bomb bay that opens up dramatically above the terrible eye of the hurricane?"

"Nope."

"Can you at least open some kind of window so my hair will blow?"

"What?"

"Never mind. Listen, do you have any kind of door or something that opens up in the floor here?"

"We have a small, auxiliary instrumentation hatch . . ."

"Great! That's wonderful! Let's call it the bomb bay," said Crease.

"But it's not—"

"I know television!" said Crease. "Now say it!"

"It's the bomb bay," Honeycutt said sarcastically.

"Good! Now here's what you're gonna do. You're going to go get the little drop-thingie and open the bomb bay, and then you're going to film me as I bravely walk to the opening—wind swirling up from the horrible storm—and release the doodad through the hole in the floor. What d'ya say?"

"No way."

Crease marched up to the cockpit and spoke urgently with Montana, who called back to Honeycutt over the intercom headsets. He explained that while Crease's request might seem unorthodox, in the larger scheme of things it was what headquarters wanted to improve the image of the air base. And it kept Crease out of his cockpit.

Honeycutt went back into the bowels of the plane, opened a panel and retrieved the dropsonde. The thunder of the engines and the storm roared all around. He handed the silver baton to Crease.

Honeycutt got down on the deck and opened the instrumentation hatch, and both men were chilled by the rush of air.

"Now remember," Honeycutt shouted above the wind, "don't release the dropsonde until I tell you we're over the eye."

"Don't worry about me," Crease shouted back. "You just make sure you get all this on tape!"

Honeycutt hoisted the video camera onto his shoulder and prompted Crease: "Readyyyyyyy, readyyyyyyy . . . three, two, one . . . now!"

Crease tossed the dropsonde underhand toward the open hatch. Flying up in the air, end over end, the twirling instrument looked like a nice shiny stick, and Toto leaped out of his pouch, took two steps and jumped. Toto caught the dropsonde in his mouth at the top of the baton's arc.

Crease's eyes bulged as Toto and the dropsonde hung suspended in the air for a split second, and then both fell through the hatch and disappeared into the hurricane.

"Ahhhhhhhhh!" Crease yelled in terror. He spun and lunged for the video camera on Honeycutt's shoulder.

"What are you doing?!" said Honeycutt.

Crease didn't answer; he pressed the eject button, grabbed the tape and gave it a quick push-throw toward the open "bomb bay" doors like a two-handed shot put. He pulled his hands back fast as if it had been a hot potato.

"Good. Nobody ever needs to see *that* footage."

He looked back at his cameraman. "I'll do my best to get you off the hook, Honeycutt, but it's going to be difficult explaining how you could have let such a brainless thing happen."

Honeycutt knocked him cold.

23

C. C. Flag pulled up to Hammerhead Ranch in a snow-white Hummer. He had full, pleated pants, a loose Australian bush shirt and a "USA" America's Cup baseball cap.

An hour later there was a curt rap on the door of Flag's motel room.

"Coming," said Flag.

But Zargoza didn't wait and opened the door with his own key.

Flag now wore a bloused white-cotton Banana Republic shirt, beige slacks and amber shooter's glasses. He had a crystal bourbon decanter in his hand and a svelte Asian-American call girl on his lap. Flag pushed the hooker up off his knees and gave her a light spank. "Got some business, baby. Why don't you wait at the bar? I'll be done soon and then *me love you long time*."

"Whatever," she said in an accent more American than Flag's. She lit a Tiparillo and strolled sensually out of the room, leaving Zargoza and Flag in her ex-

haust cloud of arrogance and contempt that made
both of them hate her guts and want to marry her.

"Bourbon straight with ice-water chase?" Flag
asked as he poured.

"We've got problems," said Zargoza. "You gotta
get back out to the nursing home."

"But I went yesterday."

"You have to go again," said Zargoza. "I just heard
a TV crew is starting an investigative series."

"I thought they only did sex scandals," said Flag.
"Since when are they *reporters*?"

"I know, I know. You can't count on anything these
days," said Zargoza. "I got enough on my plate with
the stolen beepers and cocaine . . ."

Flag stuck his fingers in his ears. "I didn't hear
anything. I'm a respectable businessman."

"Shut the fuck up!" said Zargoza. "You're worse
than any of us. You're a slimy salamander with gon-
orrhea, a pustulating sea slug, a mucous-tracking
gastropod in a construction site Porta-Johnny!
You're a—"

"I get the picture," said Flag. "What do you want
from me?"

"Glue a smile on your face and go meet the TV
crew. Put a sympathetic face on this thing. America
trusts you, God help 'em."

"I speak to their wants and dreams. . . ."

"Bullshit!" said Zargoza. "They're zoned out! A
little old lady is blown to bits and all anyone can
think about is this TV dog that wears funny clothes."

"Aren't you connected to the people who killed the old lady?" asked Flag.

"That's not the point," said Zargoza. "I'm talking about the big picture here. This is a terrible comment on our society."

An old but reliable Ford Fairlane chugged across the bridge to the barrier islands of Tampa Bay, hot on the trail.

Paul, the Passive-Aggressive Private Eye, wished it was the forties. He carried everything he needed in a fifty-year-old dark-checkered suitcase. When he checked into a motel, he pretended he was Philip Marlowe getting a room above a greasy spoon where the night manager was a junkie who looked like William Burroughs, and there was a harsh red neon sign flashing through his window all night. He'd shave with a porcelain cup and brush, pack his piece and go down to the greasy spoon for a short-order slice of meat loaf and a cup of joe and imagine he was in an Edward Hopper painting.

It didn't dispel the illusion a bit that Paul was staying at the Toot-Toot Tugboat Inn on St. Pete Beach and dining at The Happy Clam. Paul took a mug shot of Art Tweed with him everywhere and showed it to everyone.

While good with inanimate objects, Paul was inept and annoying when questioning people about Art. His relentless passive-aggressive inquisition merely bugged some, while others called the police and alerted the media.

On his third day in Tampa Bay, Paul was showing the mug shot to a woman who rented cabanas on the beach. She shook her head no. Two squad cars arrived and the cops asked Paul what he was doing.

Paul told them the whole story until the cops said he was getting on their nerves and they left. As the cruisers pulled away, a silver van that had been waiting on the side of the parking lot pulled up. It had sprigs of antennas and a rotating dish. On the side, in giant letters: "Florida Cable News." Underneath was a smiling portrait and a script banner: "Featuring Blaine Crease."

The side panel of the van slid open and Crease climbed out wearing Desert Storm camouflage. He walked purposefully to Paul.

"I've been doing some checking up on you," said Crease. "You're a private investigator. Your name's Paul. My sources tell me you've been showing a photograph all over the beach—you're tracking some kind of desperado."

Crease grabbed Paul's hand and shook it hard, then looked away. "The cops ain't giving me shit. But I figured it out. It's because they don't *have* shit."

"There's nothing for them to have," said Paul.

Crease held up a hand for Paul to stop. He leaned closer and whispered, "Between you and me, you're the man! I can tell by the way you hold yourself. You're running circles around the cops. You probably have the whole thing figured out already—just tying up loose ends now. I heard a rumor it's a hit man. That true?"

"That's the stupidest thing—"

"Don't try to be modest," interrupted Crease. "You've got a style. Reminds me of . . ." Crease tapped his head like he was on the edge of recollection. Then he opened his eyes wide. "Philip Marlowe! That's it! You've got this whole Robert Mitchum quality goin' on."

Paul blushed and looked at the ground.

"So, tell me, who are you tracking? Who's the bad guy?" Crease said, rubbing his palms together. "Come on. I'm dying to know."

"You've got it wrong. I'm not after a bad guy," said Paul.

"Great! Love it! An equivocal story—the amoral universe!" said Crease. He made two *L*s with the thumb and forefinger of each hand and put them together in a square to frame an imaginary picture in the air. "The mass murderer with a heart of gold! Finally, a villain we can root for in the new millennium!"

"No, that's not what I mean—"

"Paul, it's me! Blaine!" Crease thumped his palm over his heart.

"Really," said Paul. "I don't know where you're getting this stuff."

Paul told him all about Art Tweed and the mixup at the hospital and being hired to track Art down and give him the good news. "Art Tweed is no hit man."

"Right. I gotcha," said Crease, and he gave Paul a knowing wink.

*   *   *

A black Jeep Eagle raced through the unsettled countryside east of Tampa. The Jeep was plastered with Boris and Blitz-99 bumper stickers, and it sailed through a red light at the Four Corner intersection of State Road 674 in the phosphate mining depot of Fort Lonesome. The radio was on full blast.

"So remember: Vote yes on Proposition 213! . . . because they have weird accents!"

"Now that guy is focused!" said the Jeep's driver. "He's the only one with the guts to stand up for people like us!"

"Amen!" the two passengers said in unison.

The driver had shoulder-length blond hair in dreadlocks, the front passenger's head was shaved, and the guy in back hanging on the rollbar wore an *F Troop* cavalry hat with a plastic arrow through it. The three high school students dressed in punk rags from the Salvation Army and talked about being oppressed by minorities, but in fact they all lived in two-hundred-thousand-dollar houses in the sleepy bedroom suburb of Brandon.

After Boris's show ended, the driver tuned to a salsa dance station, which was advertising the Latin Heritage Festival that weekend in Ybor City.

"I can't believe it!" the driver exclaimed. "They're holding a party for these people when they should be tossing 'em back over the border!"

"And it's the same night as our Proposition 213 rally!" said the one on the rollbar. "What an insult!"

"Tell you what we should do," said the driver. "Go

listen to Boris at the rally, get pumped, and then drive over to Ybor and crack some heads."

"Amen!" they said again, and they raised their fists together in a Pearl Jam pose.

The three teens had yet to come up with an official name for their little think tank, but their classmates already had: the Posse Comatose.

24

$\mathcal{B}$ehind Hammerhead Ranch, just beyond the line of stuffed sharks, was the bar. It predated the motel. Originally built as a small beach house during the Florida land boom of the mid-twenties, it was gutted and renovated as a tavern during the forties. The building was wooden and sturdy, and over the years many of the beams had petrified and nails couldn't be driven into them anymore. The cracker architecture stayed intact—floor raised on stilts and a vaulted pyramid ceiling open to the joists for ventilation. It smelled salty and looked like a shipwreck. The floor was uneven with a thousand cigarette burns and stains upon splotches on top of splatters. Small blue neon letters went up in 1963 over the entrance facing the Gulf. "The Florida Room."

It hadn't resisted change as much as change had rejected *it*. No crab pot buoys made into lamps or thick rope glued around the edges of the tables. The Bahama shutters were double-thick and held up with chains. There was no AC. It stayed hot so that when there was a breeze, it reminded people that they liked it.

The Florida Room would begin filling up in the next hour. But for now, Lenny and Serge had it to themselves. Serge took wide-angle photos from each of the bar's four corners. Two sets—one flash, one natural light. The bartender wiped glasses and kept an eye on them. Serge and Lenny went back to the bar. It was quiet except for the squeaking of the bartender's wash rag and the tumbling daiquiri machine. Serge had an olive burlap shoulder bag in which he stowed camera gear, notebooks and any souvenirs that got caught in his dragnet: matchbooks, postcards, keychains, ticket stubs, brochures, swizzle sticks. He decided that now was a good time to spread the contents on the bar, reorganize and repack.

Lenny ordered a draft, Serge another mineral water.

"You ever been to the John Ringling Museum down in Sarasota?" Serge asked the bartender.

"Heard of it," he said, and continued wiping glasses.

"It's unbelievable," said Serge, turning to Lenny. "There's all the circus stuff you'd expect from his days with Barnum and Bailey. But there's also this incredible artwork, like he was trying to overcompensate for the bearded ladies and the fat guy they had to bury in a piano."

"I think you have the fat guy mixed up with the Guinness book," said Lenny.

"You sure?" asked Serge, looking up at a ceiling fan to concentrate. "Maybe I'm thinking of the guy born with his face upside down."

The bartender stopped wiping, eyed them a mo-

ment, then resumed. He was forty-eight and a Vitalis
man. He had a toothpick in his mouth and all the answers.

"They also have the Clown College down there,"
said Serge. "Heard of that?"

The bartender nodded, kept wiping.

"It's a historic institution," Serge told Lenny. "The
circus needed a school to keep their talent pool
stocked, and since the Ringling Brothers crew win-
tered there, it was the natural place. The college takes
it very seriously, just like a regular campus. Dorms,
library, cramming all night, finals. It's still there,
even though they almost closed it down after some
trouble back in the sixties."

"What happened?" asked Lenny.

"Antiwar demonstration. The National Guard
came in with Plexiglas shields. Horrible scene.
Clowns running everywhere through clouds of tear
gas; cops beating them with batons, the clowns kicking back with big, floppy shoes. At the administration building the guardsmen set up a barricade, and
thirty students rammed it in a tiny car. . . . Got a lot
of bad press. Few days later there was a news conference showing unity for the antiwar movement—a
long conference table in front of the cameras: a couple of Black Panthers, some SDS, the Weathermen,
Leonard Bernstein, three clowns . . ."

The bartender stopped wiping and studied Serge
again.

City and Country finished a rejuvenating swim in
the Gulf and bounced into the bar full of spunk. At
high tide the waves rolled twenty yards from the

back door, even closer after storm erosion. A heat wave still hadn't broken, and the water was filled with swimmers in numbers unusual for December.

The two women bellied up to the bar exuding sexual energy. The bartender immediately attached to his glass wiping the importance of a decathlete rosining up his vaulting pole. The women pointed at the daiquiri mixer. "We want two of those," City said in her British accent. The bartender poured strawberry slush with aplomb.

The pair took seats next to Lenny and smiled.

Lenny smiled back.

"What's that about?" asked Serge.

"I'm in love."

Serge asked the bartender to turn on the TV. Business began to pick up.

A Japanese man walked in with a surfboard. Serge raised his water in toast: "Tora! Tora! Tora!"

The man gave Serge a thumbs-up and smiled. "Yankee go home, shit-eater!" He took the stool next to Serge, and Serge patted him on the back and bought him a beer.

"I see you've been teaching him," said Lenny.

"Someone has to build the bridge," said Serge.

A Haitian man ran up to the bartender and talked fast in French, gesturing desperately. Captain Bradley Xeno came in seconds later. "There you are!" He threw the bartender a ten, grabbed the Haitian by the collar and dragged him off.

At a nearby table, a short, squat man was trying to sell letters of transit to a vacationing couple. "Signed by de Gaulle. Cannot be rescinded."

Serge wiped perspiration and gazed out the window and saw an armored van backed up to room five. Two men in dark suits and dark sunglasses jumped out the front of the vehicle with riot guns. Two more jumped out the back. The door of room five flew open and four more armed men in suits rushed a Mafia underboss with a beach towel over his head into the back of the vehicle, and it sped off for the next stop in the witness protection program.

As the van pulled out, a white limo pulled in. On the door were the five multicolored interlocking rings of the modern Olympics. Tampa Bay had placed a bid for the 2012 Summer Olympic games, and, although the Olympic Committee had no intention of awarding the games to Tampa Bay, they had an obligation out of fairness to show up and examine for themselves the level of local graft. Seven men of assorted ancestry got out of the limo and walked toward The Florida Room, followed by Sherpas carrying steamer trunks plastered with travel stickers. *"I love Euro-Disney," "I climbed the Matterhorn," "Hiroshima is for Lovers!"*

The International Olympic Committee wandered around the bar with confident smiles and expectant eyes, looking everyone in the face, wondering which stranger was the preordained one who would whisk them off to unimaginable wealth and human titillations.

"Hey, pencil-dicks! Down in front!"

The Olympic Committee noticed they were blocking the wide-screen TV, which was on Florida Cable News. Mug shots of City and Country were on the screen, but by the time the Olympic Committee got out of the way, FCN was into the Celebrity Rehab Spotlight portion of the broadcast.

*W*hen Jethro Maddox and Art Tweed first arrived in Tampa Bay, they got gas and Sweet Tarts at a Rapid Response convenience store. Art went inside to ask around the Proposition 213 rally. The clerk gestured to the end of the counter—a stack of bumper stickers and pamphlets with Boris's smiling face and an old car horn. On the back of the pamphlet was a map with directions to Beverly Shores. Art folded one and stuck it in his back pocket.

"You have been a noble and proud travel companion," Jethro said back at the gas pumps, "but we shall sadly depart, for I must once again rejoin my own kind."

"What?"

"I need to drop you 'cause I gotta meet the Look-Alikes for our gig. . . . Anyplace you want me to take you?"

Art looked up and saw a billboard and pointed. "Take me there."

Three miles down the road, they shook hands again and Jethro dropped Art at Crazy Charlie's Gun Store. ("Our assault rifle prices are so low because *we're absolutely insane!*") Art went inside and quickly picked out a Colt Python .357, nickel, six-inch barrel.

"That's a beaut!" said the clerk, running Art's credit card. "You can pick it up Thursday."

Art looked bewildered.

"It's the law. Three-day cooling-off period."

Art leaned forward. "No, no, no! I don't want to cool off! Cooling off is *bad*! It'll ruin everything!"

"You're preachin' to the choir," said the clerk. "Tell it to our commie government."

"Isn't there anything you can do?"

"Well, if I was a private collector selling one of my own guns—instead of a licensed dealer—there'd be no waiting period."

The clerk then looked around the store suspiciously. He took off his baseball cap embroidered with "Crazy Charlie's" and replaced it with one embroidered "Private Collector." He picked up the gun Art had selected and stuck it inside his jacket. He looked around again and then cocked his head toward the back door. "Let's take a walk."

They ended up behind the clerk's car parked in the alley. He handed Art the gun, and Art felt the weight, liked the balance. But he shook his head and handed it back. "I only have credit cards."

The clerk opened his trunk and took out a magnetic credit-card swiper and plugged it into a cell phone.

"That'll be six hundred."

"But it was only five hundred in the store!"

"I'm a private collector! I can't compete with those prices!"

Art sighed and he forked over his Visa. Then he caught a cab for Beverly Shores. They were just about done building the stage. Art cased the place. He asked someone what time Boris the Hateful Piece of Shit was supposed to arrive. The nearest accom-

modation was the Hammerhead Ranch Motel next
door. Not exactly the luxury digs he had intended,
but this was business.

He checked in with a Diners Club, tuned a radio to
Boris the Hateful Piece of Shit and began cleaning
the Colt.

25

The next morning Serge cut across the grass to the sidewalk in front of room one and turned the knob. Before he had the door open, he smelled strawberry incense; Buffalo Springfield was on the radio. Inside, the beds were pushed against the walls to create a large expanse of carpet. Everyone was sitting cross-legged on the floor. City held her breath and passed the alligator bong to Lenny, who did a double-clutch toke and passed it to Country, who then passed it around a circle of eight guys that Serge didn't recognize. They represented all races and creeds. There were coats on the beds: kabuki robe, Nehru jacket, dashiki. On top was a turban.

"What the hell's this?" said Serge. *"Get High for UNICEF?"*

"It's the International Olympic Committee," said Lenny. "They're here scouting for 2012. I wanted to do my part to bring the games here."

The men looked up and smiled at Serge and ate potato chips and salted almonds and passed the Lucite alligator.

Serge shook off the scene, then held up a video-cassette with satisfaction. "I found *The Cocoanuts,* the first Marx Brothers movie. It's about the Florida land boom back in the twenties. Groucho plays a Miami innkeeper who tries to rip everyone off." He nodded toward the delegates. "We-Are-the-World can stay, but only if they obey the theater rules."

By now Serge and Lenny had the routine down, and they began moving like a precision drill team. Serge sealed the windows with tape, and Lenny zipped around the room moving chairs and rationing out snacks. The circle of guests fanned into two rows, for optimum viewing. Serge hit the cooler, grabbing a grapefruit and mineral water. Lenny was by the TV, and Serge turned to throw him the videocassette.

"Lenny! Catch!"

"What?"

Lenny turned with the bong as the cassette zinged past his ear.

There was a scream. The videotape hit the Burkina Faso delegate in the left eye, and he grabbed his face and jackknifed in pain, right into a globe lamp. Now there was broken glass, blood and panic. A stoned Lenny picked up the videotape, stuck it in the VCR and started watching the Marx Brothers. People ran around the room in an international commotion. Groucho flicked his cigar: *"Why, when I came to Florida three years ago, I didn't have a nickel in my pocket. Now, I have a nickel in my pocket. . . ."*

Serge's jaw fell. Then came anger. "Everyone out! Now! Come on, let's get!"

Serge held the door open as they filed by, smiling, bowing and thanking Serge.

Serge looked over at City and Country, who were back into the pot.

" 'Ere," City said without exhaling, handing the smoking bong to Country. "This is some nuclear weed!"

"You, too!" Serge yelled. "Be gone, young dope fiends!"

Country didn't leave. Instead she sidled up to Serge with a whimsical, sexy swagger.

"How 'bout it, big boy?" She was feeling mischievous and wanted to toy with Serge—see him go slack-kneed. But she saw something entirely different in his eyes. Serge took a step forward, and it was Country who went invertebrate. Serge whisked her up in his arms like he was carrying a bride across a threshold. She put her arms around his neck to hold on, scared but feeling his energy.

Serge marched quickly to the bed and threw her on her back, and she bounced a foot and a half. He turned to Lenny and City. "Would you excuse us?"

It was not tender lovemaking. It was the kind of vigorous workout described in brochures for expensive isokinetic machines. Country was noisy in bed. She moaned and yelled and screamed. Lots of "Yes! Yes! Yes!" Soon they were drenched in perspiration, bodies sliding all over. They were going so hard that Serge was constantly in danger of sailing off the bed like a luge taking a turn too fast. Country writhed with her eyes closed and whipped her head side to side, her golden hair a damp mop, and it matted on her cheeks and fell in her mouth.

Suddenly she reached up and grabbed Serge by the back of the head. Breathing hard, she rocked her hips into him, parted her wet lips and gave Serge a predatory, squinting look that would send most men's prostates flying like a tee shot.

"What are you thinking about?" she asked, hyperventilating.

"Pioneer landmarks, historic graveyards, Andrew Jackson . . ." he said, keeping pneumatic rhythm. ". . . East Martello Tower, Pigeon Key, Stiltsville, the Don Shula Expressway, Larry Csonka . . ."

"Csonka? You gay?"

"I'm not picturing him *naked*. I'm imagining him splitting the linebackers in the Orange Bowl."

"Oh, I've heard of guys thinking stuff like that to prolong sex."

"I'm not," said Serge. "I'm trying to accelerate it."

Country started to give him a weird look, but Serge thrust again and hit pay dirt, and Country's eyes rolled back in her head. Then her eyelashes began to flutter. They reached simultaneous peaks, and Country surprised herself by making a squeaking sound like someone repeatedly stepping on a cat toy.

Serge arched up. "Remember the *Maine*!"

And they collapsed together in an exhausted, panting tangle.

Serge became something of a guru to City and Country. They were mesmerized by his patter on All

Things Florida, especially when they were high. They started following him everywhere like ducklings, and Serge accommodated with a running commentary as a kind of Florida docent-at-large.

The next day, about noon, he led them into The Florida Room, and they walked around the inside of the place at museum pace, taking inventory of the stuff on the walls. Dominant were the trophy fish. None of the taxidermy work looked newer than fifty years—chipped, faded scales and yellowed eyes. Serge identified the largest over the bar—blue marlin, swordfish, sea bass and mako shark—and the midsized stuff on the north and south walls: sailfish, tarpon, white marlin, wahoo. Then, above the western windows facing the water, the "small" fish: bull dolphin, king mackerel, barracuda, permit.

"Check out these great photos!" he said. They were in old wood frames mounted on the wall running down to the restrooms. The earliest were war era, group shots of people at tables in sailor and soldier uniforms. There was a close-up of a whiskered chief petty officer next to a teenage recruit, both smoking cigars. Most of the women in the photos looked like the Andrews sisters. There was raucous swing dancing and an old Bally jukebox that was later mothballed for twenty years in a warehouse in Dalton, Georgia, and now sat restored under a tenth-floor apartment window overlooking Central Park. The photographs were arranged chronologically. Lots of fishing snapshots and local parades; Hank Aaron and Stan Musial during spring training; and a party photo with a banner, "Happy New Year 1959."

Next was the memorial photo corner dedicated to some local photojournalist named "Studs" Allen, 1921–1971. Serge didn't need to read the captions.

"This is a young Cuban baseball pitcher sitting at a lunch counter on Tampa's Kennedy Boulevard, before the president's assassination, when it was still called Lafayette Boulevard. He was in town raising money to oppose Fulgencio Batista. His name was Fidel Castro."

Serge moved a step sideways and the girls followed. "This is an angry shot of beat author Jack Kerouac at the Wild Boar lounge on Nebraska Avenue in Tampa. . . . Here he is again, a little happier this time, standing outside his home on Tenth Avenue North in St. Pete, where he lived from 1964 to 1966. . . . And this is a photo of a St. Petersburg Junior College student named Jim Morrison performing at the Beaux Arts Coffee House in Pinellas Park."

Country whispered something in City's ear, and City came up with some kind of excuse to leave.

Country turned back to Serge. "Did I hear you have some kind of moon rock back in your room? I'd love to see it."

Three minutes later they were back in the room: Country kneeling on the foot of the bed, eyeing Serge—Serge completely missing the point, sitting in the middle of the bed, wrapped up in his storytelling. Country's gaze intensified, and she began to feel wet. Serge waved the rock around in the air, making rocket sounds.

"Did I ever tell you that Dade County was sup-posed to be named *Pinkney* County?"

She shook her head no.

"It's true, the Florida legislature was forming the new county down in Miami and they had the name all picked out. It was 1835. About the same time, Major Francis Lanhorne Dade began leading one hundred and ten soldiers from Fort Brooke in Tampa up to Fort King near Ocala. We had just screwed the Indians over but good, trying to ship 'em out West, so they attacked Dade's men. It was Florida's version of Little Big Horn. Only three survived. . . ."

Anyone else would have understood the look in Country's eyes. But Serge was on, well, Planet Serge.

". . . Word got back to the legislature, and they changed the name of the new county to Dade. Here's a cool epilogue. Some of the maps at the time placed Dade County north of Tampa because some of the mapmakers mistakenly thought the county was where the massacre had taken place. . . . Anyway, so now we're all pissed at the Indians, and we started the Second Seminole War. But their leader is the brave Osceola—for my money, possibly the greatest Floridian of all time. And the Indians are playing hit-and-run out of the Green Swamp, which feeds the river that runs through Tampa. All the European colonists take refuge at the fortified coastal installa-tions, which is why today we have all these cities with names like Fort Lauderdale, Fort Myers, Fort Pierce. . . ."

Country could wait no longer for Serge to come around. She pounced and pulled his pants off. Then she pinned his shoulders and got on top, wiggling down onto him with a chirp.

". . . Finally, General Thomas S. Jessup offers a flag of truce to Osceola to talk about peace. When Osceola arrives in St. Augustine, Jessup has him imprisoned, where he died in a year under brutal conditions. The attending physician cut off Osceola's head and took it home, and whenever his young boys would misbehave, he got out the head and hung it on their bedpost. . . ."

Country was sliding up and down rapidly, mouth open, breathing hard. A shock of blond hair on each side of her head swung back and forth in rhythm, brushing Serge's cheeks.

". . . Everyone wanted something done about the Indians, but not like *this*. There was no honor to it, and everyone told Jessup he was a rat the rest of his days. Finally, it all came full circle. An Orlando-area legislator took up Osceola's cause, and years later when they were naming a new county—you guessed it! And that's how Florida got a Dade *and* an Osceola County. . . ."

Country's breathing became increasingly shallow. Then she stopped breathing altogether, bowed up and quivered for ten seconds like she'd been harpooned—and collapsed on Serge's chest.

". . . Did I ever tell you Winston Churchill once stayed in Tampa as a young journalist? . . ."

Lenny and City were outside the room with their ears pressed against the door.

"What's going on in there?" whispered City.

"I don't know," said Lenny. "I think they're watching the History Channel."

Serge awoke the next morning to find a naked Lenny sitting in a chair with a toy squirt gun in one hand and his cock in the other. He had them pressed together, end to end.

"Jesus Christ!" yelled Serge. "What kind of sickness is *that*!"

"I'm squirting a cocaine solution up my urethra," said Lenny.

Serge shrugged. "I'll never understand the drug culture."

A half hour later, Serge was at the writing desk, playing with a Junior Wizard chemistry set he picked up at Toys "R" Us during the previous day's supply run. Different-colored liquids and powders filled the beakers and flasks and a rack of test tubes. In the middle of the desk was a glass distillation chamber over an unlit Bunsen burner.

Lenny asked to borrow the magnifying glass to examine his dick because "something's not right."

Serge didn't answer. He concentrated on tweaking the ratios of isotopes he had extracted from household cleaning products and fast food. Sodium palmitate, paraffin, naphthene hydrocarbons. Then he poured in a test tube filled with Bacardi 151.

"What's that?" Lenny asked as Serge added another test tube containing a clear, unidentified syrup.

"Eleven herbs and spices."

He lit the burner, and the solution began to boil and snake through a coiled glass tube into the condensate vapor trap.

Lenny sniffed the air. "Smells like bananas and coconuts."

"Then I must be close," said Serge. He looked out the window and saw the sun setting, so he killed the burner and let the solution cool. He grabbed his camera bag and a thick three-ring binder from one of the desk drawers and headed out the door for the water.

Zargoza sat near the shore in a cheap beach chair with frayed straps. He still wore his business suit, but his shoes were off and his toes deep in the sand. He was blinking and swallowing fifty percent more frequently than the average person, and his blood pressure made his head feel like a thermometer bulb. His left thumb had developed a slight involuntary shake. He drank haughtily from a large tumbler decorated with scuba flags, trickles of fluid running out each side of his mouth. The tumbler was filled equally with rum and Coke, and Zargoza constantly checked his watch, impatient for the alcohol to take effect and deliver him from the anxiety attack. It was a half hour till sunset, and he was as far up to the water as the fluffy, dry sand went. In front of him was the damp, packed sand of the littoral and the beach's pedestrian traffic. The day crowd was gone, the young body-watchers and pickup artists and beer guzzlers. This was the sunset club, a slightly higher sensibility. Beachcombers in their forties and fifties, joggers, people setting up camera tripods and long lenses. They walked down from their beach houses and condos and rentals and motel rooms; most had light jackets or sweat pants rolled above their calves.

Behind Zargoza were two goons/bodyguards, also in street clothes, sitting on a beach blanket playing poker.

The goons saw someone violate their no-fly zone, and they went for rods inside their jackets. Zargoza turned when he heard the commotion. "It's okay. Let him through."

Serge pulled up a stray beach chair and sat alongside Zargoza. He stuck his camera bag under the chair and set the three-ring binder in his lap.

"What do you have there?" asked Zargoza.

"My sunset album."

"Hmmmmmm."

"The pictures are arranged geographically," said Serge. "That's up in sawgrass at Yankeetown, and these are the flats off Homosassa. Here, the sunset reflects in the bayou at Tarpon Springs, and here it is from the Hurricane bar just down the road. This is over Lido Key, and here's Siesta Key and Boca Grande through the sea oats. . . ."

Zargoza was looking, not listening. He felt spiked walls closing in.

Serge began pulling all the photos from their slots and rearranging them chronologically and then alphabetically, then by hue. He took them out again and shuffled them and stuck them back in the book under some other criteria. He looked at it, shook his head, and started pulling the photos out again.

Zargoza reached over and slammed his palm down on the book. "Stop it! Just stop it! I'm nervous enough as it is!"

"No problem," said Serge. He put the book under his chair and pulled out his camera bag. Five minutes to sunset, the beach foot traffic slowed and then stopped. They produced binoculars and camcorders.

Serge aimed his camera at the sea and focused. He didn't like the lens. He changed it, then changed it back and refocused. He adjusted the aperture. He tried the camera body vertical and horizontal. Then tried it both ways again with the other lens.

Zargoza didn't even turn to face Serge. He hissed through his teeth: "Just take the picture or so help me I'm gonna hammer-throw that fucking camera in the ocean!"

Serge pressed the shutter button. Click. Again. Click. Advancing the film. Click, click, click, click, click. Zargoza closed his eyes and strangled the armrests of his beach chair.

26

The next day, Boris the Hateful Piece of Shit was wrapping up his morning shift in the heavily air-conditioned broadcast studios of radio station Blitz-99. "Remember, don't let your parents give you any crap, because they don't know squat! This is Boris the Hateful Piece of Sh—AHH-OOOO-GAH!"

As he stepped into the station's parking lot, he pressed a button on his keychain and his new Corvette beeped that it was unlocked. Boris planned to head over to the beach and the Proposition 213 rally, where he was scheduled as the main speaker that evening. Boris was not political, but he latched on to the Proposition 213 spearhead when he found it was a great way to score with bigot babes, who tended to be easier.

Because of his bulk, Boris could only get into his Corvette through a deliberate, time-consuming insertion like Wally Schirra. It was at least a fifteen-minute effort, and that was with the custom detachable steering wheel that snapped back on the column once he was in place. Boris didn't mind. The

Corvette's sleek lines and sharp, bullet exterior concealed the gelatinous lines of Boris's decidedly
parabolic fuselage. He had the driver's seat rigged
extra low, with as little of him visible above window
level as possible. Once inside, Boris the Hateful
Piece of Shit became Boris the Disembodied Head in
a Sexy Sports Car. He pulled out of the parking lot.
His bumper sticker read: "It sucks to be you."

A crowd gathered immediately when Boris's
Corvette cruised into the parking lot at the Calusa
Pointe condominiums. Boris got out of the car wearing dark sunglasses and a size XXXXXL metallic
silver jogging suit that was designed to deflect heat
and sometimes caused Boris to show up on radar.
There were two Cuban cigars in the shirt pocket of
the jogging suit, and he removed one and lit it. He
signed dozens of autographs with a simple circle as
he headed straight for the bar next door behind the
Hammerhead Ranch Motel.

The Proposition 213 rally wasn't for another four
hours, and the bar was as good a place as any to get
chicks. He walked inside and didn't take off his sunglasses. He took a seat against the wall, leaned back,
crossed his arms and thought: Come to Papa.

Boris had a few nibbles in the first hour. The
teenage girls had been star-struck, but not quite
enough to overcome the gag reflex to Boris's appearance and hygiene. After the last gaggle walked away,
Boris looked out the window to check the progress of
the workers preparing the outdoor stage for the rally
behind Calusa Pointe. He looked closer up the beach

and saw smaller, separate preparations under way for another function—a VIP waterfront luau for the visiting Olympic delegation. There were a few rows of beach chairs, a small podium and a giant wok-shaped dish that was a replica of the Olympic stadium torch and doubled as the barbecue.

Boris heard some laughing in the bar and turned his attention to City and Country. He liked what he saw. He realized they weren't going to come to him, so he chugged another beer and began working his way to his feet.

"What's shakin'?" Boris asked when he arrived at their table.

Country turned around and let out a startled yell upon first seeing Boris, which he did not take as a good sign. They tried to ignore him, but Boris couldn't take a hint, and he hovered over their table like a weather balloon.

Art walked into the bar and sat down three tables away from City and Country. He placed a zippered leather pouch on the table and stared at Boris.

Serge sipped a mineral water at the end of the bar and heard a rumpus over in the corner. Boris was trying to grope Country and had her by the arm. It looked like he was leaning in to administer a hickie.

"Let go!" Country yelled, and pulled her arm away.

"Lesbians!" Boris shouted, and stormed out of the bar.

Boris went out on the beach, where a crowd again formed. A guy on a beach lounger was made to get

up and offer his seat to Boris, who took off his jogging outfit to reveal an inadequate bathing suit, and
he reclined in the glow of adulation.

Art picked up his zippered leather pouch and
walked out of the bar down onto the beach. He got
inside a portable toilet set up for the Proposition 213
rally.

Boris was having the time of his life. Teenage girls
in bikinis surrounded him. Boris snapped his fingers
and someone materialized with a cell phone. Boris
chewed someone out for a minute, then tossed the
cell phone over his shoulder. His Man Friday caught
it on the fly, and a young girl handed Boris a fresh
drink and her phone number.

Art Tweed peered out a small, screened vent in the
side of the portable toilet. He ripped the screen out of
the way. He unzipped his leather bag, took out the
Colt Python and rested the barrel in the vent hole. An
easy shot at that distance. Art began squeezing the
trigger.

A high-pitched Latin twang came from the direction of Hammerhead Ranch. Boris and his retinue
turned around to see where it was coming from. Art
let off the trigger and withdrew the gun. He pressed
his eyeball to the vent hole to get a wider view of
what was going on.

"Lotion boy! Lotion boy!" said Serge as he
hopped light-footed down the beach wearing a small,
incredibly fake mustache. He stopped next to Boris's
lounger and set down a canvas beach bag. He pulled
out towels and tubes of lotion.

"I didn't know this place had a lotion boy," said Boris, glancing back at Hammerhead Ranch.

"*Sí! Sí!* Lotion boy!" said Serge, rubbing lotion vigorously over his palms and smacking them together.

Boris laid his head back on the lounger and closed his eyes. "In that case, it's about fucking time!" he said. "Give me the full treatment and make sure you get the pecs. But no faggot stuff or I'll snap your neck."

For the next five minutes, Serge lathered up Boris good, not missing a spot.

"Say, that doesn't smell too bad," said Boris. "Like bananas and coconut."

"*Sí! Sí!*"

When Serge was done, he just stood there, and Boris finally opened his eyes.

"Oh, you must be waiting for a tip," said Boris.

Serge nodded fast and smiled. "*Sí! Sí!*"

"Okay, here's your tip: Speak the fuckin' language!" Boris laughed at his own joke and looked around, and everyone else started laughing, too.

Serge smiled and nodded some more. "*Sí! Sí!*"

"What are you smiling about?" said Boris. "I just insulted you!"

"*Sí! Sí!*"

"Stop that!" yelled Boris. He leaned and shoved Serge in the chest. "Get the hell away from me! You give me the creeps."

"*Sí! Sí!*" Serge said and hopped away.

With Serge gone, Art had a clean shot, and he

lined up the Colt's barrel again in the vent hole. One of the girls moved farther out of the way, giving Art an even better shot. He couldn't miss. He closed one eye, carefully aligning the sight.

Boris pulled the last cigar from his shirt pocket and stuck it in his mouth. He looked around with a smirk at his fan club and nodded in the direction Serge had departed. "Man, those spics are stupid."

The kids laughed again. Art began squeezing the trigger. Boris raised a gold Zippo to his cigar. The Colt's hammer was all the way back. Boris flicked the Zippo.

Everyone was momentarily blinded as if a giant flash bulb had gone off. When they could see again, Boris was on fire from head to toe as if he was covered in napalm. Serge's new bananas and coconut island-scent napalm to be exact.

"Farts!" said Tweed, and he put his unfired gun away in disappointment.

Boris ran screaming for the nearest body of water—the pool only yards away behind Calusa Pointe. The incredible shrinking mayor of Beverly Shores saw Boris coming, and just as Boris reached the pool fence, the mayor slammed the gate shut. "Residents only!"

"Auuuuugh!" screamed the flaming Boris, and turned for the Gulf of Mexico. He reeled frantically toward the water, but he was beginning to succumb, stumbling on fire through the sand.

The president of the chamber of commerce was at the beach podium reading a proclamation welcoming the Olympic delegation when Boris staggered up and belly-flopped into the Olympic torch/hibachi, igniting a magnificent blue-orange flame. There were several oooooh's and ahhhhh's and then a polite round of clapping.

The delegates lined up and grabbed paper plates. The Viennese delegate spooned out potato salad and whispered to the representative from the Maldives: "Saw better special effects at Universal Studios."

Shhhhhh! Everybody shut up!" yelled Zargoza, pulling a chair up in front of the television in the boiler room. He clicked the set over to Florida Cable News. The goons gathered around.

Zargoza had sent C. C. Flag out to Vista Isles that afternoon to calm things down. The place was getting a lot of bad attention from all the missing Alzheimer's patients. State officials everywhere, going through files, interviewing people. The investigative TV crew showed up unexpectedly. That was because Zargoza had tipped them off personally—told them the famous Daddy-O of Rock 'n' Roll, C. C. Flag, would show up to answer questions.

It was Zargoza's attempt to staunch the bleeding. There had been a damning, week-long series of TV reports about the nursing home. Zargoza was sick and tired of seeing some stupid factotum at Vista Isles acting defensive on television, stuttering, vacillating, giving wrong answers or, worst of all, running and hiding in a closet. This was the real problem, thought Zargoza. It couldn't possibly be that he was kidnapping patients. He was convinced that investigators had descended on the home for one reason and one reason only—the staff wasn't telegenic.

He was right.

Zargoza wondered how deep into the newscast Flag would be. Maybe fourth or fifth item. Third if they were lucky. He couldn't wait to see Flag confidently lying on the air. That ought to call off the state agencies. What's fair is fair.

To Zargoza's surprise and delight, Flag led off the news. There he was, filling out the screen in his safari jacket and pith helmet. Zargoza heard cheering and clapping in the background.

"All right, Flag!" Zargoza said. "Way to go!"

On TV, Flag stepped to the microphone again and held up his hands for everyone to be quiet. ". . . And another thing," he barked, "I say cut off their benefits. And what are their kids doing taking up valuable space in our classrooms when they should be out in the fields picking tomatoes? And if they don't like subminimum wage, they should have chosen another country to sneak into, and learn what real oppression is . . . like Canada!"

The applause was overwhelming.

"What? What the hell's *this*?" said Zargoza.

The television camera pulled back to show C. C. Flag on a large stage.

This isn't Vista Isles, thought Zargoza. This is the condominium next door. Standing onstage next to Flag, applauding his every word, was Malcolm Kefauver, the incredible shrinking mayor of Beverly Shores. Behind them hung an American flag and a giant banner: "Proposition 213."

"Holy shit," Zargoza yelled. "This is that stupid anti-immigration thing. This can't be happening!"

The TV panned over the large crowd in front of the stage. Several people waved signs: *"They don't look right!"* *"Different is evil!"* and *"If you can't understand something, kill it!"*

Zargoza leaped to his feet in front of the TV. "You bastard! You stupid, stupid bastard! What are you doing to me! Somebody give me a gun so I can kill myself."

One of the goons handed him a gun.

"No, you fool!" He slapped the gun away. "Go get Flag, now!"

Three goons ran out the door.

Zargoza squatted like Yogi Berra in front of the TV set, punching a fist into an open hand. On TV, there was a commotion up onstage. Flag struggled with three men, then disappeared off the back of the scaffolding.

Moments later the door to Zargoza's boiler room slammed open, and the goons hustled C. C. Flag inside and pushed him to the ground.

"You wanted to see me?" Flag asked, standing up and brushing off his pants.

"Have you lost your mind! What do you think you're doing!"

"I met the mayor. Real nice guy. His main speaker for the rally didn't show, so he asked me to fill in."

"Shut up! I know what you were doing. But why? We've got state and federal investigators all over us, the Diaz Boys are running around like the James Gang, there's probably a hit man after me, and I send

you to fix a little problem and you turn up on TV
coming off like Son of Sam!"

"That might be a little strong."

"I want you to stop it! Now!"

"I can't."

"What did I just hear?!"

"I can't stop it. It's grown too big. My charisma
has become a force to be reckoned with."

Zargoza knocked Flag to the carpet and began
kicking him in the rear. "Reckon with this foot in
your ass, you ultra-nationalist prick! Now get over to
the nursing home!"

27

C. C. Flag slammed two more shots of Irish whiskey from the decanter in the office at Vista Isles. The press was gone; and so was the Vista Isles staff. Zargoza had ordered Flag over to the home after the Proposition 213 fiasco. He'd done his best to explain away all the missing Medicare patients by changing the subject and bashing immigrants. Now he deserved a reward. He hit the intercom and called the night nurse.

She arrived in his doorway with her medication cart. "You buzzed me?"

She was young and curvy with long sandy hair. Not too hard on the eyes, Flag thought.

"Come over here and have a drink with me," he said.

"I'd love to, but I have to make my rounds."

"Don't worry about your rounds. I have a lot of pull around here."

"But these are prescription medications. These residents are on a very rigid schedule. Some of their lives depend on it."

Flag picked up a medicine container. "Oooooooh! Dilaudid!" He dumped the pills in the breast pocket of his safari jacket.

"Hey! Those are for a patient who's gonna die from cancer!"

"My point exactly."

"Wait!" she said. "I've seen you on TV. You're the Proposition 213 guy. You're my hero. You really tell it like it is. I'm so tired of how migrant workers keep exploiting us."

She strolled over to the desk. "Well, I guess one drink won't hurt anything."

"Now you're talkin'!" Flag poured her a double over rocks.

By the time the first drink hit her bloodstream, she was on her third. Then Flag forced more liquor into her. Then she was bent over Flag's desk without panties. Then she was bent over the toilet, hair hanging in the water. Funny, thought Flag, I could have sworn she was more attractive earlier.

"Hey, baby. I gotta use the restroom," said Flag, banging on the door. "Get a move on."

She only moaned and her head lolled over the bowl.

"Damn," said Flag. Already smashed, he poured another. When she was still in there fifteen minutes later, he could wait no longer. He decided to use the restroom down the hall. He was down to his underwear and socks, so he grabbed a Vista Isles bathrobe from the closet and headed out the door.

* * *

A little after midnight a brown panel truck pulled up outside the veranda of Vista Isles and two of the Diaz Boys climbed out.

They flashed corporate ID at the front desk and made their way to the third floor and poked around.

Weaving up the hallway toward them was an old man in a Vista Isles robe. They watched him smack into a doorjamb and bounce off a fire extinguisher.

The man walked up in his bathrobe and socks, and he put out his hand to shake. "How ya doin', young fellas. I'm C. C. Flag. Hope ya'll will vote for Proposition 213. Take the state back from the fuckin' Latins."

The two Diaz Boys looked at each other and smiled.

"I'm the Daddy-O of Rock 'n' Roll. I'm a famous radio personality, loved and admired by millions," said Flag, swaying off balance.

One of the Diaz Boys whispered to the other: "Classic dementia."

The second one turned to Flag. "Sir, are you a Medicare patient?"

"Medicare?" said Flag. "Absolutely! I'm an American. I deserve my Social Security and my Medicare, goddammit!"

The two looked at each other again and grinned. This was too easy.

They slapped electrical tape over Flag's mouth and carried him down the fire escape to the waiting truck.

* * *

An hour later, Flag's Vista Isles robe was gone and he was dressed in homeless rags in anticipation of his drop at the Tampa bus station. The Diaz Boys took the Twenty-second Street exit on Interstate 4 so they could catch a little of the Latin Heritage parade on their way downtown. They pulled onto a side street next to Seventh Avenue and found a parking space with a good view.

The parade hadn't started yet, but the two Diaz Boys were already talking excitedly about the Gloria Estefan Revue. "It's supposed to sound exactly like her," said Juan.

They turned around and looked behind them. The back doors of the van were open and Flag was gone. The two looked at each other and shrugged. Bus station, Ybor City, what's the difference? They looked back out the windshield and waited for the parade.

Three Latin Heritage Festival officials were at the parade staging area on the east end of Seventh Avenue, going over their clipboards. Everything was ready except the grand marshal hadn't arrived and two road-tour members of Miami Sound Machine were still in the can. The officials saw an old bum in tattered rags wobbling toward them.

One pointed with his clipboard. "What's this comin' at us?"

Another official was about to run the bum off when he felt a twinge of recognition. "Hey, you're someone famous. . . . I got it! You're that guy on the sweepstakes envelopes! . . . C. C. Flag."

The chairman of the Latin Heritage Festival grabbed Flag's hand and pumped it enthusiastically. "I'm a big fan."

"Is he our grand marshal?"

"He's got to be," said the chairman. He turned to Flag. "You done parades before?"

"Of course I've done parades."

"I dunno," said the first official. "That's not what it says on my clipboard. It's supposed to be someone from the mayor's office."

"That's got to be an out-of-date program," said the chairman. "You want somebody's nephew when we can have a bona fide celebrity?"

"So what's with his rags?"

"You idiot! He's supposed to be one of the refugee rafters," said the chairman. "That's this year's theme. Weren't you at the meeting?"

The official threw up his hands in surrender. "Whatever you say." He turned to the parade's support crew and clapped his hands to get their attention. "Okay, let's get this show on the road." He turned and yelled at the row of blue portable toilets: "Miami Sound Machine—time to shit or get off the pot!"

The festival chairman waved over two assistants, who placed a silk sash across Flag's chest and helped him up on the grand marshal float.

The Diaz Boys were enjoying the parade immensely, especially the Gloria Estefan Revue, which featured a prerecorded tape of Gloria regretting that she couldn't appear at the festival in person and then cuing her latest album while bitter members of the Miami Sound Machine danced and played backup.

Then came the next float, carrying a realistic replica of a Cuban refugee raft. Standing in the middle of the raft and waving to the crowd was C. C. Flag, wearing a gold satin sash that read "Mr. Latin Heritage—Tampa Bay."

Juan and Rafael Diaz suddenly recognized the man on the float going by, and they exchanged worried glances.

"Whoops," said Juan.

He started up the van to get the hell out of there. He was about to pull out of the parking space when a black Jeep Eagle sped by and skidded up to Seventh Avenue. Three members of the Posse Comatose jumped out of the Jeep, charged through the spectators and climbed up the grand marshal's float. They began whaling on Flag.

Because of concerns of violence surrounding the upcoming vote on Proposition 213, the parade was attended by a contingent from the militant Hyphenated-Americans Defense League. For security reasons, the members attended the parade in disguise. And when C. C. Flag came under attack, the brass section of the Miami Sound Machine jumped down from its float and charged the Posse Comatose. It was a near-riot. Flag fell off the back of the float and was scooped up and pulled to safety by unlicensed gypsy nacho vendors working the skirt of the crowd.

28

The day that City and Country left Alabama for Florida, they didn't know they were going until they were already driving.

Friday, nine A.M., City began her shift at Piggly Wiggly on register eighteen, ringing up an economy box of candy corn, off-brand hair spray and ninety-nine-cent false eyelashes. Back at the apartment, Country put on her uniform and nametag and walked out the front door. On Monday, Country's Pinto had blown a gasket, whatever that meant. The mechanic had put the Pinto on the lift, wiped his brow with a greasy rag and undertaken the highly technical diagnostic procedure of trying to guess the maximum amount Country would agree to pay. The figure was way off, and the Pinto had sat ever since in a sea of disabled, gutted cars and free-range dogs behind Big Al's Garage and Beverage at the county line on State Road 67. When their boss, Mrs. Frigola, learned that Country depended on City for transportation, she staggered their shifts an hour, and Country was forced to buy a fifteen-dollar banana bike with a loose chain at Crimson Tide Pawn. For the third day, Country climbed on the high-handlebar child's bike and pedaled off for work four miles away. The first two days, Country arrived at the supermarket sticky, tired and late. Frigola said if it happened again, she was fired.

Ten A.M., City rang up a sack of pork rinds and checked her watch, then the front door. No Country. She looked over at Frigola, who was watching the door with a blend of rage and delight.

Ten-forty A.M., City saw Country through the front window of the Piggly Wiggly, drenched, walking a banana bike dragging a broken chain, forty minutes late. Country leaned the bike against the shopping carts and walked through the automatic door. Frigola waited until she was well inside and loudly fired her in front of everyone.

City bit her lip. She prayed: Country, don't say anything. Don't hit her, and *definitely* don't cry.

Country didn't. She just turned and walked out. City stopped ringing up items mid-customer and ran after her.

Frigola yelled, "You leave and you're fired, too!" but City never looked back.

Ten P.M., City and Country were peeling the labels off their fourth beers at The Hole in the Wall, a dive on the far side of town from campus favored for the eighty-five-cent longnecks. City's Torino was two hundred yards down the road from the bar, where it also had broken down. All in all, not a good week for the girls. As the house band mangled "Brown

Sugar," City and Country resigned themselves to the most constructive course of action. Unwind, maybe get a little wild, and put the day's events behind them. Get a good night's sleep and start checking the classifieds.

The bar was bare bones. Every surface was wood and had been gouged and regouged with large knives. There weren't any windows, just thick wire mesh and roll-down shutters. In the men's room, the urinal was a long trough along one wall filled with ice and disinfectant cakes, and the sink was a large rounded trough on the other wall. There was a sign above it: "This is a sink!"

It was a loud crowd and City and Country had to shout to talk. The crowd was almost all locals, but there was a table against the side wall with two frat boys and a sorority chick who'd decided to go slumming. From the trio's plurality of affections, it was clear neither of the guys was the woman's steady, but both wanted in her pants. It was also clear that Sorority Sister was a damn fine juggler, holding both their interest without committal. City nudged Country and pointed. One of the guys was looking their way, then both were looking. Soon they were waving City and Country over.

The guys didn't look too shabby, kinda young and adorable—Andrew McCarthy types—and City winked at Country and they stood up.

City and Country counted ten empty longnecks and the dregs of five pink poodle drinks as they arrived at the table. The frat brothers stood and held out chairs as City and Country sat down, but Sorority Sister's body language said the fur was standing up on her back.

The sister was an eye-catching Marilyn Monroe blonde with a name straight from the heart of Dixie—Billie Joe Bob ("Bo"). She was five-six with a string of add-a-beads, a cute little Valerie Bertinelli nose, big tits showcased in a tight pink sweater. But in the end, she was a peroxide-and-pancake makeup beauty, whereas City and Country were the Real Mc-Coys, and everyone at the table knew it.

Five minutes into the conversation. "So you girls work at Piggly Wiggly . . ." said Billie Joe, and she let a snicker escape. "That's just lovely. How bucolic."

The men were overcome with beer-chuckles and grinned at Billie Joe.

City smiled, too, as she noticed the three triangles of the Delta Delta Delta sorority on the woman's sweater.

"I heard a good joke," said City. "If you can't get a date, *tri*-Delta."

The guys broke up laughing even harder this time and turned to the unamused Billie Joe, and the guys' expressions retreated to serious.

The band rolled into "Born on the Bayou," and the guy on the left shouted, "I love this song!" He started to ask City to dance, but Billie Joe clamped onto him and nuzzled into his neck. Before she knew it, the other guy had taken Country's hand and headed for the dance floor. One of the juggling balls had just fallen.

When that guy got back from the dance floor and

sat down, Billie Joe put a hand on his thigh under the table—and the other guy popped up and asked City to dance. It went on this way for hours; Billie Joe could keep a grip on either one she wanted, but not both. A game of sexual brinksmanship, the old bird-in-the-hand dilemma, and the longer it went on, the more Billie Joe knew she risked losing both.

The alcohol kept coming—more longnecks and poodle drinks—everyone getting seriously bent. Billie Joe leaned over the table to Country. "Want a taste of this? It's really good." As she leaned, she whispered "bitch" and dumped the whole pink drink square in Country's chest.

Everyone was on their feet, suddenly awake. "I'm such a klutz," said Billie Joe. The guys were grabbing napkins from nearby tables. Billie Joe smirked at Country.

Then things took an unexpected turn. In the chaos, both frat boys were soon leading City and Country to the dance floor as the band began "Long Cool Woman" by the Hollies. Billie Joe was aghast—all the juggling balls had hit the floor.

"... *Saturday night I was downtown, working for the FBI . . .*"

Both couples had their arms around each other's neck. Back at the table, Billie Joe found an unfinished beer and drained it, grabbed her purse and got up.

On the dance floor, Country broke off from her date. Under the influence, she closed her eyes and did a sexy grind in the middle of the floor. She threw her hips in synch with the music and ran her hands slowly down the outside of her legs.

"... *Suddenly we heard a siren, and everybody starting to run—jumpin' up across the table when I heard somebody shootin' a gun* ..."

Space cleared around Country and everyone else's dancing slowed. The floor was in dim red light, and Country now started running her hands up the inside of her thighs. Her hips gyrated in a slow circle to the song's chorus. Her eyes were still closed but her full lips had opened wide and hungry. One of the Andrew McCarthys took a step back and said, "God *damn!*" Even the band was distracted.

Then, just as her hands reached the tops of her thighs—in perfect time with the tempo change in the last verse—Country's arms shot up over her head, and she began shaking her shoulders and hips like a go-go dancer.

With that signal, everyone else joined in and danced their heads off.

"... *I told her don't get scared cause you're gonna be spared—I'd rather be forgivin' if I wanna spend a livin' with a long cool woman in a black dress* ..."

At the end of the number, everyone on the floor cheered and clapped for themselves. City and Country pecked the men on the cheeks and excused themselves for the ladies' room, giggling along the way like schoolgirls.

Inside, they examined themselves in the mirror to see how hammered they looked. Everything was checking out fine when they heard a weird noise coming from one of the stalls.

City and Country looked at each other puzzled and then back at the stall. Some kind of chaos inside, bumping around, then cursing. A leather bag hit the floor and the contents of a woman's purse scattered under the stall door and onto the tiles of the restroom: lipstick, hairbrush, dispenser of contraceptive foam, car keys, cocaine vial.

More cursing.

The stall door opened and Billie Joe started to reach down for her belongings. When she saw City and Country, she stopped and stood up straight. She held a small lacquer tray and a steak knife she had gotten from the short-order kitchen, to chop at a Peruvian pebble. Her jeans were around her ankles and panties at her knees. Powder all over her nose and smeared on her left cheek. She was wreckage.

City and Country were stunned silent, but Billie Joe looked at them and yelled, "Youuuuu!"—accusation, verdict and sentence all in one syllable. She pointed the steak knife at them and charged, except her clothes were still around her legs and she was only able to manage a ridiculous waddle. City and Country had to hold each other up they were laughing so hard. Then Billie Joe ran out of steam and toppled forward on her face.

City and Country fell into hysterics. They resisted looking back at Billie Joe because it would only bust them up again; their sides were aching and they were having trouble getting air.

City finally looked back and her face changed. "Wait! What the hell is this!" A deep purple pool was spreading out from under Billie Joe. Country leaned forward and saw the tip of the steak knife sticking out the back of Billie Joe's neck.

"Jesus!"

She flipped Billie Joe over, pulled the bloody knife out of her throat and flung it aside. When the blade came out, the severed jugular squirted all over Country, and she grabbed the woman's neck trying to stop the bleeding. The more life leaked out of Billie Joe, the harder Country squeezed.

It was no use; blood was still getting out, and it was over in seconds.

Country stood and saw blood on her hands and wiped them on her jeans.

City was jumping up and down. "Oh my God! We're dead!"

"What are you talking about?" shouted Country.

The pair did a quick once-around the restroom. Knife with bloody fingerprints under a toilet, more bloody fingerprints on the bruises on Billie Joe's neck, and blood all over Country.

She began to shake. "We didn't do anything!"

"Listen to me!" said City. "This is Alabama—I know about separate justice. She's some rich bitch and we're poor trash."

"We didn't do anything!"

City looked at the door and pointed. "Lock it!"

Country ran for the dead bolt and turned it fast, and City started scooping the contents back into Billie Joe's purse.

"What are you doing?" asked Country.

"We gotta get outta the state. There's some money here."

"Neither of us has a car."

"She does," said City, holding up the set of keys with an Alfa Romeo fob. "There can't be more than one Spider outside in the lot. Let's just hope the guys didn't drive."

There was a pounding on the door, a woman's voice. "I gotta pee!"

City opened the door fast and both of them knocked over the waiting woman as they ran out. They turned down a side hallway, away from the dance floor, and burst out the plywood back door and into the parking lot.

29

$\mathcal{T}$he mood at Hammerhead Ranch had gone sour.

The heat wave continued. The excitement of just arriving at the island motel had turned to the bitter drudgery of washing clothes at the island Laundromat.

There was a stifling funk that hung heavy like ozone. The place was getting listless yet jumpy. There was the feeling of the end game.

The wind had almost completely stopped. People languished in The Florida Room, drinking more, talking less. There was little movement except the tapping of fingers on tables. The bartender was getting divorced and stopped wiping glasses. People held their drinks up to the light, looking at water spots. Serge was at a table with a jeweler's magnifying glass stuck in his eye, trying to sell a plain rock for ten thousand dollars to two members of the Olympic Committee.

C. C. Flag staggered into the bar with half his clothes torn off, welts up and down his torso, and a shredded gold sash hanging off his shoulder.

"What the hell happened to you?!" asked Zargoza.

"Tampa Bay is a primitive place," Flag said and wobbled to the bar.

A hesitant private investigator from Alabama named Paul checked into the motel and started snooping around, showing a picture of Art to people in the bar. Everyone dummied up. They grabbed his private eye badge and threw it on the roof.

Five Navy SEALs paddled ashore in a black raft and sprinted silently between the beach blankets and sand castles up to room four, hoping to surprise a band of arms dealers. The SEALs lobbed concussion grenades through the window, knocked down the door with a fiberglass truncheon, ran inside and neutralized the occupants in three point two seconds with the Vulcan nerve pinch. Except the arms dealers were in the next room, and the SEALs had subdued a vacationing family from Akron. A TV camera crew from Florida Cable News's *Cops and Robbers— Live!* charged into the room after the SEALs to incriminate the Ohio residents in their underwear before millions of viewers.

Nobody in the bar gave a damn.

Vacation had turned into a grind. The sexual tension was gone. Exciting, mysterious strangers became tired, irritable neighbors with uninteresting secrets. Even City and Country were starting to look rough. They had taken to sitting at their regular corner table and openly smoking dope the whole day. They stared puzzled and angry at their joints. "What's wrong with this shit? It doesn't work anymore!"

Lenny wandered into the bar.

"Hey, asshole," the bartender yelled at him. "You wanna get your two friends out of my bar and into some kind of twelve-step program?"

"What's the matter?" asked Lenny.

"What's the matter?! You've turned them into pot gnats!"

"Marijuana is nature's medicine."

"You got to get 'em out of here. They keep bugging me to hook 'em up with a better connection. They say your stuff's no good. Quote: 'It's a bunch of shitty brown Mexican shake that doesn't even get you high—and there's too much lumber.' Where did they learn to talk like that?"

"I don't know why it doesn't get them high."

"Because they smoke it round the clock! They're burnt out! It's like the Fabulous Furry Freak Brothers over there!"

"Have you asked them to cool it out?"

"They're *your* monsters—*you* drive 'em back into the sea!"

The Florida Cable News weather report came on the television over the bar.

"Hey, that's not Toto!" said someone at the bar.

He was right. There was a new dog on the set. Looked a lot like Toto, but the audience was too familiar with the real thing to be duped. The new weather dog was called Toto II, with no mention of what happened to Roman numeral one.

Toto II danced on a large storm-tracking map on the floor of the studio. Hurricane Rolando-berto had crossed the Caribbean Sea. It was supposed to hit the Yucatán but unexpectedly curved up into the Gulf of

Mexico. Revised projections had it heading north and passing Tampa Bay in twenty-four hours, missing it by a hundred miles to the left and making landfall somewhere between Pensacola and New Orleans.

"Where's that storm going now?" asked weatherman Guy Rockney. Toto II danced on the map in a little pirate outfit as a ceiling camera filmed the dog from overhead.

"Looks like it's still heading north," said Rockney, *"so you can breathe easy, Tampa Bay."*

*U*p the coast of Florida and around the horn to Alabama, Mississippi and Louisiana, a pre-hurricane custom was under way. Journalists flocked to the beach communities, facing out to sea, moving laterally along the coast like fiddler crabs as landfall predictions changed by the hour—trying not to be the guy who missed by two hundred miles last year and now served mashed potatoes with an ice cream scoop in the Action News 9 cafeteria. They stood on seawalls and piers and jetties and beaches, in bright raincoats, in even brighter sunshine, from Biloxi to Panama City.

A reporter in a hazard-orange raincoat stood on a wharf in Pascagoula. Her image filled the screen of the TV set anchored high on the wall of the crew lounge at MacDill Air Force Base on the south end of the Tampa peninsula. The crew of *The Rapacious Reno* had been deployed to Tampa for public relations duty, and they lay around the lounge drinking coffee, smoking and eating out of vending machines. They drew doodles and worked crosswords.

Ex–Lieutenant Colonel Lee "Southpaw" Barnes lit a Pall Mall. Milton "Bananas" Foster kept saying, "I got a *baaaaaad* feeling about this mission!"

Marilyn Sebastian was turned on as William "The Truth" Honeycutt beat the crud out of a vending machine whose corkscrew didn't drop his Jujyfruit.

"Nine-letter word beginning with *G* for a colorless syrup used in food preservation and skin lotions," said weather officer "Tiny" Baxter.

"Glycerine," said Major Larry "Montana" Fletcher, and Baxter leaned over and jotted in his newspaper.

An oscillating siren went off. The crew jumped up and ran out the door and across the runway in their flight suits.

When they got inside the plane, most were stunned to see three dozen old men with white beards sitting on a long bench in the cargo bay, wearing parachutes and drinking beer.

"Jumpin' Jesus!" said Barnes. "I'm not believin' my motherfuckin' eyes!"

"Easy now. Everything will be all right," said Montana. "This has all been officially approved by headquarters. These are the Flying Hemingways."

"The *what*?"

"You've heard of the Flying Elvises? Same thing, only different."

"Those were professional skydivers who dressed like Elvis. But *these* guys—" They all turned to see the Look-Alikes chugging beer, bumping into each other, farting and belching in graded octaves like a pipe organ.

"These orders come from the top," said Montana. "PR duty just like when we do flyovers for air shows, holidays and funerals of large political donors. Before we do recon on the hurricane, we're supposed to fly over the beach and drop the Hemingways as the entertainment for something called the Proposition 213 Jamboree."

"What's that?"

"No idea. But the mayor of a place called Beverly Shores apparently has a lot of clout. He pulled the strings."

Twenty minutes later, they were at ten thousand feet, almost directly over the Proposition 213 stage. The back gate of the Hercules dropped open. A green light in the cargo bay came on. The Hemingways struggled to their feet and clipped their static lines to an overhead cable. They were pressed together in a tight line, with only seconds to all get out of the plane once the signal was given. Jumpmaster Jethro Maddox stood by the open doorway and gave the high sign. The line began to move. He smacked each on the butt as they ran past and dove out of the plane. "Go! Go! Go! Go! Go! Go! . . ."

It was not a precision team, and by the sixth jumper their legs tangled and they started going down in a chain reaction. A few at the front made it out of the plane, but the rest of the line snarled, and the Look-Alikes toppled over on the floor into a big blob like a single brainless organism, a giant polyp of Papa-plasm. Honeycutt radioed Montana what was going on, and Montana pulled the nose of the Hercules up as high as he could, pouring the rest of the Hemingways out the back of the plane like a margarita.

They left the Hercules at all angles, on top of each other, arms and legs spindling. Down at the rally, spectators watched with binoculars. It looked like the jump the night before D day, when bad weather sprayed the pre-invasion force all over the countryside, everywhere but the target. Some Hemingways landed hundreds of yards out in the Gulf, others on the boulevard and in the shopping plazas. One chute snagged on a sailboat mast. Another Hemingway came down behind the walls of a N.O.W. retreat and was beaten severely. Jethro Maddox ended up hanging from the tallest palm tree on the grounds of Hammerhead Ranch. He pedaled his legs in the air until he was exhausted. Then he began consuming the six-pack that was stored in the pack usually reserved for the emergency chute. He fell asleep in his harness.

An hour later, *The Rapacious Reno* was somewhere in the middle of the Gulf of Mexico. "You can't fly for shit," Barnes told Montana. "And another thing . . ."

Montana held a hand up for Barnes to be silent as weather officer Baxter called the pilot over the intercom. Montana turned the plane over to Barnes and joined Baxter at the weather console. They studied the instruments with concern.

Baxter looked up. "Sir, we have a change of direction in the storm."

"Better call Miami," said Montana. "Give 'em the news."

𝒟ue to global warming, El Niño, La Niña, and a host of end-of-the-millennium volcanic eruptions, mud slides and biblical floods, the National Hurricane Center in Miami was only mildly surprised that a catastrophic hurricane had caromed ninety degrees and was about to make landfall. Officials at the center got a late jump reacting, but quickly made up time and issued the warning. Along Florida's west coast, every major television and radio station put out the word that a force-four hurricane was hooking right into Tampa Bay.

Except one.

At Florida Cable News, things hadn't gone so well during Toto II's second day on the job. The dog had been dressed in the uniform of a Tampa Bay Lightning hockey player, and the crew had worked much of the morning trying to get it to hold the miniature hockey stick. Just before airtime, a stagehand wrapped a rubber band several times around the stick and Toto II's right front paw.

Instead of doing the weather dance, Toto spent the better part of the segment trying to chew his leg off.

"He looks like he's in a lot of pain," said the anchorwoman.

"No, no, no!" weatherman Guy Rockney said with a chuckle. "He wants to play hockey! He's trying to get a better grip on the stick."

"His paw is turning blue!" said the woman. "Help him!"

"You're overreacting," said Rockney. He attempted to prop the dog up and make it dance like a marionette on top of the anchor desk.

"Guy, what's the forecast?" said the annoyed male anchor, watching the production clock.

"Oh, everything will be fine. Sunny. Lots of sun," Rockney said without looking up from Toto II, who finally bit Rockney between the thumb and forefinger.

"Owww! Dammit!" said Rockney, and he grabbed Toto II by the hair on the back of his neck and snapped his head back. Toto growled and yelped, and Rockney said "Fuck" on the air. He struggled with the dog and fell off his chair, and they both disappeared behind the anchor desk, where there was more growling and cursing. The anchorman dropped his face into his hands; the anchorwoman froze with her mouth open. The station's switchboard lit up.

Three dark government sedans raced in single file across the state on Interstate 4 toward Tampa Bay. The occupants wore suits, sunglasses. Stern faces, nobody spoke.

Lenny and Serge made their standard supply run to Island Grocery in the afternoon, oblivious to the hurricane fear gripping the rest of the population.

"What's happening?" said Lenny, standing in an

aisle, looking at the empty shelves. "It's like communism!"

Canned goods, bottled water, potato chips—all gone. Lenny whimpered when he saw the empty beer section.

"We better get moving," said Serge. They drove to the mainland and hit three grocery stores, but the story was the same. They kept driving around.

"We're in luck!" said Serge, pointing. "The video store's still open."

Lenny hit the brakes and swung into the parking lot.

The place was empty, and the pair had their pick of movies. Serge grabbed *Palmetto, Strip Tease, Out of Sight, The Mean Season, Ruby in Paradise, Body Heat, Some Like It Hot* and *Key Largo*.

"This is great!" said Serge. "All Florida, from camp to classic."

They jumped in Lenny's Cadillac and headed back to the island. Nobody was going in their direction—everyone was coming the other way over the bridge, the cars in a solid line, standing still. People got out of their vehicles to see the cause of the holdup. Someone's car had stalled at the foot of the bridge. Over the driver's protests, six people pushed the vehicle off the road and it rolled down the embankment into the water. The driver yelled. A weeping woman held a swaddled infant on the shoulder of the causeway. The car was full of clothes and personal belongings that floated up in the passenger compartment as the water line rose in the car. Then just the top of the roof showed, and a bunch of bubbles, and it went under. The traffic resumed without a skipped note, indifferent to the stranded family.

"I smell panic," said Serge. "These are different animals now. They're starting to winnow out the weak at the fringe of the herd. We need to hurry or this could affect our snack situation."

"Affirmative," said Lenny, and he accelerated. They raced around to convenience stores, grabbing whatever was left, packs of cheese and crackers, Fiddle Faddle, fortune cookies.

They tooled along the Gulf Coast, bobbing their heads to the radio, riding the *now*.

Serge suddenly bolted up in his seat, and tremors made high-frequency waves in his cheeks. Spitfoam bubbled at the corners of his mouth.

"What's wrong?" Lenny asked. Serge couldn't answer, and Lenny pulled over and made an emergency stop on top of a stray cat.

Serge looked like he might be swallowing his tongue, so Lenny grabbed his head and started jimmying his clenched jaws with the car keys. Serge's muscles began to uncoil and the spell soon passed. Lenny released.

Serge returned to normal and looked around as if he had been rudely awakened.

"What was that?" asked Lenny.

"Flashback."

"Vietnam?"

"No. The Garo Yepremian pass."

Lenny quickly remembered and shook with the willies.

"The game was in the bag!" said Serge. "Fourteen-zip in the fourth quarter—I was dick-dancin' on broken glass . . ."

"We still won," said Lenny. "Let it go."

Serge reached in his pocket and pulled out the crack vial that had stored his street tranquilizers. "I'm all out."

"You want me to try to find a drug hole or maybe break into a veterinary clinic?"

"No way," said Serge. "This is the only way to experience a natural disaster—throw a little schizophrenia in the soup."

As they drove, they saw plywood up everywhere. A few people sat outside in chairs and cradled rifles and shotguns, ready for the early-bird looters. It was getting lonely and eerie, like one of those bad sixties sci-fi movies Serge had seen as a child, life after the nuclear war.

Some people had spray-painted the numbers of their insurance policies on the plywood. Others wrote messages directed at the hurricane itself: "Go away, Rolando-berto!"

"Who's picking the names for these storms?" said Lenny.

There were no other cars anymore, and Serge and Lenny continued on toward the motel, sitting low, rocking out to Peter Gabriel's "Big Time" blasting from the stereo and echoing off the empty buildings, the only sound in the streets.

*W*hen Lenny and Serge made it back from the supply run, Florida Cable News was playing on the tele-

vision over the bar. But everyone in The Florida
Room was facing the other way, looking out the windows at the purple sky and the pounding surf rolling
in from the Gulf. The waves were enormous and the
largest splashed near the back steps of the bar.

"You think something's going on we haven't heard
about?" asked Lenny. "A tropical storm or maybe a
hurricane?"

"No way," said Art Tweed, pointing back at the
bar. "We've had the TV on all day. They would have
said something."

So all they did was close the shutters on the windward side and devote themselves to the haste of
drinking that accompanies inclement weather at a
tropical resort.

An hour later, however, they could ignore the signs
no longer. They were faced with the most accurate
predictor yet of hurricane landfall.

The surfers showed up.

30

*T*oday the hurricane arrived.

Events stacked up fast, and suddenly it was too late.

It began dark, breezy and chilly. Looked awful but no serious wind yet. Then, in the span of a minute, a stinging rain came onshore and the shallow area of the beach began to roil with whitecaps. The wind increased unevenly. It moved onto land in a series of body-punching gusts. People can brace and still walk against a steady wind, but the sudden bursts caught a dozen guests at Hammerhead Ranch between buildings and made them stumble like they were drunk.

The surfers were swept out to sea, cheering with delight.

Lenny wandered stoned out of the bar and across the parking lot, staring up at the dark sky. Just then, three black sedans with NASA emblems on the doors raced down Gulf Boulevard and whipped into the parking lot of Hammerhead Ranch.

All the sedans' doors opened at once, and a platoon of G-men in mirror sunglasses jumped out.

Dark suits, white shirts, wires running from tiny transistor earphones into their collars.

"We're looking for Lenny Lippowicz."

"You found him."

Lenny was gang-tackled.

"Where's our moon rock?" They stuffed him inside the lead sedan and drove away.

The wind increased.

Some motel guests jumped in cars and tried to get off the island, but the bridges were barricaded and it was a challenge getting back, their cars pushed sideways lane to lane. A power line popped loose and snaked and sparked at a bus stop. The windshield wipers couldn't keep up with the load, and the faint outline of large objects started moving across the road. A blow-up kiddie pool sailed in front of a car like a flying saucer. The cloth awning from the entrance of a pizza restaurant came off, aluminum frame and all, and tumbled across Gulf Boulevard. Crazy stuff suddenly appeared out of the blinding rain, plastered on the windshields. Shoe insole, Turkish menu, colostomy bag, Hemingway.

One of the guests missed the driveway and struck a sign support at Hammerhead Ranch. He jumped out of the car, left it running and sprinted for the motel. The rest of the guests were already barricading the rooms. They slid dressers to the doors and pulled mattresses off the box springs, leaning them against the windows. The electrical fuses blew in sequence like a zipper, with a loud *pow-pow-pow*. The lights went on and off several times and then out for good.

Zargoza and his men stacked steel desks along the western side of the boiler room, trying not to show fear. City and Country hid in their closet. The International Olympic Committee was jammed into another room, praying in a symphony of tongues. Art Tweed stood in an open doorway, watching the storm approach, not afraid to die.

In room one, Serge chomped with appetite from the bag of fortune cookies. "What a rush!"

The door of room ten was barricaded with cardboard boxes containing thousands of zebra-striped beepers. Huddled in the bathroom were the Diaz Boys, except for Juan, who was curled on the floor outside the door holding a metal garbage can lid for a shield.

Juan pounded on the locked door. "C'mon, let me in!"

"No room."

"It's because I'm the cousin, isn't it?"

"Ridiculous!"

Twenty minutes after the first gusts, everyone was packed in tight wherever they had decided to ride it out. Some sat with knees up against their chests, rocking nervously. It was five P.M. and pitch black. Without power there wasn't just no light, but no artificial noise—no TV or air-conditioning, no radio, no hum of electronic anything. Nobody was talking either. Nothing left to do but hang on. The wind howled against the building and the trees, and waves slapped the pylons of The Florida Room down on the beach. Every few seconds the noise of something unidentified breaking or snapping off was heard in the distance—people in the rooms trying to identify the sound of what just went. The concrete construction of Hammerhead Ranch inspired confidence, but the building was still producing far too many noises for anyone to relax. It didn't sound like something of cement, more like a wooden ship. There was a rolling, creaking sound—twenty carpenters with claw hammers slowly prying galvanized nails out of soft pine. Glass broke and then a scream—the window in someone else's room giving out.

It was Johnny Vegas's room, and the scream was from the beautiful naked woman who ran in the bathroom, refused to come out and started crying.

Hammerhead Ranch was in the worst possible location. The center of Hurricane Rolando-berto was coming ashore fifteen miles north at the Pasco County line. As the storm spun counterclockwise, the deadliest bands of wind tightened and whipped around from the southeast corner of the system right into Hammerhead Ranch. The creaking of the building increased, and more glass shattered. The wind rushed around the motel and jammed up under the eaves. The sound was a roar now, and attention stayed on the windows. Once the glass goes, the hurricane is inside the room, and everything becomes a missile. The panes of rooms thirteen and fourteen shattered, and books and cups and letter trays assaulted Zargoza and his goons. There was a final crash-bang drumroll, and the roof peeled off the motel like the tongue of an old boot. It hung straight up for a second, the guests staring into the sky in disbelief. Then it cracked in half and the top part did a backflip into the side of the condominium next door. Two more gusts and the rest was gone too.

Now everyone was trapped in their rooms by their own barricades, and they tore at the desks, tables, dressers, chairs and mattresses blocking the exits. The same idea hit everyone at the same time: Get to the bar!

The bartender was already inside, quaking in the kitchen. The shutters were fastened hard, and he had no way of seeing the wave of refugees heading his way. Zargoza was first to arrive, and he didn't mess with preliminaries. He blew the lock with a .44.

The guests piled in, and Serge and Zargoza slid an arcade game in front of the door. Some of the guests had quieted down, some still whining, many clearly a short push away from a total crack-up.

Serge took charge.

"Please calm down," he said, confidently strolling to the middle of the room. "I want everyone to just chill. What happened to the motel is not going to happen here. This place was built like Gibraltar. The wood's half petrified. It's heavy as lignum vitae— some of it won't even float anymore. Those joists are true four-by-sixes, and the builders cross-nailed it for extra strength. Look at this . . ."—he walked over and pointed up at the angle joints where the roof met a corner of the room—". . . this is ship construction. It's meant to survive storms at sea, so I think it's a safe bet it'll make it on land. You don't need to worry at all. We got our own generator out here and some stored water. We're in good shape. . . ."

People let out sighs. They gave Serge eye contact,

nodding in agreement as he spoke—Serge reining in their hysteria, getting the runaway stagecoach back under control.

Zargoza leaned against the cash register, arms crossed, still holding the .44 in one hand. He thought: This guy's *good*.

A small boy raised his hand.

Serge pointed to him. "We have a question in back?"

"What's the difference between a hurricane and a typhoon?"

"I'm glad you asked that, son," said Serge. "You see, both hurricanes and typhoons are cyclonic storms. Hurricanes occur in the Atlantic Ocean, and typhoons in the western Pacific region, often in the South China Sea. Did you know that cyclonic storms turn counterclockwise in the northern hemisphere but clockwise in the southern?"

"Wow!" said the boy. "No, I didn't."

"Want to see something neat?" said Serge.

"Sure do!"

He followed Serge into the bathroom. Serge raised the lid of the toilet and flushed.

"See?" he said. "It flushes counterclockwise, just like a hurricane. That's because we're in the northern hemisphere. You go down to Argentina or Chile, and all the toilets flush clockwise."

"Wow!" said the boy.

They walked back into the main bar area. Serge looked over at the goons and the Diaz Boys, and he noticed Zargoza was having a rough time keeping a lid on them.

"Will you listen to the man!" Zargoza pleaded. "He was right about this building, wasn't he? It's holding up like a missile silo! Not a creak."

He caught Serge in the side of his vision. "Serge! Hey, come here! You talk to 'em. You're good with that sort of thing. Tell 'em there's nothing to worry about."

"He's right," said Serge. "Everyone's going to be okay. This your first hurricane party?"

The Diaz Boys and the goons nodded.

"Good, good," said Serge. "Nothing to it. I was telling Lenny about my first hurricane party back in '65. That was Betsy, killed seventy-four. Donna, back in '60, killed one forty-eight, but I wasn't born yet. Then there was Okeechobee in '28, killed eighteen hundred out at the lake, but the big one was Galveston in 1900, *six thousand* perished."

The men turned a whiter shade of pale.

"Oh, I'm sorry," Serge said with an awkward laugh. "Getting off-track. Like I was saying, you want to keep thinking good thoughts. My first hurricane party was a blast. We were over on the east coast in Riviera Beach, just above West Palm. When she started to blow, we cut the power in the house so there wouldn't be a fire. We lit candles and played Monopoly in the hallway. We had a big metal drum of Charles Chips and we listened to our little transistor radio for the mounting death toll down in Fort Lauderdale and Miami . . ."

The goons went green.

"Oops, sorry again," he said. "How about a movie? The VCR still works 'cuz of the generator and I just happened to bring some great Florida flicks."

He held up a gym bag full of videocassettes.

Serge got the VCR going and popped in a tape. "The important thing now is to keep your minds occupied, not to think about your situation."

Serge hit play and they began watching *Key Largo,* the story of a group of criminals riding out a hurricane in a Florida motel.

Everyone in the bar fell quiet as the wind roared around The Florida Room.

Edward G. Robinson was getting nervous on the screen, asking Lionel Barrymore about the hurricane.

"Hey, old man, how bad can it get?"

"Well, worst storm we ever had was back in '35," said Barrymore. *"Wind whipped up a big wave and sent it busting right over Matecumbe Key. Eight hundred washed out to sea."*

Zargoza looked worried. He turned to Serge. "They're kidding about that hurricane, aren't they? I mean, that's just Hollywood movie fiction, right?"

"Oh, no," said Serge. "It was the real thing—the only force-five hurricane ever to hit the state."

Serge let it sink in. The building was solid, but the wind hummed all around, and now that they were in an elevated structure, it blew under them too. The shutters held fast, but when the wind was at the right pitch, they resonated with a loud rat-a-tat.

Zargoza stared at Serge with eyes that had stopped blinking.

"They sent a train down from the mainland to evacuate those in the path," said Serge. "But it got a late start, and the engineer decided in Miami to turn the train around. He said, 'I ain't goin' down there and loading up a bunch of people and then *back* out of a force-five hurricane. When I'm leaving, I'm gonna be balls-out, facing forward.' So he puts it in reverse and heads on down, and the train gets to Snake Creek, which divides Plantation Key from Windley Key, where they now have that Tropical Isle place. You've been there, haven't you? It's like if Disney had a spring break exhibit. But before it was like the Florida I remember as a kid." The lack of medication floated Serge in a sea of memories. ". . . just-mowed lawns on a Saturday afternoon, splitting coconuts open on the sidewalk, catching stingrays . . ."

"What about the hurricane?" snapped Zargoza.

"Oh, yeah. So the train picks up a bunch of people at Snake Creek. The front edge of the storm is already over them, blowing like mad, and the barometer is something insane like twenty-six inches. It's solid monsoon conditions, but the engineer presses on. There are more helpless people up ahead in the Matecumbe Keys. The hurricane thickens when they get to the last stop, and the engineer loads up the rest of the stranded residents. Then he stokes his engines and fires them full speed, back to Miami.

"They only get a few miles when the meat of the unnamed hurricane slams the islands. The Keys aren't any more than six or eight feet at their highest elevation, and the railroad trestles aren't any higher. They were wide open. . . ."

Serge took another sip of water. He studied
Zargoza; the hook was set.

"As the train races out of the Keys, the passengers
are petrified. The train seems big and heavy and safe,
but outside the wind is building to two hundred miles
an hour. Nobody knows what the passengers might
have seen—maybe a thirty-foot wall of water coming
at them at fifty miles per hour. Or maybe they had no
warning at all—the next thing they knew, the train
was slapped off the tracks like a toy. . . ."

Zargoza's mouth had gone dry from hanging open.

"They couldn't dig graves fast enough so they set
fire to big mounds of bodies back at Snake Creek.
The sky was black with the smoke. The islands were
flat, and every tree was uprooted or snapped. There
was one family who survived because the hurricane
knocked their whole house off the foundation in one
piece and it surfed the storm surge out into Florida
Bay."

"*. . . And for months afterward corpses were
found in the mangrove swamp,*" said Barrymore.

The Diaz Boys began talking excitedly among
themselves.

Serge pointed at the TV. "Hey, you're missing the
movie."

31

Jethro Maddox awoke in his parachute harness in the middle of a hurricane, twisting and swinging wildly from the tallest palm tree behind Hammerhead Ranch. Every third or fourth swing, he hit the tree trunk. "Owww! *Galanos!*" He heard a loud, ripping sound and looked up.

"Oh, Mr. Temple, you're hopelessly old-fashioned," said Bogart. *"Your ideas date back years. You still live in the time when America thought it could get along without the Johnny Roccos. Welcome back, Rocco, it was all a mistake. . . ."*

The Diaz Boys listened intently to the movie, and Zargoza began thinking about the briefcase. It wasn't safe in the storm—he had to move it. No, that was more risky. No, move it. Don't. Move it. Don't. It was driving him insane. He stood and grabbed the back of a chair for support until he calmed down. Then he started walking slowly around the bar in a state of utter paranoia.

"Yeah, that's me, sure! I was all those things—and more!" said Edward G. *"When Rocco talked, people*

shut up and listened. What Rocco said went. Nobody was as big as Rocco!"

Serge picked up Zargoza's vibe. Rope-a-dope was working. Serge's gut told him it was time to make his move. Serge stuck his pistol inside his belt and covered it with his untucked tropical shirt. He turned the sound down on *Key Largo* and stuck the TV remote in his back pocket, and he began a wide circle around the bar, tracking Zargoza.

Zargoza picked up Serge in his peripheral vision. *So that's it! He's the Judas!* Zargoza patted his lower stomach, making sure his Colt was secure. He began counter-circling Serge.

Serge and Zargoza continued their pas de deux until each had circumnavigated the inside of the bar three times.

"All right!" shouted Zargoza. "Fuck this noise!"

He pulled the Colt and leveled it at Serge, who simultaneously went for his own piece. Except that Serge had become distracted by a historic photo of Tennessee Williams on the wall, and Zargoza beat him to the draw.

"Drop it! Now!" Zargoza shouted. Everyone flattened on the floor.

Serge froze in front of Tennessee's picture. Just as he realized Zargoza had gotten the jump on him, other voices began yelling.

"You drop it, Fiddlebottom!" It was the Diaz Boys, aiming TEC-9 submachine guns.

Zargoza dropped his weapon. "I asked you not to call me that," he said demurely.

"Where's the five million?" shouted Tommy Diaz, standing with his back to the big-screen TV. "We know you've been holding out on us!"

"What five million?" said Zargoza.

"Don't play simple!"

On the other side of the room, Serge furtively slid the TV remote out of his back pocket. He knew *Key Largo* by heart. At the right moment, he pressed the volume button.

"Drop it or I'll blast ya!" yelled Edward G. Robinson.

The Diaz Boys bolted upright. They dropped their guns.

"Now kick 'em away," said Robinson.

They did, and the guns skittered across the wooden floor.

Almost as soon as they did: "Freeze!"

Serge turned and saw Zargoza had gotten his gun back and was pointing it at him.

"But I just helped you!" said Serge.

"Helping yourself to my money is more like it!" said Zargoza.

"What are you talking about?" said Serge.

"You know damn well . . ." By the end of the sentence, Zargoza was talking to himself and pacing, waving the gun distractedly, and Serge and the Diaz Boys ducked each time he did.

Tommy Diaz heard more dialogue behind him and he turned his head and peeked. "Hey! That was just the TV set! Foul! We get our guns back!"

Zargoza squeezed off a shot into the roof and

mocked Tommy. *"Foul! We get our guns back!*
Where'd you learn to be a hood? Everything's in-
bounds!"

*"That big gun in your hand makes you look grown
up—you think!"* said Barrymore. *"I'll bet you spend
hours posing in front of a mirror."*

"Turn down that fucking TV," Zargoza shouted
over his shoulder, and Juan Diaz leaned and held
down the volume button on the TV console until all
the yellow bars marched to the left of the screen.

When Zargoza turned back around, he found
Serge chatting socially with Art Tweed.

"Hey! This is a no-talking zone! Knock it off and
move over there!" Zargoza motioned to Serge with
the gun. "I thought we were pals, but you double-
crossed me! You are *so* dead!"

"No, you're dead!" said Serge, pointing a finger at
Zargoza.

"No, you are!"

"You are!"

"No, you are!"

The other motel guests glanced at each other in
terror, Serge and Zargoza still yelling in the background—"You are!" "No, you are!"—Here we go, a
bloodbath.

"No, you are!" said Zargoza.

"Behind you!" said Serge.

"You already used that trick! It's the oldest in the
book!"

Serge reached behind his back and pressed the
volume button on the remote.

"Drop the gun now!"

Zargoza turned around and saw Humphrey Bogart on TV. He yelled at Juan Diaz again. "Turn that fucking thing down!"

Juan marched the little yellow bars across the TV, and just as he was done, Serge pressed the remote and marched the yellow volume bars back the other way.

"What do I care about Johnny Rocco, whether he lives or dies?" said Bogart. *"I only care about me—me and mine. I fight nobody's battles but my own."*

"I said, turn that goddamn thing down!"

Juan turned it down, and Serge turned it back up again.

"Please, God, make a big wave, send it crashing down on us. Destroy us all if need be, but punish him!" said Barrymore.

"Jesus Christ!" yelled Zargoza. "I'm the one with the gun. That counts for something!"

"No it doesn't," said Serge.

"WILL YOU SHUT UP!"

"Uh . . . no."

A new voice: "Drop it!"

Everyone turned.

It was Aristotle "Art" Tweed, trying to look mean. He had a gun and he wasn't afraid to die.

Zargoza dropped his pistol. "Where'd you get the piece?" he asked Art.

"It's the gun Serge tossed away. There, under that table"—Art pointed to a spot a few feet to his right. "Serge whispered for me to get ready. He was going to make you look at the TV, and when you did, I was to grab the pistol."

Zargoza snapped his fingers and winced. "Fell for the oldest trick in the book."

Jethro Maddox, swinging in his parachute harness, was half stupid from repeatedly slamming into the trunk of the palm tree. He heard a ripping sound again and looked up. "Uh-oh."

"I finally decided what I wanted to do with my life before I committed suicide," said Art Tweed. "I was trying to figure out who was the worst human being I could kill and make the world a better place. But that DJ got himself burnt up before I could get to him. Guess who that leaves?"

Art stretched out his arm and aimed the gun at Zargoza. "Get ready to meet your maker, shithead!"

"Ahem? Excuse me?" Another voice. Everyone turned.

It was the short, thin man in a charcoal suit and black fedora who had checked into the motel two days ago. He had a brown leather briefcase in one hand and a piece of paper and a fountain pen from the forties in the other. He took a few steps into the middle of the room.

"Mr. Tweed," said Paul, the Passive-Aggressive Private Eye. "I've been looking all over for you." Paul looked down at Art's gun and then at Zargoza. "I thought I'd better say something before it's too late. I'm a private investigator representing Montgomery Memorial Hospital up in Alabama, and we seem to have had a little problem." He forced a chuckle. "It's really quite embarrassing. You see, the daughter of one of our employees, she sort of played a little prank. The bottom line, Mr. Tweed, is that you're not going to die. Pretty good news, wouldn't you say? Now, if you'll just sign this disclaimer releasing the hospital of all responsibility and liability . . ."

There was a terrible crashing sound as Jethro Maddox smashed through one of the Bahamian shutters, landing on top of Art Tweed. *"Galanos!"*

"That settles that," said Zargoza. He quickly picked up his pistol off the floor and aimed it at Serge and the others. He ordered two goons to push one of the cabinets from the kitchen in front of the broken shutter. The generator failed for a second and the lights dimmed. Zargoza jumped. "What was that?"

"You don't like it, do you, Rocco? The storm?" said Bogart. *"Show it your gun, why don't you? If it doesn't stop, shoot it."*

"Will you turn that fucking movie off!" said Zargoza. "My nerves are shot as it is!"

Zargoza reached over and swiped the remote control from Serge. "Gimme that thing!"

As he did, he heard a new voice from behind.

"Drop it!"

Zargoza rolled his eyes at the ceiling. *"Now what?!"*

It was C. C. Flag, aiming a pistol. He grabbed a small boy from the group of innocent visitors clustered by the bar and used him for a human shield.

"I'm gonna walk outta here real slow, and nobody's gonna move a muscle or the kid gets it," said Flag. He turned to Zargoza. "I know you've been planning to use me as the fall guy. I can't go to jail!"

"You're talking crazy!" said Zargoza. "It's the storm. It's making you crack."

"Fuck everyone!" said Flag as he backed out of the room, pressing the gun harder up under the boy's chin.

"Coward!" shouted Zargoza.

"Dung-weasel!" shouted Serge.

"You won't get away with it, Rocco!"

C. C. opened the door. The hurricane's eye was just making landfall and the winds calmed. He backed out the door and across the beach behind Hammerhead Ranch and the neighboring Calusa Pointe condominiums.

Everyone put aside their differences and ran to the door, worried about the boy. C. C. walked backward, a hundred yards away, with the gun still to the boy's head.

Suddenly, a desperate scream erupted from C. C., and he dropped the child. He stumbled in a circle, grabbing his neck and hollering, suffering the abrupt onset of a mystery affliction. The boy ran as fast as he could toward the bar. But C. C. still had the gun, and he fired in all directions as he spun.

Everyone hit the deck as slugs splintered through the walls and door; one pinged off the antique cash register and knocked a wahoo to the floor. The gunfire seemed to go on forever. The pistol had a hundred-cartridge rapid-feed jumbo banana clip heavily stocked in weapons boutiques across Florida in the NRA's continuing crusade to level the playing field for duck hunters. The boy's little legs were not making good time, and from the spray of suppression fire C. C. was laying down, it was clear the boy was riding blind luck.

Nobody knew what was happening to C. C.; everyone in the bar was just yelling for the boy to run.

Art Tweed broke from the back steps and sprinted and met the child halfway on the beach. He scooped him up and turned and shielded the boy with his body and ran back to The Florida Room. There was a big cheer when Art bounded up the steps. Lots of back-slapping, even Zargoza.

Everyone's attention went back to the beach. C. C. was clicking an empty gun now, still twirling and grabbing his throat with his free hand. They could make out something stuck in his neck, and blood running down his shirt. The foreign object was big and colorful.

The wind picked up again all at once, gusting hard, like when the hurricane had begun.

"The eye's passing," said Serge. "We're getting the backside now. Everyone take cover!"

In the midst of the gale, they noticed someone else was now out on the beach, moving from the condo toward C. C. Flag.

"You sonuvabitch!" the new person yelled as he approached Flag. "You stay the hell offa my property!"

Malcolm Kefauver, the incredible shrinking mayor of Beverly Shores, had just nailed Flag in the throat with his last lawn dart.

The dart had missed Flag's major arteries, but he was getting light-headed from the sight of his own blood. He twirled out into the water and fell to his knees. Waves crashed over him, and he rolled in the shallow surf like a porcupine fish.

The mayor of Beverly Shores advanced toward the water, taunting him. Flag's wound wasn't mortal, but his buoyancy was now a problem. He was in danger of being carried off by the surf. Flag was on his back, losing the fight, and another wave crashed over him and dragged him farther off the beach. He was in only two feet of water, but he was tossed like a cork. With a last, great effort, Flag rolled onto his stomach and dug his fingertips into the sand. Thus anchored, Flag slowly clawed his way back toward safety.

Flag was most of the way out of the water when the incredible shrinking mayor ran right up to him at the edge of the surf and resumed shouting. He yelled in a measured cadence—one word to emphasize each time he stomped on Flag's fingers—*"Let . . . go . . . of . . . my . . . beach!"*

Flag shouted and pulled his hands back to his chest in pain. A large wave knocked the mayor on his back and swallowed Flag.

Flag was quickly a hundred yards out, and his cries were sucked into the growling wind as he bobbed steadily toward Mexico. The mayor turned and headed back to the condo. The wind gusted harder, and the mayor had to lean at an acute angle. He made it to the stage set up on the beach for the Proposition 213 rally and grabbed one of the corner lighting poles for balance. He tried to rest a second. The wind kept picking up, eighty, ninety, a hundred miles an hour. The mayor had continued shrinking since his election and his suit was baggier than ever, catching an enormous amount of wind. Hundred and ten. Hundred and twenty. The Proposition 213 banner over the stage tore loose and flew away.

The guests in The Florida Room had to shut the door again, but Serge and Zargoza took turns watching through the hole where Zargoza had shot through the lock.

When the wind hit one-thirty, the mayor's feet went out from under him, but he held on to the lighting pole with both hands—flapping horizontally like a yacht club pennant.

At one-forty, it was too much. His baggy suit was fully deployed, and the mayor lost his grip. He sailed out over the Gulf, never touching the water, dipping and lifting and looping like an autumn leaf carried up and away in a strong breeze.

"Look, he's flapping his arms," said Zargoza.

"That's only making it worse," said Serge. "It's giving him more lift."

There was a long moment of quiet, and Serge continued staring out the hole in the door until the mayor faded to a speck and disappeared. When Serge finally turned around, he saw Zargoza pointing a gun at him again.

"You realize this is a cry for help," said Serge.

"Shut up! I'm tired of your talk!" snapped Zargoza. "I'm taking the money and getting out of here. . . . Sorry . . ."

Zargoza leveled the revolver at Serge's heart and thumbed back the Colt's hammer. He stiffened his arm and began squeezing the trigger.

There was a bang and Serge clenched his eyes

shut. But he didn't feel anything. He slowly opened them and inventoried his body. Nothing. He looked up and saw Zargoza with a silly grin on his face. Serge's eyebrows twisted in puzzlement. Zargoza was still grinning as he fell forward and hit the floor.

When he did, it revealed Country, standing directly behind him with one of the TEC-9s the Diaz Boys had kicked away.

"What have you done?" Serge yelled.

"I thought you'd be happy," said Country.

"I had everything under control," said Serge. He got down on the floor and rolled Zargoza onto his back. He slapped Zargoza's cheeks lightly. "Wake up! Wake up!"

Zargoza barely opened his eyes.

"Look! I turned the TV down like you asked. Can I get you anything?"

Zargoza smiled calmly and started to close his eyes.

"Wait! Wait! Don't go yet! Listen, buddy, since we got to know each other so well, why don't you tell me where the money is—so I can make sure it gets to your favorite charity."

Zargoza smiled a little broader and said in a weak voice, "You always did make me laugh."

When Zargoza closed his eyes that last time, Serge's yell of anguish shook the heavy wooden shutters of The Florida Room.

After Zargoza died, Serge, Art and the Diaz Boys sat down at the tables, guns all over the floor, not having the spirit to fight each other. There was a bond from the common goal of saving the boy, and of the ordeal that still lay ahead. The storm was back up to full strength, whipping around and under the bar again.

They looked over each other's faces with resignation.

Art floated the question. "What do we do now?"

Serge picked up the remote control and hit the volume button. "We watch the rest of *Key Largo*."

Time went by in exhausted silence until the sound of the wind outside wasn't as loud.

"Storm's passing," said Lauren Bacall.

"A torn shutter or two, some trash on the beach," said Bogart. *"In a few hours there will be little to remind you of what happened tonight."*

Epilogue

*H*urricane Rolando-berto was more remarkable for its insurance totals than loss of life. Prompt evacuation warnings by all but one of the local media outlets averted certain tragedy. Several stretches of the beach roads remained impassable for a week. Tow trucks dragged palm trees out of the streets, and the state flew in snowplows from New England to clear sand drifts. The Department of Insurance threatened to freeze the assets of six companies that tried to pull out of Florida.

In the hours immediately following Rolando-berto, a rookie police officer who lived on the island and owned an all-terrain cycle responded to the 911 distress call from Hammerhead Ranch. Everyone had decided not to mention Country's shooting Zargoza. The officer wrote diligently in his notebook for five minutes before he shouted for everyone to stop talking at once.

"Hold it. Hold it!" he said. "Let me see if I understand. The motel owner was really a gangster. A guy named Lenny was pretending to be Don Johnson. The short fella over there wants to be a private eye from the forties. And this guy thinks he's Hemingway. Do I have all this straight?"

Everyone nodded.

"What kind of a crazy motel is this?" asked the cop. "Is there anyone here who's what they're supposed to be?"

"I am," said Serge, raising his hand. "I'm a one-hundred-percent, made-in-Florida, dope-smugglin', time-sharin', spring-breakin', log-flumin', double-occupancy discount vacation. I'm a tall glass of orange juice and a day without sunshine. I'm the wind in your sails, the sun on your burn and the moon over Miami. I am the native."

And with that he grabbed two of his special bags and dashed out the door.

The remaining guests unlatched the shutters and propped them open. It was getting light out as sunrise approached. The air was still and cool and sandpipers scurried along the edge of the water. A dorsal fin moved offshore in the calm surface. The generator still had plenty of fuel, and, like at all good parties, everyone eventually ended up in the kitchen. They raided the refrigerator to cook breakfast.

The mother of the boy Art saved continued to profusely thank him. Said her name was Sally and it was so hard raising a boy alone. Tommy Diaz started the CD jukebox and picked the Rolling Stones, *Let It Bleed*, cuing up the whole album. "Gimme Shelter" boomed through the bar, making everyone jitterbug and jive as they walked around.

*E*mergency-management officials set up a triage center at the old Coliseum in St. Petersburg to handle an unusually large number of cut and bruised old men found wandering the streets in a confused state in the wake of the hurricane.

About half were ultimately identified as nursing-home patients who had apparently strayed from their facilities. The other half were members of an entertainment troupe who had parachuted out of a WC-130 shortly before the storm.

Five Look-Alikes were sent against their will to geriatric care at Vista Isles, where they were soon placed under psychiatric guard and sedated with Thorazine for demanding they be allowed to travel to Pamplona. Five Alzheimer's patients went on a tour of Europe and performed flawlessly for the centennial celebration of Ernest Hemingway's birth.

*T*he heavy rain from Rolando-berto filled the Myakka River to flood stage as it wound through Sarasota County. Johnny Vegas had taken his four-by-four into the state park. He was on an idyllic bird-watching hike deep into the hardwood hammocks and palmettos with a pretty twenty-two-year-old nature mama. For once, it was a constructive activity for Johnny, an educational experience, a communion with the environment in the company of a wholesome, healthy woman. Johnny had met her on-line, in the Horny Hot Singles Chat Room.

They were eight miles down the trail when the woman and Johnny began exchanging silly double-entendre small talk. Hot damn, thought Johnny, I'm gonna be in those tight beige L.L. Bean hiking pants before you can say—he checked his Audubon field guide—man-o'-war frigate bird.

Johnny started buttering her up. "There's just such a fresh, open-meadow feeling about you."

She giggled and threw him a coy glance.

"You're like a field of lilacs."

She gave him another look. Was she touching her breast like that on purpose?

"You're like little kittens and all-natural ice cream."

She stopped on the trail and started taking off her backpack. At last he had arrived at Score City.

"You're such a refreshing change from all those loser girls these days with tattoos. . . ."

She froze in the trail. Oh no, thought Johnny. He gave her a fast up and down and saw just a tiny bit of green ink peeking out from under the right side of her shorts. "Did I say tattoo?"

"Yes, you did! And you'll never see this one," she said, slapping the right side of her ass. She reversed direction on the trail, angrily marching past Johnny in high gear back toward the four-by-four.

"Poop!" Johnny said to himself. Not only am I not scoring, but now I have to walk eight miles back to civilization in stinging silence.

A phone rang.

Johnny pulled the cell phone off his hiking belt. "Talk to me."

It was If. "Oh, hi there!" said Johnny. He never thought he'd hear from her again after the night they got stranded on top of the Sunshine Skyway bridge.

They had a nice convivial confab. Turns out, If was just her nickname. Her real name was Inez Fawn Rawlings—I. F. Rawlings in her *Tampa Tribune* byline—a Vassar grad, Northeastern intelligentsia, rising reporter. She thought that Johnny, though not too mature or bright, looked dreamy in his tux that night at the aquarium. She would make the other women sick with jealousy when she showed up on his arm at the annual Tampa Bay media awards banquet. She told Johnny she had been nominated for the area's highest journalistic honor, the Hubert Higgins Memorial Award, named after one of the area's finest local writers, who was killed protecting a teenager from a mob attack on a lunch counter sit-in during the sixties. Actually, it was the *former* Hubert Higgins award. It was supposed to be named after Higgins in perpetuity, but in response to a tremendous outpouring of grief over a recent tragedy, it was changed this year.

I'm up for the Toto!" If told Johnny as they entered the banquet hall at the Performing Arts Center in downtown Tampa. She wore a sheer black dress, backless, almost down to her divide, with the thinnest of straps. She held Johnny's arm tight and waved and smiled at her friends, trying to get their attention, make them mad. She leaned up to Johnny's ear and whispered: "Winning journalism awards gives me better orgasms." She gave the center of his ear a quick poke with her slender tongue. Johnny's legs went to rubber, and he almost went tumbling, but If caught him and they made it to the table with their place cards.

The lights went down and the four-ounce portions of boneless glazed chicken were served. After dinner, the sea of faces turned to the podium, where master of ceremonies Blaine Crease worked his way through a prodigious list of honors.

In the late twentieth century, a new corporate philosophy to all but blow the shareholders had ravaged newspapers and TV stations, bleeding off staffing, experience and standards until what was left of the profession was a karaoke rendition of itself. The Old Guard of journalism came to the rescue by increasing the number of awards and self-congratulatory fetes until journalism officially passed bowling for most trophies per calorie burned.

Crease was deep into the "best lighting on a weekend anchor desk" stretch of the honor roll. An elegant woman came up to If and whispered, "You got the Toto! I was backstage. I saw the engraving in the trophy."

Johnny thrust a fist into the air in front of him. "Yessssss!"

Crease built his pace. Only one more category before the climax of the night, the Toto. If and Johnny leaned forward in anticipation. Crease moved into the copyediting awards, announcing the best headline on a breaking weekend news feature.

Rookie copy editor Kirk Curtly heard his name
called out and arose with his Montblanc graduation
gift clipped securely in his jacket pocket. He walked
up to shake Crease's hand and accept the solid-gold-
plated trophy.

Up in the closed-off balcony was recently termi-
nated state safety officer Chester "Porkchop" Dole, a
Remington .30-06 scoped rifle, and one of those bottles of Jack Daniel's with a handle. He drank the
bourbon out of a filthy coffee cup that read, "Ask
someone who gives a shit!"

Everyone in the banquet hall heard a clear-as-day
but enigmatic phrase yelled from the direction of the
balcony. "Write this headline, motherfucker!"

Shots rang out and the podium was strafed. People
screamed and scattered. Others dove under tables.
Dole leaned over the railing to get a better angle on
the fleeing Kirk Curtly, who was now three Kirks in
Dole's rifle scope, thanks to the miracle of modern alcohol. Dole leaned too far and went over the railing,
doing a half-gainer onto Johnny's and If's table, collapsing it. If began crying and threw down her napkin.
"My special night is ruined!" And she ran away.

Johnny snapped under the strain of involuntary
virginity. He began beating the hell out of the half-
conscious Dole, which was the image the cameras
caught when the TV lights went on. Johnny didn't
know it yet, but he was about to become an instant
media hero.

An hour later he was in a bar on Zack Street
drowning his sorrows. At 11:07 P.M.—seven minutes
after the eleven-o'clock newscast began—a stat-

uesque blonde came over to Johnny. "That was you I just saw on the news, wasn't it? You were great! So *big* and *brave*!" She leaned closer and suggested they call it a night and go back to her place. She didn't have to ask Johnny twice.

"Do I know you from somewhere?" he asked. "The movies?"

She smiled. "No, I'm not in movies, but I love to *watch* movies."

Hubba-hubba, Johnny thought. He got up and put an arm around her waist and they strolled out the door and into the streets of downtown Tampa.

"So, what kind of movies do you like?" asked Johnny.

"You ever see *The Crying Game*?"

C. C. Flag was never found. Neither was the mayor of Beverly Shores, and the crime scene tape remained across the door of his condominium at Calusa Pointe from when Mrs. Edna Ploomfield was blown up through his floor.

Neighbors began hearing movements and a voice from the unit—someone having one-sided conversations in the middle of the night. One of the bolder residents, a retiree named Cecil, knocked on the door.

A tall, lean man with dark sunglasses answered. He flipped open a billfold to display a gold police badge. Cecil leaned forward to read it, but the man flipped it closed. The man had a clipboard in his other hand, and he began writing on it without making an introduction.

"What is your name and address?" he asked Cecil, who stood nervously outside the door, trying to peek around the man into the condominium.

"Would you have any information we can use about the mayor or Mrs. Edna Ploomfield?"

Cecil shook his head.

"You wouldn't be trying to obstruct this investigation, would you?"

Cecil shook his head again, more vigorously this time.

"Good. We'll call you if we need you," Serge said and closed the door, and Cecil walked away confused, glancing back at the unit a couple of times.

Serge tossed the badge on the dining-room table and flopped down on the couch. Florida Cable News was on the tube. Serge propped his feet up on the glass-top coffee table and resumed writing on the clipboard. The key to life, Serge knew, was the diligent keeping of lists. The clipboard was Serge's newest tether to reality. There were so many loose ends in Serge's life, relentless injustices, endless chores, unphotographed historic sites. He felt a sense of control over things he had no control over by listing them. At the top of the clipboard: "Find 5 million." After that, in smaller letters, "Visit Fort DeSoto, buy batteries/film, Egmont Key (rent boat?)"

The condo was a great setup, and Serge knew it would have to end all too soon. The sunsets were stunning from the balcony, and that was important to Serge. It had a cozy little walk-in kitchenette and a breakfast bar, where he liked to take his scrambled eggs and juice with the morning paper. He paced all day in the condo like a caged cheetah, barefoot on the shag carpet, talking to himself while holding the clipboard or newspaper or TV remote or all three. The AC was down as low as it would go, constantly giving Serge that just-showered feeling. He even liked the thick carpet under his toes, although to him Florida would always be terrazzo country.

The sun was on its way down again. According to routine, Serge dropped the clipboard and picked up his camera and walked out on the balcony. He leaned a little over the rail and looked north and saw a small crane lowering something on top of the sign next door at Hammerhead Ranch. A small neon top deck was being added to the old sign, so that it would now read "The Diaz Boys' Hammerhead Ranch Motel."

The three surviving Diaz Boys stood proudly in the road watching the sign go up. "I'm glad we finally got out of the cocaine business," said Tommy Diaz with a large hoop of room keys around his neck.

The Diazes moved out of the driveway and waved at a departing white limousine with the five interlocking rings of the modern Olympics. The International Olympic Committee's advance team grinned and waved back. They had a decision to make. Once back in Lausanne, Switzerland, they would weigh the rabid bigots, oppressive heat, armed criminals and hurricane against the quality of Lenny's weed and the stunning sight of City and Country, and they would immediately leapfrog Tampa Bay into the front-runner position for the 2012 Olympic Games.

Serge watched the Olympic limousine pulling away down Gulf Boulevard, and he strolled back in from the balcony and onto the carpeting. Blaine Crease was on TV, standing at the roadblock that prevented looters from coming on the island. He was interviewing *"the man who has cracked this case wide open!"*

The man on TV with Crease tried to hide his face. "Please leave me alone. Get away from me." It was Paul, the Passive-Aggressive Private Eye, who was bad with people but great with inanimate objects, and he was holding the handle of an attractive silver Halliburton briefcase.

Serge slapped his forehead in astonishment. "How the hell?"

He was in awe of Paul's mystical gift. Then he saw Paul break free of Crease and climb into a Malibu driven by Jethro Maddox, who had hung in a palm tree the night before the hurricane and had an unobstructed aerial view of the Hammerhead Ranch grounds when Zargoza went running around in his pajamas hiding the briefcase for the last time.

Serge went over to his toiletry bag and grabbed his electronic homing device. He banged it on the table and it began beeping.

Cecil the neighbor arrived at the door with two officers. "Open up, police!"

Serge grabbed the toiletry bag and ran across the room and, a second before the officers kicked in the door, he jumped down through the hole in the floor made by Edna Ploomfield.

As fear of crime continued to grip the residents of Florida in the late 1990s, legislators in Tallahassee examined the problem in exhaustive detail and finally saw it for what it actually was: an opportunity to exploit for votes.

In a selfless display of bombast, certain lawmakers brought back the tradition of the roadside chain gang. These same legislators then took a valiant stand against tax-and-spend liberals by steadfastly refusing to fund the chain-gang program.

On the first day of the new year, a group of prisoners in a medium-security detail collected trash down the hot median of I-275 on the underside of Tampa Bay. Their chains had never been purchased, so they walked around freely, and escapes were epidemic. In the middle of the shift, something began making a light beeping sound. One of the prisoners pulled a zebra-striped pager from under his baseball cap and read the alphanumeric message: "Crockett, we're on!"

Over a small hill in the highway came the unmistakable theme song of the smash-hit TV show *Miami Vice*. A dented-up pink Cadillac containing Serge, City and Country flew over the hump and skidded to a stop next to the work detail. Lenny dropped the pager and sprinted up the incline of the median and dove into the convertible as the guard fired a round of buckshot. Serge hit the gas and the car accelerated east toward Interstate 75.

*S*ean Breen and David Klein were gone fishing again. Sean had bought a new Chrysler New Yorker with the insurance money after reporting the maniac who had stolen his car at the brush fire down in the

Everglades. The new Chrysler was pulling a new, loaded fishing skiff, purchased with the advance on book rights to their harrowing story in the Florida Keys. ("I can see it now," said their agent. "We'll call it *Florida Road*–something.") They were headed across the state to the Banana River, and the weather couldn't have been nicer. The sky was blue and clear except for a string of popcorn clouds marching their way across the southern horizon.

A pink Cadillac convertible pulled up alongside. The driver waved and accelerated past. Sean and David looked at each other and then shook their heads and said together: "Nawwww."

Serge steered the Caddy with his knees and fiddled with the homing device. It pointed him directly at Cocoa Beach.

A hundred miles ahead, a short, rumpled man and his stout friend with the white beard lounged poolside at the Orbit Motel, sipping drinks out of coconuts.

Country played with the radio, turning up Billy Preston, "Will It Go Round in Circles."

"*. . . I got a story ain't got no moral, with the bad guy winnin' every once in a while . . .*"

Serge planned to hang loose and play it by ear. No big rush. If they didn't find Paul and Jethro right away, there were plenty of things Serge needed to photograph over there. And of course he'd have to give Lenny, City and Country the A-Tour, starting with the John F. Kennedy Space Center, where thousands of people lined up every day to peer inside a bulletproof exhibit case proudly displaying a rock from the driveway of the Hammerhead Ranch Motel.

Enjoy an excerpt from
Orange Crush by Tim Dorsey

Prologue

With three weeks to go in the Florida governor's race, the Tallahassee morning newspaper ran the following headline: 2 HEADS EXPLODE IN SEPARATE INCIDENTS

Tallahassee is the capital of Florida, up in the north end of the state near Georgia. The land is less flat, more wooded; the people not as hurried or transient. In the eighteenth century the population centers of old Florida were Pensacola in the panhandle and St. Augustine on the Atlantic—too far apart to be managed under a single provisional government. Officials went looking for a spot in between. But the

Talasi Indians were already on that spot, so the officials told the Indians they needed to borrow their village for about three hundred years.

Tallahassee was established the capital in 1823. East Tallahassee High School was established in 1971. On a balmy October evening in 2002, a banner hung in the high school's auditorium: GO FIGHTING SENATORS! Another hung over the stage: WELCOME GOVERNOR CANDIDATES.

A smattering of people sat in the sea of folding chairs on the basketball court. Technicians taped electrical cables to the parquet floor and checked the sound system. Agents swept the school with bomb-sniffing German shepherds. Reporters shuffled around in a tight herd, stepping on each other's shoelaces, interviewing The Man on the Street, then each other, looking for that fresh Pulitzer angle. The debate was less than two hours away.

*T*he majestic old Florida Capitol building, with its trademark red-and-white Kentucky Fried Chicken awnings, stands proudly at the foot of the Apalachee Parkway. Behind it is Tallahassee's only skyscraper, the new Capitol, a sterile monolith built of the finest materials someone else's money could buy.

At 5:46 P.M., a man in a dark suit and dark sunglasses stepped out a side service door of the Capitol and held it open. A platoon of ten identically dressed men jogged out of the building. The tallest one had a stopwatch and wireless headset, and just as he reached Pensacola Street, a black super-stretch limo screeched up to the curb. The man with the stopwatch opened the back door of the limo, scanned the surroundings, and turned to the rest of the men, who had taken up sentry positions across the Capitol lawn. He twirled a finger in the air, followed by a series of third-base-coach signals. A clutch of elegantly dressed men and women emerged from the service door. The array of sentries collapsed around them to form a circle of human shields, then hustled the group to the curb and shoved them in the back of the limo, which sped north on Monroe Street. A pair of forest-green Hummers joined the limo, an escort in front and a trail vehicle in back. Two small flags snapped in the wind on each side of the limo's hood. The flag on the right corner displayed the seal of the Florida governor's office. The flag on the left used to have the same seal but now read: "The Outback Steakhouse Florida Governor's Race."

Local law enforcement was worried about security. Due to the state's proliferation of military assault weapons, violent narcotics gangs and middle-aged loners in one-bedroom apartments, the capital police force reported it was no longer capable of providing what it deemed was adequate security for the governor, lieutenant governor and their families and mistresses. They said they knew of only one group who could get the job done.

The governor's office hired the people who handled security for the Rolling Stones.

The governor and staff were violently tossed left, then right as the limo slalomed the back roads of Tallahassee in textbook U.N. convoy maneuver. The governor and his campaign manager faced each other in the posh opposing backseats. The manager flipped flash cards.

A bright yellow card: "Wetlands Despoilment."

The governor scratched his head. "We for or against that?"

"For," said the manager. "You feeling okay? That's the third easy one you've missed."

The governor nodded, but his thoughts were elsewhere. A political world that had been second nature his entire life now seemed alien, oblique, clumsy. He felt light-headed, and the periphery of his vision dissolved with a hallucinatory tinge. He looked around the spacious interior of the limo, which was packed with the usual suspects. The leather bench seating seemed to go on forever, all the way up to the chauffeur's soundproof partition, like a hall of mirrors. The governor squinted and took a hard look for the first time. Who the hell *were* all these people? They stared back at him, smiling and nodding—handlers, trainers, therapists, linguists, donors, spokesmen, media consultants, speechwriters, image makers, spin doctors, crisis teams, spiritual gurus, food tasters, pollsters, pundits, wags, wonks, interstate bagmen, unindicted co-conspirators, miscellaneous hangers-on, and three bimbos who looked like the Mandrell Sisters.

The campaign manager snapped his fingers in front of the governor's face.

"Wake up! I have some people I want you to meet."

The manager patted a bald man on the back. "Governor, this is Big Tobacco." The manager then pointed to others who had wiggled their way back from the forward seats and now crowded shoulder to shoulder in the rear of the limo. "And this is Big Oil, Big Sugar, Big Insurance and Big Rental Car . . ."

The limo approached a sprawling compound north of the Tallahassee limits. A guard waved them through the twin white metal gates with musical notes that replicated the entrance at Graceland. The vehicle entered a tunnel of nineteenth-century oaks. The residence sat on an elevated bluff—ten thousand square feet, three stories, brick, with portico and columns of federal architecture. One hour until the debate, one last stop. Fund-raising. A high-end cocktail reception at the home of a man who needed no introduction other than "Perry."

Periwinkle Belvedere, the most influential lobbyist and political tactician in the state of Florida, who only drank mint juleps.

Perry would have been imposing, even frightening, if it wasn't for his gamma-ray smile. Six-four and full head of obscenely red hair. He was trim, but his hands and head were extra-large, and he greeted everyone with a fluid personal manner and a handshake that—through years of practice—precisely matched the pounds per square inch of his guest's.

Power was everywhere in Tallahassee. Political, industrial, sexual. Puddled up all over the city. Periwinkle simply connected the puddles and organized the water. Soon he had a raging river on his hands, which he dredged, dammed, reservoired and viaducted according to his fee schedule.

But the times were changing. Laws limiting gifts, requiring disclosures, a full public accounting. The fun had already started to wheeze out of the capital balloon. Perry was mingling in the library, trying to hide his irritation at the legislators peeking through the blinds and curtains every few minutes, keeping an eye out for reporters like lookouts at a safe-cracking. Journalists, thought Perry, now there's an attractive bunch. They could put a damper on an orgy.

If ever a place had an orgy in mind, it was Perry's. The Roman fountain in the foyer pumped Dom Pérignon. Inside the dining hall and out on the torch-lit patio: tables almost collapsing under Keys lobsters, beluga caviar, perigord truffles, Peking duck and Alaskan salmon. All top-shelf, except for the two Sterno trays at the end of the banquet table, specially ordered by Periwinkle to cater to the particular tastes of the Florida speaker of the house. Pigs-in-a-blanket and Beenie Weenies.

When the lawmakers first reached the buffet tables, there was aggressive jockeying, the bright glint of cutlery and serving ladles, and finally a blinding pirana frenzy. In minutes, it was quiet again. The aftermath was chilling. Salmon stripped to the spinal column. Blue cheese chunks bobbing in the punch bowl. Beluga flung across the linen like coffee grounds. Cocktail sauce splattered mob-hit-style.

But what really inspired Perry's awe was their Light Brigade desiccation of the open bar. "My God," he said in a reverent, hushed tone. "They're worse than sportswriters."

No matter how many parties Perry threw, he couldn't get over one of nature's marvels, the sights and sounds of lawmakers at the trough, storing up complex carbohydrates for the winter in their wood-chuck cheeks and distensible pelican throats. Early on, Perry learned that perks had a curious Bermuda Triangle effect on lawmakers, sending the instrument needles spinning in their judgment cockpits. It worked out to about a dime on the dollar. Fifty bucks of complimentary food, drink and knickknacks bought as much influence as a five-hundred-dollar campaign contribution.

Despite the adorable government-in-the-sunshine reforms, Perry's soirée tonight began to show signs of life, and a smile crossed his face as the foyer echoed with the hollow din of clinking glasses, self-important laughter and cell phones.

Another cell phone went off, and a half-dozen people at the petit fours checked their jackets and purses. The ones who came up with nonringing phones winced in public shame; the one with the ac-tivated phone smirked.

The smirk belonged to Todd Vanderbilt, who an-swered his cell phone loudly for the benefit of those around him: "It's your dime!"

Todd was Perry Belvedere's top lobbyist, and his cell phone rang every five minutes because he told his personal assistant to "call me every five minutes."

"What do I say?"

"You don't say anything."

"I don't understand."

"I know."

Between phone calls, Todd's beeper went off. So

did his Palm Pilot, Sky Pager and self-correcting wristwatch, receiving microwave data from the Atomic Clock in Colorado.

Another alarm went off somewhere on Todd. He reached in his jacket, pulled out an e-gizmo and grinned at the crowd. "Stock split!"

"Ha!" countered a rival. "The market's closed!"

"Tokyo," said Todd.

"Oooooooooooo," the impressed crowd responded, then clapped.

Todd was everything Tallahassee was looking for: young, handsome, ambitious and completely full of shit. From his wardrobe to his manicure, everything was consciously in place. Except for one puzzle piece. The girl on his arm. His date was Sally Brewster, Perry Belvedere's accounting wizard. She was twenty-three, which was right in Todd's usual kill zone, but that's where it ended. Sally had scored something like a million on her SATs and graduated magna cum laude from Princeton, where she had a full scholarship and no dating life. There were a number of reasons. Her long hours studying left little time for extracurricular activity. And she had a nose like a stromboli.

Consequently, Sally remained awkward and frumpish. Her brown hair was straight and stringy, and her clothes looked like the uniform at a Cracker Barrel. She was also sweet as they come. And when a girl is as intelligent and nice as Sally, nature—with its charming brand of whimsy—makes her have a crush on a guy like Todd.

Sally had hovered around Todd for months, running to get him coffee, baking him cookies and banana bread, laughing at jokes that were at her expense. He routinely took out frustrations on her because she was the path of least resistance, and she forgave him.

Last Friday morning, Todd checked the market action on his office computer and chewed with his mouth open. Sally stood demurely with a baking tray.

"Killer brownies," said Todd, still chomping. "Hey, you wanna go to Perry's party with me next week?"

Todd thought Sally had gone into anaphylactic shock.

He got her a chair and a glass of water. "Tell me if you're gonna be sick, okay? 'Cause I can't get anything on this tie."

Sally spent the next week shopping. She ran up charges for clothes, her hair, everything. Even was fitted for contact lenses so she could ditch the granny glasses.

It would be nice to say the change was stunning, and that Sally emerged like a beautiful swan. It was not to be. She looked as natural and graceful as a rusting robot, stiffly hobbled on high heels, blinking rapidly from new contacts and bumping into things.

$\mathcal{P}$eriwinkle Belvedere glanced from his watch to the doorway, waiting for the governor. Standing with him was Elizabeth Sinclair, Perry's office manager. Todd Vanderbilt may have been Perry's hottest lobbyist, but Elizabeth was the glue of maturity that held his staff together. Dignified dark business suit and pearl stud earrings. Blond hair in a short, conservative Meg Ryan cut. She was forty-eight years old, wondered why she was still single, and remembered why every time she came to one of Perry's parties.

"You certainly look nice tonight," said Perry.

"Thank you," said Elizabeth.

"Although we talked about your clothes."

"I know."

"I really wish you'd wear something a little more . . ."

"More what?"

"You know."

"No, I don't."

Perry sighed. "Why can't you be a team player like Todd?"

Elizabeth and Perry looked over to the faux fireplace, where a series of electronic beeps, pulses, tones and buzzers were going off all over Todd, who smiled and produced a device in each hand and announced: "The sound of success!" He flicked open the cell phone. "It's your dime!"

Elizabeth turned to Perry. "Your star pupil."

Perry shook his head. "Look, I'm depending on you—" Something across the room caught his eye and he perked up. "Here comes the governor. Try to be nice."

Heads turned as the state's chief executive crossed the ballroom. His campaign manager and press secretary trailed close behind, whispering over his shoulders, overlapping each other, identifying people just before the governor shook their hands.

"There's Helmut von Zeppelin, mega-developer . . ."

"And that's Marshall Bellicose Leghorn, cattle baron . . ."

"Here's 'Little Tony' Mezzanine, local organized crime . . ."

"And this is Elizabeth Sinclair, Belvedere's office manager . . ."

Sinclair smiled with professional distance. "Pleasure to see you again, Governor."

She braced as they shook hands, determined to keep grinning through anything. She remembered shaking hands with him at the last party. "Wow, lady, that's some grip you got on ya. Bet it comes in handy, if you know what I mean." Wink.

The memory made her shiver.

Tonight, the governor shook her hand deferentially and averted his eyes. "Nice to see you again."

That's weird, she thought.

Suddenly, the governor and Elizabeth were knocked off balance as Sally Brewster crashed into them. The pair steadied Sally before she could topple off her high heels.

"You okay?" asked the governor.

"New contacts," said Sally.

Elizabeth fixed Sally's bra strap so it wouldn't show. "Let's get a glass of wine." She turned back to the governor: "It was nice seeing you again."

The women moved to the bar and ordered cabernet.

"I've got some comfortable shoes out in the car," offered Elizabeth, her bunched eyebrows betraying acute sympathy for her spastic friend.

"No, I've got to do this."

"You're way too smart and pretty for a jerk like Todd. What do you see in him, anyway?"

Sally just gave her that smitten look. It reminded Elizabeth of her own youth. Easier to reason with a wild bandicoot than a crush.

"You got it bad," she said, and they touched wineglasses.

They sipped quietly next to a row of potted ficus flanking the bar. A familiar voice boomed from the other side of the trees.

"Come on, guys, fork it over! We had a bet!"

Elizabeth and Sally peeked through the leaves. It was Todd and two of his buddies, who pulled currency from their wallets and handed it grudgingly to Todd.

"Okay, okay, you win," said one of the buddies. "You definitely have the dorkiest date at the party."

Sally put a hand over her mouth, started crying and ran from the party, but not before slamming into the governor again and taking an ugly tumble down the front steps.

Elizabeth marched around the end of the trees. "You son of a bitch!"

"What?" said Todd, then turned to see people running to help Sally. "Oh, her? She'll get over it. She didn't honestly think someone like *me* would actually go out with her. You see the honker on that chick?" Something began beeping. "Hold on, I got a call." He flicked open his phone. "It's your dime!"

Elizabeth dumped her glass of cabernet on his chest.

"Hey! My shirt!"

She stomped off.

Todd stared down in horror at the purple stain spreading like a gunshot wound. Something walked by that made him forget about laundry. His eyes followed the lithe figure across the room. She was a Latin beauty with short hair and a nametag from the Brazilian embassy.

"Salsa!" Todd said to himself. He licked his index finger, touched it to an imaginary location in the air and made a hissing sound. "Spicy hot!"

He trotted after her.

In the next room, a senator from Hialeah peeked through the blinds and saw what he had been dreading all night—a reporter talking to the guard in the driveway, gesturing at the house with his notebook. The first ant at the picnic.

A minute later two more reporters arrived, then a few more, and soon a large motley throng clamored in the driveway. The senator closed the blinds and discreetly informed his colleagues:

"RAID!"

They scattered in all directions. People ran into each other; women lost their heels. The Florida speaker of the house stuffed a handful of pigs-in-a-blanket in each coat pocket, gripped another in his mouth, and joined the stampede spilling across the mansion's driveway.

Cars patched out, fishtailing on the lawn. Senator Mary Ellen Bilgewater was ambushed before she could get to her Saab. She came up swinging. "How dare you ruin this party! We deserve this! People don't understand the sacrifice it takes . . ."—starting to sob—"... you don't know how hard it is being a lawmaker! You just don't get it!"

A half hour later, on the other side of town, the crowd that had gathered for the gubernatorial debate was growing restless in the auditorium of East Tallahassee High School. They began stomping their feet and singing. "... *We will, we will rock you!* ..."

A network cameraman turned to a sound technician. "I hate that fucking song."

The governor's limo approached the auditorium, where a mob waited at the stage entrance: a tight flock of reporters, obsessed followers, and demonstrators with pickets. "Free Cuba!" "Medical Marijuana Now!" "Pick Me, Monty!"

The Reform Party candidate, Albert Fresco, was outside protesting that he wasn't allowed to participate in the debate. Fresco and his staff wore T-shirts with his campaign slogan in large type: "I'm Madder Than a Sumbitch!"

The limo stopped as scripted a block from the auditorium. The head of Rolling Stones' security spoke into his voice-activated headset. "Send in Jagger."

A Mick Jagger impersonator got out of a sedan across the street from the auditorium and sprinted for another door around the side of the building. The mob shrieked and ran after him. The limo pulled up to the unattended stage entrance, and the governor's entourage was whisked inside without incident.

The audience in the auditorium piped down as the event's moderator, Florida Cable News correspondent Blaine Crease, laid down the League of Women Voters' ground rules for the debate.

The candidates stood at identical podiums thirty feet apart. The Democratic challenger was the Florida speaker of the house, Gomer Tatum, a fifty-eight-year-old portly, perspiring William Howard Taft–shaped man. He had fine black hair and an emerging bald pate. During commercial breaks in the debate, his dandruff blizzard would be carefully vacuumed and tweezered off the shoulders of his navy-blue suit by a crack staff who worked him like a Daytona pit crew. But they could only do so much. Under the television lights, Tatum appeared pasty and wilting.

The Republican incumbent wore an identical blue suit, but a longer, slimmer cut. Governor Marlon Conrad, thirty-eight years old, and everything about him projected confidence, success and high poll numbers—from the sound of his name to the Richard Gere good looks and Kennedy hair. If that wasn't enough, there was the family legacy. Great-grandfather Cecil Conrad, citrus magnate whose vast landholdings north of Lake Okeechobee were still in the family, the source of its embarrassing wealth. Grandfather "Two-Fisted" Thaddeus Conrad, twenty-term congressman who earned his nickname on the McCarthy committee. Father Dempsey "Tip" Conrad, former attorney general and current state Republican Party chairman.

Moderator Blaine Crease signaled thirty seconds to airtime.

Tatum's campaign manager looked out onstage and saw something that almost gave her a stroke.

"Where did he get *that*?" The manager ran onto the stage and snatched a pig-in-a-blanket from the speaker's mouth and stormed off. The speaker glanced furtively at his manager, then produced another pig-in-a-blanket from a coat pocket and resumed chewing.

Conrad's people, along with everyone else, had considered the campaign a slam dunk. Marlon was supposed to put Tatum out like a wet cigar in the early weeks.

Then the stumbles, the missed opportunities. Conrad hadn't been himself lately. The timing was gone, and there had been no knockout punch. Tatum managed to hang ten to twelve percentage points back, a distant second, but still in range.

Tonight at East Tallahassee High, the televised debate was the first major statewide event of the campaign. Conrad's staff was hopeful. Their man had been the stuff of vigor all day, and television was his medium. It certainly wasn't Tatum's.

As the debate opened, the governor's people stood behind the stage curtains, leaning forward on the balls of their feet, waiting for the kill. Instead, Conrad sleepwalked through the event, dazed.

Near the end of the debate, moderator Blaine Crease was handed a note by a network aide. There had been a problem at the prison in Starke. Something with the state's electric chair. Child torturer-murderer Calvin Rodney Buford had been set for execution at seven sharp. But one of the guards forgot to put the conductive jelly on the ankle strap. Also, they had failed to account for a metal plate in

Buford's head, which acted as a giant capacitor and heat sink. Two big jolts. Then a third. Still alive, although much more irritable. At 7:12 they gave it everything they had for four minutes, at the end of which Buford's head let go like a stuffed pepper in a microwave.

The state of Florida had retired the electric chair two years earlier in favor of lethal injection. But in the last legislative session, a number of key incumbents faced a massive no-bid contract scandal that was only eclipsed by the revelation that they had blown thousands of taxpayer dollars on Internet pay sites involving humiliation and discipline. The issues wouldn't go away. So, in the middle of the ethics hearings, the legislature brought back the chair, and all was forgotten.

Moderator Crease recounted the news from Death Row for the candidates. "Gentlemen, in light of tonight's development, and indeed a whole series of botched executions, wasn't it a mistake to reinstate the electric chair?"

Backstage, Conrad's manager smiled and pumped a fist. "Perfect timing! This is his best bully pulpit!"

Onstage, Conrad stared at his hands. He looked up. "It's something to think about."

"What the fuck!" yelled his manager. He threw down a sheaf of papers. "It's a no-brainer! I can answer that one in my sleep: 'I hope all their heads explode! Then maybe they'll think twice before they commit crimes in Florida!'

Crease turned to Tatum. "What about you, Mr. Speaker?"

The camera caught Tatum off-guard—eyes wide, bulging in terror, a pig-in-a-blanket protruding from his stuffed mouth. He inhaled it, gulped hard and hit himself in the chest with a fist. "Uh . . . I hope all their heads explode? . . . Uh . . . then maybe they'll think twice before they commit crimes in Florida?"

The audience went wild. Tatum looked around, startled at first, then grinned.

Florida Cable News had arranged for home viewers to register opinions live during the debate with special keypads. At East Tallahassee High, the results were displayed on the auditorium's basketball scoreboard. After the electric chair question, Tatum's stock slowly began rising . . . and kept rising. . . . The audience gasped when the numbers finally leveled off.

Three weeks left in the campaign, it was a dead heat.

$f$our hours after the debate, the auditorium swarmed with police. Shortly after the governor and audience had left the building, there had been an explosion.

The Tallahassee police detective in charge of the scene directed forensic photographers and gloved technicians through the debris in the balcony.

A tall man in a rumpled tweed jacket ducked under the yellow crime tape at the top of the stairs and approached the detective. He flashed a gold badge. "Mahoney, homicide."

The detective studied the badge. Miami Metro–Dade.

"Mahoney, it looks like you're out of your jurisdiction."

"It's all one big, sick jurisdiction now."

"I hear ya."

"Miami sent me up here because of a case we had. Miami thinks we may have a match."

"Miami thinks a lot of things."

"What do you think?"

"I think I have a dinner at home getting cold."

"It's a cold world."

"Never heard that."

Mahoney stared down at the lumpy sheet on the balcony floor. "What's the skinny?"

"A witness says he saw the victim come up here with a young woman. My guess is he was trying to score a little nooky."

"Nooky?" said Mahoney. "They still have that around these parts?"

"If you know the right people."

Mahoney nodded. He pulled an antique silver flask from his tweed coat and took a pull, then offered it to the detective.

The detective waved off the flask. "I'm on the wagon."

"What wagon's that?"

"A big red one with stripes. What do you care? You're Mr. Hot Shit from Miami."

"Please, drop the mister." Mahoney pointed down at the sheet. "We got a make on the vic?"

The detective flipped open a notepad. "One Todd Vanderbilt."

Mahoney leaned down and lifted the sheet. The

body was missing the head and right hand.

The detective held up a clear evidence bag filled with minuscule plastic chips and semiconductor shards.

"Cell phone?" asked Mahoney.

The detective nodded. "My guess would be C4 plastique explosive hidden in the speaker and wired to the answering button."

Mahoney stared off into space. "I'd say he had the wrong calling plan."

"A janitor was sweeping down below when it happened," said the detective. "Claims he heard someone say, 'It's your dime!' then *kaboom*. The victim's head took off across the auditorium like an Olympic volleyball serve."

Mahoney shook his head. "Isn't that always the case?"

"Look at this." The detective opened the victim's shirt to reveal something written on his chest in Magic Marker:

Kiss me—I just voted!